# THE LITIGATION
# PROTOCOL

# THE LITIGATION PROTOCOL

## A PATENT WARS NOVEL

TAREK N. FAHMI

PRIOR ART PRESS, LLC

"One may smile, and smile, and be a villain."
*Hamlet*, Act I, Scene 5 (Shakespeare)

---

"The strong do what they can,
and the weak suffer what they must."
Thucydides, *History of the Peloponnesian War*,
Book V (Melian Dialogue)

# ONE

"Look at it," Alex said, his voice trembling with pride and exhaustion. "Our first patent. We're official now."

The hum of old fluorescent lights filled the converted warehouse that NovaTech called home. It wasn't glamorous. Peeling paint on the walls, mismatched chairs scavenged from Craigslist, and a coffee machine that hissed like a dying engine, but to Maya Singh and Alex Carter, it was the beating heart of possibility.

Maya stood before the whiteboard, marker still in hand, staring at the framed certificate Alex, CTO and mind behind their breakthrough, had just hung on the wall. The patent number gleamed under the cheap glass frame like a badge of honor, the only thing in the room that caught the morning light and threw it back with pride.

Alex grinned, hands jammed deep into the pockets of a hoodie that had endured too many late nights. It was the kind of grin that threatened to crack into tears if examined too closely.

Maya smiled, though exhaustion tugged at the corners of her mouth. She set the marker down and crossed her arms, letting herself lean against the whiteboard. This patent wasn't just a milestone; it was their lifeline. Without it, NovaTech was just another hopeful name in a crowded field. With it, they had a chance; a slim one, maybe, but real.

Without thinking, she reached out and straightened the patent's frame, a nervous habit she'd picked up in the early days, whenever the future felt uncertain. "It's not just a piece of paper, Alex. It's our shield and our sword."

Alex's eyes sparkled. "You always said we'd get here. I didn't believe it until I saw the number."

Maya looked over at him. "This patent isn't just protection; it's a promise. We play fair, they play fair."

Alex asked playfully, "And if they don't?"

"Then we remind them why laws exist," Maya said, her voice low.

Alex laughed, running a hand through his unruly hair. "Our ticket out of this dump."

The two of them had spent years chasing this moment—late nights fueled by ramen and ambition, endless prototypes that failed spectacularly before one finally worked. Now, the technology they believed could change the industry was legally theirs.

Ethan Brooks, the youngest of NovaTech's founding trio, poked his head in from the hallway, a mug of coffee in one hand and a sheaf of printouts in the other. "Did you two sleep here again?" he asked, his tone teasing, but tired.

Alex shrugged. "Define 'sleep,'" he replied with a half-smile.

Ethan rolled his eyes, but there was affection in it. "I brought the latest stress test results. We're still seeing a bottleneck at high input rates, but the transform layer holds."

Maya took the printouts, scanning them with practiced efficiency. "We'll need to address that before we pitch. No surprises."

"We're close." Alex said. "I can feel it."

"You always say that," Ethan replied, rolling his eyes.

"And I'm always right, eventually."

Ethan grinned. "You said that about the last three prototypes, too."

"Fourth time's the charm!" Alex proclaimed.

Maya's phone buzzed on the desk. A text from her husband: *Don't forget dinner tonight. We need to talk.* She ignored it for now, tucking the phone beneath a stack of papers. Tonight was meant for celebration; not another argument over missed anniversaries and broken promises.

She turned back to the team. "Let's take a minute. This is a win. We should at least pretend to celebrate."

Ethan raised his mug, tapping it twice against the others; a tradition they'd begun after their first all-nighter. "To NovaTech."

Alex retorted, "To the weirdest family I've ever had."

They stood in silence, the three of them, letting the moment settle. The pride in the room was real, but so was the fear. Fear that it could all slip away. Outside, the city was waking up; delivery trucks rumbling down the street, the distant wail of a siren, the low murmur of rain against the windows. Maya glanced at her team, sensing the fragile hope lingering in the room. "We're not just here to survive," she said softly. "We're here to prove that you can build something honest and win. That's what this patent means. That's what NovaTech means."

Still, she couldn't shake the sense that their victory was fragile. She'd heard stories, startups with bright ideas, chewed up by giants who played by different rules. She pushed the thought aside, yet it lingered, a shadow at the edge of the morning light. The rain outside blurred the city into streaks of gray and gold, and for a moment, she was back in that other storm, two years ago, when everything nearly fell apart.

----

Rain battered the windows of a cheap diner. Maya slid into the booth, a folder of sketches under her arm. Alex was already there, stirring cold coffee, eyes rimmed with exhaustion.

Maya tried for a smile. "You look like you haven't slept in a week."

Alex managed a crooked grin. "I haven't. But I think I've got it. The transform layer: it's not just normalization; it's adaptation. Like a language that learns as it listens."

Maya spread out business plans, market analyses, a list of potential investors, most of whom had already said no. She tapped the folder, voice low. "If we're going to do this, we need more than code. We need a story. Something people can believe in."

Alex's gaze flickered. "I believe in it. Isn't that enough?"

Maya shook her head, gentle but firm. "It's a start. But we need a team. Someone who can build with us, not just for us."

The bell over the door jingled. Ethan, a young engineer barely out of college, appeared, drenched from the rain, clutching a battered laptop.

Ethan was still catching his breath. "Sorry I'm late. The bus broke down. Twice."

"You're hired," Alex said, eyes alight.

Maya laughed, the sound surprising even herself. "And you don't even know what the job is."

Ethan shrugged, grinning. "Does it matter? I want in. I've seen your code, Alex. And Maya, your pitch deck is the only one that doesn't make me want to run."

"See?" Alex asked rhetorically. "That's the spirit."

"You're both insane," Maya said, a playful edge in her voice. "But maybe that's what it takes."

They shook hands over cups of cold coffee and a plate of soggy fries.

"So, what do we call ourselves?" Ethan asked.

Alex replied without hesitation. "NovaTech. New technology, new rules."

"NovaTech it is," Maya agreed.

That night, NovaTech was born. Not in a boardroom, but in a diner, among people with more hope than resources.

As the weeks blurred together in a haze of late nights, cheap takeout, and mounting pressure, the optimism born in that diner was soon tested by the kind of crisis that could break a fledgling team.

Three months later, at 2:00 a.m., the office was a mess of tangled charging cables and the sharp scent of burnt coffee. The team was younger then, and the world felt both wider and more precarious.

Alex hunched over his laptop, eyes bloodshot, muttering lines of code under his breath. "It doesn't make sense! The simulation was clean. Why is the live data crashing the transform?"

Ethan paced in tight circles, clutching a notebook. "It's the input variance. The hospital's telemetry isn't normalized. We're getting spikes the test suite never saw."

Maya stood at the whiteboard, marker in hand. "Can we patch it?"

They'd spent months preparing for the demo. A live pilot with a major hospital network. If it worked, NovaTech would have its first real customer, a lifeline to keep the lights on. If it failed…

Alex shook his head, frustration etched deep. "Not in time. We'd have to rewrite the parser."

Ethan frowned. "If we fudge the input, we risk corrupting the output. They'll see right through it."

As the fluorescent lights hummed overhead like they were running on the same frayed nerves as the team, a soft knock broke through the noise.

"Please tell me that's caffeine," Ethan groaned without looking up.

"It's better," a familiar voice said.

Maya turned. Ravi, her husband, stood in the doorway holding two paper bags and a thermos, hair wind-tousled, smiling in that soft way that cut straight through her armor.

"Midnight snack delivery," he said. "Though based on the vibe in here, maybe it's triage."

Ethan blinked. "Oh thank God. Are you a saint? You might be a saint."

Ravi laughed and handed him one of the bags. "Eat something that didn't come from a vending machine."

Then he crossed the room to Maya, lowering his voice. "Hey."

She hadn't realized how tightly she'd been holding herself until she saw him. The tension in her chest eased just a little. "You didn't have to come."

"I know." He unscrewed the thermos lid and offered it to her. "But you forget to take care of yourself when things get bad."

She took a sip; hot chai, warm and spiced, liquid grounding. "God, that's good."

"Of course it is," Ravi teased. "It's not your coffee."

For a moment, just a moment, she smiled. Really smiled.

Ravi brushed a loose strand of hair from her forehead. "How's the crisis?"

"Unfolding," she said. "We're close. I think. Maybe."

"You don't need to pretend for me," he said gently.

Maya exhaled, shaky. "I'm scared we'll lose the pilot. If we do, the investors—"

"Then you'll adapt," Ravi said. "You always do."

She leaned into him, forehead resting briefly against his shoulder.

For one suspended moment, the noise and panic fell away, leaving only warmth, breath, and the possibility of a life not measured in deadlines. In her mind, she saw her mother behind the counter of Singh's Market, slipping free fruit to kids who looked hungry, never asking for thanks. She could almost smell the spices and fresh bread, hear the bell over the door, feel the warmth of their hope. She remembered her mother's words, spoken late at night after the store closed: "Build something that lasts, Maya. Not just for you, but for everyone who comes after."

But after a moment her thoughts ran to the payroll due in a week, the investors waiting for good news, her parents and every sacrifice that had brought her here. "I wish I could come home," she whispered.

"I know." Ravi held her a beat longer. "I just wanted you to know someone's waiting when you do."

Alex called out from across the room, "Maya! I think we're on to something."

She straightened, startled back into urgency.

Ravi stepped back, smiling without bitterness. "Go. You're needed."

Maya squeezed his hand. "Thank you."

"Always," he said — and he meant it then.

He left as quietly as he'd arrived, warmth trailing behind him.

"What did you find?" Maya asked as she approached Alex and Ethan.

Ethan was slumped in a chair, rubbing his eyes. "I blew it. I should have tested with messier, more real-world data."

Maya knelt beside him, her voice gentle. "We all missed it. That's how you learn."

"So, what do we do now?"

"We call them," Maya said. "We tell the truth."

Alex looked up, startled. "We can't."

Maya was firm. "We have to. If we fake it and they catch us, we're done. If we're honest, maybe we get another shot."

"I'll make the call," Alex sighed. "It's my code."

Maya put a hand on his shoulder. "We do it together."

The next morning they dialed in, voices trembling. The hospital's tech lead listened silently as they explained the failure, the gaps in their testing, and their promise to fix it.

There was a long pause. Then: "You're the first vendor who's admitted a problem before we found it. Fix it, and we'll reschedule."

When the call ended, the team sat in stunned silence. Relief mingled with shame and, unexpectedly, something new: trust.

Ethan let out his breath. "We survived."

Alex managed a tired smile. "Barely."

"Next time," Maya declared, "we test with the messiest data we can find."

"I'll write a generator for chaos." Ethan said.

Alex took up the thread. "I'll rewrite the parser from scratch."

"And I'll make sure we never promise what we can't deliver," Maya finished.

They laughed, the sound shaky but real, and started again. Wiser, humbler, and more determined.

———

The memory receded, leaving Maya with the familiar ache of old lessons and new risks. The patter of rain against the windows tethered her to the present, the office's quiet hum a reminder that the stakes had only grown.

She blinked and glanced at Alex and Ethan, older now, scarred by setbacks but unbroken. She remembered the promise to build something that mattered.

"We've been here before," she said softly. "We're not just building tech. We're building a place where people can be brave. Where failure isn't the end."

Alex looked up from his laptop, catching the echo in her voice. "You know why I stayed? Not for the patent. Not even for the code. I stayed because you made me believe we could do this the right way."

Ethan grinned. "And because no one else would put up with your variable names."

"Hey, my variable names are poetry." Alex said.

"Your poetry crashed the build last week."

"That was a metaphorical crash."

Maya just shook her head. "You two are impossible."

"We'll get through this." Alex said, certain it was true.

Ethan grinned. "As long as we don't run out of coffee."

Maya smiled. For a moment, the weight of the world lifted. "Let's get to work."

———

The patent certificate was still gleaming on the wall when Maya's phone vibrated with the calendar alert: *Board Call—11:00 a.m.* She gathered her notes, steadied her breath, and dialed in.

The screen flickered to life with a grid of faces; some familiar, some new, all expectant. Alan, the lead investor, appeared first. His background was a study in curated power: mahogany shelves, a framed Wharton diploma, and a model yacht.

"Morning, Maya. Congratulations on the patent. Now, let's talk about what it means."

Priya joined next, her voice warm but her eyes sharp behind rimless glasses. "It's a milestone, Maya. But milestones don't pay salaries."

A third window popped up. Jonas, the numbers guy, already frowning at a spreadsheet. "I've run the projections. Even with a licensing deal, you're out of cash by Q3."

Maya forced a smile. "Good morning, everyone. I appreciate you making time. The patent is a foundation. We're moving quickly to leverage it."

Alan wasted no time. "Let's get specific. You mentioned Titan Corp in your update. Where do things stand?"

"We've reached out. We're positioning for a partnership—preferably a licensing deal, but we're open to joint development. If they bite, everything changes."

Jonas didn't look up from his screen. "Leverage is only useful if you use it. What's your fallback if Titan strings you along?"

"And what's your plan if they walk?" Priya joined in. "We can't afford another year of 'strategic conversations.'"

Maya's pen tapped against her notepad, a nervous metronome. "We have a shortlist of secondary targets. Mid-tier OEMs, a couple of healthcare platforms. If Titan doesn't move, we pivot fast."

Alan was skeptical. "Define 'fast.'"

"Thirty days. If we don't have meaningful engagement, we shift focus."

"And if Titan launches a competing product?" Jonas asked.

"We're protected. The patent is strong, and we're prepared to enforce it."

Priya shook her head. "Litigation is expensive, Maya. Are you prepared to go to war?"

Maya hesitated, feeling the weight of the question. "If we have to. But the goal is partnership, not conflict."

Alan steered the conversation back to a deal. "Let's talk numbers. What's the minimum deal you'd accept?"

Maya tried to sound confident. "Seven figures upfront, plus royalties. Anything less, and we walk."

Jonas frowned. "And if they counter with equity?"

"We'll consider it, but only with board representation and clear milestones."

"What about the team?" Priya asked. "Can you keep morale up if this drags out?"

"We've been through worse. The team believes in the mission."

Alan's tone softened, but only slightly. "Belief is good. Payroll is better."

A tense silence settled. Maya felt the weight of every eye on her.

Priya broke it, her tone softer. "You've done well to get this far, Maya. But this is the moment. Don't blink."

Maya nodded, voice steady. "I won't."

Alan started to wrap up the call. "You have two weeks. Show us traction, or we'll need to revisit the funding plan."

"And Maya," Jonas cautioned, "no surprises. If there's a problem, we hear it from you first."

Maya nodded. "Understood."

The call ended, the grid of faces vanishing. Alone again, Maya let her shoulders sag. The pressure from the board felt like a weight pressing down on her chest, heavier than any late-night debugging session or missed anniversary. She wondered, not for the first time, if she was leading her team toward triumph or disaster.

———

Alex and Ethan huddled over the server rack, their voices rising and falling, sometimes sharp, sometimes playful, always threaded with the shorthand of people who had built something together from scratch.

Alex tapped a diagram on his tablet, eyes bright with the thrill of a new idea. "If we move the normalization upstream, we can cut latency by half."

Ethan shook his head, arms folded. "And double the risk of data loss. We need stability, not just speed."

Alex grinned, undeterred. "We can have both. Watch—if we buffer here—"

Ethan cut him off, rolling his eyes. "You're chasing ghosts. The bottleneck isn't in the transform, it's in the I/O. I checked the logs twice."

Alex opened his mouth to argue, but Maya stepped in, her tone decisive. "We need both. Alex, run the numbers. Ethan, check the logs for anomalies. I want a clean demo."

Ethan nodded, already turning to his laptop. "You got it, boss."

Alex gave a mock salute. "On it." As he turned back to his laptop, Alex doodled a tiny circuit diagram in the margin of his notebook, a ritual that helped him think.

Ethan, meanwhile, unwrapped a bag of wasabi peas and offered them around, grinning at their groans. As Maya walked away, he lowered his voice and said, "You know she's right."

Alex sighed, a reluctant smile tugging at his lips. "I know. Doesn't mean I have to like it."

Ethan grinned, the tension easing. "Fourth time's the charm, right?"

"Don't jinx it."

They bent over their screens, the quiet hum of the servers filling the space between them; a rhythm as familiar as their arguments.

———

The apartment was quiet when Maya let herself in, the only light coming from the kitchen where Ravi, her husband, sat at the table, a half-eaten dinner growing cold. The air was thick with the scent of turmeric and disappointment.

"You missed it," Ravi said, not looking up.

Maya set her bag down, guilt prickling at her skin. "I know. I'm sorry. The patent came through. We're prepping for Titan."

A long silence settled. "You said you'd be here. I cooked your favorite."

Maya hesitated, glancing at the untouched plate. "I lost track of time. The team—this is a big moment for us."

Ravi's voice was flat. "It's always a big moment. There's always a reason."

Maya sat across from him, exhaustion settling into her bones. "This is everything we've worked for. If Titan bites—"

"And if they don't? What then, Maya? Another late night? Another 'just one more quarter'?"

Maya looked down at her hands, fingers stained with whiteboard ink. "We're so close. I can feel it."

Ravi pushed the plate away. "I can't keep doing this. I can't keep coming second to your company."

Maya reached for his hand, but he pulled away. "I'm trying. I really am. I want this to work, for us."

Ravi's eyes were tired, rimmed with worry. "I know you're trying. But I don't know if you're happy. You don't laugh anymore. You barely sleep. You talk about the company like it's your whole life."

Maya's voice was barely a whisper. "Sometimes it feels like it is."

A silence stretched between them, heavy and fragile.

Ravi finally spoke, softer now. "I miss you, Maya. I miss us. I miss when you used to dream about more than just surviving."

Maya blinked back tears, her throat tight. "I want that too. I just... can't let go. Not now. Not when we're this close."

Ravi stood, gathering the plates. "I'm going to bed. Don't stay up all night."

Maya watched her husband disappear down the hallway, the ache in her chest sharper than any investor's rebuke. As she sat alone in the dim kitchen, the memory of the hospital pilot and Ravi's unexpected arrival at the office felt like a vanishing echo and she wondered when she had stopped letting him carry even a little of the weight. The heavy silence of her home no longer felt like refuge. The patent was meant to be a beginning; instead, it felt like a weight. One she'd chosen, one she couldn't set down.

She pressed her palms to her eyes, fighting the urge to call Alex and to bury herself in work. But the silence pressed in, heavy and unrelenting. She gave in, opened her laptop and checked Teams, the company's collaboration platform. Of course, Alex was on-line and Maya opened a video call.

Back at the office, Alex was in the server room, hunched over his laptop, headphones on. The glow of the screen painted tired shadows across his face. Ethan had left hours ago, but Alex couldn't sleep. Not tonight.

"Can't sleep?" Maya asked.

Alex blinked, then managed a sheepish smile. "Just... thinking."

He'd pulled up the patent document, reading it line by line, searching for reassurance in the legal language. Every now and then his eyes would flick to the whiteboard, crowded with equations and half-erased notes. He'd thought about the years spent chasing this dream, the friendships forged and tested, the moments when it all seemed impossible.

"I've been sketching ideas for the Titan integration. Optimizations, new features, ways to make us irresistible."

Maya sat at her kitchen table, her posture mirroring his fatigue. "Do you ever worry we're in over our heads?"

Alex hesitated, then nodded: "Every day. But then I remember. Nobody else built this. We did."

Maya's gaze drifted to the window, where city lights shimmered in the rain. "That's what scares me," she admitted.

Alex's voice was gentle. "We'll figure it out. We always do."

Maya let out a breath she hadn't realized she was holding. "You know, sometimes I wish I could just... stop. Just for a day."

Alex grinned, the old spark returning for a moment. "You? Stop? I'll believe it when I see it," he joked.

Maya smiled, shaking her head. "Maybe in another life."

Through the video chat they sat together in silence, the weight of the future pressing in, the hum of the servers their only company.

"Get some sleep," Maya said, then closed her laptop. Tomorrow, she promised herself. Tomorrow, she'd find a way to make it all worth it.

————

The next morning, the sun rose behind a curtain of rain, the city washed clean and new. Maya arrived early, brewing a fresh pot of coffee and reviewing the draft of the email to Titan, reading each line as if it might change the future.

Ethan arrived, bleary-eyed but determined, a backpack slung over one shoulder. "Logs are clean. No weird access. We're good."

Maya offered a grateful nod. "Thanks, Ethan. Let's keep it that way."

A moment later, Alex pushed through the door, balancing a box of pastries from the corner bakery. "Bribery," he announced, setting the box on the table. "For morale."

Ethan grinned. "If you're trying to buy my silence, it'll take more than a cruller."

"You say that now but wait until you try the chocolate one."

Maya smiled, the tension in her shoulders easing just a little. "Let's eat, then get to work. Today's the day we make them notice."

On her way back to her desk, Maya walked by Jamie Tran, a young programmer. He was on a headset, and she could hear his voice as careful as a tightrope walker. "––Yes, out-of-network was emergency only. We submitted pre-auth. I... understand. Can you escalate?"

The screen on Jamie's phone screen displayed a portal marked with red banners: *Coverage Pending*. A thumbnail photo—small hand in a hospital wristband—peeked out from behind a spreadsheet.

Maya paused. "Everything ok? Do you need time off?"

Jamie muted the call, the smile too bright. "All good. Just fighting forms."

"Tell me if we can help."

"Really, I'm okay," Jamie said, then unmuted and read a policy number like a prayer.

On her way out, Maya wrote herself a note she'd later misplace: *Stipend for emergency care fund. Ask Alan.*

Two hours later, Maya, Alex and Ethan gathered back around the conference table, the patent watching over them. Maya read the email aloud one last time. "To whom it may concern at Titan Corp: We are pleased to announce the issuance of U.S. Patent No. —"

Alex nodded. "Send it."

Maya hesitated, then hit **Send**. The email vanished into the ether, a message in a bottle tossed into a sea of giants.

They waited, the silence heavy with hope and dread. Outside, the city moved on, unaware that three people were betting everything on a single idea.

———

The board call was scheduled for noon, a week after the Titan email had gone unanswered. Maya dialed in, her notes spread before her, a knot of dread tightening in her stomach.

Alan's face appeared first, jaw set. "We're still waiting, Maya."

Maya tried to keep her voice steady. "We followed up with Titan's business development lead yesterday. No response yet, but—"

Jonas cut her off, his tone sharp. "You promised traction. We're burning cash. What's the plan if Titan ghosts you?"

Priya's voice was cooler than before. "We're hearing rumors Titan is talking to your competitor. Are you aware?"

Maya swallowed, forcing herself to sound confident. "We're monitoring the market. We have meetings lined up with two other OEMs next week."

Alan shook his head. "That's not enough. We need a signed letter of intent, or we start looking at alternatives. You have one week."

Maya's grip tightened on her pen. "We're doing everything possible. The team is—"

Jonas interrupted, not unkind but unyielding. "The team doesn't pay the bills. Results do."

A silence fell. Maya felt the walls closing in.

Priya said quietly: "We believe in you, Maya. But belief has its shelf life."

The call ended. Maya stared at her reflection in the black screen, the pressure mounting in her chest.

———

The rest of the day was a study in anticipation. Every email ping made them jump. Every phone call felt like a potential lifeline.

Ethan leaned back in his chair, drumming his fingers on the desk. "What if they just ignore us?"

Maya didn't look up from her laptop. "They won't. Not with what we have."

Alex glanced at the clock, then at the silent phone. "And if they do?"

Maya closed her laptop, her voice steady but tight. "Then we make them notice."

The rain eased, the city brightening steadily outside the window. Maya stood for a moment, watching the world move on, indifferent to NovaTech's hopes and fears.

She turned back to her team, gathering resolve. "We built something real. That matters. No matter what happens next."

Alex managed a small smile. "To the next step."

Ethan raised his mug. "To not getting crushed."

They laughed, the tension breaking for a moment before the silence settled in again, heavy with hope and dread.

———

As night fell, Maya lingered in the office, the frame around the patent certificate glowing in the lamplight. The building was quiet, just the hum of the refrigerator and the distant tick of the wall clock.

She thought about her family, her team, the risks they'd taken. The silence pressed in, heavy and unyielding.

Maya traced the edge of the frame with her finger, remembering the hope she'd felt when they first hung it on the wall. Now, it felt less like armor and more like a dare.

She whispered to the empty room, "We play fair. They play fair."

But even as she said it, a chill of doubt crept in. Was it ever that simple? She'd heard stories about Titan; how they'd swallowed smaller companies whole, leaving only empty promises and regrets behind.

Outside, city lights flickered against the night sky, indifferent to the fragile dreams kindling in the battered room. Maya stared at the patent one last time, feeling its weight. Not just as a victory, but as a promise. A promise she intended to keep, no matter the cost.

Maya straightened the frame, squared her shoulders, and walked to the whiteboard. Tomorrow, she would draft a new plan, one that didn't wait for permission or validation. If Titan wouldn't answer, NovaTech would make itself impossible to ignore. She picked up the marker and wrote: "No one forgets us."

# Two

THE RIDESHARE CAR glided off the main road and onto Titan's private drive, the city's noise fading behind a wall of manicured greenery. For a moment, Maya thought they'd taken a wrong turn. Surely no tech campus could be this serene, this insulated from the world outside. But then the trees parted, and Titan's headquarters rose before them, a monolith of poured concrete and glass set like a challenge in the landscape.

Maya still couldn't quite believe it. She remembered the email that had arrived just after midnight a few days ago, subject line: *NovaTech Proposal – Meeting Request*. Claire Donovan, Titan's business development officer, had written with the brisk efficiency of someone used to making decisions at speed:

*We've reviewed your materials.*

*Product Strategy would like to meet.*

*Can you be at Titan HQ Thursday at 10:30?*

No pleasantries, no promises; just a window, and the unspoken message that this was the only one they'd get.

The timing felt almost surreal. Maya had been drafting a last-ditch update for the Board when the notification appeared; her relief so sharp it left her dizzy. She'd forwarded the invite to Alex and Ethan with a single word: "Go."

Now, as the car glided up Titan's drive, Maya scrolled back to the message, as if to reassure herself it was real. The Board's deadline was hours away. Somehow, they'd made it in under the wire.

The building stood out in brutalist fashion: sharp angles and shadow, its mass both defiant and deliberate. Around it, the grounds were a study in curated eco-theater: native grasses swayed in the breeze, a reflecting pool mirrored the sky, and solar panels gleamed atop a parking structure shaped like a folded origami crane. The message was clear: Titan had money to burn, and it would spend it on whatever made the company look both progressive and untouchable.

Alex stared out the window, his voice barely above a whisper. "It looks like a fortress."

Maya nodded, her jaw tight. "I think that's the point."

The car rolled to a stop at a circular drive, where a minimalist sign— just the word TITAN in matte black steel—stood guard over the entrance. No slogans, no mission statements. Just the name, as if that alone was enough.

A valet in a slate-gray uniform opened their door. "Welcome to Titan. Are you here for the 10:30 with Product Strategy?"

Maya stepped out, smoothing her jacket again. "Yes. Singh and Carter, NovaTech."

The valet nodded, expression unreadable, and gestured toward the main doors. As they approached, Maya felt the building's presence pressing down, a weight in the air, a hush that made her want to lower her voice.

Alex's grip tightened on the demo binder. He leaned in, voice low. "If we get out of here alive, I'm buying you lunch."

Maya almost smiled. "If we get out of here alive, you're buying the company lunch."

The entrance was a slab of glass set into concrete, so tall it seemed to slice the sky. As they passed through, the doors whispered shut behind them, sealing them into a world where everything was designed to make visitors feel small.

The lobby was a canyon of stone and light. Polished basalt floors stretched to distant walls, broken only by islands of living moss and the occasional sculptural bench that was more art than furniture. Overhead, a skylight ran the length of the space, but the sun's warmth was filtered and cold, diffused by a grid of solar shades that cast shifting patterns on the floor.

A living wall of ferns and orchids climbed one side, but even the greenery felt curated, as if nature itself had been tamed and put on display. The air was cool and faintly scented with something expensive and unplaceable.

At the far end, a reception desk rose from the floor like an altar. The receptionist's suit was a shade lighter than the stone, her posture perfect, her smile practiced.

"Welcome to Titan," she said, her voice echoing in the vastness. "Names, please?"

Maya forced herself to breathe evenly. "Maya Singh and Alex Carter, NovaTech," she replied, her voice steady but quiet.

The receptionist's eyes flicked over her screen. "You're expected. Claire Donovan will meet you in the executive lobby. May I offer you coffee, tea, sparkling water?"

Alex, nerves showing, shook his head. "Just water, thanks."

Although her mouth was dry, Maya said, "Nothing for me."

"Please proceed to the elevators. Claire will be waiting on Level 21."

As they crossed the lobby, Maya felt eyes on them. Security, perhaps, or just the building itself, watching. The walls were hung with abstract art in muted colors, each piece signed by an artist whose name Maya recognized from auction headlines. Everything here was meant to impress, but also to unsettle. You are not one of us, the space seemed to say. You are here on our terms.

The elevator bank was set into a wall of black glass. As they approached, one door slid open without a sound. Inside, the car was lined with pale wood and brushed steel, the controls a single touch panel. No buttons, no floor numbers. Just a glowing prompt: *Executive Lobby*.

Alex glanced at Maya, his voice low. "I feel like I should have worn a tie."

She managed a small smile. "You look fine. Just remember, they want what we have. That's why we're here."

The elevator rose in silence, the city shrinking away beneath them. For a moment, Maya caught her reflection in the glass: composed, professional, but with a flicker of uncertainty in her eyes. She straightened her jacket, squared her shoulders.

The doors opened onto a smaller lobby. Still grand, but warmer, with walnut paneling and a view that stretched to the bay. A wall of glass let in the morning light, but the furniture was arranged to keep visitors standing, not settling in. A single piece of sculpture, a twisted column of reclaimed metal, stood in the center. It was both beautiful and vaguely threatening.

Claire Donovan was waiting, tablet in hand, her smile genuine but tinged with the briskness of someone who had already triaged three crises before breakfast. She extended her hand. "Maya, Alex, so glad you could make it. Welcome to Titan."

Claire's handshake was cool and firm, her eyes bright with intelligence and something harder to read. Curiosity, perhaps, or calculation. "Thank you for having us," replied Maya.

Claire gestured toward a corridor. "The boardroom's just finishing up. Can I get you anything while you wait?"

Alex shook his head. "We're good."

Claire's eyes lingered on Maya, as if searching for something. "An impressive building, isn't it? Designed to be both sustainable and intimidating, they say."

Maya allowed herself a small, wry smile. "Mission accomplished," she said.

Claire laughed, the tension easing for a moment. "Come on, I'll show you to the executive lounge. We'll bring you in as soon as they're ready."

As they followed Claire down the corridor, Maya glanced back at the lobby, at the city beyond the glass. For a moment, she felt very far from home.

Claire led Maya and Alex down a corridor that seemed to stretch forever, the hush broken only by the soft click of Maya's heels and the muted thud of

Alex's sneakers on the basalt floor. The walls here were lined with vertical slats of walnut, their grain running in perfect, unbroken lines—nature, disciplined and domesticated. Every few feet, a recessed alcove displayed a single object: a fossilized ammonite, a chunk of meteorite, a minimalist sculpture in polished steel. Each piece was labeled with a tiny plaque, as if to remind visitors that even time and the cosmos could be curated by Titan.

The corridor opened into the executive lobby; a space designed to impress and unsettle. The ceiling soared two stories overhead, but the lighting was subdued, casting long shadows that made the room feel both vast and intimate. One wall was a continuous sheet of glass, offering a panoramic view of the campus grounds. Native grasses rippling in the wind, the reflecting pool catching the sky. Beyond that, the city skyline, distant and faintly unreal.

The furniture was sparse and severe: a pair of low, angular couches in charcoal wool, a coffee table of blackened oak, and a single armchair upholstered in something that looked like sharkskin. A sculptural column of twisted bronze dominated the center of the room, its surface catching the light in unpredictable ways. The only color came from a bowl of impossibly perfect green apples on the table. So flawless they looked artificial.

Claire gestured for them to sit. "They're running a few minutes behind. Always the way with these things."

Maya perched on the edge of the couch, back straight and hands folded neatly in her lap. Alex sat beside her, fidgeting with the zipper on his laptop bag, eyes darting from the sculpture to the view and back again.

Claire settled into the armchair, crossing her legs with practiced ease. "Can I get you anything? We have a full espresso bar, or something herbal if you prefer."

Alex shook his head. "I'm good, thanks."

Maya just said, "We're fine."

Claire's smile softened so that it was a little more genuine now. "You know, the first time I came up here, I was terrified. I spent the whole wait rehearsing my pitch in my head, convinced I'd forget my own name."

Maya allowed herself a small, conspiratorial smile. "I know the feeling."

Silence settled, not quite comfortable. The room seemed to absorb sound, making every movement and every breath feel amplified.

Alex leaned forward, voice low. "Is it always this quiet?"

Claire glanced at him, a hint of amusement in her eyes. "Only when you're waiting. Once you're inside, it's all voices and opinions and too many slides. But out here? You're meant to feel the weight of it."

Maya studied the view, searching for any sign of life on the campus below. A groundskeeper in a green jumpsuit moved along the edge of the reflecting pool, his figure dwarfed by the building's bulk. A pair of ducks landed on the water, sending ripples across the perfect surface. Even nature, it seemed, was permitted only on Titan's terms.

A digital display above the reception desk scrolled through the day's schedule: *9:00—Legal Review; 10:00—Product Strategy; 10:30—Nova-Tech Partnership Discussion.* The letters were crisp, impersonal, a reminder that they were just one item in a long day of power plays.

Alex cleared his throat. "How long have you been at Titan, Claire?"

She considered. "Almost eight years. I started in product marketing, moved to partnerships. It's... a world unto itself."

Maya asked, "Do you like it here?"

Claire hesitated, then smiled. "Some days. It rewards ambition, but it can be... a lot."

Alex looked around the space. "It feels like a spaceship. Or a museum."

Claire laughed. "Both, sometimes. The building was designed to make a statement. You're not supposed to forget where you are."

---

Claire's mind drifted back to her first week at Titan. It had felt like stepping onto a different planet. She remembered the way the lobby's polished stone seemed to swallow her footsteps, the way the glass walls reflected her own nervous smile back at her. On her first day she'd arrived early, clutching a new leather bag and a notebook filled with ideas, determined to make an impression.

Her new manager, a brisk woman named Evans, awaited her at the elevators. "You'll be shadowing me for the first few days," Evans said, barely glancing up from her phone. "We move fast here. Don't worry about asking too many questions, just keep up."

Claire tried to keep up. The days blurred together: onboarding sessions, security briefings, a whirlwind tour of the product labs. She was introduced to the team. Engineers with MIT hoodies, product managers with perfect hair, a legal counsel who seemed to know everyone's secrets. At lunch, she sat with a group of new hires, all of them wide-eyed and eager, trading stories about their last jobs and their hopes for this one.

That first Friday, she stayed late, reviewing partnership proposals in a glass-walled conference room that overlooked the city. The skyline spread out in a grid of lights, and for a moment, Claire felt exactly where she belonged. She believed in Titan's mission, at least, the one they put on the website. She wanted to help build things that mattered.

Evans stopped by on her way out. "Settling in?" she asked, her tone softer than usual.

Claire nodded. "It's a lot. But it feels good. Like I can actually make a difference here."

Evans smiled, just a little. "That's what I thought, too. Just remember, Titan rewards ambition but doesn't always reward idealism. Pick your battles."

Claire laughed, but the words stuck with her. That night, as she rode the elevator down to the parking garage, she promised herself she'd be both ambitious and idealistic. She'd find a way to do the right thing, even if it meant bending the rules. She didn't know then how hard that would become.

———

A chime sounded from Claire's tablet. She glanced down, then back up. "They're ready for us. Shall we?"

Maya stood, smoothing her jacket, and exchanged a glance with Alex. He nodded, tucking the binder under his arm.

As they followed Claire toward the frosted glass doors at the far end of the lobby, Maya felt the weight of the building settle on her shoulders. A reminder that in this place, everything was calculated, and nothing was left to chance.

The doors slid open with a whisper, revealing the heart of Titan's power. The boardroom was a study in engineered intimidation: a long, black-glass table stretched toward a wall of windows, the city sprawling far below. The ceiling soared, but the lighting was focused. Spotlights illuminated the table, leaving the corners in shadow.

Maya's heels clicked on the polished floor as she entered, Alex close behind, clutching the demo binder. The air was cool, faintly scented with ozone and something sharper, like the tang of ambition.

Around the table sat Titan's product strategy team: a half-dozen men and women in tailored suits, their faces composed, eyes sharp. Laptops open, styluses poised, they watched Maya and Alex with the polite wariness of predators sizing up unfamiliar prey.

Claire took her seat near the head of the table, offering a reassuring nod. "Everyone, this is Maya Singh, CEO of NovaTech, and Alex Carter, CTO. They're here to present a technology we believe could be transformative."

A few polite nods. One engineer, a man with silver hair and a jaw like a chisel, didn't bother to look up from his tablet.

Maya set her laptop at the far end, connecting to the room's display. The NovaTech logo appeared on the massive screen, dwarfed by the Titan branding in the corner.

She took a breath, steadying herself. "Thank you for having us. We know your time is valuable. What we're presenting today isn't just an incremental improvement. It's a new architecture for real-time telemetry normalization. We believe it can unlock significant performance and reliability gains across your product lines."

Alex brought up a schematic. A flow diagram, color-coded, with callouts for each subsystem.

He spoke, voice clear but tight. "Our transform layer adapts dynamically to input variance. Instead of flattening all data streams, it preserves the unique characteristics of each source—what we call 'signal accent'—while still normalizing for downstream analytics."

A Titan engineer, young, sharp-eyed, with a badge reading "S.

Patel," leaned forward. "Isn't that just a fancy way of saying you're running a weighted average on the input?"

Alex shook his head, smiling. "No, it's more nuanced. We use a topology-preserving transform. Think of it as a choreography, not just a blend. The system learns the relationships between data streams and adapts the mapping in real time."

Patel's lips twitched. "So, a neural net?"

"Not exactly," Alex explained. "It's a hybrid. Statistical mapping with a feedback loop, but interpretable. You can audit the choices."

A woman in a navy suit, Titan's head of platform integration, spoke up, skeptical. "How does it handle failure modes? If you get a spike in telemetry, what's the fallback?"

"We chose stability over speed. The system queues and breathes, letting latency rise slightly to avoid catastrophic loss. Here—" He pulled up a graph. "You can see the inflection point. We let the system absorb the shock, then recover."

The silver-haired engineer finally looked up. "We've been running our own experiments with adaptive transforms. Most of them break under real-world noise. What's your outlier rejection strategy?"

Maya stepped in, voice calm. "We use a two-stage filter: first, a statistical threshold based on historical variance, then a context-aware gate that flags anomalies for review. It's not perfect, but it's robust."

He raised an eyebrow. "And what's the computational overhead? Our systems run at the edge. Every millisecond counts."

Alex took this one. "We've profiled the code on QCore GPUs. The transform layer adds less than 5 percent overhead compared to your current pipeline, but the reduction in downstream error more than compensates."

Patel responded dryly: "That's a bold claim. Did you use our test suite?"

"We used public benchmarks and a synthetic set modeled on your published specs. We'd be happy to run a pilot with your data."

A third engineer, arms folded: "And what about integration? Our stack is proprietary. We don't have time to refactor for someone else's architecture."

Maya jumped in. "We anticipated that. The core module is

containerized and modular, with adapters for your API. You can run it as a sidecar or inline."

The head of platform integration exchanged a glance with Patel. "We've heard that before. It's never that simple."

Alex responded quietly. "We're happy to work with your team to prove it."

Silence fell. The Titan team conferred in low voices, not bothering to hide their skepticism.

Just as Maya was about to speak the door opened and Richard Hale strode in. Tall, silver at the temples, his suit immaculate and unwrinkled. He didn't apologize for being late; he didn't need to.

He scanned the room, eyes sharp. "Maya, Alex. Welcome to Titan."

He took his seat at the head of the table, folding his hands. "I see we're in the thick of it. But I have to ask. Why should Titan license from NovaTech, rather than build our own solution? Our engineers are among the best in the world."

Maya met his gaze, steady. "Because we've solved a problem your team is still wrestling with. And because we're willing to share, not just sell."

"Partnerships are built on trust. Are you prepared to be transparent?"

"We're prepared to share what's necessary—under NDA."

"Of course," Richard said. "Send us the technical specs. Our engineers will want to dig deeper."

Patel added with a faint smirk: "And we'll want to see the code. Not just the slides."

Alex nodded. "We can set up a sandbox environment. You'll see the performance for yourself."

The silver-haired engineer looked at him. "And if it doesn't live up to the hype?"

"Then you walk away," replied Maya. "No harm, no foul."

Richard's smile widened, but it didn't reach his eyes. "Excellent. Claire, coordinate the details. We'll be in touch."

The meeting ended with handshakes and polite promises. As Maya and Alex gathered their things, the Titan team was already conferring in low voices, their skepticism sharp and palpable.

As they left, Maya again felt the weight of the room pressing down. A reminder that in this world, validation was never freely given. It had to be wrested, line by line, from those who believed they'd already invented everything worth having.

The boardroom doors closed behind them with a soft, pneumatic sigh; a sound that felt, to Maya, like the sealing of a vault. The corridor outside was empty, the hush almost oppressive after the tense energy of the meeting.

Alex exhaled, shoulders sagging as if he'd held his breath for the entire pitch. He clutched the demo binder to his chest, knuckles white.

Maya glanced back through the glass. Inside, the Titan team had already clustered at the far end of the table, heads bent together, voices low and urgent. Richard Hale was speaking, gesturing with a slow, deliberate hand. No one looked their way.

Claire Donovan caught up with them, her expression apologetic but unreadable. "You both did well. Don't let the grilling get to you. Our engineers are... thorough."

Alex managed a weak smile. "Is it always like that?"

Claire hesitated. "Sometimes. They're proud of what they've built. Outsiders have to prove themselves."

Maya nodded, her voice steady but quiet. "We expected pushback. We're used to it."

Claire offered a small, genuine smile. "I'll be in touch soon. I'll make sure the NDA and pilot details move quickly."

They shook hands. Maya's grip firm, Alex's a little clammy. Claire lingered for a moment, as if she wanted to say more, then turned and disappeared back into the boardroom.

Maya and Alex walked in silence toward the elevator, the echo of their footsteps swallowed by the expanse of the corridor. The grandeur of the executive floor felt colder now; the art, the glass, the curated nature all parts of a machine designed to remind them of their place.

Inside the elevator, Alex finally spoke, his voice barely above a whisper. "They hated it."

Maya shook her head. "Not hated. They're defensive. They want to believe they're the smartest people in the room."

Alex stared at the floor. "Did we give them too much? Not enough?"

"We gave them what we had to," Maya replied. "If they want more, they'll have to earn it."

The elevator descended in silence, the city rising to meet them. Alex's hands trembled as he tucked the binder back into his bag.

"I kept thinking, if we blow this, it's over," he said, voice raw.

Maya reached out, squeezing his shoulder. "We didn't blow it. We showed them something they can't ignore. That's all we can do."

The elevator doors opened onto the lobby, the vast space now feeling even more cavernous and impersonal. The receptionist's smile was gone, replaced by the neutral efficiency of someone already on to the next task.

As they stepped outside, the air was sharp and bright, the city's noise a relief after the hush of Titan's world. Maya paused on the steps, looking back at the building—a fortress of glass and concrete, indifferent and immense.

Alex followed her gaze. "Do you think they'll call?"

Maya's answer was quiet, but resolute. "They have to. If they don't, we find someone who will."

They walked toward the street, the weight of the morning settling on their shoulders. For a moment, neither spoke. The future was uncertain, but for now, they had survived the gauntlet.

———

The doors had barely closed behind Maya and Alex when the atmosphere in the boardroom shifted from polite formality to something sharper. Like the air after a thunderclap.

Richard Hale remained at the head of the table, fingers steepled, gaze fixed on the NovaTech slides still glowing on the wall. The rest of the team relaxed their postures, the masks of hospitality slipping away.

Patel spoke first, voice dry. "They're smart. I'll give them that. But we've been down this road before. We could build something similar if we wanted to."

Anita, arms folded, didn't look up from her notes. "We've been saying that for a year. We haven't done it yet."

Patel's jaw tightened. "Because we've been busy with real priorities. Their 'breath' policy is just a queue manager dressed up in a PR campaign."

Dr. Lasker, silent until now, finally looked up. "It's more than that. The way they handle ghost streams and explain their decisions—there's engineering discipline there. And humility. The system knows when to wait, when to degrade, and it tells you why. That's rare."

The head of platform integration frowned. "Their modularity claims are optimistic. Our stack is a beast. Plug-and-play is a fantasy."

Gabe, Security, scrolled through his logs. "No credential leaks. No hidden calls. Their honeytokens are obvious if you're looking, but not malicious. They're careful."

Anita nodded. "And their adapters worked. Our weirdest payloads didn't break them. The pass-through on failure is honest. I'd rather have a system that admits when it's out of its depth than one that fakes it."

Patel pressed. "But do we want to depend on an outside vendor for something this core? Once we integrate, we're stuck negotiating on their terms."

Lasker countered. "Or we negotiate from strength, because we know what works and what doesn't. We can always build our own, but it'll take time. And time is the one thing we don't have if we want to hit Q3."

Claire, who had been quietly observing, finally spoke. "They're not asking for a blank check. They're offering a pilot, a price, and transparency. We can set the terms. And if we walk away, we do it with our eyes open."

Patel shook his head. "I still don't like it. Not invented here."

Anita's tone sharpened. "Not invented here is why we're behind on this feature. We can't keep pretending we're the only smart people in the room."

Gabe closed his laptop. "I want a longer security audit, but I'm not seeing red flags."

Lasker nodded. "I want to see how it scales. If it holds up under real load, we have to consider it."

Richard Hale rejoined the group. He looked around the room, reading the faces.

"Well?" he asked.

"They're good," Patel offered. "Maybe too good."

Lasker looked at him. "They're honest. And their system works."

Richard nodded, considering. "We'll keep them in the sandbox. Push them harder. If they break, we walk. If they don't, we negotiate. But we don't show our hand until we're sure."

He paused, then added, "And in the meantime, I want a parallel effort. If we can replicate their approach, we do it. If not, we buy what we need. But we don't let them set the price."

Patel asked dryly, "And if it works?"

Richard's smile was thin. "If it works, we'll see how much we can learn before we talk about licensing. No reason to pay for what we can build ourselves."

Dr. Lasker shook his head. "There's always a reason. Time to market, liability, optics. But yes, let's not get ahead of ourselves."

The head of platform integration closed her laptop. "I'll assign a team to review their API adapters. If they want to play in our sandbox, they'll have to play by our rules."

Richard nodded, his tone final. "Good. Claire, keep them hopeful. We want them eager, not desperate. And make sure legal tightens the NDA. No code until we say so."

Claire hesitated, then nodded. "Understood. I'll keep the lines open."

Richard's smile was thin. "Good. Let's see how brave they really are."

As the team filed out, Richard lingered, staring at the city beyond the glass. For the first time, NovaTech was more than an outsider, they were a problem. And maybe, just maybe, a solution.

———

The ride back to NovaTech was quiet, the city's bustle a distant hum behind the glass. Maya watched the world slip by. Strip malls, food trucks, a mural of a hummingbird on a cinderblock wall. Each one a reminder of the world they were fighting to stay in.

The NovaTech office felt even smaller after Titan's cathedral of glass and stone. The familiar clutter greeted them: whiteboards crowded with almost indecipherable scrawl, a tangle of charging cables, the battered coffee machine hissing in the corner. The patent certificate on the wall caught the afternoon light, a badge of hope and defiance.

Ethan was waiting, perched on the edge of a desk, eyes bright with anticipation. "Well?"

Alex dropped his bag and slumped into a chair. "They grilled us. Hard."

Maya hung her jacket, forcing a steady tone. "They were skeptical. Defensive, but they listened."

"Did they get it? Did they see what we've built?"

Alex rubbed his eyes. "They picked apart every detail. Called our transform a 'fancy average.' Wanted to know if we'd tested on their stack, their data, their everything."

"It was a gauntlet," Maya said. "But we held our ground. They want a pilot. NDA first, then maybe a sandbox."

"That's good, right?" Ethan asked anxiously.

Maya hesitated, searching for the right words. "It's not a no. But it's not a yes, either. They're proud. They don't want to admit someone else solved their problem."

Alex frowned. "They'll try to break it. Or rebuild it themselves."

Ethan looked at him. "So what do we do?"

Maya looked at her team, her family really, and felt the weight of the day settle in her bones. "We prepare. We lock down our code, document everything, anticipate every attack vector. We show them we're not just smart, we're resilient."

Alex managed a tired smile. "We've been here before."

Ethan grinned. "And we're still standing."

Maya nodded, resolve hardening. "We don't let them define us. Not Titan, not anyone. We built this. We know what it's worth."

A silence settled, not quite comfortable but full of shared understanding. Outside, the sun dipped behind the city's skyline, painting the office in gold and shadow.

Late that night, Maya sat alone in her office, replaying the meeting in her mind: Richard's smile, Claire's empathy, the engineers' skepticism. She thought of her parents, of every sacrifice, of the promise she'd made to herself and her team.

She opened her laptop and drafted the follow-up email to Claire, careful, precise, every word a negotiation.

Before sending, she paused, staring at her reflection in the dark screen. "We play fair," she whispered. "They do the same."

But even as she said it, she felt the first chill of doubt.

———

By late afternoon the office had shifted from adrenaline to procedure, the way a body settles after a sprint and starts repairing the microtears. Maya wrote *PILOT – WEEK 0* in block letters across the whiteboard and underlined it twice. The marker squeaked, as if protesting the weight of those words.

"Three tracks," she said, ticking them off on her fingers. "Security lockdown. Integration scaffolding. Performance harness. And a fourth that touches all three: story. We don't just prove it works; we prove why it matters."

Ethan spun his chair to face the board, a mechanical pencil tapping against his notebook. Alex leaned back, eyes closed for a beat, then opened them and pushed himself forward as if the chair had a spring.

"Lockdown first. No code leaves the building that we can't afford to lose. No secrets. No keys. No surprises."

Ethan nodded, already typing. "SBOMs for every module, signed artifacts only, ephemeral credentials. I'll rotate keys and kill the long-lived ones. Vaulted secrets, not env files."

"Tripwires," Maya added. "Honeytokens in the readmes and sample configs. If they touch what they shouldn't, we get an alert."

Alex's eyebrows lifted. "Subtle," he said. "I like it."

"And provenance," Maya said. "We generate attestation for every build. If anyone says, 'we built it ourselves,' we show the timeline of our choices."

She turned to the other half of the board, where an outline of boxes and arrows already formed a nervous system. Alex stood and took the marker without asking; it felt less like interrupting and more like finishing a sentence together.

Alex drew the transform layer as a river. A thick blue stroke that branched and rejoined. "We're not giving them internals," he said, "but we need to show confidence. Containerize the core, expose just enough at the edge."

He outlined the modules, labeling them with neat, compact handwriting:

- **ingest-gateway** (adapters: REST/GRPC/MQTT)
- **pre-normalize** (schema sniffers, basic guards)
- **transform-core** (topology-preserving map, adaptive weighting, feedback loop)
- **stability-orchestrator** (breath/queue control under surge)
- **audit & explain** (decision traces, hash-linked)
- **metrics & kill-switch** (SLOs, trip thresholds)

Ethan added a small box at the bottom: **license-sentinel**. "We watermark at runtime," he said. "Not just a string—behavioral fingerprinting. Tiny, harmless timing signatures on specific code paths. If we ever need to prove lineage, we can."

Maya raised an eyebrow. "Defensible?"

"Documented, reproducible, and nondestructive," Ethan said. "Invisible unless you know where to look."

Alex capped the marker and stepped back. "We'll offer them two integration paths: sidecar and inline. Sidecar gets us in fast. Inline is more efficient but riskier." He underlined *SIDECAR*. "We pitch it as 'your stack, our lungs.'"

The whiteboard filled with boxes and arrows, a nervous system taking shape. The team stood back, surveying the architecture. Part shield, part invitation, all theirs.

Ethan prowled the office, sleeves pushed up, eyes scanning lines of code like a detective at a crime scene. The hum of the servers was a comfort. Steady, predictable, unlike the world outside.

He muttered to himself as he typed, fingers flying. "CI only from signed commits. No direct pushes. Strip secrets, scream if someone forgets." Each rule was a shield, each warning a scar from battles past.

Alex watched from across the room, half-amused, half-admiring. "You treat the pipeline like it's a fortress."

Ethan didn't look up. "It is. Or it better be." He paused, then added, "Titan's sandbox gets the gateway, nothing else. Rate limits, anomaly flags. If they try to scrape, we'll see it."

Maya leaned against the whiteboard, arms folded. "Don't show we're watching. Let them feel trusted. But don't trust them."

Ethan's lips twitched—a smile, almost. "Trust is a log line with a timestamp." He pinned a fresh printout to the corkboard: *PILOT READINESS CHECKLIST*. Boxes for SBOMs, signatures, vault audits, key rotations. At the bottom, he added *HONEYTOKEN STATUS*, a row of empty squares waiting to be filled.

He stepped back, surveying his handiwork. "Checkboxes are cheap courage," he said quietly, but he checked them anyway. Each tick was a promise: not today, not on my watch.

Alex wandered over, peering at the checklist. "You ever sleep?"

Ethan shrugged. "Sleep's for when the logs are quiet."

Maya smiled, just a little. "We're lucky you're paranoid."

Ethan grinned, the tension easing for a moment. "Paranoia's just pattern recognition with a bad attitude."

He turned back to his laptop, eyes sharp, mind already racing ahead. The world outside was full of giants, but inside these walls, Ethan was the sentry. Watching, waiting, ready.

The office had adopted the rhythm of a lab. Cables curled like sleeping snakes across the floor; laptops hummed and warmed palms; whiteboard residue misted the air with the faint mineral smell of erasable ink.

Alex opened a terminal, summoned the demo topology, and spoke without looking up.

"How about a sidecar that safely ingests multi-protocol streams, normalizes them, adapts under load, and self-protects when SLOs or integrity are at risk? We'll favor data correctness over uptime with a hard stop on any data loss.

"Adapters first. We'll meet them where they live."

Ethan pulled up a spec sheet, sketched a quick diagram. "REST adapter: idempotent POST for batches, streaming GET for continuous. GRPC: bidirectional stream; flow control with credits. MQTT: QoS 1, retained messages off. We gate all three through ingest-gateway so we can swap internals without them knowing."

Alex nodded. "Schema sniffers in pre-normalize. We detect basic shape: time, source, payload, tags. And wrap anything unknown in a safe envelope. If a stream is pathological, we pass it to quarantine, not to the core."

He typed, the code scrolling in clean, deliberate bursts:

```yaml
# pilot-sidecar-config.yaml
    ingest-gateway:
    listeners:
    - name: rest
    port: 8443
    tls: required
    auth: mTLS
    - name: grpc
    port: 7443
    tls: required
    auth: mTLS
    - name: mqtt
    port: 1883
    tls: starttls
    auth: token
    pre-normalize:
    schema:
    required_fields: [timestamp, source, payload]
    coercions:
    timestamp: iso8601|epoch
    payload: json|binary
    quarantine:
    drop_on: [malformed_timestamp, payload_overflow]
    transform-core:
```

```
mode: adaptive
explainability: on
stability-orchestrator:
queue:
max_depth_ms: 300
surge_threshold: p95(latency) > 180ms
breath:
policy: "favor_integrity"
metrics:
export: prometheus
slo:
latency_p95: 150ms
data_loss: 0
kill_switch:
thresholds:
hard_stop: data_loss > 0
soft_degrade: cpu > 85% && latency_p95 > 180ms
```

"This won't be the exact file we hand them," Maya said, reading over his shoulder, "but it contains the soul of it."

Alex glanced up at her. "The soul without the arteries."

Ethan added, "We'll watermark at runtime. Behavioral fingerprinting. If we ever need to prove lineage, we can."

Maya nodded, her resolve sharpening. "Adapters, schema guards, tripwires. We meet them on their terms, but we keep our lungs breathing."

Alex smiled, the tension easing for a moment. "Let's make sure the lungs don't cough."

The team bent over their screens, the hum of the servers filling the space between them. A rhythm as familiar as their arguments, and as vital as their hope.

Maya moved to a different whiteboard and drew a square labeled REALITY.

"Performance isn't a number," she said. "It's a story. What are our beats?"

Ethan spoke before Alex could. "Golden set first. Our clean lab data. Then Dirty Twelve. Twelve streams with the worst behavior we've seen: out-of-order timestamps, skewed clocks, bursty payloads, embedded NaNs, duplicated IDs, nested array-of-arrays nonsense, BSON pretending to be JSON, huge payloads with tiny useful signals, and a stream that flips encoding mid-sentence because why not."

Alex grinned despite himself. "Don't forget the ghost stream. The one that goes to sleep for 93 seconds every 10 minutes, just long enough to convince a naïve heartbeat it's dead."

Ethan snapped his fingers. "Ghost is thirteen. The Dirty Baker's Dozen."

Maya wrote them down, the list becoming a kind of poetry. "Metrics?" she asked.

Alex rattled them off as if they'd been living in his throat for weeks. "Latency: p50, p95, p99. Throughput in events per second. Loss rate zero, obviously. Transform fidelity—distance between source structure and normalized shape measured by map entropy. Stability under surge —breath cycles, queue depth area under the curve. Explainability coverage—the percentage of decisions with trace. Footprint—CPU, memory, network overhead."

Maya underlined *Explainability*. "If they ask why it worked, we tell them in one sentence. If they ask how, we show them the trace. If they ask, 'could we have done this ourselves,' we make it clear what choices we made and why we made them then."

"Without giving away the sauce," Ethan added.

"Sauce is a verb, not a noun," Alex said, and began scripting the load generator.

Ethan popped in earbuds and began his other favorite game: breaking things he loved to keep them honest. He wrote adversarial test flows in terse lines that looked like curses:

- **stutter**: pause streams unpredictably; jitter clocks by ±300ms; burst payloads at 3× steady state.
- **flood**: slow, then hurricane; watch queue fall to its knees, then stand again.

- **salt**: inject subtly malformed fields that parsers typically "helpfully" coerce.
- **mirror**: create a near-duplicate stream with a single structural mutation to test topology sensitivity.
- **mask**: hide a critical tag in a nested object two layers down to test sniffers.

He wired each into the harness with switchable flags, added observer hooks, then paused at **salt**, chewing the inside of his cheek before adding a line:

- **malice**: attempt to probe endpoints beyond gateway; log and blackhole.

As the first test runs began, the team gathered around the screens the way people gather around a campfire. Drawn to heat they can't touch. Lines climbed and bent and held. The stability-orchestrator pulsed under surge, breath policy favoring integrity. Queue depth swelled, then eased. Latency curves rose and didn't panic.

Ethan watched the numbers, eyes sharp. "Look at p99," he said. "She flirts with 190ms, then... breathes."

Alex spoke almost as in wonder, "She knows when to wait."

A warning light blinked and died. **Salt** found a parser that tried to be too helpful, coercing a malformed timestamp instead of rejecting it. Alex cursed under his breath, opened the module, and made the fix. A two-line change that toggled a guard from permissive to skeptical.

"Fail loudly," he said, committing the patch. "We're not the lenient uncle."

Maya smiled, tension easing for a moment. "Let's make sure reality doesn't break us before Titan has the chance."

The harness ran on, the office quiet except for the whir of server fans and the steady beat of hope.

Maya wrote across the top of another whiteboard:

WHAT THEY WILL SAY → WHAT WE ANSWER.

*"Isn't this just optimization?"* → "Optimization assumes a known axis. We created the axis then chose mercy over speed under surge."

*"We've tried adaptive transforms; they break."* → "They break when you flatten humans into averages. This preserves accents, explainability on."

*"Plug-and-play never is."* → "Sidecar by design. Adapters meet your dialects; the lungs breathe at the edge."

*"Prove it."* → "Dirty Baker's Dozen. Your data next."

She stepped back, the board a choreography of provocation and reply. "We need a single slide that reads clearly in a hallway," she said. "One that holds the shape of the truth."

Alex pulled up a template: no gradients, no stock people high-fiving. A simple diagram with streams entering left, a river in the middle, clear shape exiting right. He added a red dot where the breath policy engaged.

"Here's the heartbeat," he said. "We tell them when and why we slow down."

Maya drafted the email to Claire. Tone: collaborative, not deferential. Details: mTLS certificates issued per service; a sandbox endpoint with narrow ingress; a proposed data dictionary for the pilot. She attached a one-page *Pilot Guide*. A map without the treasure.

Before hitting send, she looked to Ethan. "Tripwires?"

"Honeytokens sprinkled and sleeping," he said. "If they lift a sample config verbatim into production or a public repo, we get an alert. If they scrape, the gateway coughs politely and logs it."

"And if their engineers are just thorough, not malicious?"

"Then the tripwires stay bored," he said. "Bored is my favorite state."

She sent the email. The whoosh sounded more final than it ought to.

They rehearsed like a band about to record live. Ethan played Titan. Blunt, smart, and easily bored.

"Why weighted?" he threw across the table. "Why not a simple Kalman filter?"

"Because your sources lie in different ways at different times," Alex answered. "Our weights aren't constants; they're context, and the transform explains itself as it changes."

"Explain without hand-waving," Ethan said, tone clipped.

Alex pivoted to the trace viewer. A decision tree unfolded like a polite autopsy: "Source A skewed 120ms; downweighted by 0.15; Source C stable, promoted; breath policy engaged at 182ms; queue depth peaked at 270ms; loss prevented."

"Miles better," Ethan said. "Now do it without talking."

Alex tapped once. The tale assembled in five words and a curve. Ethan nodded, satisfied and a little cruel. "Again."

He pushed on risk. "What happens if stability-orchestrator itself fails?"

"We're stateless," Alex said. "Heartbeats fall back to safe lane. Kill switch trips and we drop to pass-through with tagging so you know we degraded."

"Show me," Ethan said, and Alex did, the line flattening, honesty over bravado.

They swapped roles; Maya took the questions with the grace of someone stirring an argument into a story. When Ethan said, "This is just plug-and-play marketing," she answered, "No, plug-and-prove," and let the numbers fill the space after.

———

Night took the city and then the building, leaving the office in a blue quiet. The coffee machine gave one last sigh and went to sleep.

Alex stayed with the transform's heart. Flamegraphs bloomed and cooled; he shaved a handful of microseconds from a hot loop with a cache hint and the removal of a poetic but unnecessary allocation. He commented the change with a single sentence: *Mercy still fast.* He smiled at his own softness and left it in.

Ethan pulled a chair into the server closet and listened to the fans like they were waves. He combed the logs, eyes snagging on small irregularities the way a tongue finds a cracked tooth. He tuned the anomaly detector, nudged thresholds, and wrote himself a sticky note: *Trust is a log line with a timestamp.*

Maya walked the quiet office, fingertips grazing the backs of empty chairs, the edges of whiteboards. She stopped at the patent certificate and the space beside it where, one day, a second frame might go. She imagined the pilot going right, then wrong, then right again in an unpredictable pulse. She imagined the day Titan would say "we'll be in touch" and mean it. She imagined the day they wouldn't.

Her phone vibrated on the desk. A reply from Claire:

*Got it—clean and thoughtful. Legal will turn NDA tonight.*
*Proposing sandbox window Wed–Fri. Our data set will include mixed sources.*
*Thank you for the clarity on scope.*
*—C*

Maya forwarded the note to Alex and Ethan with a single word: *Green.*

———

Morning broke in thin bands. The building smelled like burnt coffee and dry-erase marker and a little like hope.

The checklist on the corkboard wore more ink than box. **SBOM** checked. **Signatures** checked. **Vault audit** checked. **Honeytokens** blinking a polite, contented gray.

Alex had added a handwritten line at the bottom: *Teach the lungs to sing.* Ethan had drawn a tiny set of eyes beside **tripwires**, and under it wrote: *We're watching the watchers.*

Maya updated the agenda: *WED – Titan Sandbox: 10:00 a.m.* She drew a thin rectangle around the time slot, then shaded the edges like a boundary.

"All right," she said to the room that was also a team and sometimes a family. "We're ready. Or we're as ready as anyone gets before a giant decides who they are today."

Ethan cracked his knuckles. "Dirty Baker's Dozen loaded."

Alex took a breath, then another. He smiled at Maya, small and real. "Lungs are warm."

Maya looked at the whiteboard river, the one that had carried them from idea to now. She capped the marker and set it down as if laying a tool on a table between surgeries.

"Let's breathe."

———

The office looked different at 9:57 a.m. Not cleaner or bigger, but more intentional, as if the furniture had taken a position. Cables were coiled, coffee cups exiled to the back counter. On the wall screen, three panes waited: **Metrics**, **Traces**, and **Titan**. A video tile with the Titan logo and a spinning wheel.

"mTLS certs in place," Ethan said, checking the green ticks. "Sandbox endpoint fenced. Honeytokens bored."

Maya stood behind him with a legal pad she wouldn't need. Beside her, Alex rolled his shoulders and flexed his fingers as if about to play an instrument. The clock ticked to 10:00. Titan's tile resolved into faces.

Claire appeared first—brisk, kind eyes, a nod that said *let's do the work*. Then Patel, expression a bar of steel. Dr. Lasker slid into frame, silver hair immaculate, gaze neutral. Two more tiles joined. **DevOps—Anita** (platform integration) and **Security—Gabe** (who looked like he didn't laugh often on the clock).

"Good morning," Claire said, her eyes brisk but kind. "Thanks for the tight prep. We have a two-hour window and a mixed set ready. Shall we?"

"We're ready." Maya confirmed. "Scope as agreed: sidecar only, adapters on REST, GRPC, and MQTT. We'll start with our Golden Set for baselining, then you drive."

"We'll drive," Patel said, leaning forward.

"Perfect," Maya said. "We'll breathe."

Ethan toggled a switch. **Pilot Sidecar** came online—one container blossomed into a constellation. The **Metrics** pane lit with first numbers. Flat lines waiting for data.

Alex started the pilot. "Publishing SLOs. You'll see them pinned left —so we can argue from the same sheet of music."

SLOs:
latency_p95 <= 150 ms
data_loss == 0
explainability_coverage >= 95%
cpu <= 85% (steady), <= 90% (surge)

Patel nodded. "Noted."

NovaTech pushed the Golden Set. Clean lab streams meant to show the shape of success before reality set in. Graphs rose and held, blue veins pulsing with traffic.

**Metrics** scrolled:

10:03:11[1]() ingest_eps=15,200 p50=46ms p95=118ms
p99=141ms
10:03:11[2]() loss=0 queue_depth_ms=24 breath=off
10:03:11[3]() explainability_coverage=100% export=healthy

"So far, a brochure," said Dr. Lasker.

"Exactly," Maya said. "Now your turn."

Anita unmuted. "We'll start with a mild spike and some clock drift. Realistic day, before the alarm bells."

On NovaTech's board a lettered icon slid into the stream (T-01). The p95 curve lifted to 129 ms and stayed. Queue depth wobbled and settled.

Alex narrated without theatrics. "Clock skew detected at 112 ms on Source D; down-weighted 0.15; stability-orchestrator idle; no breath."

"You're weighting the source because of time drift?" Patel asked, voice tight with accusation. "Risky. Data could be right and the clock wrong."

Alex switched to **Traces**, clicking the top line. A tidy card expanded: five bullet decisions and an annotated mini-timeline.

TRACE: stream:D span:transform-core@7421

- clock_skew: +112ms (threshold 80ms) → weight: -0.15
- corroboration: sources A/C aligned within 12ms → weight: +0.05 to A/C
- structure_preservation: maintained (entropy drift 0.02)
- surge_state: false (p95=129ms < 150ms SLO)
- decision_signature: 8f1b:ca62

"Clock wrong, data intact," Alex said. "We preserve the data's accent and tell you why."

Gabe cut in. "Fingerprint in that decision signature?"

Ethan smiled a fraction. "Only for trace integrity. No PII, no hidden beacons."

Patel waved it off, voice clipped. "Next."

Anita lifted her eyebrows, seeking permission. Richard wasn't on the call, but his ethos was. Patel nodded. Anita pressed keys.

"T-04," Ethan said softly. "Here comes the salt."

The p95 line firmed at 141 ms; p99 flirted with 168 and eased. Then a small red pulse appeared: **breath on**. Queue depth rose and fell like a lung.

The log stream ticked:

1 {"ts":"10:09:26.114","module":"pre-normalize","event":"coercion_refused","field":"timestamp","value":"2025-11-13T10:09:26.1z","reason":"malformed_fraction","action":"quarantine"}
2 {"ts":"10:09:26.132","module":"transform-core","event":"surge_policy","state":"ON","trigger":"p95>150ms?false, p99>180ms?false","breath":"micro"}
3 {"ts":"10:09:26.210","module":"audit","event":"decision_trace","id":"c7a5..",
"coverage":"100%"}

Patel pounced. "You're dropping the bad timestamps."

"Quarantining," Alex corrected. "Tagging, not trashing. You decide later."

Dr. Lasker watched the breath pulse. "Micro-breath buys you integrity. You pay latency."

"Yes," Alex said simply.

Lasker nodded slightly. "Good."

Patel's mouth tightened.

Anita queued a proprietary payload—nested arrays of arrays, one object flipping encoding mid-stream. Ethan's eyebrow arched. "Dirty Nine plus Ghost."

The queue depth grew and smoothed; explainability held at 100%. CPU climbed to 74%.

**Metrics:**
10:16:03[4]() ingest_eps=28,900 p50=52ms p95=146ms p99=181ms
10:16:03[5]() loss=0 queue_depth_ms=163 breath=on (duty=0.18)
10:16:03[6]() cpu=74% mem=63% export=healthy explainability=100%

"Show adapter behavior," Anita said. "Where exactly do you unwrap our nonsense?"

Ethan opened a slim pane in **pre-normalize**. No code, just a human-readable decision tree:

ADAPTER PATH: ingest-gateway → rest → pre-normalize
- schema sniff: found ["timestamp","source","payload"] ✓
- payload: nested arrays depth=3 → path: flatten:2 preserve:1
- encoding flip: utf8→latin1 at offset 4092 → normalized (tag: encoding_flip)
- quarantine: none

Patel remained unimpressed. "Still looks like... good plumbing."

"Plumbing that doesn't flood the house," Ethan said.

Gabe unmuted, voice pure compliance. "We're going to push a surge—a real one. If something breaks, we want to see it now."

"Understood," Maya said. "We'll show everything."

Traffic doubled in four seconds, then doubled again. The p95 scraped 152 ms, p99 jumped to 211, and the breath indicator glowed steady. A visible exhale. Queue depth swelled to 310 ms and began its way back.

A hard ding hit the log. A different tone. Ethan's eyes flicked left.

1 {"ts":"10:22:17.019","module":"gateway","event":"anomaly","class":
"exploration","vector":"/metrics/_all","src":"10.54.7.28","action":"blackhole",
"note":"sandbox ingress only"}

Gabe said nothing. His mouth tilted half a degree, a professional admission, *we were going to check.*

Alex narrated over the surge. "Breath policy at duty 0.27. No loss. Transform fidelity within drift 0.05. Export steady."

"You're still hiding cost," Patel noted. "Show CPU."

"Front and center," Ethan said as CPU hit 83% and leveled. Memory rose to 71%. SLOs remained green, except **latency p99**, amber for eleven seconds, before snapping back to green.

Maya remarked: "We slow instead of bleed. That's the core choice."

"Your core choice," Patel said. "Others choose differently."

"Others choose dropped patients," Maya said, and let the sentence hang.

The session continued, each test a new challenge, each metric a measure of NovaTech's resolve. The team watched the numbers, the traces, the breath cycles. They knew every decision, every line of code, was being weighed by giants.

The flood subsided to a heavy rain. Titan shifted from assault to deposition.

Patel leaned in, voice sharp. "We've prototyped adaptive transforms. What you're doing looks like weighted regression wearing a marketing halo."

Alex didn't flinch. "If you don't need topology preservation, yes. This is just flavor. But when misalignment matters, the halo is the heart."

Patel pressed. "You're not using a Kalman filter."

Alex answered. "No."

"Why not?"

"Because Kalman assumes noise with a shape. We map noise that changes its mind."

Gabe cut in. "Decision trace. Can you redact that in production? We have regimes where even reasoning becomes sensitive."

Ethan answered, steady. "Toggle per field and per stream. Coverage SLO is yours to set. We'll still log hashes, so you know a decision happened when it happened."

Anita, platform integration, challenged. "Plug-and-play. Our stack is brittle by design. How many adapters will you write before you ask us to shift?"

"We'll meet your dialects at the gateway," Ethan said. "Inside are our lungs. You don't move your bones for us."

Claire watched it all, a silent judge of tone more than content. She caught Maya's eye with a small you're-doing-it nod.

Maya stood her ground, voice calm but unyielding. "We built this to survive the worst. If you want to break it, you'll have to get creative."

Patel's mouth tightened, but he didn't look away.

The questions kept coming, each one a test, each answer a line drawn between trust and skepticism. NovaTech held the line, their choices exposed, their logic on display.

Anita whispered to someone off-camera and then: "Okay. Ghost stream. Not because we think you'll fail. Because we expect it to."

Traffic normalized. Then, as if bored, one stream went to sleep for 93 seconds. Heartbeats flattened to a line. Many systems would declare death.

NovaTech's queue did not panic. The breath indicator dimmed and stayed on the edge of on.

The trace showed why:

TRACE: stream:GHOST span:stability-orchestrator@219
- heartbeat: missing (t=+81s) → hold: lane=warm
- policy: do not rehome; do not rebalance (ghost profile matched)

- resume: t=+93s → reintegrate with weight: -0.08 for 12s
- decision_signature: ee73:b1d9

Dr. Lasker leaned in, his first genuine movement of interest. "You've fingerprinted ghostliness."

Alex's voice was steady. "We've learned to wait for the right absences."

Lasker didn't smile this time, but the corners of his eyes softened into something human. "Good."

Patel stared at his own notes, unwilling to grant ground in public. Eyes narrowed, voice clipped, he said, "Turn off explainability and run the surge again."

Maya met the challenge head-on. "Why?"

Patel didn't blink. "Instrumentation hides sins."

Ethan toggled a profile, fingers steady. "Explainability traces off; counters on. Same surge."

Numbers rose; breath came on sooner by two seconds, latency p95 rose three milliseconds, p99 by five, CPU fell by one percent. Ethan showed the diff like a weather map.

"Overhead's one to two percent," he said. "Sinless enough?"

Gabe barely glanced up. "Turn it back on." Not a request; policy asserting itself.

Ethan toggled. "Back."

Alex watched the numbers settle, tension easing just a little. "Transparency is a choice. We built for scrutiny."

Patel's mouth twitched, almost a smile. "We'll see how much scrutiny you can handle."

Maya stood her ground, voice even. "We're not hiding. If you want to see the bones, you'll have to trust the lungs."

The room was quiet, the challenge hanging in the air. NovaTech's system had survived another test, but the real scrutiny was only beginning.

Anita leaned forward, voice measured but insistent. "We'd like to peek at the transform loop. Just to validate assumptions."

Maya didn't hesitate. "We can't share source. Not for a pilot."

Patel pressed, arms folded. "Then you're asking us to trust the black box."

Alex met the challenge, calm but firm. "Not black. Translucent. You can see the choices; you can't take the lungs home."

Patel's tone sharpened. "Home is where we're going to build them anyway."

A brief silence. Maya held her ground. "Then this pilot proves one of two things. That you don't need us. Or that you don't want to need us."

Claire stepped in, voice gentle but authoritative. "Let's stay inside scope. We agreed to traces, metrics, and adapters. For today, that's enough."

Patel didn't argue, but the line was drawn. NovaTech's boundaries held. Transparency, but not surrender.

Alex glanced at Maya, a silent confirmation passing between them. The code would stay home. The lungs would keep breathing, on Nova-Tech's terms.

At 11:41, Dirty Eleven slithered in. A payload with a nested number that exceeded a boundary no one had seen in six months. Pre-normalize balked and quarantined; then transform-core threw a soft error and tripped the kill-switch to safe lane for twenty-three seconds.

The big screen flipped to a red banner that said nothing more dramatic than DEGRADED—PASSTHROUGH + TAGS.

Maya didn't move. "Thank you for breaking reality where we could see it."

Ethan opened the trace of the failure as if showing a bruise. He pointed with a pen, not a cursor. "This is the guard that chose honesty. If you'd rather we limp, we can argue. We chose to walk."

No one spoke for three seconds. Then Anita: "You held your SLOs. That matters."

Patel exhaled in a way that sounded like a word he didn't say.

Alex watched the numbers settle, relief and pride mingling with fatigue. "We built for failure. Not for hiding it."

Maya nodded, her voice steady. "We'd rather show you the bruise than pretend we never fall."

The room was quiet; the failure exposed and accepted. NovaTech's system had bent but not broken and the team stood a little taller for it.

Dr. Lasker cleared his throat, leaning in for the first time with genuine interest. "Run the ghost again, but with salt and a minor time skew. I want to see the breath hesitate and then choose."

NovaTech ran it. The red dot breathed, paused, and resumed. A choreography that felt like intention.

Lasker nodded, almost to himself. "Okay."

It wasn't applause; it was acceptance of a kind that mattered more.

Ethan watched the metrics, a small smile flickering. "She hesitated. She chose."

Alex exhaled, tension unwinding from his shoulders. "We taught her to wait for the right absences."

Maya caught Lasker's nod, the subtle shift in the room. "Sometimes the win is quiet," she said, voice low but certain.

The team let the moment settle, knowing that in a room full of skeptics, a single nod could mean everything.

Claire glanced at the time. "We're at two hours. Any last requests?"

Gabe spoke up. "Export a scrubbed trace bundle: no payload, decisions only, with timing. Our audit needs to see."

Ethan nodded. "We'll ship hashes and choices. No secrets."

Anita added, "Leave the sandbox up for the afternoon? We'll do quiet runs. If we find anything dull, we'll let you know."

"Please do," Maya said, her tone steady.

Patel's face reappeared front and center. "We'll debrief internally. Claire will be in touch. If we continue, we'll want a scale test. And a price."

Maya didn't hesitate. "Both are prepared. Price follows value; scale, courage."

Patel's mouth twitched—the closest he got to a smile that day. "We'll see how brave we feel."

The Titan tiles blinked out until only Claire remained. "Good work," she said, and meant it. "I'll move the paperwork."

The screen went black.

———

The office was quiet, the tension replaced by a fragile sense of accomplishment. Ethan leaned back, finally letting himself breathe. Alex closed his laptop, exhaustion and pride mingling in his eyes. Maya stood for a moment, letting the silence settle.

Ethan finally spoke, voice low. "Honeytoken #3 woke up for twelve seconds." He shrugged. "Curiosity, not theft."

Maya glanced at the corkboard, where the checklist was now mostly inked in. "Bored again?" she asked.

Ethan nodded. "Nicely bored."

Alex leaned back, closed his eyes, then opened them with a wet shine he blinked away. "Did we... convince them?"

Maya watched the blank screen, the silence stretching. "We showed them breath," she said. "Some people only respect speed. Lasker respects breath."

"That's one," Ethan said.

"One is how you start counting," Maya answered.

Her phone buzzed on the desk. Claire:

*Pilot complete. Thanks for the trace bundle. Platform team is reviewing. Will circle back after internal debrief.*

*Will keep you posted if there are next steps.*

*—C*

Maya read it twice, searching for meaning in the corporate brevity. No promises, no next steps. Just a polite acknowledgment and a vague timeline.

She forwarded the note to Alex and Ethan, her words brief: *Green light, for now.*

Alex underlined *SIDECAR* on the whiteboard one last time. Ethan reopened the logs, eyes scanning for patterns in the quiet.

The team let the moment settle, hope flickering in the silence. Outside, the city moved on. Inside, NovaTech waited. Uncertain, but still believing.

# THREE

THE FIRST MORNING after the pilot, hope lingered in the air, fragile but persistent. Maya woke before dawn, her mind already racing. She checked her phone. Nothing from Titan, nothing from Claire. She scrolled through Ethan's overnight logs, searching for reassurance in the numbers.

At the office, Alex was already at his desk, dark circles under his eyes, a half-empty mug cooling beside him. "I couldn't sleep," he admitted, voice thin. "Kept replaying the sandbox. Did we tune the breath policy too aggressively?"

Ethan shrugged, trying for confidence. "It held. If they want more, they'll ask." He tapped at his keyboard, sending another round of logs to Maya, as if proof could conjure a reply.

The team clung to routine, buoyed by the memory of the successful pilot. They refactored code, updated documentation, ran new tests on the "Dirty Baker's Dozen." Maya drafted a follow-up email to Claire, then deleted it, then drafted it again. She told herself patience was a virtue, yet it felt more like surrender.

By noon, optimism began to fray. The office was too quiet, every conversation brittle. Alex tried to rally the team with a new performance metric, but the numbers felt hollow, like applause in an empty theater.

Ethan grew restless, pacing between his desk and the server rack, muttering about latency curves and anomaly flags.

Maya checked her email every hour, then every half hour, then every ten minutes. She scrolled through investor updates, news alerts, anything that might explain the silence. She watched the patent certificate on the wall, waiting for it to shine again with the promise it once held.

A text buzzed on Maya's phone: *Dinner tonight? Or should I just eat alone again?*

She stared at the message, thumb hovering over the reply. She typed, deleted, typed again. *I'll bring dinner home. Nine.* She hit **Send** before she could second-guess it, guilt already gnawing at her resolve.

Day blurred into night. The city outside moved on, indifferent to NovaTech's hopes and fears. Maya lingered in the office long after sunset, the hum of the servers her only company. She replayed the pilot in her mind. Titan's engineers, the metrics, the subtle win. She remembered Claire's nod, Patel's grudging respect. Surely, she thought, they would call.

But they didn't.

———

Ravi was curled at the far end of the couch, one ankle tucked under him, the TV's glow flattening the room into blue and gray. A bowl of popcorn sat untouched.

The door clicked. Maya stepped in, breath caught in the collar of her coat, takeout bag swinging from her wrist. "I'm home," she said softly.

"You said nine," Ravi answered. Not angry, just tired. The kind of tired that comes from waiting without knowing why.

11:38 blinked on the stove. "I know," she said. "I'm sorry. Titan—. " She lifted the bag, trying for a smile. "I brought dinner."

"I ate," he said, a small apology tucked inside the words.

She sank beside him, the couch breathing out a sigh. She wanted to ask about the movie, to put her head on his shoulder and let the day slough off.

Her phone buzzed. Alan: *Any update from Titan? Their silence is spooking the board. Need reassurance before Monday's call.*

Maya's thumb hovered. The responsible thing, the only thing, was to answer before the rumor mill found its own oxygen.

Ravi muted the TV. "You hear me," he said quietly, "but I don't know if you're actually here."

Guilt flared. "Ravi—"

He clicked the screen dark. The room went still, the takeout bag cooling between them.

For the first time, a thin thread of fear tugged at Maya: some emergencies didn't announce themselves until they'd already rearranged the furniture.

———

There were no calls from Titan the next day nor the one thereafter.

The silence grew heavier, filling the office with tension that made every gesture feel rehearsed. Ethan snapped at small mistakes, slamming his laptop shut when a test failed. "Why do we even bother?" he muttered, his voice sharp enough to sting.

Alex retreated into his code, headphones clamped tight, rewriting modules that didn't need rewriting. At lunch, he stared at his untouched sandwich, lost in thought. "What if we missed something?" he whispered to Maya. "What if they found a flaw?"

Maya kept up a brave front, her optimism thinning with each unanswered message. She sent another email to Claire, this one shorter, more desperate. She didn't expect a reply.

By the end of the week, hope had curdled into bafflement. The team gathered for morning standup, but the energy was gone. Alex stared at the whiteboard, lost in thought. Ethan barely spoke. Maya tried to reassure them, but her words felt insubstantial, like mist.

A calendar alert flashed on Maya's screen: *Board call—Monday, noon.*

She closed the notification, feeling the knot in her stomach tighten.

Still, they waited. Still, they believed. But the cat was out of the bag, and NovaTech was left behind, watching as the world moved on without them.

———

On the third day, Maya arrived early, her desk littered with notes, spreadsheets, and half-drunk coffee. She rehearsed her talking points for the board, but the knot in her stomach only tightened.

The screen flickered to life, faces appearing in neat rows. Alan, jaw set; Priya, eyes sharp behind her glasses; Jonas, already frowning.

Alan spoke first, voice clipped. "Three days, Maya. Not a word from Titan. What are we supposed to tell our LPs?"

Maya forced a steady tone. "The pilot went well. Titan asked for a trace bundle and a short SOW for a load test. We delivered everything on time. Claire said they'd circle back."

Jonas interrupted, voice tight. "Circle back? That's not a commitment. You said this pilot would be the turning point. Instead, we're bleeding cash and getting ghosted."

Priya's tone was icy. "We're fielding questions from the fund. They want to know if we're chasing vapor. Titan's silence is making us look desperate."

Maya's throat tightened. "We're still in the running. I'm following up, but—"

Alan cut her off. "You need to stop waiting for them to call. What's your plan if they walk? And don't say 'pivot.' We've heard that before."

Jonas leaned forward, frustration clear. "We're seeing chatter that Titan's platform team is benchmarking other vendors. Are we even on their radar anymore?"

Priya added, "We need something concrete, Maya. Not another story. Not another promise."

Maya hesitated, searching for words. "We have meetings lined up with two other OEMs. I'm pushing for a letter of intent."

Alan's voice was flat. "You have five days. If there's no traction, we'll have to consider winding down. I'm not risking another quarter on hope."

The call ended abruptly, leaving Maya staring at her own reflection in the black screen. The office felt colder, the patent certificate on the wall looking more like a tombstone than a trophy.

———

Maya stepped into the apartment, shaking rain from her hair. The kitchen was quiet, but not peaceful. Ravi was at the counter, sorting through a stack of unopened mail. He glanced up, his expression unreadable.

"You got something from the insurance," he said, holding out an envelope. "And a letter from your mother."

She took them, setting them aside. "Thanks. Sorry I'm late."

He shrugged, but his movements were clipped. "I didn't know if you'd be home. I ate."

Maya opened the fridge, searching for something to say. "The board call was brutal. Titan's still not responding. I spent half the day trying to keep the team from falling apart."

He leaned against the counter, arms folded. "You know, I tried calling you. Twice. Just wanted to hear your voice. I ended up talking to your voicemail."

She winced, guilt flickering. "I'm sorry. I was in meetings all afternoon. I should have checked."

He shook his head. "It's not about the calls, Maya. It's about feeling like I'm on the outside looking in. I hear more about NovaTech's problems than about us."

She closed the fridge, empty-handed. "I don't know what to say. Everything feels urgent. If Titan ghosts us, we're done."

He softened, just a little. "I get that. I do. But you're not the only one with things falling apart. My project's getting cut. I might be out of a job next month. I wanted to talk about it, but—" He trailed off, the words lingering between them like fragile glass.

Maya stepped closer, reaching for his hand. "Tell me. I want to know."

He let her take his hand, but his grip was loose. "I just want to feel like we're in this together, not merely surviving side by side."

She nodded, the weight of his words settling in. "I'm sorry. I've been so wrapped up in NovaTech, I didn't see what was happening here."

He squeezed her hand, finally meeting her eyes. "I miss you, Maya. Not the CEO. Just you."

For a moment, Maya let herself be vulnerable. "I miss who I am too."

He smiled, tired but genuine. "Shall we try again tomorrow?"

She nodded, hope flickering. "Tomorrow."

He headed for the bedroom, pausing in the doorway. "Don't stay up all night."

Maya lingered in the kitchen, the unopened mail a silent reminder of everything she'd neglected. For the first time in weeks, she didn't reach for her laptop. She just stood there, listening to the quiet, wondering if tomorrow would be different.

———

The next morning, the office was quieter than usual. The rain had stopped, but the tension hadn't. Maya arrived early, hoping to set the tone, but even the coffee machine seemed reluctant to start.

Alex was already at his desk, headphones on, staring at lines of code that refused to yield any comfort. Ethan wandered in late, his usual energy dulled, eyes flicking to the empty inbox on his phone.

Maya tried to rally the team. "Let's run the numbers again. Maybe there's something we missed in the pilot logs."

Alex didn't look up. "We didn't miss anything. The system worked. The metrics were clean."

Ethan slumped into his chair. "So why aren't they calling? We gave them everything. It's like we vanished."

Maya forced a smile. "Claire said they're reviewing. Maybe it's just bureaucracy."

Alex pulled off his headphones, rubbing his temples. "Or maybe they're reverse-engineering our code right now; figuring out how much they can take before we notice."

Ethan's voice sharpened. "We set tripwires. If they lift anything, we'll know."

Alex shook his head. "Tripwires don't stop a giant. They just tell you when you've been stepped on."

A silence settled over the office, heavy and brittle. Maya glanced at the patent certificate, its glass catching the morning light. It looked less like armor and more like a dare.

She opened her laptop, scrolling through emails. Investors asking for updates, her husband's message from last night still unread, Claire's brief note: *Platform team is reviewing. Will circle back after internal debrief.* No questions. No feedback. Just the digital equivalent of a polite nod.

Ethan broke the silence. "I hate this. The waiting. The not knowing. I'd rather get a rejection than nothing."

Alex nodded, voice low. "At least then we could move on. This . . . this is like being stuck in limbo."

Maya tried to sound confident. "We're not done. We keep building. We show them we're not desperate."

But inside, she felt the cracks spreading. Every unanswered email, every silent phone call, every day without news was a new fracture in her resolve.

Ethan spun in his chair, staring at the ceiling. "You ever think we should've just gone with the smaller OEMs? Titan's too big. Too slow. Too proud."

Alex shrugged. "Maybe. But nobody remembers the company that played it safe."

Maya closed her laptop, the weight of leadership pressing down. "We didn't come this far to be forgotten."

———

Ethan lingered at his desk after the others had left for lunch, eyes fixed on the security dashboard. The tripwires he'd set before the pilot, little digital landmines meant to alert him if anyone poked where they shouldn't, had been quiet, mostly. But today, a single alert blinked in the corner of the screen: "Low priority. Internal credential. 2:17 a.m."

He frowned, scrolling back through the logs. The access looked routine. A system health check, maybe, or a backup script. Still, something about the timestamp nagged at him. Most maintenance jobs ran at midnight or four, not in the dead zone between.

He flagged the entry and added a note: *Odd timing. Check later.* But the office was tense, and Titan's silence was louder than any anomaly. Ethan closed the dashboard, telling himself it was probably nothing.

Later, as the team regrouped, Ethan mentioned it in passing. "One of the tripwires pinged last night. Probably noise, but . . ."

Alex barely looked up. "We're all running scripts at weird hours. Probably just the backup."

Maya nodded, distracted. "Let's focus on the pilot fallout. If it's real, we'll see more."

The office fell quiet again, but Ethan's unease lingered and he made a mental note to dig deeper when things calmed down. For now though, NovaTech had bigger problems.

Then Ethan spoke, voice low but urgent. "What if we leak the pilot results? Not the code, just the metrics. Get the word out that Titan's interested, even if they're not. Stir up some buzz. Maybe force their hand."

Alex looked up, startled. "That's risky. If Titan finds out, they'll shut us out for good, and investors might see it as desperation."

Maya didn't answer right away. She traced a finger along the edge of her laptop, thinking of the board's warnings, the investors' impatience, the silence that had settled over everything. The idea was reckless, but it was movement. A way to break the stasis.

Ethan leaned forward, urgency sharpening his words. "We're ghosts in our own story. If we wait much longer, we'll disappear."

Alex's voice was quieter now, almost pleading. "If we do this, we do it clean. No names, no fingerprints. Just numbers, just buzz."

Maya nodded, her decision slow but certain. "Draft something. Anonymous. Just the facts. If we're going to risk it, we do it on our terms."

Ethan's fingers hovered over his keyboard, the weight of the moment settling in. "I'll keep it tight. No details Titan can trace."

Alex watched him, tension in his jaw. "We're betting the company on a rumor."

Maya met his gaze, steady. "We're betting on being seen. On not letting them erase us before we've begun."

But she didn't move from her spot at the head of the table. Instead, she turned to Ethan, her voice measured. "Draft it, but don't send anything. Not yet. I want to see every word."

Ethan nodded, the urgency in his posture tempered by Maya's authority. "I know a couple of journalists, tech blogs, some industry newsletters. I can keep it anonymous. Just the metrics, just enough to get people talking."

Alex frowned. "How do we know it won't blow back? What if Titan traces it?"

Maya considered, her mind working through contingencies. "We don't mention Titan by name. We frame it as 'a major enterprise pilot.' Just enough for the right people to guess, but not enough for legal to bite."

Ethan opened a blank document, fingers poised. "I'll pull the cleanest numbers from the pilot. Latency, throughput, explainability. No code, no architecture. Just results."

Maya stepped closer, reading over his shoulder. "And the contact?"

Ethan hesitated. "There's Sofia Martinez at Tech Ledger. She's got a reputation for digging, but she's fair. Or we could go smaller; an industry newsletter, something that flies under the radar."

Maya shook her head. "Not yet. We don't go big until we're ready for the fallout. Draft the note, but I'll decide where it goes. If anyone asks, it comes from me."

Alex relaxed, just a little. "That's the right call."

Ethan nodded, already shifting gears. "I'll keep it tight. No fingerprints."

Maya watched the words appear on the screen, each one a calculated risk. She felt the weight of leadership. Every choice, every consequence. This wasn't just about being seen; it was about surviving the silence, and making sure NovaTech's story didn't end before it began.

Outside, the city moved on, indifferent. Inside, the team worked in quiet conspiracy, the leak no longer a reckless whisper, but a deliberate signal. Crafted, measured, and waiting for Maya's final word.

———

A week passed. Then another.

Titan sent occasional requests. *Can you clarify this metric? Can you run one more test with this payload?* But each felt less like progress and more like a fishing expedition. The team complied, but hope faded with each new ask.

Investor emails grew sharper. *If Titan won't commit, we need to pivot.*

Maya replied, *We're close. I can feel it.*

The answer came back: *Feelings don't pay bills.*

At home, Ravi stopped waiting up. The distance between them grew; not in miles but in missed dinners and unspoken fears. The patent, once a symbol of hope, now felt like a relic. A promise that meant nothing without power to enforce it.

In the office, the mood was brittle. Ethan's jokes landed flat. Alex grew quiet, retreating into his code. Maya kept up a brave front, but inside, she was unraveling.

One evening, the team gathered around the conference table, the city outside fading into dusk. Ethan slid a draft across to Maya. A short, clinical summary of the pilot metrics, stripped of names and context, but unmistakable to anyone in the know.

Maya read it twice, her mind racing through consequences. She thought of the board, the investors, Titan's silence, the team's fraying resolve. She thought of the risk, and of what it meant to be erased.

She nodded, finally. "Send it."

Ethan didn't hesitate. He opened a secure browser, pasted the text into an encrypted form, and sent it to a trusted industry newsletter. One that specialized in enterprise tech rumors, the kind that moved quietly through inboxes and Slack channels before surfacing in the open.

Alex watched the screen, tension in his jaw. "It's done?"

Ethan nodded. "It's out there. No fingerprints. Just a whisper."

Maya exhaled, the decision settling over her like dust. "Now we wait." For the first time in weeks, she felt something new. Not relief, not hope. Just the certainty that they had chosen action over silence, and that the story would move, one way or another.

It didn't take long.

The next morning, Ethan arrived early, his usual caffeine-fueled swagger replaced by a nervous energy. He refreshed his inbox, then the industry newsletter's site, then his inbox again. Nothing. For an hour, the office was suspended in anxious quiet.

Then, just before nine, Alex's phone buzzed. He glanced at the screen, eyes widening. "It's out."

Ethan dived at his laptop. The newsletter's headline was subtle, but unmistakable:

### TECH LEDGER | SOFIA MARTINEZ
**Rumors Swirl Around NovaTech and Titan: Did a Leak Tip the Scales?**

In the world of enterprise telemetry, whispers travel faster than code. This morning, an anonymous leak of pilot metrics has set the industry abuzz, with speculation centering on a possible partnership, or rivalry, between NovaTech, a rising startup, and Titan Corp, the sector's perennial heavyweight.

The numbers, stripped of names but not of ambition, tell a story: latency, throughput, and explainability metrics that suggest a breakthrough in real-time data processing. For NovaTech, the leak is both a lifeline and a risk. Investors are circling, but so are lawyers.

"Leaks like this are a double-edged sword," says Jordan Reyes, an intellectual property attorney not involved in the deal. "They can force a conversation, but they also raise questions about confidentiality and trust."

Titan's silence is strategic, but insiders say the company is reviewing its options. The stakes are high. Both for the technology, and for the story that will shape public perception. In the battle for innovation, sometimes the loudest voice is the one that whispers first.

**Sidebar: What's a Pilot, and Why Do Leaks Matter?**

A "pilot" is a trial run. A chance for a startup to prove its technology in the real world, often under strict confidentiality. When metrics leak, the consequences ripple outward: partners get nervous, investors get bold, and the line between rumor and reality blurs. In this case, the leak may have forced Titan's hand or simply exposed a fault line that was always there.

NovaTech declined to comment for this story. Titan did not respond to multiple requests for clarification. As the dust settles, one thing is clear: the next move belongs to the giants and to the upstarts bold enough to make them blink.

No mention of NovaTech. No mention of Titan. Yet Maya's stomach tightened, the coffee in her hand suddenly bitter. Sofia didn't bury the lede. She sharpened it. And anyone who knew the space would quickly read between the lines. The comments section was already filling up: speculation, skepticism, a few insiders dropping hints. On Slack, a private channel pinged. An old contact from a mid-tier OEM, asking if NovaTech was behind the story.

Ethan grinned, relief and adrenaline mingling. "People are talking. It's working."

Alex was less certain. "It's working for now. But if Titan connects the dots—"

Maya cut him off, her voice steady. "We knew the risks. Now we see what comes next."

Her phone buzzed. A message from Claire at Titan:

*Saw the newsletter. Please confirm if NovaTech is involved.*

Maya hesitated, weighing every word. "We don't respond. Not yet." Another buzz. Investors, already circling like hawks. She silenced it, forcing her voice steady. "This changes the game. But it also raises the stakes."

The team watched the metrics spike: website traffic, inbound emails. The silence was broken, but in its place came noise: questions, rumors, the first hints of opportunity and threat.

Ethan leaned back, a smile tugging at his lips. "We're not ghosts anymore."

Maya nodded, her resolve hardening. "No. Now we're a target." She stared at the headline again, the words blurring for a moment. She drew a breath, feeling the weight of leadership settle like armor. "We need to play this smart. For now, we say nothing."

Alex nodded, but his eyes were shadowed. Ethan leaned back, a grin tugging at his lips. "We wanted noise. We got it."

Maya's gaze drifted to the patent. It looked less like a shield and more like a dare. She braced for the next move knowing that the story was no longer theirs alone.

———

Inside the cathedral of glass and steel that was Titan's headquarters, the air in the boardroom was anything but serene.

Claire Donovan had been the first to spot the newsletter, the metrics too familiar to be coincidence. She'd forwarded the link to Richard Hale, subject line terse:

*Possible NovaTech leak?*

Richard had read the article in silence, jaw set. The numbers matched the pilot, down to the decimal. He didn't need confirmation. He knew.

He'd called an emergency meeting, and the product strategy team had assembled in the glass-walled room. The city sprawling below, indifferent to the drama unfolding inside.

Claire spoke first. "It's out there. No names, but the metrics are ours. Someone's talking."

Patel, arms folded, scowled. "They're trying to force our hand. Make us look slow. Or desperate."

Richard's voice was cold, measured. "Or they're panicking. Either way, we don't let them set the narrative."

Gabe from Security chimed in. "We need to audit the sandbox logs. See if anything was exfiltrated. If they breached NDA, we go legal."

Anita was already scanning the pilot traces. "No code, no architecture. Just results. It's clever. But it's a shot across the bow."

Richard leaned back, considering. His voice was calm but laced with steel. "We respond, but not on their terms. Claire, draft a statement— neutral, noncommittal: 'Titan routinely evaluates emerging technologies. No decisions have been made.'"

He turned to Gabe. "If you find evidence of a leak, escalate. I want options. Legal, PR, technical. We don't reward stunts."

Claire nodded, already typing. "Do we reach out to NovaTech?"

Richard's eyes narrowed. "Not yet. Let them sweat. If they want a war, we'll show them what it means to pick a fight with a giant."

The meeting ended with a flurry of action: emails, audits, calls to legal. Titan's silence was no longer passive; it was strategic, calculated, and laced with threat.

———

The buzz from the leak hadn't even settled before the first investor emails arrived. Maya's inbox filled with subject lines that read like demands:

*Pilot Rumors. Clarify Immediately*

*Are We Involved?*

*Next Steps—Urgent*

Alan called before noon. His voice was clipped, all business. "Maya, I'm seeing chatter about a breakthrough pilot. Is this us? Is this Titan?"

Maya kept her answer measured. "We're running pilots with several enterprise partners. The metrics are ours."

Alan didn't buy it. "You know how this looks. If Titan thinks we're leaking, they'll shut the door. If the market thinks we're bluffing, we lose leverage. You need to control the narrative."

Priya chimed in, her tone sharper than usual. "We're getting inbound interest, but it's all speculation. Some are asking if we're desperate. Are we?"

Maya felt the pressure mounting. "We're not desperate. We're strategic. The silence was killing us. Now we have momentum."

Jonas, always the numbers guy, cut in. "Momentum is good. But if Titan retaliates, we need a backup plan. What's our next move?"

Maya promised a board update by the end of day, but the call ended with more questions than answers. The investors wanted clarity, certainty, and Maya had neither.

Back in the bullpen, the mood was volatile. Ethan was energized, almost triumphant. "We did it. People are talking. We're not invisible anymore."

Alex was less convinced. He paced by the window, arms folded. "We're not invisible, but we're exposed. Titan could crush us for this. Or just walk away."

Ethan shrugged. "Let them. At least now we have options. The smaller OEMs are sniffing around. We can pivot."

Alex shook his head. "We built for Titan. That was the plan. If they slam the door, we're back at square one."

Maya watched the two of them, feeling the fault lines in the team. Ethan wanted action, Alex wanted caution. Both were right, and both were wrong.

She gathered them at the whiteboard, marker in hand. "We need to be ready for fallout. If Titan calls, we play it cool. If investors push, we show them the numbers. No panic. No apologies."

Ethan nodded, already scanning his inbox for replies. Alex just stared at the patent certificate, jaw tight.

Maya capped the marker, her voice steady. "We chose risk. Now we own it."

The team fell into a tense rhythm. The leak had broken the silence, but it had also broken something else: the illusion that they were in control.

# FOUR

**TECH LEDGER | SOFIA MARTINEZ**
**From Whispers to Shockwaves: NovaTech Leak Sparks Industry Frenzy**

What began as a quiet rumor at dawn has erupted into a full-blown debate across boardrooms, Slack channels and investor calls. The leaked pilot metrics, latency curves, throughput benchmarks, and explainability scores are now being dissected by analysts who say the numbers point to a technology that could redraw the map for real-time telemetry.

Titan Corp issued a brief statement this afternoon: "Titan routinely evaluates emerging technologies. No decisions have been made." The neutrality did little to calm speculation. Several venture firms confirmed they are "actively monitoring developments," and at least one mid-tier OEM hinted at outreach to NovaTech.

Behind the scenes, sources suggest Titan's legal team is reviewing the leak for potential NDA violations. "If they find a breach, expect fireworks," said one industry insider. Others argue the move was strategic. A calculated gamble to force Titan's hand.

For NovaTech, the spotlight is both opportunity and peril. The question now isn't whether the leak made noise. It's whether that noise becomes music or a funeral march.

"I'm telling you, we're fine." Ethan paced, waving a printout. We didn't leak code, just metrics. That's not a violation."

The office felt tense, the air thick with burnt coffee and worry.

Alex shook his head, frowning at the NDA on his laptop. "You didn't read the fine print. Look: *Section 3.2. Recipient shall not disclose, publish, or disseminate any Confidential Information to any third party, except as expressly permitted in writing.* That covers everything. Even the numbers."

Ethan stopped, exasperated. "How can it cover everything? Some of that information is ours! We built it, we ran the tests. How does Titan get to claim all of it?"

Alex sighed, rubbing his temples. "That's how NDAs work, especially with big companies. Anything you learn, build, or measure while working with them, even if you did most of the work, can be considered confidential. The language is intentionally broad."

Maya nodded. "It's not about what's fair. It's about what you agreed to when you signed. They want to make sure nothing leaks, so they write the NDA to cover every possible angle. If there's any doubt, the lawyers will argue it's theirs."

Ethan frowned, glancing at the screen. "So, we're just supposed to sit on everything? Even our own results?"

Alex shrugged. "Unless they give you written permission, yeah. That's the deal. One wrong move and you're in legal quicksand."

Ethan muttered, "We scrubbed the names. No one can prove it's Titan unless they already know."

Maya's tone was measured but sharp. "We play it smart. No more leaks. No more risks. If Titan comes after us, we need to show we acted in good faith. Facts, not panic. Remember, they have the lawyers. We have... hope."

Ethan snorted, "Feels like we're playing chess with half the pieces missing."

Alex closed his laptop with a snap. "Next time, we run everything by legal, even if it slows us down."

Ethan murmured, "If we had a legal department."

Maya managed a tired smile. "We have me. And I say: no more surprises."

———

By midday, Maya's inbox was a battlefield. Investors wanted answers. Analysts wanted quotes. Amid the chaos, one message stood out, cryptic, seductive:

> **Subject:** Saw the numbers. If you're the team behind them, let's talk.
> **From:** Daniel Cho | VP Strategy, Helios Systems
> We've been watching the chatter. If those metrics are yours, we should connect. Big opportunity here. Can you jump on a quick video call today?

Maya stared at the screen, pulse ticking faster. Helios wasn't Titan, but they were no lightweight. A mid-tier OEM with deep pockets, they had a reputation for moving fast when they smelled blood in the water.

She tapped **Reply**, her fingers steady despite the adrenaline.

*Daniel—thanks for reaching out.*
*I can do 2:30 p.m. Pacific. Sending a Teams link now.*

She hit **Send**, then opened her calendar and dropped in the invite. The act felt like a lifeline. A thread of control in a day unraveling at the edges.

Behind her, Ethan grinned like a man who'd just hacked gravity. "We did it," he said, spinning his chair toward the big screen where Tech

Ledger's latest article glowed like a beacon. *From Whispers to Shock-waves* was everywhere now. LinkedIn, Twitter, Slack threads Maya didn't even know existed.

Ethan glowed. "We're the story."

Alex didn't share the thrill. He paced by the window, arms folded tight, eyes on the city beyond the glass. He half expected to see a black SUV with *Titan Security* plastered on the side screech to halt in front of the building.

Maya forced calm into her movements. Though her pulse was a drumbeat, she turned to the whiteboard, uncapped a marker, and wrote in bold: **CONTROL THE NARRATIVE.**

The team gathered around, tension crackling like static. Ethan leaned forward, still riding the high. "We go loud. Interviews, panels, podcasts. Make it impossible for Titan to ignore us."

Alex shook his head. "That's suicide. If they think we leaked, they'll shut the door. Hard."

Maya capped the marker, her voice steady but sharp. "No. For now, we say nothing and let the numbers speak."

Her phone buzzed again, Claire's name flashing on the screen. She silenced it without looking. The weight of leadership pressed down like armor, heavy but necessary.

———

The NovaTech conference room was barely big enough for the three of them, but now it felt crowded with possibility. Alex was at the whiteboard, sketching fallback plans. Ethan hovered by the window.

Precisely at 2:30 p.m., the call connected and the Helios logo bloomed on the screen. Crisp and confident, cobalt blue against a white field. Daniel Cho appeared a second later. Early forties, charcoal blazer, the kind of smile that belonged to someone who'd closed deals in rooms where oxygen was scarce.

"Appreciate you making time, Maya," he said, voice smooth but urgent. "I'll cut to the chase. If those metrics are yours, you've built something extraordinary. And if Titan is dragging its feet, that's our opening."

Maya kept her expression neutral, even as her pulse raged beneath her skin. "We're exploring options," she said carefully. "What did you have in mind?"

Daniel leaned in, eyes bright. "A pilot. Fast-track. We've got infrastructure that can showcase your tech at scale. And we move quicker than Titan ever will. You'd have executive sponsorship, budget, and a clear path to deployment."

Ethan, sitting just out of frame, mouthed *Say Yes*, like a kid at Christmas. Alex stayed silent, jaw tight, eyes flicking between Maya and the screen.

Maya measured every word. "We're interested. But we need clarity on scope, timelines, and—" she paused, letting the weight of the next word settle, "terms."

Daniel smiled as if the future had just tipped unmistakably toward him. "Fair. I'll send a draft proposal tonight. Let's make this happen."

The Helios logo faded from the screen, leaving the room in a charged silence. Ethan bounced his knee, unable to sit still, his grin so wide it threatened to split his face. "This is it," he whispered, as if afraid to break the spell. "Titan can't kill us if Helios gets there first."

Alex's arms were folded so tightly his knuckles blanched. He stared at the scuffed carpet, voice low and brittle: "Or they kill us faster for playing both sides."

Maya let the silence stretch. The air felt thick, humming with possibility and dread. She pressed her palm to the whiteboard, the cool surface grounding her. CONTROL THE NARRATIVE glared back, the letters blurred where her fingers had lingered. For the first time all day, hope flickered, but it was edged with steel, and something colder beneath.

———

Claire Donovan remained in the glass-walled conference room long after the others. The city sprawled below, glittering and indifferent. The hum of the building's HVAC was the only sound. A mechanical heartbeat, steady and cold.

She stared at the table where Richard's directives lay like cold steel:

*Audit. Escalate. No contact until we decide.*

She scrolled through the Tech Ledger article again, the metrics sharp and undeniable. NovaTech had built something real. Something worth more than Titan's posturing.

Patel's voice echoed in her memory: *"We'll bury them if they play games."*

Claire's jaw tightened. She'd heard that tone before. At other companies, in other boardrooms; the language of winners, of people who believed the world was a chessboard and every piece expendable. She had joined Titan to build, not to crush. She remembered the first time she'd met Maya. Nervous but brilliant. Stubborn perhaps. The kind of founder who made you want to believe.

But Titan didn't believe. Titan calculated.

She closed her eyes, feeling the weight of it settle in her chest. Was this partnership or predation? Was she here to shepherd innovation, or to snuff it out before it could threaten the giant.

Her tablet chimed. A calendar invite: *Board Strategy Session: Friday, 9:00 a.m. Topic: Build vs Buy vs Bury.*

Claire's thumb hovered over the **Accept** button. She wondered if anyone else in that room would ask the question she couldn't shake: *What if the right move isn't the ruthless one?*

She imagined herself speaking up, suggesting a partnership, a path where both companies could win. She could already hear the silence that would follow, the polite dismissal, the subtle tightening of Richard's jaw.

She looked out at the city, lights blurring in the glass. She thought of the engineers on her own team, the ones who'd stayed late to test Nova-Tech's code, who'd whispered that maybe, just maybe, the little company had done something special. She thought of the emails she'd sent, the promises she'd made. Both to herself and to the idea that tech could be more than a zero-sum game.

A knot of doubt twisted in her gut. If she stayed silent, she'd be complicit. If she spoke, she'd be alone.

The city below was vast, but the room felt smaller than ever.

———

The office was quiet by midnight, the hum of servers the only sound. Maya sat alone at her desk, drowning in investor decks and draft responses. Every ping felt like a demand, every unanswered call like a judgment.

Ethan scrolled through the security logs for the third time, his eyes gritty with exhaustion. He'd set the honeytokens and tripwires before the pilot and checked them afterward, but the logs had been a blur of routine noise and false alarms.

Except for one thing. He filtered the logs again, isolating the window during the pilot. He found a single alert, timestamped 2:17 a.m., flagged as *low priority*.

Ethan's heart thudded. He drilled down. The honeytoken had been accessed, but the request was masked as a system health check. Not impossible, but odd. He checked the source. An internal credential, but one that shouldn't have been active at that hour.

He swore under his breath and called out, "Maya, you need to see this."

She forced herself upright, joints protesting, walked over to Ethan, and looked at his screen. Barely noticeable in the corner of Ethan's anomaly dashboard she saw:

*Tripwire Event: Low Priority. Timestamp 02:17 a.m.*

Ethan spoke, his voice tight. "See this?" His finger hovered just above the screen, not quite touching. "One of the honeytokens triggered during the pilot. I thought it was noise. But the access was masked, and the credential's wrong."

Maya squinted, her mind foggy. "It's probably just a glitch, Ethan. Like Alex said, we were all running scripts at weird hours." Maya's voice lacked conviction.

Ethan shook his head. "No. This was deliberate. Someone knew how to hide. Someone inside."

Maya leaned in, her face tense. "Are you sure?"

Ethan nodded. "Not one hundred percent. But if someone slipped through, they could've taken anything."

A heavy silence settled over them.

Maya straightened. "Check everything. If there's a hole, we need to find it."

Ethan's fingers flew over the keyboard, adrenaline sharpening his focus. "If there's a mole, I'll find them."

Maya watched him, worry etched deep. "Let's hope you're wrong. But let's not bet the company on it."

Later, alone, she looked at her phone. Ravi's message glowed on the lock screen:

*Can we talk tomorrow? Or are you still married to the company?*

She stared at it, thumb hovering, then let the phone fall to the desk. The silence in the office was absolute, broken only by the distant pulsing of the servers. A lullaby for the sleepless.

------

Friday morning. Titan's executive boardroom gleamed like a blade: black glass table, skyline sprawling beyond the windows, sunlight fractured by steel.

Richard let the silence settle for a moment. The slide behind him read *Q3 Launch Window* in letters large enough to feel like a deadline. "Let's get to it," he said.

Patel spoke first, sharp and certain. "We build. Their architecture isn't magic. We can replicate it in-house. Give us six months and a dedicated team, we'll match it."

Anita shook her head, eyes on her tablet. "Six months is fantasy. Their metrics aren't fluff. We can ship something, but their breath policy... our stack can't mimic that without a rewrite."

Dr. Lasker simply went over the options. "If we buy, we get the humane choice now. If we build, we'll default to speed."

The Finance representative was not happy. "Licensing puts optics on Titan paying a startup, and gives them leverage in PR."

"NDA gives us cover either way." The Legal rep seemed indifferent. "No code exchange; sandbox only. Low risk of claims."

Richard's gaze flicked to Gabe. "Security?"

Gabe's tone was flat. "No breach evidence yet. But the leak was surgical. If they did it, they're careful. If they didn't, someone wants us paranoid."

Claire cleared her throat, voice measured. "We could negotiate. A licensing deal buys time and keeps us ahead of the market."

Patel snorted. "And make them a partner? Hand them leverage? No. We bury them. Quietly."

Richard leaned back, considering. "Optics matter. We don't want headlines about crushing startups; we want headlines about innovation."

Dr. Lasker spoke softly. "Innovation isn't just speed. It's trust. If we burn NovaTech, the ecosystem notices."

Richard's smile was thin. "The ecosystem notices winners. Here's the math: If we build it's costly and the timeline is risky. If we buy, it's cheaper, but we risk dependency. If we bury them, people notice. But it's manageable."

He tapped the table, each word a verdict. "We don't pay for what we can build. We proceed with the internal build. Keep NovaTech in the sandbox for now; just enough hope to keep them cooperative in case we run into issues. Claire, you'll handle the soft touch."

He paused. "And we do not miss Q3."

Claire nodded, though her stomach tightened. The only audible sound was a ventilation hiss that felt like a verdict.

Richard's voice was steel. "Draft the message. Make it polite; final enough to freeze them, but vague enough to keep them waiting."

The meeting ended with the quiet efficiency of power. Outside, the city glittered. Inside, Titan had chosen its weapon.

———

Richard let himself into his home, the city's lights flickering through the windows. He loosened his tie, the silk rough against his throat, and set his briefcase down with a dull thud. The only sound was the low, steady hum of the refrigerator coming from the kitchen.

His wife sat at the kitchen table, her posture rigid, a half-eaten dinner congealing on her plate. "You missed it," she said, not looking up.

Richard hesitated in the doorway, suddenly aware of the ache in his feet, the weight of the day pressing down. "I'm sorry. The launch—"

She cut him off, her voice brittle. "It's always the launch. Or the board. Or the next big thing. Sandi asked where you were tonight. I didn't know what to tell her."

He looked away, jaw clenched. "I'm doing what I have to. For all of us."

She pushed her chair back, the legs scraping the tile. "Are you?"

He didn't answer. The silence stretched, thick as the city's fog.

Later, alone in the dark, Richard sat on the edge of the bed, scrolling through old family photos. His thumb hovered over a picture from a birthday party years ago. Sandi's gap-toothed grin, his own face younger, unlined. He wondered, not for the first time, if winning was worth what he was losing.

———

In a much smaller home, with far fewer windows, Ravi stood in the bedroom doorway, shoulders slumped, tie hanging loose like a surrender flag. Maya was perched on the edge of the bed, laptop balanced on her knees, a mess of spreadsheets and emails reflected in her tired eyes.

"Hey," Ravi said softly. "You got a minute?"

Maya looked up, but her gaze was fogged with numbers and unknowns. "Yeah—sorry. Just finishing something." She closed one tab, then another. "How was your day?"

He hesitated. "Rough."

A brittle laugh. "They cut the Chronicle module. Called it a 'reprioritization.' You know what that means."

Maya's expression softened. "Ravi, I'm so sorry."

He nodded, but the motion was slow, weighted. "I get it. Everyone's cutting. Everyone's scared." He took a breath. "But I thought maybe we could talk tonight."

"Of course," she said, but her phone buzzed on the nightstand before the sentence finished.

She glanced down.

**Alan:** *Any update from Titan? Burn rate is rising. We need traction soon.*

Maya exhaled through her nose, tension rippling across her shoulders. "They're still silent," she murmured. "If they walk away, we're... we're in trouble."

Ravi stepped inside the room, voice quiet. "Maya, I'm not mad. I just—" He swallowed. "I feel like things are breaking on my side too, and there's never a good time to say it."

She closed her laptop halfway, not fully. "I know. I promise I'll be more present once we know where Titan stands."

Ravi's eyes flicked to the half-closed laptop, to her phone still glowing with Alan's message.

"Yeah," he said gently. "That's what I'm afraid of."

He turned off the light on his side of the room. Left the door ajar. Not closed, but not open either.

———

Early Saturday morning and Maya was in the office before sunrise; the city still draped in gray. Her inbox reeled from the week, but she hunted for Helios' follow-up. She barely noticed the new subject line until it burned like a fuse:

**Subject:** Next Steps
**From:** Claire Donovan | Titan Corp

She clicked. The words were clean, surgical:

*Maya—thank you for your efforts during the pilot. Titan is continuing to evaluate strategic priorities and will not be moving forward with additional engagement at this time. We appreciate your professionalism and wish you continued success.*

No warmth. No ambiguity. Just the corporate equivalent of a guillotine.

Maya read it twice, then a third time, as if repetition could change the meaning. Her pulse was a hollow drum. Behind her, Ethan laughed at something on Slack, oblivious.

Her phone rang. Alex.

"Did you see—"

"Yes," Maya said, voice flat.

"Two years' work... for this?"

"They used us," she whispered, her throat tight. "Every spec, every test result. They bled us dry."

———

When Alex reached the office, Maya was at the conference table. A legal pad lay untouched, her pen still.

He lingered in the doorway, uncertain. "You want coffee?" His voice was low.

She shook her head. "No. Thanks."

He hesitated, then crossed the room and sat opposite her. For a while, neither spoke.

Finally, Maya broke the silence. "I keep thinking there should have been a sign. Something we missed."

Alex's reply was gentle. "We saw what we wanted to see. That's not a crime."

She nodded, but her jaw tightened. "I hate that it ended with an email. After everything."

Alex looked down at his hands. "We're still here. That counts for something."

Maya managed a thin smile. "Does it?"

He met her eyes. "It has to."

A message pinged on her laptop. It was Alan. *Board Call—ASAP.*

She sighed and spun the laptop so Alex could read Alan's summons. "He's pissed."

Alex said nothing. For a moment, the silence between them felt like solidarity, not defeat.

———

By noon, the calm had shattered.

The faces of Board members flickered across Maya's screen—pixelated, impatient—voices overlapping in a rising tide of panic.

"This is catastrophic," Alan barked. "We need an exit strategy."

Priya's tone was clipped, her background a blur of city lights. "Sell. Before Titan crushes us."

Jonas, ever the numbers guy, tried to interject: "Let's look at the burn rate—"

Maya gripped the desk's edge, knuckles white, the wood biting into her skin. "We're not selling."

Alan's face loomed, filling the screen. "You don't have leverage."

Maya's voice was ice, though her heart hammered. "If we don't fight, we're already dead."

The call ended in a cacophony of voices. The screen went black with a final, accusing click, leaving Maya in a hush so deep she could hear the tick of the wall clock and the faint, uneven hum of the city beyond her window. She let her hands fall to her lap, fingers numb, the imprint of the desk's edge still pressed into her skin.

She looked up at the patent. In the half-light, the glass was smudged with fingerprints, the gold seal faded to dull brass. Once, it gleamed like a shield. Now, it looked brittle; an artifact from a war already lost.

Maya stood, her chair scraping softly against the floor. She crossed the room and pressed her palm to the glass, feeling its chill seep into her skin. For a moment, she closed her eyes and let the silence settle around her.

When she opened them, she straightened the frame, squared her shoulders, and whispered to the empty room,

"Not yet."

# FIVE

THE LIVESTREAM BEGAN at noon sharp, an hour chosen for maximum impact, when the world's attention was measured in trending hashtags and the pulse of a thousand notifications. Titan Corp's stage glowed like a temple to innovation: LED walls pulsed with shifting colors, drones hovered for sweeping camera shots, and a sea of executives, influencers, and journalists filled the front rows, their faces lit by the blue glow of anticipation.

Back at NovaTech's cramped office, Maya, Alex, and Ethan huddled around a battered laptop, the sound of applause echoing through tinny speakers like distant thunder. The contrast was cinematic: Titan's world was all glass and steel, NovaTech's was cluttered with coffee mugs, tangled charging cables, and a faded cat poster that said, "Hang In There." The air smelled of burnt coffee and rain.

On screen, the Titan logo shimmered, then faded to reveal Richard Hale, every inch the conqueror. He strode onto the stage with the confidence of someone who'd already won, his voice booming as he welcomed the world to "the future of real-time intelligence."

"Today," Richard declared, "Titan redefines what's possible. Our new platform delivers unprecedented performance, reliability, and insight. Built for the world's most demanding environments." The specs flashed across the screen: throughput numbers, latency curves, and a sleek device that looked like it belonged in a sci-fi film.

It was theirs. Every line, every breakthrough, every sleepless night distilled into Titan's triumph.

Alex's breath caught. "That's our architecture," he whispered. "Our algorithms. Even the way they're visualizing the data. It's ours."

Ethan's jaw clenched. "They didn't even bother to change the terminology. Look—'breath policy,' 'topology-preserving transform.' That's straight from our pilot."

Maya muted the stream for a moment, her hands trembling. The applause faded, but the rage roared louder. "They gutted us," she said, voice low, lethal. "And dressed it in their colors."

The stream cut to a glossy video segment: engineers in Titan-branded polos stood in a pristine lab, discussing the platform's capabilities. Patel, standing to the side and in front of the polo-wearing flock, gestured to a wall of monitors. "With Titan's adaptive transform layer, we handle clock drift and outlier rejection in real time. Our system learns from every data stream, preserving signal accent while normalizing for analytics."

Another engineer chimed in, "We chose stability over speed. When telemetry spikes, our orchestrator lets latency rise slightly to avoid catastrophic loss. See the inflection point here? Our system absorbs the shock, then recovers. No more dropped inputs, no more silent failures."

A third added, "We've benchmarked against every major competitor. Our transform layer adds minimal overhead, and the reduction in downstream error is unmatched. Others claim plug-and-play; we deliver it."

The video cut to animated graphs. Latency curves, throughput metrics, and a side-by-side comparison with "Competitor A" and "Competitor B." The names blurred, but the implication was clear: Titan's line soared above the rest, a blue ribbon of victory.

Ethan grunted. "Notice how NovaTech isn't mentioned. They're erasing us even as they steal our work."

Alex's hands shook as he recognized his own code, variable names, and even the structure of the demo. "They didn't even bother to change the variable names," he muttered. "It's like watching your own house on a real estate ad."

The livestream shifted to customer testimonials:

A hospital CIO appeared, beaming. "Titan's platform transformed our telemetry. We went from daily outages to seamless integration. Our staff can focus on care, not troubleshooting."

A logistics manager: "We used to lose shipments to data errors. With Titan, our system breathes through the chaos. It's like having a nervous system for our business."

A startup founder: "We tried everything. Titan solved problems we didn't know we had. Their team listened, adapted, and delivered."

The applause swelled. Richard returned to the stage, flanked by engineers and happy customers. "We're not just building technology," he said. "We're building trust. Titan's platform is the result of relentless innovation, rigorous testing, and a commitment to excellence."

A final video played. A montage of Titan's engineers high-fiving, code scrolling across screens, and the product in action: monitoring patient telemetry, optimizing supply chains, powering smart cities. The music soared, the visuals dazzled, and the message was unmistakable: Titan was the future.

———

Back at NovaTech, the silence was suffocating. The Titan launch had been a masterclass in dominance, and the weight of it pressed down like a storm cloud. Rain streaked the windows, blurring the city lights into smears of gold and gray. The muted glow of Titan's logo still lingered on the laptop screen like a taunt.

Maya's phone buzzed. A message from Sofia Martinez:

*Maya, this is Sofia at Tech Ledger.*
*Can you comment on Titan's launch? Industry's watching.*

She stared at the screen, thumb hovering over **Reply**. The world wanted a soundbite, a reaction, a sign of life. For a moment, she considered typing something, anything, but the words wouldn't come. Not yet. Not when Titan had declared war. She snapped the laptop shut, the sound ringing like a gunshot.

For a moment, no one spoke. The hum of the HVAC filled the void.

Ethan was the first to break. "Well," he said, pacing between the whiteboard and the window, "that was... spectacular. If you're into theft dressed up as innovation." He smirked, but his voice cracked at the edges. "All in all though, I give it six out of ten. Needed more jazz hands."

Alex snorted into his coffee, the brief levity breaking the tension for a heartbeat. He rubbed his temples, eyes hollow. "They didn't just copy us. They improved the optics. The messaging, the polish... they made it look inevitable."

Maya leaned against the desk, arms crossed, her voice low and cutting sharp. "Optics don't win lawsuits. Facts do. And the fact is, they stole our architecture."

Ethan grunted, spinning a marker between his fingers like a blade. "Tell that to the investors. They're going to see Titan trending worldwide and assume we're yesterday's news."

Alex spun his chair around, frustration boiling over in slow, smoldering waves. "We should've launched first. We had the tech. We had the edge. And now—" He gestured toward the laptop like it was a crime scene. "Now we're the footnote."

Maya's gaze hardened. "We're not a footnote. We're the origin story. And origin stories matter. Especially in court."

Ethan stopped pacing, his voice dropping to a bitter whisper. "Court? You think litigation is going to save us? Titan's got an army of lawyers and a war chest big enough to buy the judge's golf club."

Maya straightened, her tone cutting through the despair. "Then we fight smarter. We document everything; every commit, every timestamp, every patent claim. We make it undeniable."

Alex hesitated, then asked the question hanging in the air: "And if the Board doesn't back us?"

The silence that followed was heavier than before. Outside, thunder rolled like distant artillery.

———

The video conference grid flickered to life, a mosaic of faces framed by curated backdrops: mahogany offices, sterile home setups, and the occasional blurred bookshelf. Titan's launch was still trending, its hashtag pulsing like a warning light. Even through pixels, the panic was palpable.

Alan's voice cut through first, clipped like a scalpel. "Let's get straight to it. Titan just ate our lunch. What's the plan?"

Maya leaned forward, spine rigid, fingers gripping the edge of the desk until her knuckles whitened. Her eyes locked on the camera, steady and unflinching. "We fight. Patent enforcement. Immediate injunction."

A ripple of groans. Someone muted, then unmuted. The amplified sigh filling the silence like static.

"Litigation?" scoffed Jonas, his tone dripping with disbelief. "Do you have any idea what that costs? Titan will drag this out for years."

Ethan leaned into frame, jaw tight, voice edged with fury. "Do you have any idea what it costs to roll over and die? They stole our architecture. If we don't push back, NovaTech becomes a cautionary tale."

Jonas shot back, smooth and surgical. "Emotion doesn't pay bills. Cash flow does. And right now, ours is bleeding."

Alex cleared his throat, voice shaky but determined. "We have time-stamps, commits, design docs. We can prove origin. If we file fast, we can freeze their rollout."

Alan's laugh was cold. "Freeze Titan? Son, they've got more lawyers than engineers. They'll bury us in motions before lunch."

Maya's tone sharpened, slicing through the noise. "Then we make it public. Press release, social amplification. We frame this as theft, as betrayal. Titan wants to play dirty? Fine. We'll drag them into the light."

A younger board member leaned forward, eyes bright with opportunism. "Public fight means risk. If we lose, we look incompetent. If we win, we look vindicated. But broke."

Priya folded her arms. "What if we approached them about an acquisition? Their system has to have been rushed. It has holes. If they buy NovaTech they cure any issues and our cashflow problems disappear."

The words hung like smoke. Ethan slammed his palm on the desk. "Sell? After what they just pulled? That's not a deal. That's surrender."

Maya's voice dropped to a lethal calm. "If anyone here thinks selling is an option, say it now. Because if that's the consensus, I'll walk. And I'll take the engineering team with me."

The silence was electric. Faces shifted, some avoiding eye contact, others calculating angles. Alan finally spoke, tone softer, almost paternal. "Take it easy, Maya. Priya is just throwing out an option."

Maya didn't flinch. "If we don't fight, we're already ashes."

Alan exhaled, "Okay, okay. Where are things with Helios?" What do they have to say about this?"

Maya's jaw tightened. "I haven't heard from Daniel yet, but he's my next call. Helios controls the distribution pipeline. If they side with Titan, we're boxed out."

Alan nodded, his voice turning to command. "Keep us updated."

The call ended with curt goodbyes and the hollow chime of disconnect. Maya stared at the blank screen, her reflection fractured in the glass. Outside, rain hammered the windows like a countdown. Inside, the storm was already gathering, and she was ready to meet it head-on.

———

Across town, in Titan's glass fortress, Richard Hale toasted with his inner circle. Champagne fizzed in crystal flutes as screens replayed the launch highlights.

"To victory," Richard said, his grin sharp as a blade.

Claire Donovan raised her glass, but her hand trembled. She forced a smile, swallowing guilt with the champagne. Silence was safer for now.

———

## Tech Ledger | Sofia Martinez
### Did Titan Steal NovaTech's Secret Sauce?

The gloves are off in the enterprise telemetry wars. Titan Corp's latest product launch has industry insiders raising eyebrows and questions. The new platform's architecture bears a striking resemblance to NovaTech's patented technology. The timing has fueled speculation that Titan's new platform is more than just a parallel innovation.

"Patent infringement isn't just about who files first," explains Jordan Reyes, an IP litigator. "It's about what the claims cover, and whether the new product actually uses the invention."

Sources confirm that NovaTech's technology was recently tested in a pilot with Titan, under strict confidentiality. Now, with Titan's launch echoing NovaTech's design language and technical choices, the question of inspiration versus imitation is front and center.

NovaTech's CEO, Maya Singh, declined to comment, but sources say the company is weighing its legal options. Meanwhile, Titan's PR team insists that all development was done in-house.

For the market, the story is as much about ethics as it is about innovation. Investors are watching, competitors are recalibrating, and customers are left to wonder: Is this a classic case of David versus Goliath, or just business as usual in Silicon Valley? As the legal battle looms, one thing is clear. In the fight for the future, the lines between invention and appropriation have never felt blurrier.

Maya's laptop reflected the harsh glow of the Tech Ledger article's headline as she waited for Daniel Cho to connect. The world wanted a David-and-Goliath story, but Maya knew David rarely wins. She needed Helios to come through.

A new window opened and a high-definition PDF labeled *Term Sheet – Accelerated Pilot* came into view.

Daniel's face was crisp in a small square above the document, his tone all business. "We're prepared to move fast, Maya. Here's what we're offering." He clicked, and the term sheet filled the shared screen.

Columns of legalese, highlighted cells, and a signature block already waiting.

"Accelerated pilot, full funding for the duration, and a clear path to deployment if you hit the metrics," Daniel said. "But we need optics. SOC 2 posture, chain of custody for all artifacts, and exclusivity for the vertical during the pilot. Reporting cadence is weekly, with compliance reviews at every milestone."

Ethan, arms folded, muttered just loud enough for Maya to hear, "Translation: they want to own us for the quarter."

Alex, hunched over his own laptop, scrolled through the PDF. "Exclusivity clause is tight. If we sign, we can't talk to anyone else in healthcare until the pilot's over. That's our whole runway."

Maya kept her voice steady. "And if we walk?"

Daniel didn't blink. "We'll wish you well, but we'll move on. The market's watching, Maya. This is your window."

Maya scanned the highlighted clauses. "The reporting cadence... weekly is aggressive. We're a small team. If we hit the metrics, can we revisit the exclusivity before the pilot ends?"

Daniel's smile was polite, but unmoved. "If you overdeliver, we'll talk. But for now, our board needs certainty. We can't risk a competitor getting your tech mid-pilot."

The printer in the corner coughed, spitting the first page of the term sheet onto the desk. Maya glanced at it, the paper still warm, the words *Chain of Custody* bolded at the top.

Ethan shook his head. "We need the money. But if we sign, we're betting everything on Helios playing fair."

Alex's voice was low. "It's a leash, but it's gold-plated."

Maya looked at her team, then back at Daniel. "We say yes and we stay clean. No shortcuts, no gray areas. If Helios wants transparency, they get it. But we don't give up our soul."

Daniel nodded, a small smile flickering. "Onboarding starts in an hour. My compliance team will send the kickoff invite."

The call ended. The printer spat out the last page. Maya gathered the stack, feeling the weight of each clause and every hope pressing down. The team sat in silence, the hum of the HVAC filling the room.

Outside, the rain had finally stopped. Inside, NovaTech was about to step into the light, or the fire.

———

The conference room still smelled faintly of last night's pizza. Ethan and Alex sat at the table, laptops open, as the Helios Security Engineer shared a screen filled with checklists and dashboards. The cursor moved with metronome precision, ticking through log ingestion, artifact tagging, and documentation bucket review windows.

"As part of our standard onboarding, we run a full retrospective scan of access logs for the pilot window," the SecEng intoned. "It's routine. Just making sure the history matches the present. We'll need your SBOMs, signed artifact manifests, and a list of all ephemeral credentials used in the last thirty days."

Ethan nodded, already making notes. "We can export logs in JSON or CSV. Our artifact pipeline tags every build with a hash and timestamp."

"Perfect," the SecEng replied, barely glancing up. "We'll also need access to your documentation bucket for review windows. Our compliance team will flag any anomalies for follow-up. And we'll need full audit trails for all pilot-related systems."

Ethan hesitated. "Full trails? That's a lot of data. Our logs go back months, and some of it is archived. Can we scope it to just the pilot window?"

The SecEng's tone was polite but firm. "We understand the lift. But for onboarding, our policy is full trails for the relevant systems. At least for the last ninety days. If you need more time to retrieve archives, let us know. We can stagger the upload."

Maya, watching the exchange, interjected, "We'll get you what you need, but we'll need a day to pull the oldest logs from cold storage."

"That's fine," the SecEng said. "Send what you have now and update us as the rest comes online. Our goal is transparency, not disruption."

Alex scrolled through the onboarding checklist, frowning at the "confidence in optics" policy. "Do you need application-level traces too, or just system logs?"

The SecEng nodded. "Both, if possible. We want to be able to reconstruct any event chain if there's an audit."

Maya stood, quietly gathering her things. "I'll leave you two to the technical details. Ping me if you need sign-off." She slipped out, the door closing softly behind her.

In the hallway, Maya paused to check her phone. She typed a quick message to Ravi: *Another late night. Go ahead and eat without me.* She hesitated, then hit **Send**.

She made her way to the bullpen, where Jamie was hunched over his monitor, headphones on. Maya tapped the desk gently. "Hey. How's it going?"

Jamie pulled off his headphones, blinking. "Just wrangling some test data. All's good."

"If you need anything, time off, help with the insurance forms, let me know," Maya said, keeping her tone light.

Jamie managed a tired smile. "Thanks, Maya. I'm okay... just fighting the usual bureaucracy."

"Let me know if that changes," she said, then moved on.

Back in her office, Maya drafted a quick update to the Board: *Helios offer accepted, onboarding in process. Compliance review underway. Will update as soon as pilot window is confirmed.*

She hit **Send**, then leaned back, listening to the muffled voices from the conference room and the faint hum of the printer spitting out onboarding checklists.

———

The launch party was winding down, but the echo of applause still lingered in the glass-walled executive lounge high above the city. Titan's headquarters glowed with celebration: Caterers clearing away champagne flutes, clusters of executives laughing too loudly, the city skyline a glittering backdrop.

Richard Hale stood alone at the window, his reflection superimposed on the city lights. The launch had gone off without a hitch. The product was live, the press was buzzing, and the board was already talking about market share.

He swirled the amber liquid in his glass, the ice clinking softly. On the coffee table, a stack of congratulatory cards and a glossy launch brochure caught the light. He picked one up, flipping through the pages. NovaTech's architecture, rebranded and polished, stared back at him.

He set the brochure down, harder than he meant to.

His phone buzzed. A message from home:

*Saw the livestream. You looked great. Proud of you.*

He typed, *Thanks. Big day*, then hesitated, thumb hovering. He deleted the words and locked the screen.

A junior PR rep poked her head in, eyes bright. "Mr. Hale, the Board wants a photo with you."

Richard forced a smile. "Give me a minute, will you?"

The door closed. Silence settled. He walked to the bar, poured another finger of whiskey, and stared at the city lights. For a moment, he thought of Maya's last email, her hope, her trust. He remembered the first time he'd met her, the way she'd shaken his hand, eyes clear and unguarded.

He wondered, not for the first time, if there had been another way. If winning always had to feel like this. Hollow, heavy, and a little bit cold.

He set his glass down beside the untouched stack of launch brochures, then pressed his palm to the cool glass of the window, watching the city pulse with possibility.

Inside, Richard closed his eyes and listened to the quiet, waiting for the feeling of victory to arrive.

———

Three days after onboarding, the pilot felt like a wave they could finally ride. Alex and Ethan fielded questions on signal fidelity and surge behavior; each answer landed clean. During a recent call a Helios engineer even let slip, "Your curves are beating our internal target. If this holds, we might actually outrun Titan."

The morning's check-in was supposed to be routine: previous night's run, delta notes, next payload set.

The Helios SecEng's voice came thin over the speaker, professionalism with distance. "Before we begin, we need to address an optics flag."

A screenshare flickered to life. The audit report was clinical:

- **Summary:** Historical Access Anomalies—Documentation Bucket
- **Severity:** Yellow (Pause Required)
- **Findings:**
  - 7 instances of masked health-check API calls between 2:00 and 2:20 a.m., spanning three consecutive Fridays
  - Source: Internal credential, flagged as "service account"
  - Access pattern: Read-only, but with metadata pulls and download attempts
  - Masked as routine system health checks, but timing and frequency inconsistent with scheduled maintenance
  - No corresponding entries in NovaTech's maintenance logs

The SecEng's cursor hovered over a timeline graph. "Your present controls look clean," he said. "But your history raises optics risk. See here?" The cursor highlighted a narrow band on the timeline, then zoomed in on a documentation bucket. "Each spike at 2:13 a.m. corresponds to a masked health-check accesses against your documentation store. Signature repeats on a cadence. Our compliance policy requires us to flag any undocumented or unexplained access to sensitive documentation."

Ethan leaned forward and pinched the bridge of his nose. The graph was a quiet confession: touches that looked like maintenance if you didn't squint; too clever if you did. "Masked as health checks," he muttered. "It looks routine if no one asks why."

"Those are before we rotated credentials and locked down the bucket. The service account was supposed to be dormant."

Maya's voice was steady, but her jaw was tight. "We can remediate. Send us the artifact list."

A pause. Keys clicked, clinical. "Remediate optics?" the SecEng asked, and the word landed like cold rain. "Our board will see risk."

Ethan's chair creaked. "They're calling courage 'dirty' because the paper trail hiccupped," he said, too low for the mic, just loud enough to bruise the room.

"We're pausing your fast-track pilot," the SecEng continued, voice steady. "Pending chain-of-custody remediation and audit alignment. Your present posture is acceptable, but your history must be made legible. We'll follow up with an audit summary before kickoff."

In the corner of Maya's screen, the calendar tile flipped from blue to gray. *Canceled.*

"Pause doesn't mean never." The SecEng said, sounding apologetic. "It just means no headlines with risk."

The office's ancient coffee machine hissed like a cat. Ethan reached over and smacked the power switch; the hiss died, leaving the fluorescent ballast to fill the silence with a thin, mechanical buzz.

Maya kept her voice level. "We'll remediate chain of custody. Send the exact windows, scope, and artifact list. We'll provide full trails for the ninety-day window."

"Understood," the SecEng said. "Expect the compliance packet within the hour. Thank you."

The call ended. The screenshare dissolved. For a breath, no one moved.

The printer coughed out an audit memo, edges warm. Alex watched it slide into the tray like a mouth refusing to swallow. The header was bold: **Helios Compliance Review—Pilot Pause Notification**. Below, the findings repeated in bullet points, each one a bruise.

Maya's phone buzzed; she didn't look at it. "We fix the record," she said. "And we make the past look like the truth it should have been."

Ethan opened the tripwire board, the screen filling with muted red and yellow timestamps. He traced the 02:13 signature with a finger he didn't let tremble.

"History matches the present," he said, more vow than observation. "Or we find who made it lie."

The room held its breath. Outside, the city kept moving. Inside, NovaTech faced the kind of pause that felt like drowning with a rope in reach.

———

Maya had retreated to her desk and now stared at her laptop. A blank email draft waited for her to explain the unexplainable.

She typed, deleted, then typed again. In the end, she kept it short, blunt, and almost surgical:

**Subject:** Update: Helios Pilot Paused
Helios pilot paused by compliance optics. Historical access anomalies flagged; remediation is underway. Will update within 24 hours.

She hit **Send** before she could soften it. The truth was a blade, and she had no time for polish.

Her phone vibrated almost immediately. Alan. The message held a Teams link and nothing else.

She dialed in. The grid of faces was sharper than usual, the backgrounds more curated, the tension almost visible.

Alan spoke first, his voice clipped. "Maya, what the hell happened? 'Optics'? What does that mean? Why are we hearing about this now?"

Maya kept her tone even. "Helios flagged undocumented access in our historical logs. Masked as health checks, but the timing was off. They've paused the pilot until we remediate and provide a full audit trail."

Jonas leaned in, eyes narrowed. "Is this a security breach? Are we exposed?"

"No evidence of exfiltration," Maya replied. "But the pattern is irregular. We're pulling full trails for the ninety-day window. Ethan is on it."

Priya's voice was icy. "You said onboarding was clean. Now we're paused, and we're blindsided. What else haven't you told us?"

Maya's jaw tightened. "We moved fast to secure the deal. The compliance review surfaced legacy access. Service account, supposed to be dormant. We're investigating. I'll have a complete report within 24 hours."

Alan's expression was unreadable. "How long have you known about this? Because this is the first we're hearing about anything suspicious."

A silence stretched. Maya chose honesty. "We've seen anomalies before. Nothing conclusive. This is the first time it's impacted an external partner. We're treating it as a top priority."

Jonas shook his head. "This is a disaster. Helios was our runway. Now we're paused, and the optics are—" He didn't finish.

Priya cut in. "You need to control this. Our LPs are already asking if we're compromised. If there's a breach, we need to know now."

Maya's voice was steady, but her hands shook beneath the desk. "You'll have answers. I'm not hiding anything. But I won't speculate until we have facts."

Alan exhaled, the sound sharp. "Twenty-four hours, Maya. Fix this. And no more surprises."

The others clicked off but Alan's tile lingered, his background shifting as he settled closer to the camera.

He spoke quietly, the edge gone from his voice. "Maya, I went to bat for you with Priya. Talked her down from selling. Told her you always deliver. Now I look like a fool."

Maya met his gaze, unflinching. "Don't lose faith, Alan. We're working around the clock. I've never let you down before. I'll get to the bottom of this, and I'll report back directly."

Alan's disappointment was palpable, but so was his exhaustion. "You'd better. I can't keep burning capital on hope."

Maya nodded. "You backed me because I deliver. I will. But I need you to hold the line for one more day."

Alan hesitated, then nodded once. "Twenty-four hours. That's all I can give."

He disconnected and Maya sat in the silence. The audit memo was still warm in the printer. She pinned it to the wall. In thick marker, she wrote: *No secrets, especially when it's scary.*

She stared at the words, willing herself to believe them. Then she turned back to her laptop, the cursor blinked, the clock already counting down.

After a minute she found Ethan in the server closet, sleeves pushed up, eyes fixed on a wall of monitors. The room remained stubbornly cold, the fans breathing in sync with Ethan's tension.

She closed the door behind her. The latch clicked like a verdict.

Ethan didn't look up. "I heard the call. We're on the clock."

Maya nodded, settling onto the only empty chair, her knees brushing a tangle of network cables. "Walk me through what you've got."

Ethan showed her his screen. "Here's the audit window Helios flagged. Seven hits, always between 2:00 and 2:20 a.m., three Fridays in a row. All masked as health checks, but the cadence is off. No matching entries in our maintenance logs."

He pulled up a timeline, the spikes at 2:13 a.m. glowing like wounds. "Service account credential. Supposed to be dormant since we rotated keys last quarter. But someone woke it up."

Maya leaned in, scanning the logs. "Could it be a backup script? Something legacy?"

Ethan shook his head. "I checked every scheduled job. Nothing matches. And the access pattern. Read-only, but with metadata pulls and download attempts. It's too careful."

A silence stretched. Maya broke it. "You think it's internal?"

Ethan's jaw tightened. "If it's not, we have a bigger problem. But the signature's local. Whoever did this knew our hygiene. Knew how to hide."

Maya exhaled. "We need to know if anything left the bucket. Can you reconstruct the artifact list for those windows?"

"I'm on it," Ethan said, already scripting. "I'll cross-reference every access with our artifact manifests. If anything was touched, I'll find it."

Maya watched him work, the monitors' glow casting tired shadows across his face. "Ethan, if this is a mole, if it's someone on the team... are you ready to follow it all the way?"

He paused, hands hovering over the keys. "I have to be. We can't fix the record if we don't know where it broke."

Maya nodded, her voice softer. "No secrets, especially when it's scary. That's the rule now."

Ethan managed a tired smile. "I'll pin it to the board when I'm done."

A beat passed. Maya stood, placing a hand on his shoulder. A rare gesture. "You're the reason we still have a shot. Don't burn out before we get there."

He nodded, eyes never leaving the screen. "I'll sleep when the logs fall silent."

Maya left him to the cold and the code, the door clicking softly closed behind her. In the hallway, she checked her phone. Another message from Ravi, unread. She let it go for now. There were too many ghosts in the system, and only so many hours left to find them.

———

The Tech Ledger office buzzed with the low-grade panic of a newsroom on the edge. Phones rang, monitors flickered, and the air smelled of printer toner. Sofia Martinez barely had time to drop her bag before her editor's voice cut through the din.

"Sofia. My office."

The glass-walled office was a fishbowl of tension. Her editor slid a letter across the desk. Heavy paper, a law firm's logo embossed at the top.

"Titan's lawyers are circling," the editor said, voice low. "If you're wrong, we're exposed. They're threatening to sue if we publish anything defamatory or based on confidential information."

Sofia scanned the letter, jaw set. "I have the documents. The truth matters."

Her editor's gaze was steady, but tired. "Just make sure your sources are bulletproof. We can't afford a lawsuit, not on a maybe."

Sofia nodded, determination hardening. "I'll stand by every word. I've triple-checked the chain. If they want a fight, they'll get one."

The editor leaned back, exhaling. "Just don't get reckless. We need you in the newsroom, not in court."

As Sofia left the office, her phone buzzed. A new message, subject line blank, sender unlisted. She opened it, heart ticking faster.

*You're asking the right questions. There's more to find.*

Sofia lingered by the newsroom window, the anonymous message reverberating in her mind. The stakes had never felt higher. Somewhere, someone wanted the truth out. But the cost was rising for everyone who touched it.

———

The apartment was dark except for the faint spill of streetlight pushing through the blinds. Maya slipped inside, closing the door with a softness that felt like apology. She hadn't meant to work this late. She hadn't meant to miss dinner. She hadn't meant for any of it.

But meaning to and doing were two different worlds now.

Ravi sat on the sofa, a book open but unread in his lap. He looked up as she entered. Not startled. Not expectant. Just... watching.

"You're home," he said quietly.

Maya managed a tired exhale. "Yeah. Sorry. Helios paused the pilot. They found anomalies in the logs. Maybe nothing, maybe a misconfigured gateway, we're not sure. I've been putting out fires all day."

Ravi nodded once. "I figured it was something big."

A beat.

"It's been days."

The words landed with a dull weight, not an accusation but a simple truth.

Maya set her bag down. "I know. I'm sorry. Everything's—everything's falling apart."

Ravi closed the book gently. "And I've been trying to give you space to handle it. I really have."

He swallowed, choosing his next words carefully.

"But I think I need you to hear something. Really hear it."

Maya lowered herself into the armchair across from him, exhaustion pressing like gravity. "Okay."

He leaned forward, elbows on his knees. "I've tried to be patient.

I've tried to not make demands. I've tried to wait until things 'calm down,' even though we both know they never do."

A soft, sad laugh. "I told myself Titan launching would be the worst of it. Then Helios came. Now the anomalies. Every time I think we've hit bottom, there's another layer."

Maya rubbed her eyes. "Ravi—"

He shook his head gently. "Please. Let me finish."

She fell quiet.

"I love you," he said, voice low. "More than I've ever loved anyone. But the last few months... I don't think I've been in your life. Not really. I think I've been orbiting it."

His voice grew even softer. "And three days ago, when Titan launched, I thought maybe you'd come home early. Or call. Or text. Just... something."

A pause.

"You didn't."

Maya felt her throat tighten. "I was drowning."

"I know," he said. "That's the thing. I know. And I kept telling myself it would change. After the pilot. After the leak. After Titan. After Helios."

He met her eyes across the dim room.

"But it doesn't change. And I'm losing parts of my life too. My project's gone. My job's on the line. I'm scared, Maya. And I can't even tell my own wife without competing with a dozen crises."

Her phone buzzed in her bag as if summoned.

They both looked at it.

She didn't reach for it.

But the damage was already done.

Ravi exhaled, something inside him deflating. Not anger. Not frustration. Just weariness.

"I think you need to keep fighting your fight," he said finally. "I think you have to. It's who you are. It's what this war demands."

His voice cracked, barely audible.

"But I can't keep losing mine while you're out there winning or losing battles I can't even see."

Tears blurred in Maya's vision before she could stop them. "Ravi, please... I'm trying."

"I know." He stood. Slowly. "That's what makes this so hard."

He took a step toward the hallway, then hesitated. "I'm not leaving tonight," he said. "But I don't know how many more nights like this I have left in me."

Her breath caught. "Are you—are you ending this?"

"No," he said softly. "I'm saying this is the moment before the ending. Unless something changes."

He walked down the hall, the dim light catching the slump of his shoulders. "Maya?"

She looked up, silent.

His voice was barely a whisper. "Loving you shouldn't feel like waiting for a storm to pass."

He disappeared into the bedroom, closing the door gently behind him.

Maya sat alone in the dim room, listening to the soft hum of the refrigerator and the muted rain outside. Her phone buzzed again and again in her bag.

She didn't reach for it. Not this time.

———

Across the city, in Titan's executive suite, the cost of loyalty was being tallied in a different way.

The air tinged with ozone from the laser printer and the faint metallic tang of rain on the window ledge. Richard Hale sat at the head of the conference table, reviewing the latest cost-cutting spreadsheet. HR had flagged several names for potential layoffs. Mid-level managers, engineers, and one executive: Claire Donovan.

Smyth from Finance, his accent crisp and his tie askew, leaned in. "Claire's been advocating for NovaTech since the beginning. She's not aligned with the new direction. If we're trimming, she's an obvious candidate."

Patel, arms folded, didn't look up from his tablet. "She's good with partners, but she's been second-guessing the engineering roadmap. If we're closing ranks, we need people who are all-in."

Richard scanned the list, his jaw set. Claire's name was highlighted in red. He remembered her advocacy in the early meetings, her quiet integrity, the way she'd tried to build bridges instead of walls.

He hesitated, pen hovering over the approval line. "Claire's good at what she does. She understands both sides of the table. We need that, especially now."

Smyth frowned. "She's a risk. If she's not with us, she's against us."

Richard shook his head. "She stays. For now. We need stability, not more chaos."

He signed off on the rest of the list, leaving Claire's name untouched. The meeting moved on, yet Richard lingered, eyes fixed on the spreadsheet. Sparing Claire felt right, but it also felt dangerous. A crack in his armor, a choice he couldn't explain.

Later, as he passed Claire's office, their eyes met through the glass. She looked up from her screen, uncertainty flickering across her face. For a moment, neither spoke. Then Claire nodded, grateful but wary. Richard nodded back, the gesture brief, almost imperceptible.

He told himself it was just business. But deep down, he knew it was something more. A refusal to destroy someone who still believed in doing the right thing.

# SIX

THE SERVER ROOM was small and stubbornly cold, as if someone had bottled winter and let it loose among the racks. The wheeze of fans filled the space. A mechanical breath Ethan had come to find oddly comforting. He settled into the battered chair, the vinyl cracked at the edges, and pulled up the log aggregator on his laptop. The screen's glow painted his face in shifting blues and greens.

He began applying filters: time windows around every major exchange with Titan, spikes in outbound traffic, odd authentication pings. For the first hour, the logs were what they always were: poetry written by machines, indifferent to human drama. But Ethan was relentless, his mind refusing to let go of the anomaly he'd flagged weeks ago. He drilled deeper, stacking numbers until they whispered.

There. A micropattern at the edge of a dump. An API key accessing a branch that shouldn't have been touched that week, the call cloaked behind a harmless utility service. He flagged it and cross-referenced. The activity coincided with Titan's request for "clarity on optional smoothing heuristics." His pulse ticked faster.

He kept digging, the stacks of numbers leaning on one another until they began to tell a story. There: the cron job masked as a system health check that the Helios SecEng had flagged, hitting a documentation bucket at 2:13 a.m. every Friday. The signature was local. A ghost with a badge.

Ethan sat back, throat tight. The chair creaked, an old hinge telling an older story. He was alone in the cold with proof that betrayal wasn't just across town. It was in the room.

He printed the relevant lines, the paper warm against his fingers. He slid everything into a folder, labeled it by hand, *Anomalies: Access Keys / 02:13,* and felt the shape of the war change in his head.

He hesitated, then pinged Maya on Teams: *I'm making progress, but there's something else I want to check: old access keys; anomalies around the times Titan requested addons.*

Minutes later, Maya appeared in the doorway, face drawn and eyes rimmed with exhaustion. She studied him. "You think we were leaking from the inside."

"I hope not," Ethan said flatly. "But hope's not a method."

She nodded, her voice steady but tired. "Do it. Quietly."

When she left, Ethan stared at the folder in his hands. Jamie's name was on the credential. Jamie, who'd been hired not long after Ethan, who'd pulled all-nighters with him, who'd once fixed a memory leak at 3 a.m. while Ethan ranted about the unfairness of the world. Jamie, who'd brought in donuts on Ethan's birthday and covered for him when his own code broke the build.

No. It couldn't be Jamie.

Ethan set the folder aside and started over. He pulled up the HR records, badge logs, every access credential that could possibly match. Maybe the system had recycled an old credential. Maybe someone had spoofed Jamie's account. Maybe it was a script, a backup job, a ghost in the machine.

He cross-referenced every login, every badge swipe, every time Jamie had set foot in the building. He checked for remote logins, for VPN anomalies, for any sign that someone else could have used Jamie's credentials. He ran scripts to look for privilege escalation, for lateral movement, for malware. He even checked the physical access logs. Maybe Jamie's badge had been stolen, maybe he'd lost it and never reported it.

But the pattern held. The access times matched Jamie's late-night coding sessions. The files touched were the ones Jamie had worked on, the ones he'd asked Ethan about, the ones they'd debugged together over cold coffee and bad jokes.

Ethan's denial turned to desperation. He scrolled through chat logs, searching for any sign. An odd message, a missed joke, a cry for help. Anything. He found nothing but the usual: code reviews, memes, the occasional vent about insurance forms and hospital bills.

He stared at the screen, then pressed his palms to his eyes, willing the data to change. "Come on, Jamie," he whispered. "Tell me I'm wrong." But the logs remained relentless. The signature was Jamie's. The ghost was someone Ethan had trusted, someone he'd mentored. Someone he'd called a friend.

Ethan's hands shook as he opened the folder again. He felt the betrayal like a physical ache, a cold knot in his chest. He wanted to scream, to smash the monitor, to wake up and find had all been a mistake.

But the evidence was clear. There was no one else. No other explanation.

He slumped back in the chair, the cold of the server room seeping into his bones. For a long moment he sat still, listening to the fans, the mechanical breath that had always felt like safety. Now it sounded like accusation.

Finally, Ethan stood, folder in hand, and walked out to find Maya and Alex. He found them in the conference room.

He hovered in the doorway, uncertain, the folder clutched so tightly the paper creased, then stepped inside.

Maya looked up, her eyes red-rimmed but alert. Alex just stared at his laptop.

Ethan's voice was rough. "I need to show you something."

He set the folder on the table, sliding out the printouts. "I've been digging through the logs. The anomalies Helios flagged."

Alex frowned, glancing at the pages. "You found something?"

Ethan nodded, swallowing. "Every time Titan asked for clarification, they got it, from us. But also... from inside."

Maya's jaw tightened.

Ethan hesitated. "I checked everything. Badge logs, VPN, physical access, credential resets. I tried to prove it was a script, or a backup job, or a stolen badge. But it's not. The access times match late-night sessions. The files touched... they're the ones we worked on; the ones Jamie and I debugged together."

Alex shook his head, voice brittle. "Jamie? No. That's not possible. He's... one of us."

Ethan's voice cracked. "I know. I didn't want to believe it either. I ran every check I could think of. I tried to find another explanation. But the logs... they don't lie."

Maya leaned forward, scanning the evidence. "Are you sure? Credentials can be spoofed. Maybe someone got his password. Maybe—"

"I thought of that," Ethan said, almost pleading. "I checked for privilege escalation, for malware, for badge cloning. There's nothing. The access pattern is too specific. It's Jamie's account, Jamie's hours, Jamie's machines. I even checked the chat logs. He was online every time the access happened."

Alex's hands were shaking. "But why? Why would he—?"

Ethan's voice was barely above a whisper. "I found an email. Buried in his drafts. Titan offered to pay for his daughter's surgery. All he had to do was send the code."

A silence fell, heavy and suffocating. Maya stared at the printouts, her lips pressed into a thin line. Alex looked away, blinking hard.

For a long moment, no one spoke. The only sound was the distant hum of the servers. This time though, they sounded like an accusation.

Maya finally broke the silence, her voice hollow but steady. "We need to talk to him. Together."

Alex nodded, still not meeting Ethan's eyes. "We need to hear it from him."

Ethan stood silently, the folder limp in his hands, bearing the weight of every line of code, every late night, every joke, argument, and shared victory. He wanted to be wrong.

Maya pulled out her phone and typed a short message:

*Can you come to the conference room for a quick chat? Bring your laptop.*

Moments later, footsteps sounded in the hallway. Jamie entered, a puzzled look on his face, laptop tucked under one arm. "Hey, what's up? Did something break?"

He stopped short when he saw all three of them waiting, the table cleared except for the folder. The air in the room was heavy, expectant. Jamie's eyes flicked from Maya to Ethan to Alex, and in that instant, his expression changed. Confusion giving way to dread.

He didn't sit. "What's going on?"

Ethan's voice was the first to break the hush. "Jamie, we need to talk. Sit down."

Jamie hesitated, then lowered himself into the chair, his posture tense, hands gripping the edge of his laptop. He looked at each of them in turn, searching for some sign of reassurance, but found none.

Ethan opened the folder, spreading out the printouts: access logs, badge records, timestamps. "We've been investigating the compliance anomalies Helios flagged. At first, I thought it was just noise. But the pattern kept coming back. Always the same credential. Always the same files."

Jamie's eyes flicked to the papers, then away. "You think it was me?"

Alex's voice was thin, almost pleading. "Just help us understand, Jamie. If there's an explanation, we want to hear it."

Jamie shook his head, a nervous laugh escaping. "I don't know what you're talking about. Maybe someone used my account. Maybe the system glitched."

Ethan's jaw clenched. "I checked for that. I checked everything. The access times match your late-night sessions. The files are the ones you and I worked on. The ones we debugged together. The badge logs, the VPN... there's no sign of anyone else. It's you, Jamie."

Jamie's hands trembled. "No. I mean... I wouldn't—" He looked at Maya, then Alex, searching for an escape. "There has to be some mistake. I'd never—" His voice faltered, the words catching in his throat.

Maya's voice was steady, but her eyes were hard. "Jamie, we want to believe you. But the evidence is overwhelming. If there's something you need to tell us, now is the time."

Jamie's shoulders sagged. For a moment, he looked impossibly small. "I—" He glanced at Maya, then Alex, searching for an escape. "I just... I thought I could fix it before anyone noticed. I thought if I just gave them what they wanted, it would be over."

He looked up, eyes shining with tears he refused to shed. "They said they'd cover her surgery," he whispered. "Titan. My daughter's insurance denied the claim. I thought... I thought if I just sent them what they wanted, no one would get hurt. I thought I could keep us safe and save her."

Ethan's voice was raw, betrayed. "You chose them over us. You didn't even tell us."

Jamie's voice broke. "What was I supposed to do? Watch her get sicker? I didn't want to hurt anyone. I just—I was desperate. I kept telling myself I'd stop. That it was just this once. But they kept asking, and I kept... I kept saying yes."

Alex looked away, unable to meet Jamie's eyes. He remembered late nights, Jamie's laugh echoing in the empty office, the way they'd once argued over variable names and then ordered pizza at 2 a.m. Now, the memory stung.

Maya stepped in, her tone final. "No more keys, Jamie. Not until we understand everything. You're done here for now."

Jamie nodded. He slid his badge across the table, the plastic scraping against the metal. No one touched it.

"I'm sorry," he whispered. "I thought I could fix it."

"HR. Then home," Maya said quietly. "We'll tell you when you can come back. And with whom."

Jamie stood, shoulders bowed, and left without another word. The echo of his footsteps faded down the hall.

For a long moment, no one spoke. The room had gone cold. Alex leaned against the wall, staring at the floor. "I keep thinking there should have been a sign. Something we missed."

Ethan stared at the badge on the table, jaw tight. "He was one of us. I thought I'd feel angry, but mostly I just feel... tired."

Maya looked at them both, her voice barely above a whisper. "We do everything right, and it still isn't enough."

Alex nodded, hollow. "We lost more than code."

Ethan closed his eyes. "We lost our friend."

Maya straightened, gathering herself. "We tell the Board the truth. All of it. No more secrets."

They nodded, the silence between them heavy with loss.

———

The faces of Alan, Priya, Jonas and the others were arranged in neat rows on the screen. Maya sat at her desk, the folder of evidence still on her lap, her hands folded tightly to keep them from shaking. She took a steadying breath, then began.

"Thank you all for joining on short notice. I want to update you on what's happened." Her voice was steady, but the fatigue was unmistakable. "We've identified the source of the compliance anomalies that triggered the Helios pause: Jamie, one of our engineers. He accessed sensitive documentation using a dormant service account. We confronted him this morning."

Priya's voice cut in, sharp and skeptical. "Was it intentional? Was he working for someone else?"

Maya nodded, her jaw tight. "He confessed. Titan offered to pay for his daughter's surgery if he shared technical materials. He said he thought he could help her and keep us safe at the same time. He's been removed from all systems, and we're conducting a full audit to ensure there's no further exposure."

Jonas's face was grim. "So the compliance issue was an inside job. What does this mean for Helios?"

"Ethan and Alex are briefing Helios's security team now," Maya replied. "We're being fully transparent. I'll let you know as soon as we have their decision."

Priya's eyes narrowed. "If Helios walks, we're out of options. We need to talk about a sale."

Alan raised a hand, his voice softer than usual. "Let's not get ahead of ourselves. Maya, thank you for your candor. Before we discuss next steps, sale or otherwise, I want to hear what Helios decides. If they're out, we'll reconvene and make a decision."

Maya nodded, her voice barely above a whisper. "Understood. I'll keep you posted the moment I hear from Helios."

Alan gave a small, tired smile. "All right. We'll table the discussion until then. Thank you, Maya."

The call ended, the grid of faces vanishing into black. Maya sat in the silence, eyes drawn to the badge on her desk, the empty chair across the room, and the blinking cursor on her screen—waiting for the next crisis, the next decision, the next fight.

———

While Maya was on with the Board, Ethan and Alex sat in NovaTech's small conference room, laptops open, a stack of audit printouts between them. On the other end of the video call was the Helios Security Engineer.

Ethan cleared his throat. "Thank you for making time. We wanted to be fully transparent about what we found."

Alex nodded, sliding the folder into view. "We've completed a full audit of our access logs. The anomalies you flagged: masked health-check calls, documentation bucket access at odd hours. They were the result of an internal breach. One of our engineers was approached by Titan and agreed to share technical materials in exchange for help with a family medical emergency."

The SecEng's expression didn't change, but his eyes sharpened. "Was there any indication that Titan IP or code was introduced into your systems?"

Ethan shook his head. "We've checked every commit, every artifact. There's no evidence of reverse contamination. No Titan code in our stack. But given the nature of the breach, we can't guarantee with absolute certainty that nothing crossed over. We're continuing to audit, but we wanted you to have the facts as soon as we did."

The SecEng nodded, fingers steepled. "I appreciate your candor. But if we roll this out and there's even a whiff of Titan's code in your stack, we're the ones in the crossfire. That's not a place we want to be."

Alex's shoulders slumped. Ethan simply stared at the table.

The SecEng continued. "Look, this isn't a reflection on your integrity. It's just reality. I'll talk to my team, but I can't see us moving forward. If things change or if you can provide a clean bill of health in the future, we're open to revisiting. But for now, we have to step back."

Ethan nodded, voice barely above a whisper. "Understood."

The call ended with a polite click, leaving Ethan and Alex alone in the quiet conference room.

Alex closed his laptop with a sigh. "That's it, then."

Ethan just nodded, the silence between them saying everything that words could not.

———

Maya's phone buzzed. Daniel Cho's name flashed on the screen. She stepped into her office and answered, bracing herself.

Daniel's voice was gentle, regretful. "Maya, I'm sorry. I really did want this to work. For both of us. But given what you've told us, we have to assume there's a risk. If your engineer was in contact with Titan, there's a nonzero chance Titan IP could have been seeded into your codebase. Intentionally or not. If we deploy your tech and it turns out to contain Titan's proprietary material, it's Helios that gets sued. We can't take that risk. Really, I'm sorry."

Maya closed her eyes, letting the words settle. "I understand, Daniel. Thank you for being straight with me."

A pause. "If things change, if you can clear this up, call me. I mean that."

"I will," Maya said quietly.

The call ended. Maya sat for a moment in the hush, the weight of loss and responsibility pressing in from all sides.

———

It was late morning at Titan, but the office felt tense. The usual hum of conversation had been replaced by the low drone of urgent meetings and the staccato of Slack notifications. Claire sat at her desk, sunlight glancing off the glass towers outside, her inbox overflowing with updates and terse status checks.

A new memo from Richard Hale landed with a sharp ping.

*Delete all correspondence with NovaTech. No exceptions.*
*—RH*

Claire stared at the message, pulse ticking faster. She scrolled through her inbox, pausing on a thread with Maya, subject line: *Pilot Integration Questions.* The early messages were warm, hopeful, full of possibility. Now, they felt radioactive.

Her finger hovered over the **Delete** key. She hesitated, then quietly forwarded the thread to her personal email, watching the progress bar crawl across the screen. Only then did she delete the original, her pulse pounding.

She sat for a moment, staring at the empty inbox, the city beyond the glass. The silence pressed in, heavy and expectant.

Later, alone in the elevator, she caught her reflection in the brushed steel doors. She whispered, "What are we doing?"

The doors slid open. She stepped into the empty lobby, resolve hardening with every step.

———

The board call was set for late afternoon, but Maya had been ready for hours. She sat at her desk, laptop open, the folder with Jamie's badge and the audit logs beside her. When the meeting started, Maya was a bit startled to see more than the usual threesome. The entire Board, save Maya, had gathered in Alan's conference room. She couldn't recall when she had last seen some of them; probably not since the last quarterly update. For the first time, Maya felt small.

Alan opened, his voice clipped. "We got your message. Helios is out. We need to decide. Do we fight, or do we sell?"

One of the new faces, a director Maya barely knew, spoke up. "Jonas, what does the balance sheet say?"

Jonas didn't hesitate. "Sell. We're burning cash. Titan's launch is everywhere and with Helios out we can't maintain things long. If we can get a deal on the table, we'll at least return something to the LPs. But the longer we wait, the less leverage we have."

Another director, older, leaned forward. "We've all seen the numbers. If we fight, we're betting the company on a lawsuit. That's not what we signed up for."

Priya's tone was sharper than Maya had remembered. "Maya, I know what this company means to you. But we funded you and your tech, not a lawsuit. When's the last time you heard of a big tech company having to stop selling a product just because of a patent? It doesn't happen these days. Even if you win, what then? They change a few lines of code and keep on going. Meanwhile, we're the company that sues people. Who wants to do business on those terms?"

Maya's jaw tightened. "When we first came to you, you thought enough of our team and our tech to back us. You told us you were there to help us. And you have. Why do you want to throw it away now?"

Priya paused, her expression softening for a moment. "Things change, Maya. We funded you because we believed in your vision. But the market's changed. The risks are different now. We have to be realistic."

Jonas jumped in. "We're not a litigation shop. We're a startup. If we go down this road, we could lose everything. There's still value left. Let's not waste it."

A third director, who'd been silent, spoke up. "I've seen this before. You fight, you lose, and then you have nothing. Or you win, and it drags on for years. Meanwhile, the tech gets old, the team burns out, and the market moves on."

Maya's voice was steady, but there was steel in it. "You want to talk about value? What's the value of a patent if it can be steamrolled by a company like Titan? What's the point of building anything if the rules only protect the giants? This isn't just about money. It's about consequences. It's about standing up for what's right."

Priya shook her head. "You're asking us to risk everything on principle."

Maya met her gaze. "Others are tired of seeing innovation crushed. If we don't fight, we're just another cautionary tale. I can't be a drone at a company like Titan, even if it means throwing away everything I've built. I won't sell to someone who manipulated a decent guy like Jamie. I won't let them win like this."

Alan, who had been silent, finally spoke. "Let's be honest. This isn't just about business. This is about what kind of company we want to be. Do we want to be the ones who fold when things get hard, or the ones who stand up for what we believe in?"

A tense silence settled over the room. Maya could see the conflict on their faces: fear, frustration, and, just maybe, a flicker of respect.

Jonas broke the silence. "If we fight, we need to know what we're getting into. Litigation is a black hole. Are you prepared for what that means, Maya? For you, for the team?"

Maya nodded. "I am. I know what it will cost. But I also know what it will cost if we don't."

Alan leaned back, rubbing his temples as if the weight of the decision pressed down on him. "Let's take five." He went on mute, and Maya watched as the conference room disappeared from the grid, replaced by a computer-generated icon.

She sat in the quiet, staring at her own reflection in the laptop screen. Her hands trembled, but she didn't look away.

After a few minutes, Alan came back on. He looked tired, but his voice was clear.

"It wasn't unanimous," Alan said. "But we'll back you, Maya. We'll fight."

Maya let out a breath she hadn't realized she was holding. "Thank you."

Alan nodded. "Don't make us regret it."

The call ended. Maya sat in the hush, the city outside her window fading to gold as the sun set. She opened her laptop, typed a single name into the search bar: *Jordan Reyes.*

———

The sun had set by the time Maya made it home. She let herself into the apartment; the familiar click of the door echoed in the quiet. The lights were off. The air felt still, as if the rooms themselves were holding their breath.

She set her bag down, listening for the clatter of dishes from the kitchen, the low hum of Ravi's music, the faint scent of his tea. Nothing. The apartment felt emptier than she remembered.

She noticed the row of shoes by the door; Ravi's were missing. The coat rack was lighter. A mug, once his favorite, sat rinsed and upside down in the drying rack.

On the dining table, a single envelope waited. Her name, written in Ravi's careful hand.

She opened it, her fingers trembling.

*Maya—*
*I waited as long as I could. I hope you find what you're really*
*fighting for.*
*—R*

She stood for a long moment, the note fluttering in her hand. The city lights blinked through the window, indifferent. She pressed her palm to the table, steadying herself.

She had convinced the Board to fight. She had chosen her company, her principles, her team. But here, in the hush of the apartment, she realized what she had lost.

Maya sat down at the table, the note beside her, and let the silence settle. For the first time all day, she allowed herself to feel the ache. Not just of battle, but of absence.

---

Jordan's office was a minimalist's dream: a single glass wall framing the city's sprawl, pale oak floors, and a desk that resembled a sculpture more than a workspace. No family photos, no clutter. Just a single, oversized monitor, a legal pad with a Montblanc pen, and a small, perfectly tended bonsai. The only color in the room came from a Rothko print, all deep blue and tension.

Jordan embodied Silicon Valley casual, done with intent: a navy Zegna sweater, charcoal wool pants, and Italian loafers without socks. No tie, no jacket. Yet everything about him, his posture, his watch, the way he greeted Maya with a nod, radiated control and taste.

"Maya Singh," he said, extending a hand. "I've read your patent. Impressive work."

"Titan stole it," Maya said flatly. "I want them held accountable."

Jordan gestured to a chair. "You have a case. A strong one. But it'll cost you everything. Time, money, blood."

Maya sat, meeting his gaze without flinching. "Then we'll bleed."

Jordan's smile flickered and vanished as quickly as it appeared. He slid a slim, encrypted drive across the desk. "First step isn't filing. It's assembling. Every document, every commit, every email, every napkin sketch. We vet everything. Twice. Only when the record is bulletproof do we file. Then comes the war."

As he watched Maya's silhouette disappear, the city's lights started to twinkle to life outside. Jordan closed the folder in front of him, fingers lingering on the edge. He'd seen founders walk in with fire before. Most burned out before the finish. This one, though... she might just drag the whole system into the light with her.

He exhaled, slow and quiet. The weight of what was coming settled in his bones. He had told Maya the truth: it would cost everything. What he hadn't said, what he rarely admitted, even to himself, was that sometimes, the fight was worth it. Even if you lost.

He straightened his desk, already plotting three moves ahead. "Let's bleed," she'd said. He almost smiled. "Let's see who runs out first."

That night, Maya stood alone in NovaTech's office, city lights flickering through rain-streaked panes. She looked at the patent certificate, the promise that had started it all, and whispered to the empty room:

"They think they can steal our future. They're wrong."

She picked up her phone and called Alex. "Get ready," she said. "Tomorrow, we fight."

# SEVEN

THE CONFERENCE ROOM looked less like a law office and more like a command center. Three walls were swallowed by screens; the fourth vanished behind foam boards layered with diagrams, exploded schematics, and neat stacks of claim charts bound with red spines. A single glass pane overlooked the city, but no one faced it. All eyes were on the battlefield mapped across the room.

Jordan Reyes stood at the head of the table, sleeves rolled to his forearms, a pen tucked behind one ear. He moved with the calm precision of a surgeon. "We're done being reactive," he said, tapping a laser pointer against the first board. "We go feature by feature, claim by claim."

Maya sat opposite him, posture straight despite a night without sleep. Alex was beside her, pale, a sheen of sweat on his brow; caffeine had kept him upright, conviction kept him present. Ethan hovered near the back, notebook open, a line of ink already forming a restless scar down the page.

Jordan clicked to the first slide: a side-by-side comparison of NovaTech's core patent claim and a still from Titan's launch presentation. A flow diagram ran like a river between them, boxes for each step, arrows pulsing in red.

Before he could start in, Ethan raised his hand. "I know the patent describes our architecture, but what if Titan didn't actually 'copy' it? They had stuff from Jamie, but what if they tweaked things... got some places on their own?"

"That's the heart of it, Ethan." Jordan explained patiently. "A patent is like a fence. If Titan's product lives inside our fence, even if they took a different path to get there, it's infringement. We'll show the jury where their product overlaps with our claims, step by step."

He pointed to the slide. "Element 1: Input capture. Your claim language: 'receives time-series telemetry data.'" He indicated the right-hand image. "We map it to Titan's deck: 'seamless intake of multi-source diagnostic streams and flattening to a unified profile.' Different words. Same bones."

He clicked again. "Element 2: Transform layer. Your language: 'dynamically determining a required processing resource level for a transform layer operation based at least in part on the monitored characteristic.'" Another image, another red arrow. "Titan's 'container orchestration.' Different skin. Same skeleton."

"The claims of the patent define the fence line. They mark exactly what's protected." Jordan was on a roll. "Infringement isn't about copying, it's about crossing that fence line. If Titan's product uses every element described in our claims, even if the words differ, they're inside the fence. That's infringement. We'll ask the judge to define the fence line. We call it 'construing the claims.' The jury will compare each claim to the accused product using the judge's definition and decide if Titan has crossed over."

Ethan took in Jordan's explanation like an IV drip, each beat a dose of cold clarity. The vocabulary changed, the architecture did not. This was NovaTech's design set in mirrored glass.

Jordan turned, the laser dot clipping across the board like a heartbeat. "We'll package this as a claim chart; every claim limitation mapped, every piece of evidence referenced."

Ethan frowned. "No jury is going to understand this language. I could barely understand it when the patent was filed, and I wrote a lot of the code that does what that language says."

Jordan nodded. "That's why we'll use an expert. Probably a university professor. Someone who can break down complex ideas for a jury. You and Alex will have to walk them through everything, get them up to speed. In the end, the jury doesn't need to be engineers, but they will have to understand enough to decide if what the patent claims is in Titan's product."

Alex cleared his throat. "We should include stress-test traces, too. Titan's throughput curves match ours down to the inflection at scale. That—" he paused, catching the rasp in his voice, "that's not simple convergence. That's replication."

Jordan's mouth pulled into a quick, tight smile. "Exactly. That's the kind of evidence that makes the story real for a jury. We'll show them the fingerprints of design choices. Where Titan's product doesn't just look like ours, it behaves like ours, under stress, in the same ways."

He paused, letting the weight of that land.

"But remember, Titan will argue 'parallel development.' They'll say, 'We just solved the same problem, in a similar way.' That's why specificity matters. We'll map every technical choice, every tradeoff, every odd little decision that only someone following our blueprint would make."

Ethan tapped his pen, still skeptical. "But what if the jury thinks it's all just... coincidence? That in tech, everyone ends up at the same place eventually?"

Jordan smiled, but there was steel in it. "That's where the story comes in. We're not just teaching them technology. We're teaching them betrayal. We'll show the sequence: Titan came to us, asked for details, kept asking for more, then walked away and launched a product that mirrors ours, right down to the quirks. The law rides along, but the story drives."

He clicked to a new slide. A ladder titled "Narrative" with four rungs: *Promise. Extraction. Abandonment. Exploitation.*

"This is our story. Promise: the partnership. Extraction: the endless technical requests. Abandonment: the sudden cut-off. Exploitation: the launch. The jury doesn't have to be engineers. They just have to see the pattern."

Maya exhaled slowly, feeling the pinch of her ring finger, the ghost of a band she'd stopped wearing last week. She watched Jordan, this relative stranger, fighting for something that once felt like a dream and now sounded like a closing argument. For a moment, she wondered if she could trust him with the company's future, or if she had any choice.

———

Jordan's guided tour though litigation preparation lasted about an hour. When he paused, Maya leaned in.

"Pre-suit letter?"

"Already drafted," Jordan said. "Tough, but tight. Enough to put them on notice, not enough to feed them defenses. We'll file the complaint quickly, preferably within the week, ask for a scheduling conference, and push for early discovery around product design. If we get the right judge, we'll angle for a claim-construction schedule that favors us." He paused. "I know you want an injunction. We're not there yet. We need the record."

Jordan clicked the remote again. The walls bloomed with deadlines. "I'll need full technical documentation, version history, and the original slide decks sent to Titan. Anything exchanged under NDA. If there were meetings recorded, I want the transcripts, the videos if they exist. If there were hallway chats, I want the notes too."

Ethan raised a hand. "We have logs of everything we sent. I'll pull the archive."

"Good," Jordan said. "Chain of custody matters, so we keep it clean." He shifted his gaze to Alex. "Your testimony will anchor this. Explain your choices as if you're teaching a class, not defending your soul."

Alex attempted a nod; the motion cost him. "I can do that," he said, voice thin but proud. "I want them to understand why we built it this way. Why it matters."

Jordan, softer: "You okay?"

Alex's smile was brittle. "Just tired. The good kind."

Maya's eyes caught his. She offered a small, steadying nod. Gratitude, reassurance, and apology all at once.

Jordan powered down the projector, the room falling into the hush of machine fans. "Last note. Titan will hit back. They'll argue non-infringement. That what looks the same is just a veneer. 'Parallel development but a different outcome.' The cure for that is specificity. When they say 'predictable,' we answer with choices no one else would make unless they were following your map."

He capped the marker, a final sound that felt like a seal.

"So what's the next step? What do we do tomorrow?" asked Maya.

Jordan looked at each of them in turn. "Tomorrow, we start assembling the arsenal. Every email, every draft, every napkin sketch. We'll build claim charts, prep for depositions, and get our expert ready. And we'll brace for Titan's counterattack. PR, legal, technical. This is going to be fast, and it's going to be brutal."

Alex managed a tired smile. "We've been here before. Just... never with this much at stake."

Jordan's tone softened, just a fraction. "You built something worth stealing. Now, we prove it's worth defending."

Ethan closed his notebook, resolve settling in. "Let's make sure they remember who built it first."

Jordan nodded. "Let's get to work."

The team sat for a moment, letting the silence settle. Maya reached out, briefly resting her hand on Alex's shoulder, then Ethan's. "We do this together," she said quietly.

They rose, gathering their things, and headed for the door, not just as colleagues, but as comrades, bracing for the front.

———

After a few days, the war room's adrenaline had faded into the slow, relentless work of proof. NovaTech's office had become part living archive, part assembly line: tables buried under boxes of old notebooks, binders, and printouts; the whiteboard crowded with timelines and sticky notes. The hum of the scanner was constant, punctuated by the rustle of paper and the low murmur of Alex and Ethan as they pieced together the story of how NovaTech's invention came to be.

Meanwhile, Maya was collecting old emails. "Think of everything you regret sending," Jordan had said grimly. "Then find it twice." She moved through the email archive like a tide, checking, copying. Every once in a while the door would creak and she'd look up expecting something to change. It never did. The fluorescent lights hummed. The coffee machine hissed. The patent certificate watched them all in unblinking silence.

On the morning of the third day Alex sat cross-legged on the floor, surrounded by a sprawl of lab notebooks and folders. Ethan hunched over a battered laptop, cataloging files as fast as Alex could hand them over.

"Here's the original design sketch for the transform layer," Alex said, passing over a dog-eared page. "And this—" he held up a faded printout, "was the first time we hit the bottleneck in the hospital pilot."

Ethan grinned. "You even annotated the crash log. Vintage Alex."

They worked in companionable silence until Alex, digging through a box labeled "Patent Prep," froze. He pulled out a thick binder; its spine marked in red: PRIOR ART.

His heart thudded. "Oh no."

Ethan looked up. "What?"

Alex's voice was tight. "I don't remember if I gave this to the patent attorney. If we didn't disclose this, and the examiner never saw it—"

Ethan set his laptop aside and took the binder. He flipped through the tabs, then opened the laptop. "Hang on. You sent this to the attorney. Look." He turned the screen so Alex could see the message, dated months before the patent application was filed. "And here—" Ethan pointed to the cover page of the issued patent, "the examiner listed these references as considered. You're clear."

Alex let out a shaky breath, relief and embarrassment mingling. "I know the rules, but for a second I thought I'd blown it."

Ethan shrugged. "Duty of candor, right? You did it by the book."

Alex nodded, the panic fading. "Yeah. We did."

Across the room, Maya and Jordan were assembling a different kind of evidence. Jordan had already pulled slides from Titan's launch presentation, but now they pored over a stack of new finds: glossy marketing brochures, a technical brief published by Titan engineers in a trade journal, and a screenshot of a product demo video.

Jordan tapped the technical brief. "They basically describe our transform layer. Same terminology, same diagrams. They even mention the 'breath policy' by name."

Maya's eyes lit up. Finally, something was going their way.

"It's gold," continued Jordan. "We'll map every feature in their public materials to our claims. The more they brag, the easier it is to show the overlap."

Alex, sensing Maya's excitement, walked over. "And the demo video —they walk through a failure scenario that matches our architecture, step for step. It's almost like they're reading from our playbook."

Jordan smiled, sketching out how the new evidence would fit into the complaint. "This is how you win a case: not just with the patent, but with the paper trail. Yours and theirs."

"I want to cover one more thing," Jordan said cautiously. "Jamie."

He turned to Maya. "This matters for willfulness. For damages. For the narrative."

Ethan stepped forward, his voice steady. "I ran deeper forensics on our logs. There's a recurring access pattern masked as a system check, hitting documentation buckets on a cadence tied to our exchanges with Titan. There's no question, the source was internal."

The room got very quiet. Jordan moved closer, scanning the binder Ethan had handed him. "You're sure?"

Ethan pointed. "The API key changes, but the MAC address range stays within our allocation."

Jordan looked at Maya. "Jamie's testimony would be awfully hard for Titan to explain away."

Maya's face hardened, the lines of it set by something older than fatigue. "He was trying to save his daughter. He thought he had no choice."

Jordan nodded slowly. "We don't play it as theft, rather, as infiltration."

Maya exhaled, a breath that trembled once and then steadied. "Do it," she said.

Jordan gathered the papers, fanning them like a magician about to make something appear. "Titan needs to learn we're not prey."

The team pressed on, the office filling with the quiet intensity of people building a record that would have to stand up in court.

———

The boxes were stacked by the door. Binders, claim charts, and evidence files, each one labeled in Jordan's precise hand. The war room felt emptier now, the chaos of assembly replaced by a tense, expectant quiet.

Jordan stood at the head of the table, a single envelope in front of him. The team gathered: Maya, Alex, Ethan, each looking more worn than they had a week ago, but steadier too.

Jordan glanced at the boxes, then at the faces around the table. "This is it. We've done the work. Every chart, every timeline, every scrap of proof, boxed, indexed, and ready. I'm about to send the demand letter to Titan's General Counsel. Once it's out, there's no going back."

He tapped the envelope. "Here's what happens next. Titan will respond. Probably by denying everything and threatening to bury us in motions if we file. Their lawyers will posture, their executives will bluster, and their PR team will start working overtime. Expect a smear campaign. They'll call us opportunists, say we're trying to cash in, maybe even question our integrity or our invention."

He looked at each of them in turn. "You need to be ready for that. Don't talk to the media. Don't respond to rumors. If anyone calls, refer them to me. We trust the process, and we trust each other."

Alex shifted in his seat. "What if they go after us personally?"

Jordan's voice was steady. "They might. That's what bullies do when they're scared. But we have the record. We have the truth. And we have each other. Remember what you've built, what you've achieved. No matter what they say, they can't take that away."

Maya nodded, her jaw set. "We're ready."

Jordan allowed himself a small smile. "You are. I've seen many teams fall apart before the fight even starts. You're still here. That matters."

He picked up the envelope, already marked for same-day delivery, weighing it in his hand. "Once this is sent, we brace for impact. But we don't blink. We don't break. We move forward together."

He looked around the table one last time. "Any questions before we start the clock?"

No one spoke. The only sound was the hum of the lights and the distant city outside.

Jordan nodded. "All right. Let's do this."

He left to send the letter, and the team sat in silence, the weight of what was coming settling over them.

———

By noon, the letter had been copied multiple times and was making its way through Titan's executive floor. The language was measured and merciless.

*Notice of Infringement.*
*Claims asserted.*
*Products identified.*
*Remedies sought.*
*Preservation demanded.*

Titan's General Counsel was saying, *We expected this,* while one of her deputies was asking the engineering team, *What did we write that they'll read aloud to a jury?*

In the boardroom, Richard Hale paced before the wall of windows. The rooftops in the distance looking like weeds between neat rows of city streets. His voice carried the savor of victory well used to seasoning.

"They'll cave," he said. "They have to. We'll play it by the book: independent development, common techniques, generalized claims. PR says small company doing a cash grab. Keep our engineers off social. Lock down docs behind legal hold."

Claire Donovan sat near the back, fingers laced tightly. She had replayed the last few months so often the scenes had lost color. Her inbox was a mausoleum of promises.

Richard stopped. "One more thing: I don't want to see a single email that looks like coordination. If you wrote it, assume a jury will read it. If you didn't write it, don't."

A murmur of compliance rose and fell. Claire kept her eyes down. She wondered when silence had started to feel like a crime.

———

A week had passed since Jordan sent the pre-suit letter. The rain which had been pelting against the window had stopped, but the city outside

Maya's window was still slick with reflections. She sat alone in her office, quiet for once, the printer silent. Her phone buzzed. A new email, subject line: *Confidential Proposal.*

She recognized the sender: a venture capitalist who'd backed NovaTech's Series A, now rumored to have ties to Titan. The message was brief, clinical.

Maya,

There's a path to resolution here. Titan is prepared to offer a strategic partnership—generous terms, full funding for your next project, and a personal board seat.

The only condition: NovaTech drops all claims, signs a comprehensive NDA, and agrees not to discuss the dispute publicly.

This could save your company, your team, and your future. Let me know if you're open to a conversation.

—P.

Maya stared at the screen. Her hands trembled. Not with anger, but with exhaustion. She imagined what "resolution" would mean: no more late nights, no more war rooms, no more risk. Alex could go back to building. Ethan could stop chasing ghosts in the code. She could sleep.

She opened a new draft reply: *Thank you for your message. I'm willing to discuss terms.*

Her thumb hovered over **Send**. She pictured the team. Alex, Ethan, the engineers who'd trusted her. She saw their faces if she told them she'd taken the deal. Relief, maybe. But also, disappointment. The patent on the wall, the late-night strategy sessions, the fight for something bigger than survival.

She deleted the draft. The cursor blinked, accusing and patient.

A few minutes later, her phone rang.

She hesitated, then answered. "Hey, Alan."

He didn't waste time. "I saw the email. I was bcc'd."

Maya closed her eyes. Of course it would go to Alan, he and Peter had been friends since before Maya had even started college.

Alan's voice was gentle. "You know, Maya, I'm not calling to tell you what to do. God knows you've carried this farther than anyone had a right to expect. But... you've seen what this fight has already cost. You, the team, your family. I remember when you first pitched NovaTech. How much you believed in building something that mattered. You've done that. Maybe it's enough."

She was silent, listening to the hum of the city outside.

Alan continued, "I'm not saying you should take the deal. But I want you to think about what comes next. If you walk away now, you walk away with your head high, with options. If you keep going, it's going to get ugly. Titan will drag this out, and you know it. You could spend years in court, and even if you win, what's left?"

Maya's voice was quiet but steady. "If I take the deal, what do I tell Alex? Ethan? That we fought until it got hard, then took the money and let them write the ending?"

Alan sighed. "You tell them you did what you had to do to survive. That you built something from nothing, and you protected your people. That's not failure, Maya. That's leadership."

She shook her head, even though he couldn't see. "It's not enough, not for me. Not this time."

There was a long pause. Alan's voice softened. "I'll back your play, whatever you decide. Just... don't forget you have a life outside this fight. Don't let it take everything."

Maya managed a small, tired smile. "Thanks, Alan. I won't."

After they hung up, Maya sat for a long time, staring at the city lights. She poured herself a cup of cold coffee, her resolve settling like sediment.

She whispered to the empty room, "If we win, we win clean; if we lose, we lose together."

The fight would go on.

———

The office was hushed in the grey dawn, the city outside still slick from last night's rain. Light seeped through the windows, painting pale rectangles across the cluttered desks and the whiteboard still crowded with deadlines. Maya stood by the window, arms folded, watching the city begin to stir.

Alex entered, rubbing his eyes, hair still damp from the walk in. He glanced at the patent certificate on the wall, then at Maya.

"Did you sleep?" he asked, voice soft.

Maya shook her head. "Not really. Too much to think about."

Alex nodded, joining her at the window. For a moment, neither spoke. The city was waking up, indifferent to what the day would bring.

He broke the silence. "Whatever happens, we got here. That counts for something."

Maya managed a tired smile. "It does."

Her phone buzzed on the counter. A message from Jordan:

*Filed. Clock's ticking.*

She typed back:

*Good.*

She let her gaze linger on the city, the sky brightening by degrees, then walked to the whiteboard and struck off *File Complaint*.

By the time the sun cleared the rooftops, the news was everywhere.


### TECH LEDGER | SOFIA MARTINEZ
**Complaint Filed: David Goes to Court**

The quiet part is no longer quiet. NovaTech has filed a federal patent infringement suit against Titan Corp, setting up the rarest kind of tech story: one that will be decided in the open, by people in a room rather than emails in the dark.

The complaint alleges that Titan, after a much-touted pilot, "launched a product that includes every element of NovaTech's patented invention." The filing asks for an injunction, damages, and, between the lines, something harder to quantify: credibility. Titan denies any wrongdoing.

Patent cases aren't about who had an idea; they're about claim coverage, prior art, and which side can explain the technical details most clearly to the jury.

"At its core, patent litigation is about enforcing property rights," says attorney Jordan Reyes. "Just like you want to keep trespassers off your land, a patent owner wants to keep others from using their innovations. The courtroom is where we decide if a competitor has crossed the boundary and, if so, what the appropriate penalty, or 'rent,' should be."

If this follows the usual path, expect months of discovery: source code reviews, depositions, and diagrams that look like subway maps for a city that doesn't sleep.

For startups, litigation is a terrible business model but sometimes the only one left. The trial court will hear witnesses; the market will hear a story. Both audiences will decide what feels true.

NovaTech's case had landed before Judge Eleanor Price, who scheduled a video call with the parties and their attorneys almost before the printer ink had dried on Titan's Answer.

Before her appointment to the federal bench, Judge Price had been the go-to trial lawyer for inventors and industry giants alike. A partner at a leading intellectual property boutique in Boston, she tried complex patent cases ranging from biotech to software to semiconductors. She was known not just for her trial wins, often secured after surgical cross-examinations, but for her deep respect for the innovation process. Whether representing a startup or an established industry veteran, her ability to translate technical jargon for juries and her insistence on clarity and efficiency in the courtroom won the respect of clients and adversaries alike. Judges often sought her out as a neutral mediator in high-stakes IP disputes, appreciating her sense of fairness and knack for cutting through posturing to get to the heart of the matter.

All this experience made her a natural choice when the judiciary sought candidates for the fast-track patent trial pilot. She had long argued that patent cases deserved trial judges who understood both the law and the science, and who could keep cases moving without sacrificing thoroughness or fairness. Her selection was seen as a signal that the federal judiciary had listened.

The call commenced precisely at 9:00. "Let's get to the point. This district is open for business. Patent business. I've seen what Judge Bentley did in Texas, what Judge Martin is doing in Delaware. We can do better." Judge Price's no-nonsense demeanor cut through the ether like a cold November wind.

Through the screen she made eye contact with Jordan. "You want a speedy trial? How's nine months?" She looked at both of the attorneys in turn. "But you'll get no endless motions, no fishing expeditions. We do this clean and fast. Discovery is streamlined, no Daubert circus, no Markman marathons. You each get your day in court, and the market gets clarity."

Outside the view of the camera, Jordan passed Maya a note.

*We'll have to move at light speed.*

Titan's counsel interjected. "Judge, that's way too fast. We can't possibly get things done on that timeline and I have another case that is going to be going through discovery at the same time. I'll need at least twice as long."

"Counsel, I appreciate your candor about your calendar, but this court's calendar and the interests of justice come first. Patent cases have a reputation for dragging on for years. That ends here. You'll have the time you need to do the job right, but not a day more."

Trying again, Titan's counsel said, "With respect, Your Honor, there are technical experts to retain, source code to review, and—"

"I know exactly what's involved. I've tried these cases myself." Judge Price continued. "You'll get focused discovery, and if you need a prompt ruling on a real dispute, you'll get it. But I won't allow delay for delay's sake. If you have a genuine scheduling conflict, propose specific dates for depositions now. Otherwise, you'll adjust."

She leaned forward, her tone sly. "Besides, this way your client can tell the world they are looking forward to proving their product is theirs alone and not NovaTech's. Won't that be good for business?"

"Let me be clear: this pilot program was created because too many patent cases die of old age. The parties here are entitled to a decision while it still matters. If you need more resources, bring in co-counsel. If you need to prioritize, do so. But this case will be tried in nine months, barring true emergency. Is that understood?"

"Yes, Your Honor."

"Good. I expect professionalism and preparation from both sides. If you encounter a real, unavoidable obstacle, raise it promptly and with specifics, but spare me the drama. I've tried these cases. I know the difference between a real issue and a manufactured one."

She spared a glance at her docket.

"Here's how this will work:

- We'll set a schedule for disclosures and expert reports.
- Claim construction will be limited to the terms that truly matter.
- If you need a hearing, you'll get one, but be concise.
- I will not tolerate delay tactics.
- If you have a discovery dispute, raise it promptly and with specificity.
- I expect technical presentations to be clear enough for a jury, but accurate enough for me."

She leaned forward again and allowed herself the faintest smile. "And if anyone tries to bury me in paper, I promise I'll read every page. But I'll remember who sent it."

She looked to both sides. "Any questions before we set the schedule?"

———

By the time the call was done discovery deadlines, expert disclosures, and the full suite of pre-trial briefings and other items had been set.

Jordan sat back in his chair. "I've never seen that before from a trial judge. She is going to be brutal on us if we can't meet these deadlines."

"We'll meet them," Maya said quietly. "we have to."

———

## TECH LEDGER | SOFIA MARTINEZ
**Patent Wars: Speed vs. Justice**

In a move that could reshape the landscape for patent litigation, the District of New Hampshire has launched a fast-track pilot program, promising a trial within nine months for qualifying cases. For NovaTech, whose dispute with Titan Corp has captured industry attention, the accelerated timeline offers both hope and anxiety.

"A fast-track trial means less time for motions, more time in front of the jury," says Jordan Reyes, NovaTech's attorney. "It's a chance for clarity, but it also means every mistake is magnified."

Critics argue that speed could come at the expense of thoroughness. Titan's counsel, in a statement, cautioned, "Complex cases deserve careful consideration. Rushed justice is justice denied."

The program's architect, Judge Eleanor Price, is known for her technical fluency and brisk courtroom style. Whether her approach will deliver justice or simply be faster remains to be seen.

For startups like NovaTech, the stakes are existential. The outcome will not only determine the fate of its patent but could set a precedent for how innovation is protected or challenged in the years to come.

Alex hunched over a stack of technical reports, his eyes red, hands stained with ink. Jordan had a deposition prep outline and expert reports arranged into neat piles beside him. For the past few hours he had peppered Alex with questions, forcing him to go over every aspect of the patent, demanding minutiae Alex could hardly remember and frowning sternly whenever he provided too much.

"Just answer what's asked. No more, no less," Jordan demanded. "If they want more, they'll ask. If they don't understand, too bad. Let them ask a different question or the same question a different way. You aren't there to teach. You're there just to answer questions."

Alex looked up, his eyes hollow. "I have been answering questions. I'm done with answering questions."

Maya paced by the window, phone pressed to her ear as she negotiated with an impatient investor. Ethan sat at the server terminal, eyes gritty, fingers flying over the keyboard.

Jordan slid a folder across the table. "Alex, let's run through the transform layer sequence again. Remember, Titan's counsel will push you on pre-processing. Don't concede their framing."

Alex nodded, his voice barely a whisper. "Right. The transform layer only works if the data is normalized before it hits the core. Titan's algorithm—" he stopped, rubbing his eyes. "Wait. Didn't their expert say they process data differently before the transform?"

Jordan shook his head, flipping to a highlighted section in the evidence binder. "No. That's their argument, but it's not true. Look— here's the document from Titan's own pilot study. Their pre-processing is performed just as described in NovaTech's patent; it's even referred to as a preferred embodiment. You can't let them walk you into agreeing with their narrative."

Alex's jaw clenched. "Sorry. I'm just tired. I keep second-guessing myself."

Maya, listening from the window, crossed the room and placed a hand on his shoulder. "You know this better than anyone. You built it. Just breathe."

Alex shook her off, frustration flaring. "That's easy for you to say. You're not the one who has to explain every line of code to a room full of people trying to prove you're a fraud."

Maya's voice softened, but her words only seemed to make it worse. "You're not a fraud, Alex. You're exactly the reason we're here."

Alex snapped, "Then why does it feel like I'm the one dragging us under?"

A heavy silence settled. Jordan broke it, his tone brisk but not unkind. "Let's take five. Maya, could you check on Ethan? I need a word with Alex."

She paced over to where Ethan was sitting. "We need the full log archive for Jordan," Maya said, voice tight. "He wants to cross-reference every pilot trace with Titan's requests."

Ethan nodded, already pulling up the server dashboard. "I'll lock down the archive. Just in case. Don't want any surprises if Titan tries something." He typed a string of commands, double-checking the security flags. The dashboard blinked: *Archive permissions updated.*

Five minutes later, Alex was trying to pull up a copy of an old test report on his laptop. He frowned at his screen. "Ethan, I'm getting a permissions error. I can't access the archive."

Ethan's heart skipped. He tried to pull up the archive himself. *Locked.* "Wait, that's not right." He scanned the config, realizing with a sinking feeling that he'd accidentally revoked access for the entire team.

"What's going on?" Maya asked.

Alex gestured at his laptop. "We're locked out of the archive. Ethan, did you change something?" he snarled.

Ethan's cheeks burned. "I—I was trying to tighten security. Must've set the wrong flag. Give me a minute. I'll fix it."

Maya's voice was calm. "Take it easy, Alex. We're working on it."

Ethan nodded, swallowing his embarrassment. "I'll sort it out."

The next few minutes were tense. Maya tried to help, but Ethan insisted on handling it. Jordan, ever the tactician, quietly reshuffled his outline, making notes in the margin: *Deposition. Alex: clarify transform layer, pre-processing, Titan's algorithm.*

Finally, Ethan found the error. A single misplaced permission flag buried in a tangle of security protocols. He reset the access, restoring the archive for the team.

"Found it," Ethan said, voice hoarse but triumphant. "Everything's back." He exhaled, tension draining from his shoulders. "Sorry about the screw-up. I'll double-check everything from now on."

Maya nodded, grateful for the excuse to step away. She walked over to Alex. "You okay?"

He didn't look up. "We're on the clock."

Maya settled onto an empty chair, her knees brushing a tangle of network cables. "Walk me through it."

Slowly, Alex started explaining the preprocessing. It took twenty minutes, but when he was done, he smiled. "I remember working this through. It reminded me of untangling fishing line when I was a kid."

"Think of the data like fishing line after a bad cast," he said. "If you've ever tried to reel in a tangled mess, you know what I mean: you can't just yank on it and hope for the best. If you do, the knots only get tighter, and you end up with a bird's nest you'll never fix."

He tapped the diagram in front of him, tracing the path from raw input to the transform layer. "Preprocessing is where we untangle everything. Every timestamp, every field, every weird little anomaly. If we don't get it straight here, the transform layer can't do its job. It's like trying to cast with a line full of knots. The fly never lands where you want, and sometimes the whole thing snaps."

He looked up at Maya, a tired smile softening his face. "But when you're patient, when you work through the tangles one loop at a time and get everything running in the right direction, suddenly the line runs smooth. That's when the data is ready. That's when the transform layer can actually breathe. That's when the system works."

Jordan smiled. "That's the story we need the jury to hear."

A beat passed. Maya stood, smiled at Alex. "You're the reason we still have a shot. Don't burn out before we get there."

He nodded. "I'll sleep when this is over."

Maya left him to Jordan as the two started going over it again. In the hallway, she paused, leaned against the wall and breathed. Four months to go. Could they really get through this without breaking?

Back in the conference room she said to no one in particular. "We're almost there. We're going to win this together."

———

Claire Donovan stood in a restroom lit too brightly, the clang of a too-clean mirror staring back. She ran water, watched it slip down stainless steel. Her phone lay face down on the counter, vibrating once, then again.

She turned it over. The subject line had found her: *Notice of Deposition – NovaTech v. Titan.*

Her throat tightened. She thought about the first meeting, the handshake that had felt like an oath. She thought about Richard's polished assurances, the emails that were half suggestion, half directive. She thought about a folder of attachments that did not belong to her.

When she turned off the tap, she decided nothing. But the part of her that remembered why she had once loved building things from scratch, the part that had gone quiet, leaned toward the door marked *Exit* and listened for the sound of her own footsteps.

# EIGHT

Sofia's voice came on, clear and practiced.

"Welcome back to *The Ledger Podcast*. I'm Sofia Martinez. Today, we're tackling a case that's become a flashpoint for startups, tech giants, and anyone who cares about innovation: NovaTech versus Titan Corp. A battle about to play out in federal court and one that could change the rules for Silicon Valley.

"With me are two people at the heart of this confrontation. Maya Singh, CEO and co-founder of NovaTech, and Jordan Reyes, NovaTech's lead attorney.

"Thank you both for joining us."

"Thanks for having us, Sofia," Maya replied.

"Glad to be here," said Jordan.

Sofia continued. "Let's start with the basics. Maya, for listeners who haven't been following every headline, what is this case really about?"

Maya took a breath, her voice trembling just enough to betray the strain beneath her steady words.

"It's... everything. We built something from nothing. We believed that if we played by the rules, if we worked hard, we'd have a shot. Now, I wake up every morning wondering if that was naïve.

"It's about what happens when a small company tries to be transformative. We partnered with Titan, hoping for collaboration. Instead, while they shook our hand, they took what we built with the other. It's hard not to take it personally."

She paused, her voice tightening. "It's about whether companies like ours have a place at the table, or if the rules only protect the giants."

Sofia turned to Jordan. "For listeners who aren't patent lawyers, what's one thing you wish the public understood about patent law and what does it mean to 'violate a patent'? What will the jury actually have to decide?"

Jordan's passion for the subject came through in his voice.

"That patents aren't about stifling innovation. They're about rewarding it. Yes, patents come with an exclusive right to make, use, or sell an invention. But there's a trade-off. The inventor has to tell the world how they did it. In fact, they have to reveal so much detail that others, once the patent expires, can reproduce the invention for themselves.

"That's the bargain: the inventor gets a monopoly, but only for a limited time, and the rest of the community gets the benefit of having the inventor teach them something new.

"But the system only works if everyone plays by the same rules. If a competitor makes a product that is covered by someone's patent, no matter how they got there, that's infringement.

"The jury will have to compare NovaTech's patent claims, that's the part of the patent that identifies precisely what's protected, to Titan's product and decide if that product 'lives inside the fence,' so to speak."

"And what about 'willful infringement'"? Sofia asked. "That's been in the headlines."

"Willful infringement means the defendant knew about the patent and chose to infringe anyway. If the jury finds willfulness, the court can enhance the damages. In some cases up to three times the amount the jury awards. In our case, we'll show that Titan had our patent, had our confidential materials, and went ahead regardless."

"Maya, you've said this isn't just about money." Sofia tone softened. "What does a win actually look like?"

"A win means more than damages. It means forcing Titan to stop selling their infringing product. But it's also about sending a message:

that the rules apply, even to the biggest players. If we lose, it tells every startup that patents are just paper."

Sofia looked at Jordan. "Jordan, you've called this 'a test case for the American patent system.' Why?"

"Because this case is now part of a pilot program," Jordan explained. "We're on a fast-track: nine months from complaint to verdict. That's almost unheard of in patent litigation. It's designed to give clarity while it still matters. Before the market moves on or the technology is obsolete. But it also means there's no room for mistakes."

"Some critics say this is all too rushed. Are you worried about getting a fair shake?"

"We want a fair trial, not a forever trial," Maya said, her voice firm. "Innovation can't wait years for clarity. We're ready to prove our case, quickly and openly."

"Maya, what's it like to have your company and your name at the center of this storm?"

Maya's voice was quieter now, and she paused, considering.

"It's lonely. Some days, I feel like I'm fighting for every founder who's ever been told to 'just move on.' Other days, I feel like I'm letting everyone down. My team, my family, myself.

"It's also terrifying. We've had support, but also criticism. People saying we're just looking for a payout, or that we should have known better than to trust Titan. I didn't want to be a public figure. I wanted to build something that mattered."

Sofia let the silence breathe.

"What do you want listeners to understand about what's coming?"

Maya took that one. "That this isn't just about us. It's about whether the rules mean anything. Whether you can build something honest and have a chance to defend it. And that sometimes, the fight is the only way to prove you belong."

"Jordan, final word. What should people watch for as the trial begins?"

"Watch for the story behind the evidence," Jordan replied. "The emails, the timelines, the choices. Trials aren't just about documents. They're about people, and the truth that comes out when you put everything on the line."

"Thank you both." Sofia wrapped up. "We'll be following every step. For our listeners, you can find more coverage at Tech Ledger and subscribe for updates as this case unfolds. I'm Sofia Martinez, and this has been *The Ledger Podcast*."

———

The morning grey cast a pale light through the window of Claire's apartment. She sat at her kitchen table, a half-drunk mug of coffee cooling beside her. Her laptop was open and the apartment was quiet except for the faint, tinny sound of Sofia's podcast playing through the speakers.

Maya's voice came through, steady but raw:

*This isn't just about us. It's about whether the rules mean anything. Whether you can build something honest and have a chance to defend it. And that sometimes, the fight is the only way to prove you belong—even if it costs you more than you ever imagined.*

Claire closed her eyes. She pressed her palm to her chest, feeling her heartbeat. Fast, anxious. She rewound the last few seconds, letting Maya's words echo through the kitchen, filling the quiet with something sharp and electric.

Her gaze drifted to her Titan badge on the counter, the company logo suddenly looking colder than ever.

The podcast continued, Jordan's voice now:

*Patents aren't about stifling innovation. They're about rewarding it. The law says: teach the world how you did it, and you get a limited monopoly. But that only works if the system enforces the rules, even when it's inconvenient for the powerful.*

Claire's jaw tightened. She remembered the meetings, the emails, the way Richard's voice would drop when he talked about "strategy." She remembered the first time she met Maya. How hopeful she'd sounded, how much she'd wanted to believe in partnership.

She stood, paced the kitchen, then stopped in front of her laptop. Her reflection stared back at her in the dark screen. Tired, uncertain, but something in her eyes had changed.

———

A few hours later, the rain had stopped but the city's tension had only thickened. Claire's apartment was empty now, her coffee cold, the echo of Maya's voice still lingering in her chest. She'd changed into a smart, dark jacket over a graphic tee and jeans. Silicon Valley executive casual, but sharp. Her Titan badge hung from a lanyard, swinging as she walked briskly through the glass doors and into the heart of the company's headquarters.

By mid-morning, Titan's crisis room buzzed like a hornet's nest. Screens flashed headlines, tweets, op-eds. The podcast was already trending, and the words "David vs. Goliath" scrolled across a dozen news tickers. The air was sharp with the scent of burnt coffee and the low hum of too many devices.

Richard Hale stood at the center, jaw clenched, voice clipped.

"Spin it. Frame it as a shake-down. Say we're being targeted for our success, for building on what's already out there. Push the narrative: Those who can, do. Those who can't, litigate."

A PR exec nodded, fingers flying over a keyboard. "We'll seed thought pieces. Get influencers on board."

Richard's smile was thin, brittle. "And make sure every quote says, 'competition drives progress.' If they want a morality play, we'll give them economics."

At the far end of the table, Titan's General Counsel Marjorie Thorne adjusted her glasses and cleared her throat. The room quieted.

"Let's be clear," Marjorie said, her tone clipped and surgical. "No one speaks to the press without clearance from Legal. No off-the-cuff comments, no leaks, no 'anonymous sources.' I want a memo to every manager: all internal communications about NovaTech are privileged and must be preserved. If anyone asks, we're evaluating all our options and have no comment on pending litigation."

She let her gaze settle on Claire just a beat too long. "And for those who have already given depositions, remember, your testimony is on record. If there are inconsistencies, or if you've omitted anything material, now is the time to come forward. There will be no tolerance for surprises."

Claire felt heat rising in her cheeks. She remembered the questions she'd skirted, the emails she hadn't mentioned, the truths she'd left in the shadows. Her badge felt heavier than ever before.

Richard nodded, but his eyes were already scanning the headlines. "We own this story," he said. "We don't let them set the terms."

Claire sat near the back, silent. Her phone vibrated. Another new episode of *The Ledger Podcast*, the last one still open in her app. She stared at it, pulse ticking like a metronome. She thought about the emails buried in her inbox, those that could reduce Titan's defense to dust. She thought about the oath she'd taken in her deposition, and the truth she'd left unsaid.

She remembered the first time she'd met Maya, the hope in her voice, the handshake that had felt like a promise. Now, every word in this room felt like a warning.

When Richard repeated, "We own this story," something cracked inside her. For the first time in years, silence didn't feel safe. It felt like complicity.

Claire looked down at her phone, Maya's words from the podcast echoing in her mind: *Sometimes, the fight is the only way to prove you belong. Even if it costs you more than you ever imagined.*

———

Across town, NovaTech's office was a hive of noise. Reporters called. Emails stacked like bricks. Social feeds pulsed with hashtags: *#Patent-War, #TitanVsNova, #InnovationJustice.*

Ethan leaned against the doorway, scrolling through comments. "Half the internet thinks we're heroes," he said. "The other half thinks we're grifters."

Maya didn't look up from her laptop. "Let them think. The jury's the only audience that matters."

Alex sat at the far end of the room, pale under the fluorescent lights, his hands trembling over a keyboard. He typed slowly, deliberately, as if each word were a weight he had to lift. The glow from his screen made the shadows under his eyes look deeper.

Jordan strode in, phone pressed to his ear, voice clipped. "No more interviews," he said to Maya without breaking stride. "Not yet. From here out we control the narrative in court, not on cable news."

Maya nodded, though her inbox told a different story. Requests from every major outlet, offers for exclusives, promises of sympathetic coverage. She closed the laptop and rubbed her temples. The fight had spilled beyond the courtroom. Now it was a spectacle.

A Teams notification pinged. Ethan glanced at the screen. "Someone just made a meme of you, Maya. You're wearing a cape."

Alex managed a weak smile. "At least they didn't Photoshop me into a villain. Yet."

Maya forced a laugh, but it sounded thin. "Give it time."

Jordan hung up, dropping into a chair. "We're not here to win Twitter, we're here to win the record. Eyes on the trial."

Ethan tossed his phone onto his desk. "Easy for you to say. You don't have a cousin texting you every five minutes asking if you're about to be rich or fired."

Maya looked around at her team. She saw exhaustion etched into their faces, tension in every shoulder. "We keep building. We keep breathing. Let the noise be noise."

As Maya was about to close her laptop, an email notification popped up from one of her newsfeeds: *USPTO leadership rumors persist. Analysts warn of increased post-grant challenges if new Director is appointed. Monitor for impact on patent strategy.* She closed her laptop, exhaled, and looked up at the patent. For a moment, it seemed less like a shield and more like a challenge.

———

The old Titan annex was a relic from another era. An address most employees had forgotten, a building slated for "IT asset reclamation" but inside two or three servers were still quietly humming on the network. Claire parked in the nearly empty lot, her car one of only three. The rain had started again, its tap a nervous rhythm against the windshield.

She swiped her badge at the side entrance. The lock clicked open. No one had bothered to revoke access for a building that was supposed to be "offline" but still ran backups for legacy systems. Down the corridor there was no one at the front desk; the security guard was probably on break, or maybe just bored.

She moved quickly to the server room, past empty cubicles and faded posters about innovation and teamwork. The air smelled faintly of dust and ozone. Inside, she found a terminal, flicked on a task light, and noticed the layer of dust. She slipped on a pair of latex gloves. Habit, not necessity, but it steadied her hands.

She plugged her laptop into an open Ethernet port, bypassing the Wi-Fi entirely. The old rack switches still routed internal traffic, and the annex's subnet had never been fully segmented from the main Titan network. She checked the MAC address spoof on her adapter. Set to mimic a decommissioned asset from last year's inventory.

Claire ran her script, injecting a scheduled "legacy backup" job into the server's cron table, masking her admin ping as a routine rsync operation. She disabled auto-forward logs for a fifteen-minute window and set the syslog daemon to drop all non-critical alerts to /dev/null. If anyone checked, it would look like routine maintenance. Unless they looked closer.

The network was slow but still connected to Titan's internal archive. Her heart hammered as she navigated to the executive email archive. She authenticated with her own credentials, then escalated privileges using an expired service account credential she'd discovered during a compliance audit months ago. She knew exactly what she was looking for: the threads Richard had marked "strategy," the ones that could tip the scales for NovaTech. As she typed, Claire could almost hear Richard's voice, *Winners write the story, Claire.*

A security alert flashed on the screen. *Unusual admin access detected: legacy node 3B.* Just a warning, not a lockout. Claire's breath caught. She deleted the alert from the local log, wiped her script, logged out, and unplugged her laptop, her heart pounding. She'd left a shadow, but she was betting on Titan's backlog.

She transferred the files to an encrypted drive, then wiped the terminal's recent history and cleared the ARP cache. Every whir of a fan and distant clang of a door made her flinch.

As she left, she paused in the doorway, listening for footsteps.

Nothing but the steady hum of old servers, the ghosts of a company that had forgotten its own corners.

Outside, the rain had picked up. Claire hurried to her car, the stolen emails burning a hole in her bag. She glanced once over her shoulder at the darkened windows, then drove away, her hands shaking on the wheel.

Tonight, she would send the truth.

———

By the time she reached her apartment, Claire's hands had stopped shaking, but the weight in her chest remained. She set her bag on the kitchen table, powered up her laptop, and opened a new, encrypted email burner account.

For a moment, she hesitated. Her finger hovering over the trackpad, the city lights blurring beyond the rain-streaked window.

She attached the files, typing a single line in the subject: *You want the truth? Start here.*

She addressed it to Sofia, double-checked the encryption, and hit **Send**.

As the message vanished into the ether, Claire let out a shaky breath. She deleted the burner account, the blinking cursor amplifying her anxiety, and closed the laptop. For the first time in months, the silence in her apartment felt different. Not just the hush of fear, but the possibility of something honest breaking through.

Her calm didn't last long.

Her phone buzzed. A new calendar invite, appearing without warning.

**Subject:** Compliance Review
**Organizer:** [blank]
**Time:** Tomorrow, 9:00 a.m.
**Location:** HR Conference Room

Claire frowned. She hadn't heard about any review. No one else on her team was invited. She checked the details. No notes, no context, just her name and the time.

A minute later, another notification popped up.

IT Security Alert:
Your recent account activity has been flagged for review. Please ensure all correspondence complies with company policy.

Her breath caught. Was it routine? Or had someone noticed something? She considered deleting the invite, but instead marked it *Accepted*. If they were watching, she'd face them head-on.

She glanced at the laptop. The risk was no longer theoretical. Titan's systems were watching, and the walls felt closer than ever.

But Claire's resolve hardened. She whispered to herself, "If they want to talk, I'll give them the truth."

She shut off the lights, the rain tapping a nervous rhythm on the glass, and prepared for whatever came next.

———

The NovaTech office was quiet for a change, the storm of headlines replaced by the steady rhythm of work.

Jordan placed a fresh binder on the table. "We add a Jamie protocol," he said, voice matter-of-fact. "Everything touched during the window gets rehashed and recertified. The defense will call compromise; we'll answer with provenance."

Maya's knuckles blanched as she flipped through a stack of documents. "We buy time with blood," she muttered, half to herself.

Alex was at the far end of the table, cross-referencing filenames and timestamps, his pen tapping a nervous rhythm. Ethan sat beside the scanner, feeding in another stack of exhibits, his eyes red from lack of sleep.

A printer jammed, spitting out a page with a single word—NOPE —in bold, accidental type. Ethan grinned, tore it off, and taped it to the wall. "Mascot for the week," he said.

For a moment, the team paused. Outside, the rain had finally stopped, and a thin band of sunlight crept across the cluttered floor.

Jordan looked up from his checklist. "We're almost through the Jamie window. After that, it's just the usual hell."

Maya managed a tired smile. "Just the usual hell. I'll take it."

For a brief moment, the war room felt almost normal. Just a team, doing the work, holding the line.

———

Tech Ledger's newsroom was a low-lit hive of screens and printer fumes. Sofia Martinez sat at her desk, headphones on, the leaked Titan emails open in a secure window. She cross-referenced each with public filings, NovaTech's complaint, and her own notes from months of reporting. Her phone buzzed, a Signal message from her source, brief and unsigned.

Sofia's editor leaned over the cubicle wall, voice low.

"Titan's lawyers are already circling. If you're wrong, we're exposed. If you're right, we're still exposed."

Sofia didn't look up. "I have three independent confirmations. I'll redact all personal identifiers and run the story past legal before it goes live."

She encrypted her notes, deleted her chat logs, and prepared a source protection affidavit. She also set up a secure tip line for future whistle-blowers, her fingers steady even as her heart pounded. Sofia knew Titan's legal team would come after her, but she was determined to leave no cracks in her own firewall.

———

The air in Titan's war room was sharp with burnt coffee and the blue glow of too many screens. Marjorie Thorne, Titan's General Counsel, stood at the head of the table, flanked by PR and compliance officers. Her deputies arrayed along both sides of the table.

The deputy overseeing discovery was handing out copies a memo:

**UPDATE: LEGAL HOLD – NOVATECH MATTER**
Copies of all emails, chats, and documents referencing Nova-Tech have been provided to Legal. We are reviewing for sensitive information.

At the far end of the table Claire sat silently. Her phone buzzed with a reminder: *Compliance Review—9:00 a.m.*

She glanced at Marjorie. "I have to go. I have a meeting."

Marjorie looked at Claire and scowled. "Something more important than this?"

Claire's pulse ticked faster. She knew the firewall was up, but she also knew where it was thin. "Something got scheduled late last night. I have to go." Claire stood, somehow kept her knees from buckling, and walked purposefully out of the room. On the other side of the door she steadied herself against the wall and let go the breath she had been holding in.

———

Back at Tech Ledger, Sofia's editor returned, holding a letter with a law firm's logo.

"Titan's threatening to sue if we publish anything defamatory or based on confidential information."

Sofia nodded, unflinching. "I'll attribute only to 'sources familiar with the matter.' No direct quotes from internal headers. Legal gets final review."

She backed up her files to an encrypted drive, then drafted a Slack message to her editor outlining her verification steps and source protection protocols.

"If Titan sues, we have a paper trail. I'll testify if needed."

The newsroom was quiet except for the tap of Sofia's pen and the low hum of anxiety. She was ready for the gauntlet.

———

The HR conference room seemed more like an interrogation chamber, cold and cramped. Claire sat in a chair that seemed designed for intimidation.

"We noticed a spike in admin access last night," the HR officer said, voice tight and clipped. "Anything to report?"

Claire kept her voice steady. "I was prepping for the integration audit. Needed to cross-check legacy threads."

"Isn't that something that should have been done during working hours?"

Claire looked back, her voice suddenly stern. "You try getting your day job done during working hours when Legal is demanding all your files for the last ten months. I barely have time to check in with my team before they want something else. Be glad I'm not going out on stress leave and instead trying to do two jobs at once."

"Okay, okay. Just have to check these things out, you know. We have procedures too," the HR officer said, trying to placate her. "Let us know if you come across anything unusual."

Claire stood and strode out of the room, adopting an air of impatient arrogance.

In the hallway, her phone vibrated. A Signal message from Sofia:

*Got the docs. Are you safe?*

Claire watched the message disappear. Sofia must have used the minimum timer setting to ensure no trace was left. She put the phone back in her pocket, smoothed the front of her blazer, and, as she retreated to the safety of her office, hoped no one noticed her walk was more of a run.

———

By the following morning, Sofia's article detonated across the tech world:

**TECH LEDGER | SOFIA MARTINEZ**
**Exclusive: Internal Titan Emails Reveal Deliberate Infringement Strategy.**

Screenshots glared like evidence in a courtroom:

*Why pay for what we can build?*

*Keep them talking.*

*Mirror their flow. The trick is to look inevitable.*

The article spread like wildfire... first on Slack channels, then everywhere. Within minutes, *#TitanLeak* and *#PatentWar* were trending. The screenshots were already being memed, dissected, and retweeted by the time most of Silicon Valley had finished their first cup of coffee. VCs texted each other, rival founders posted cryptic emojis, and even the anonymous Twitter accounts that usually mocked patent litigation were suddenly paying attention.

At NovaTech, the effect was electric. Phones lit up with calls and texts—investors, journalists, old friends who'd gone silent during the worst of it. The company's main Slack channel exploded with emojis and exclamation points.

*"We're vindicated!"*

*"Did you see the part about 'cut bait'?"*

*"Holy shit. This is real."*

Ethan spun in his chair, grinning at Alex, who looked like he might cry or laugh or both. Somewhere in the kitchen, someone started playing *We Are the Champions* on their phone. For a moment, the office was a hive of noise and wild, nervous energy.

Maya stood by the window, watching the city blur through rain. The weight that had pressed down for months was suddenly lighter, replaced by something unfamiliar. Hope.

Her phone buzzed—a message from Jordan: *Game changer. Things just got easier.*

She typed back: *Good.*

Then she set the phone down and closed her eyes. The adrenaline was already fading, replaced by something heavier. Victory felt closer now. But so did the cost.

———

Across the city at Titan, the mood was the opposite. The war room was silent except for the relentless buzz of incoming alerts. Marjorie Thorne read the article twice, then again, her jaw set. Richard Hale stood at the window, staring at the headlines scrolling across the news ticker. PR scrambled to draft a statement, but the damage was done. The story was out, and this time, they didn't control the narrative.

"What the proverbial fuck were you thinking?" Marjorie enunciated, every syllable making others feel like they were back in the school principal's office.

Richard glared at her. "Don't give me that. We both know you signed off on things long before we launched. Don't think for a second you won't go down with me if this goes to hell."

"What do your people plan on doing about this?"

Marjorie peered over her glasses. "My people, as you call them, are doing what they can. It's a bit difficult to spin your telling Claire to 'Keep them talking' while at the same time telling Lasker and his team to hurry up and get something built."

"Just handle this," Richard growled. "I don't want to know how, just get it done." He stormed out of the room. For the first time since the initial meeting with Maya, Richard felt a cold sweat beginning to form.

———

Claire, alone in her office, watched the story break on her phone. Relief and terror warred in her chest. She knew what would come next: investigations, interrogations, maybe worse. But for the first time in months, something like courage flickered inside her. Her hands shook as she set the phone down, but she didn't look away from the screen.

———

With the sound of Richard's footsteps still echoing in the hallway, Marjorie picked up her phone and dialed her lead outside counsel. "We're going to have to open a second front in case the trial doesn't go well." Marjorie started.

"IPRs?" The voice on the other end of the phone asked.

"Yes. How soon can you get them filed?" asked Marjorie.

"We've been planning on it. The petitions are sitting on my desk, ready to go. They're good."

Marjorie's voice was cold. "They'd better be. File them today."

———

Back at NovaTech, the celebration was already giving way to planning. Ethan was fielding calls from engineers at rival startups, some congratulatory, some fishing for details. Alex, pale but grinning, started a new thread: *What's the weirdest Titan excuse you've seen so far?*

Maya opened her laptop and scanned the article again, this time as a CEO, not just a survivor. Every word felt like a weapon, every screenshot a shield. Somewhere inside Titan she had an ally. But she also saw the shadow behind the headlines, the trial was still ahead.

Outside, sunlight broke through the clouds. The city pulsed with a new reality, and so did NovaTech. The storm, finally, had broken.

———

Much later that night, Ethan hunched over his laptop, hoodie pulled tight, fingers flying. "I'm telling you, the timestamp on this build is off. If Titan claims they developed this in-house, they're lying. I can feel it."

Alex, slumped in a chair, rubbed his eyes with ink-stained fingers. "We don't have time for another wild goose chase, Ethan. We need to finish before Jordan gets here."

Maya turned, her voice rough from too many late-night calls. "We check everything. No shortcuts. This is our only shot."

The door opened with a groan. Jordan entered, rolling a suitcase behind him, his suit jacket dusted with rain. He surveyed the chaos, and with a smile that didn't reach his eyes handed Maya a checklist. "Final discovery deadlines. I want every email, every draft, every napkin sketch. If you ever wrote it down, I want it."

Maya took the list, her hands trembling. "We're on it."

Jordan's eyes softened for a moment. "You look exhausted."

She managed a brittle smile. "We are."

Alex's phone buzzed. A text from his partner: *Are you coming home tonight?* He silenced it, guilt gnawing at his chest.

Ethan stood, stretching, his back popping. "I'll grab more coffee. Anyone want anything from the vending machine?"

"Just bring the whole machine," Alex muttered.

"Wait, that's not all," said Jordan. Reaching into a bag that weighed more than it looked he handed Maya a stack of papers. On top of the pile was one that read:

*Titan Corp. v. NovaTech, Inc.*

*IPR 2026-00364, U.S. Patent No. ...*

*Petition for Inter Partes Review (Grounds 1–6).*

Beneath it, three more stacks, siblings with different middle names.

Jordan ran a finger down the caption and exhaled through his nose. "Titan just filed four Inter Partes Review petitions against our patent. Every claim, every angle. They hired at least two experts, divided by discipline but united by hindsight."

Maya pulled up a chair and sat. The title pages lay white and indifferent, footers gray with authority. She flipped through until words found shape.

*Motivation to combine...*

*reasonable expectation of success...*

*person of ordinary skill in the art...*

Ethan looked up from his laptop, brow furrowed. "What's an IPR?"

"An IPR is an administrative challenge filed at the Patent Office before the Patent Trial and Appeal Board," Jordan explained, his voice quieter than usual. "Titan's hired experts to argue our patent was obvious and never should have been granted. If the Board agrees, they can invalidate it no matter what a jury decides."

Alex slumped in his chair tea forgotten. Ethan stammered, "But... the court... the trial?"

"They're collaging our work out of strangers," Maya murmured, more to herself than the room. "They've made a map from pieces of other towns and swear it shows our street."

Alex murmured, "They'll pretend the choreography was just Lego bricks."

Jordan nodded once, rubbing his eyes. "At the Board, mosaics become maps. We must show why these pieces don't fit and why, even if they did, no one would have believed they could dance together back then."

Ethan lifted a petition like a brick. "So we're fighting in two courts at once?"

"Not quite, not yet," Jordan replied. "These petitions are just requests. The Board still has to review them and decide if there's any merit to what Titan is saying. If not, they'll deny the petitions outright."

"Any if they think there's merit?" asked Ethan.

"Then we have another kind of trial; one without a jury, just administrative patent judges and paper," Jordan said flatly.

Alex had barely looked up from the mass of paper. "They keep saying 'it would have been obvious to try.' They're describing courage as common sense."

"Obviousness by clairvoyance," Maya said, and turned another page.

The printer finally spat out a stack of documents. Maya gathered them, the paper warm and rough in her hands. She looked at her team, red-eyed but unbroken.

"Back to work," she said, voice steady now. "We're not done yet."

# NINE

THE COMFORT INN wasn't much, but it was all NovaTech could afford. The carpet in the hallway was worn thin, patterned with faded blue diamonds that had seen too many winters. The air in the lobby smelled faintly of industrial coffee and burnt waffles. A plastic fern drooped in the corner, and the "business center" consisted of a single aging desktop wedged between a soda machine and a rack of brochures for maple syrup farms and Revolutionary War sites.

Maya checked in two days before the trial, her suitcase bumping over the tile. The desk clerk barely looked up as he handed over a keycard and a Wi-Fi code scribbled on a slip of paper. "Breakfast is six to nine. Coffee's always on," he said, as if reciting a memorized spell.

She found her room: second floor, view of the parking lot and a distant strip mall. She set her bag down, took a breath, and looked at herself in the mirror. She looked tired, older than she remembered. But she was here. They all were.

Alex and Ethan arrived an hour later, Alex with a battered duffel and Ethan with a backpack and a box of cables. They met in the lobby, exchanged a hug that was more relief than celebration, and immediately started arguing about Wi-Fi speeds before they'd even found their rooms.

By nightfall, the team had claimed a corner of the breakfast area as their war room. Whiteboards leaned against the wall, witness outlines and claim charts spread across the little tables, and a tangle of charging cables snaked between power outlets and laptops. The Inn's "business center" printer jammed on the second page, and Ethan spent twenty minutes coaxing it back to life with a butter knife borrowed from the front desk.

"It's not the Ritz," Ethan muttered, eyeing the vending machine, "but at least the ice is free."

Alex grinned, plugging in his laptop. "I think the Wi-Fi's running on dial-up. I just heard it wheeze."

Maya smiled, exhaustion and adrenaline warring in her chest. "We're not here for the amenities."

At the far end of the breakfast area, Jordan was already set up at a table, a stack of folders and a laptop open in front of him. He looked up as the team approached, offering a tired but genuine smile. "Welcome to headquarters," he said. "I've been here a couple of days meeting with local counsel, trying to make sure we don't get blindsided by some New Hampshire quirk of procedure."

He gestured to the empty chairs. "Sit. I've got updates, and we need to go over the witness list again. Local counsel says Judge Price is a stickler for punctuality and hates surprises."

Ethan dropped his bag and flopped into a chair. "Any good news?"

Jordan shrugged. "The coffee's free, and the judge is fair. That's about all I can promise."

They worked late, fueled by takeout pizza and the Comfort Inn's endless supply of watery coffee. Maya reviewed witness outlines at 2 a.m. in the lobby, the hum of the ice machine her only company. Alex went over his deposition testimony for the third time, muttering lines under his breath. Ethan prowled the hallways, checking for quiet corners to take calls.

In the mornings, they gathered in the breakfast room, surrounded by families in sweatshirts and sales reps in wrinkled suits. The team huddled over laptops and cold bagels, trading nervous jokes and last-minute reminders.

On the second night, Maya stood outside the hotel, the New Hampshire rain tapping against the awning. She looked towards the neat houses across the street and wondered what it would feel like to belong somewhere so settled, so certain. Where the lights in the windows meant family dinners and quiet routines, not late-night strategy sessions and the weight of a company's future pressing down on her shoulders.

They were outsiders in this small New England town, a team of underdogs camped out in a budget hotel, holding the line together.

———

The morning was gray and close, the rain still falling in a steady, determined drizzle. Maya checked her watch for the third time in as many minutes, then glanced at the lobby clock, as if hoping the battered timepiece might offer a better answer.

Alex and Ethan emerged from the elevator, both in suits that looked slightly out of place against the faded carpet and vending machines. Ethan carried a messenger bag stuffed with cables and witness outlines; Alex clutched a battered laptop case like a shield.

Jordan was already waiting by the door, umbrella in hand, a stack of folders tucked under his arm. "Uber's two minutes out," he said. "Local counsel says parking is a nightmare, and I'd rather not have us show up looking like drowned rats."

Ethan, shifting his messenger bag, leaned in. "Still can't believe we're doing this in New Hampshire."

Jordan smiled, a little wry. "Titan's founders were Dartmouth guys. Incorporated here back in the eighties, and one of them still sits on the board. Every new general counsel tries to move them to Delaware, but the old guard won't budge. So, for better or worse, this is Titan's legal home. And now ours."

They piled into the back of a silver Toyota Camry; the driver's seat was covered in plastic and the air thickened with the scent of pine air freshener. The ride was quiet at first. Each of them lost in their own thoughts as the neat houses and rain-slicked sidewalks slid by.

Maya watched as the Warren B. Rudman United States Courthouse came into view. A hulking mass of glass and stone that looked as if it had been dropped onto the quiet street a few blocks from the Merrimack river by mistake. Its sharp lines and sheer scale dwarfed the neighboring houses and storefronts, making the whole block feel off-kilter.

As she stepped out of the car, she caught sight of the green awning of the Asian Kitchen restaurant directly across the street, its cheerful yellow script promising dine-in and take out. The contrast was almost comic: the courthouse, all severity and authority, facing down a strip-mall eatery with faded menus taped to the window.

A line of black SUVs idled at the curb, drivers in suits leaning against the hoods, umbrellas at the ready. Ethan nudged Alex, nodding toward the convoy. "Is the President in town?"

Jordan shook his head, a wry smile on his lips. "No, just Titan and its legal team."

Alex let out a low whistle. "Guess we know who's billing by the hour."

Maya adjusted her jacket, feeling the weight of the moment settle on her shoulders. "Let them have their motorcade. We've got what matters."

They huddled under umbrellas and hurried up the courthouse steps, the rain tapping a nervous rhythm on the stone. Inside, the ceiling soared, the air was hushed and cool, and the marble floors echoed with the sound of their shoes. What drew Maya's eye, and stopped the team in their tracks, was the statue.

Justice, rendered in gleaming stainless steel, perched on a granite pedestal and standing nearly ten feet tall at the center of the atrium. Unlike the familiar, passive figure with scales and sword, this Justice was caught in a moment of action: arms raised above her head, tightening the knot in her own blindfold. The steel folds of her robe caught the light, throwing fractured reflections across the marble floor.

For a moment, none of them spoke. Ethan broke the silence first. "That's... not what I expected."

Jordan set his briefcase down, looking up at the statue. "Diana Moore. She wanted to show Justice as something active, someone who chooses impartiality, not someone who has it forced on her."

Maya stepped closer. She remembered an article she'd read, years ago, about the statue and its meaning. The blindfold, it said, only became a common motif in the 17th century, when people began to believe the judiciary should stand apart from the king. Moore's Justice, the article argued, seemed free to adjust her blindfold as she sees fit.

For a moment, the team stood together in the shadow of Justice, each of them wondering what kind of impartiality, and what kind of judgment, awaited them inside.

———

The courtroom smelled faintly of varnish and old paper, scents that clung to polished benches and heavy oak doors. The lights hummed overhead, casting a sterile glow on paneled walls that had seen decades of arguments. Maya sat at counsel table, legal pad open, pen poised like a weapon she wasn't sure she'd need. Across the aisle, Titan's attorneys occupied their corner like a well-funded army: tailored suits, gleaming laptops, and the quiet confidence of people who had never lost a case they could afford to win.

The side door opened, and Judge Eleanor Price stepped in. Her robe flowed like a shadow, yet her presence was all precision: sharp eyes, silver hair pulled back, and the calm authority of someone who had spent decades navigating the labyrinth of patent law. She settled into the bench, adjusted her glasses, and surveyed the room with a look that could strip varnish.

"Counsel," she said, voice even but brisk, "we'll proceed with jury selection. You've all reviewed my questionnaire. Keep your follow-ups concise. We're not here for theatrics."

Maya had read the questionnaire twice that morning. It was pure Price. Targeted, surgical. Questions about prior exposure to intellectual property disputes, views on innovation, and whether anyone believed patents stifled progress. No fluff, no fishing expeditions. The judge had already done the heavy lifting; now it was about reading the gaps.

The clerk called for the panel and prospective jurors filed into the gallery, the small of rain fresh on their coats. A woman with a cardigan buttoned to the throat, and another with sharp eyes and a laptop bag who radiated quiet skepticism. A young man in a Red Sox cap who looked like he'd rather be anywhere else. Maya felt her pulse quicken.

Each was a cipher, and the code lay in posture, tone, and the flicker of expression when they heard the word "patent."

Judge Price spoke, her voice carrying easily in the hushed room.

"Good morning. You've been summoned as prospective jurors in a civil case. This matter involves allegations of patent infringement. Claims that Titan Corp. infringed a patent owned by NovaTech. Your role, if selected, will be to listen to the evidence, apply the law as I instruct you, and render a fair verdict.

"If you are selected as a juror, you cannot discuss the case with your fellow jurors before you are permitted to do so at the conclusion of the trial, or with anyone else until after a decision has been reached by the jury. This means you cannot talk about the case or otherwise have any communications about the case with anyone, and that includes email, text messaging, blogs, or comments, or on social media websites and apps like Twitter, Facebook, Instagram, LinkedIn, YouTube, Whats-App, and Snapchat, until I tell you that such discussions may take place. If you feel that you cannot do this, then you cannot let yourself become a member of the jury in this case.

"Is there anyone who will not be able to comply with this restriction?"

The room remained silent.

Judge Price continued. "You also cannot conduct any type of independent or personal research or investigation regarding any matters related to this case. Therefore, you cannot use your cellphones, iPads, computers or any other device to do any research or investigation regarding this case, the matters in the case, the legal issues in the case, or the individuals or other entities involved in the case.

"And you must ignore any information about the case you might see, even accidentally, while browsing the internet or on your social media feeds. This is because you must base the decisions you will have to make in this case solely on what you hear and see in this courtroom. If you feel that you cannot do this, then you cannot let yourself become a juror."

She gestured toward counsel tables. "Let me introduce the attorneys. For the plaintiff, NovaTech: Mr. Jordan Reyes." Jordan stood, nodding briefly. "And for the defendant, Titan Corp.: Ms. Marla Whitaker." Titan's lead counsel rose, smooth and polished.

Price continued, her tone brisk but courteous. "You'll be asked questions to determine whether you can serve impartially. There are no right or wrong answers, only honest ones. Please answer truthfully and completely."

She raised her hand, and the jurors followed suit.

"Do you solemnly swear or affirm that you will answer all questions truthfully and completely?"

A chorus of voices responded, "I do."

Price nodded once, satisfied. "Thank you. You've all completed my written questionnaire. I'll begin with a few clarifying questions."

Jordan leaned in, voice low. "Number seven: Ramirez. Tech background. Could lean Titan."

Maya nodded, eyes scanning the panel. *She looked sharp, analytical, the kind who reads footnotes. If Titan spun this as protecting innovation, she might buy it. But maybe fairness would resonate. Maybe.* Maya scribbled a note: *Watch her.*

Judge Price moved through the panel with the efficiency of someone who had no patience for gamesmanship. When a juror hesitated, she pressed. Politely, but firmly. Until the answer was clear.

"Mr. Collins," she said to the man in the Red Sox cap, "you indicated you work in IT support. Ever dealt with software disputes?"

He shrugged. "Not really. Just fixing printers."

Price nodded once, moved on. "Ms. Ramirez, you wrote that you follow tech news. Any strong opinions about patents?"

The woman with the laptop bag tilted her head. "I think some companies abuse the system. But... I guess it depends."

Price's eyes flicked to Jordan, then to Titan's lead counsel, as if to say: *You'll want to think about that one.*

Jordan whispered, "She's dangerous. Knows enough to have opinions."

Maya kept her gaze forward, but her mind was racing. *Dangerous, yes. But maybe she hates bullies. Maybe Titan looks like one.* She wrote: *Probe fairness. Avoid jargon.*

When Judge Price finished her questioning, she gestured to Titan's lead counsel. "Ms. Whitaker, you may proceed—briefly."

Whitaker rose, smooth as silk. "Thank you, Your Honor." Her tone was warm, practiced. "Ms. Ramirez, you mentioned companies abusing the system. Would that affect your ability to be fair in a case involving patents?"

Ramirez's eyebrow twitched. "Not if the rules are followed."

Maya caught it. *Not buying Titan wholesale. Good.*

Jordan leaned closer. "She's a thinker. Could go either way."

Whitaker moved on, asking about corporate trust, innovation, and whether anyone had worked in tech. Her questions were tight. Price wouldn't allow anything else. When Jordan's turn came, he stood, voice calm but firm.

"Mr. Collins," Jordan said, "you indicated you work in IT support. Any feelings about smaller tech companies versus larger ones?"

Collins shrugged again. "Not really. Just hope my printer works."

A ripple of laughter broke the tension. Even Judge Price had to suppress a smile.

Price kept the tempo brisk, a reprimand coming only once when Whitaker lingered too long. "Counsel, that's enough."

There were a handful of strikes, each one a calculated move. Maya watched, heart thudding, as Jordan dismissed an accountant who had nodded vigorously when Whitaker praised "corporate innovation, and a sales rep who wrote "big companies create jobs" on his questionnaire.

Whitaker struck a retired machinist who admitted to suing a credit card company. Each choice felt like a move on a chessboard, and the clock was ticking.

By noon, the panel was set. Nine strangers plus an alternate, the number having been agreed between the parties, to decide NovaTech's fate:

Helen Brooks, a retired teacher, sat upright, hands folded neatly in her lap. When Judge Price had mentioned "fairness," Helen nodded, lips pressed in a thin line of approval.

Tom Collins, still wearing his Red Sox cap damp from the walk in, slouched in his seat. When asked about software disputes, he had shrugged, eyes drifting to the clock as if already counting the minutes.

Carla Ramirez, the tech consultant, scanned the room over the rim of her glasses, her laptop bag tucked at her feet. Her fingers tapped restlessly on her questionnaire, and she tilted her head, skeptical, when patents were mentioned.

Linda Wu, a nurse, glanced at the attorneys with quiet curiosity. When asked about impartiality, she'd answered softly, voice steady but reserved.

Frank Dorsey, a postal worker, wore his uniform, still damp from the walk. He had listened intently, brow furrowed, and given a small, reassuring smile when the judge explained the rules.

Marta Alvarez, a small business owner, sat forward, elbows on her knees, eyes sharp and attentive. She jotted notes on her pad when "corporate innovation" was mentioned, lips pursed in thought.

Samir Patel, a librarian. He was the alternate. He'd placed his umbrella carefully under his chair, glasses fogged from the rain and read the oath slowly, mouthing the words as if committing them to memory.

Jenna Price, a college student, fidgeted with her phone, sneaking glances at the attorneys. When asked about patents, she admitted, "I don't really know much about them, but I'm willing to learn."

Walter Greene, a retired firefighter with hands thick and scarred, resting on his knees. He listened with a steady, unhurried gaze, nodding slightly when the judge mentioned responsibility.

Derek Foster, an auto mechanic sat with his arms folded, grease still under his fingernails. He squinted at the attorneys, as if sizing up an unfamiliar engine.

The clerk administered the juror's oath, each affirming they would try the case fairly and render a true verdict "upon the law and the evidence."

Jordan leaned in close. "We did what we could."

*Did we?* Maya wondered. *Nine strangers. Nine chances for Titan to crush us or for us to survive.*

Judge Price set her glasses down. "Counsel. Openings at 2:00 p.m. Keep it to forty minutes. No showmanship. No juror tutorials. We'll get to the evidence."

The courtroom emptied slowly, the shuffle of jurors' shoes echoing against marble. Maya gathered her notes, her pen tapping a restless rhythm.

Jordan slid into the chair beside her, loosening his tie. His voice was low, meant for her ears only. "Well," he said, "we've got Brooks. That's something."

Maya nodded, eyes still on the empty jury box. *Brooks is steady. Fairness-minded. She'll listen.*

"Ramirez?" she asked, though she already knew.

"She's in," Jordan said. "I thought Titan would excuse her, but no."

Maya exhaled slowly. *They wanted her. That means she was dangerous.* "They're playing it safe," she murmured, voice low as if confessing a fragile truth.

Jordan gave a dry smile. "That's the game. We kept Collins. Neutral, maybe bored."

"Bored is good," Maya said softly. "Bored means he won't fight us."

Jordan leaned closer, voice dropping another notch. "Look at the rest: nurse, postal worker, small business owner. No engineers, no patent lawyers. That's a gift."

Maya's pen stilled. *A gift, maybe. Or a trap. Less technically savvy jurors might lean on instinct and instinct favors the big name, the familiar brand.* "They'll sell Titan as the innovator," she said quietly. "The engine of progress."

Jordan nodded. "And we sell fairness. Level playing field. No jargon, no tech-speak. Just rules and promises."

Maya glanced at the rain streaking the courthouse windows, blurring the neat lines of the world beyond. *Fairness. It sounds so clean. But in here, it's a knife fight in velvet gloves.*

"They'll hit us on size," she said. "Make us look like opportunists."

Jordan's jaw tightened. "Then we make them look like bullies."

For a moment, neither spoke. The hum of the lights filled the silence as Maya imagined the jurors filing out, their faces already fading into anonymity.

Jordan stood, gathering his folders. "Opening statements. We keep it simple. We make it human."

Maya rose, slipping her pen into her bag. *Human. Fairness. No theatrics.* She hoped that was enough.

As she followed Jordan out into the corridor, she found herself studying the courthouse's historical exhibits. Old photographs of Concord's first federal court, a faded letter from President Washington, and a timeline tracing the District's evolution from borrowed rooms to this modern facility. She tried to imagine the first case here. A quarrel over tariffs and coffee beans. She wondered what the judges then would have thought of those stakes compared to ones now.

———

The courtroom was quiet, the air heavy with anticipation. The jurors settled into their seats, some glancing at their notepads, others folding their hands or shifting in their chairs. Maya studied them. A cross-section of New Hampshire, each carrying their own story, now holding the fate of NovaTech in their hands.

Judge Price adjusted her glasses and nodded. "Mr. Reyes, you may proceed."

Jordan stood, buttoned his jacket, and walked to the lectern. He paused, allowing the silence to settle before starting.

"Good afternoon. As Judge Price told you, my name is Jordan Reyes, and I represent NovaTech. This case is about fairness. It's about whether the rules that protect innovation apply to everyone; whether a small company can stand on equal ground with a giant."

He glanced at the jurors, his voice steady but earnest. "NovaTech is a company built on ideas. Our engineers developed technology that changed the way telemetry is processed. Telemetry is the automatic collection, transmission, and analysis of data from remote sources."

Jordan paused, noting the quizzical looks on the jurors' faces. "You're familiar with it. Think of a weather station. It has sensors to measure things like temperature and pressure. Or a hospital ER, where doctors and nurses use sensors to measure a patient's vital signs like heart rate and blood pressure. Telemetry is the name for sending that data to a central location for monitoring, analysis, and informed decision-making. Organizations depend on telemetry data to monitor and gain insights into the health of their systems and processes, detect and diagnose issues, optimize performance, and make informed decisions."

The jurors seemed to relax. Collins even looked away from the clock and for the first time seemed interested in what Jordan had to say. This wasn't going to be that hard to understand after all.

Jordan continued. "NovaTech invented a unique way to process telemetry and protected that invention with a patent, just as the law allows. Titan Corp., a much larger company, was interested in NovaTech's creation. They commissioned a pilot. A trial run. To see how NovaTech's system would handle both routine data flow and data flow that was wildly unusual. It's when the data is coming in unusual patterns or timing that NovaTech's invention really shines, and Titan was impressed with the results.

"But Titan didn't want to give NovaTech the credit it was due. Rather than sign a deal to license NovaTech's technology, Titan kept asking for just one more test, just one more report. All the while Titan was racing to build its own solution, knowing that NovaTech had already patented it. After seeing just how good it was, Titan used NovaTech's technology without permission. They didn't ask. They didn't pay. They simply took it."

Jordan's tone softened. "We're not here to punish success. Titan is a respected company. But the law is clear: when someone invents something new, they have the right to protect it. That right belongs to everyone, big or small."

He gestured to the monitors in front of the jury box. "Over the next few days, you'll see documents, hear testimony, and learn how NovaTech's invention works. You'll hear from experts, engineers, and witnesses who will explain what was created, how it was protected, and how Titan used it."

Jordan's gaze swept the jury. "At the end of this trial, we'll ask you to find that Titan infringed NovaTech's patent. Not because they're a big company, but because the facts and the law demand it. We'll ask you to uphold the rules that make innovation possible for everyone."

He nodded, stepped back, and returned to the counsel table.

Judge Price turned to the defense. "Ms. Whitaker?"

Marla Whitaker rose, her movements precise, her expression composed. She approached the lectern, her voice smooth and confident.

"Thank you, Your Honor. Good afternoon, ladies and gentlemen. My name is Marla Whitaker, and I represent Titan Corp."

She smiled, measured and reassuring. "Titan is proud of its record of innovation. We invest in research, we develop new technologies, and we compete fairly. The story you just heard is not the whole story."

Marla's tone sharpened but remained calm. "NovaTech claims Titan took something that wasn't theirs. Their engineers are talented, and their contributions matter. But Titan's team worked independently and developed its own technology. Lawfully. The similarities NovaTech points to are just that. Similarities, not theft."

She held the jury's gaze steady. "Patents are important. They protect inventors. But they do not give anyone the right to block progress or stifle competition. Titan respects the law. We did not infringe NovaTech's patent."

Marla gestured to her team. "You'll hear from our engineers and experts, and you'll see the documents that show how Titan's technology was developed. You'll see that Titan played by the rules."

She paused, letting her words settle. "At the end of this trial, we'll ask you to look at the facts, apply the law, and find that Titan did nothing wrong."

She returned to her seat, her expression unchanged.

Judge Price looked to the jury. "Thank you, counsel."

She glanced at the clock, then addressed the courtroom with her usual brisk authority. "Ladies and gentlemen, we will recess for the day."

Looking at the jurors, she continued, "Please remember: you are not to discuss this case with anyone, not even each other. Nor are you to conduct any research or read about the case in any form, including online or on social media. Do not form or express any opinions until all the evidence is in and you have heard my instructions on the law."

She looked over her glasses, making eye contact with counsel. "We will resume promptly at 8:30 a.m. tomorrow. Please be on time. Court is adjourned for the day."

The jurors rose, gathering their notepads and shuffling out in a quiet line, the bailiff guiding them through the side door. As they left,

Maya searched their faces for any sign. Sympathy, skepticism, even curiosity would be ok.

For a moment, the courtroom was filled with the rustle of papers, the scrape of chairs, and the low murmur of people conferring in hushed tones.

Maya closed her notebook, feeling the adrenaline ebb into exhaustion. Jordan gathered his files, stacking them with practiced efficiency. Alex unplugged his laptop, hands trembling just slightly, while Ethan coiled up a tangle of charging cables and stuffed them into his backpack.

They exchanged a few quiet words, a joke about the judge's punctuality. Maya glanced back at the jury box, now empty, and felt the weight of the day settle on her shoulders.

As they made their way down the aisle and into the corridor, the courthouse felt at once immense and strangely intimate. A place where everything mattered, and nothing was certain.

Outside, the rain had eased to mist. The NovaTech team stepped into the gray evening, the courthouse doors closing behind them with a heavy, echoing thud.

# TEN

THE COMFORT INN's hallways were quiet except for the distant hum of the ice machine and the faint, persistent scent of burnt coffee that seemed to seep from the wallpaper. Alex sat at the small desk in his room, the glow of his laptop screen painting tired shadows across his face. Outside, the rain had started again, tapping a nervous rhythm against the window as if the world itself was waiting for the trial to resume.

On the bed behind him, a precarious stack of witness outlines and patent diagrams teetered on the edge of spilling onto the floor. Alex had read them all. Twice. He'd highlighted passages, scribbled notes in the margins, then, in a sudden fit of nerves, erased half of them. Now, he stared at the blank page of a legal pad, trying to remember what it felt like to believe in the work, not just defend it.

A knock at the door. Jordan entered with a gentle nod, carrying a slim folder and the kind of calm that comes from years of late-night strategy sessions.

"Couldn't sleep?" Jordan asked, easing into the room's only chair.

Alex shook his head. "I keep replaying the questions. What if I freeze? What if I say too much, or not enough?"

Jordan smiled, setting the folder on the desk. "That's why we practice. Forget about winning arguments, Alex. Your job is to teach. The jury's looking for the person behind the patent, not just the diagrams. They want to know what kept you up at night, what problem you refused to ignore, and how you found your way through the mess. The math matters, but the story is what sticks."

Alex nodded, though his hands twitched nervously at the edge of the legal pad. "What if they ask about the prior art? Or the emails? Or why I said something was 'easy' in a message two years ago?"

"Tell the truth," Jordan said. "If you don't know, say so. Don't guess. Don't speculate. Listen to the question, answer only what's asked, and stop. If you need a moment, pause. I'll object if the question is improper. And remember, on direct, look at me and then at the jury. On cross, look at the lawyer. But always, always be the teacher."

Alex tried to steady his breath. "I'm not Edison. I'm not Ford. I just... built something I thought would help."

Jordan's smile softened. "That's exactly what they need to hear. The myth of the American inventor isn't about being a genius. It's about seeing a problem, refusing to accept the easy answer, and working until you find a better one. That's your story. Let them see it."

He opened the folder, revealing a copy of the patent: diagrams, claims, the language that had become both shield and target. "Walk me through it, Alex. Like you're explaining it to someone who's never written a line of code."

Alex took a breath, tracing the lines of the transform layer with his finger. "We built a system that could breathe. When data spiked, it didn't panic. It queued, waited, adapted. We didn't flatten the signals; we let them keep their accents. That's what made it work."

Jordan nodded. "And when they ask about dynamic scalability?"

Alex found his footing. "It's not just about adding servers; it's about knowing when to scale, how to keep the system honest. We monitored queue lengths, CPU, memory. When the system was overwhelmed, it called for help. When things calmed down, it let go. It was about resilience, not just speed."

Jordan flipped to a page of handwritten notes. "And if they press you on whether that was obvious?"

Alex shook his head. "The pieces existed, sure. But no one put them together this way. We tried the obvious paths; they failed. What worked was the sequence, the choices, the willingness to let the system wait instead of break. That wasn't in the textbooks."

Jordan closed the folder. "Good. Tomorrow, you'll get questions meant to rattle you. They'll try to make you angry, or confused, or small. Don't let them. Stay calm. Be patient. If you need to, pause. Remember, your credibility is your most valuable asset."

Alex looked up, the weight of the moment settling on his shoulders. "What if I mess up?"

Jordan's voice was gentle but firm. "You won't. And if you do, we'll fix it. The truth is on your side, just tell it."

A silence settled between them, broken only by the rain and the distant sound of a vending machine coughing to life. Alex closed his laptop, set aside the outlines, and let himself breathe. Slow, deliberate. Like the system he'd built.

Tomorrow, he would teach. Tonight, he would try to sleep.

———

Outside the courtroom, the hallway buzzed with voices and the distant rattle of a vending machine. Alex leaned against the cool marble wall, steadying his breath. In a few minutes, it would be his turn to speak. Not just for NovaTech, but for every line of code that had ever kept him awake at night.

Maya stood a few feet away, phone pressed to her ear, her posture rigid. The voice on the other end was clipped, urgent. A board member, by the sound of it.

"Maya, there's still time. A settlement would show the board you're pragmatic."

Maya's grip tightened on her phone as she watched Alex, then the rain. "Pragmatic? Or just giving up? I didn't come this far to fold when it matters."

"Be practical."

"I am," Maya replied, ending the call with a tap that echoed louder than it should have in the hush of the hallway.

For a moment, she just stood there, her reflection blurred in the glass, the city beyond washed in gray. Her phone buzzed again. Three messages from numbers she didn't recognize, one from a number she once knew by heart and hadn't blocked. Instead, she pressed her palm against the window until the cold steadied her.

Jordan appeared beside her, a folder tucked under his arm, his tie slightly askew. "They're about to open the doors," he said quietly. "Fifteen minutes."

Maya nodded, her voice barely above a whisper. "Alex is ready?"

Jordan glanced at Alex, who was still leaning against the wall, lips moving in silent rehearsal. "As ready as anyone ever is."

Maya crossed to Alex, her heels clicking softly on the marble. He opened his eyes, meeting hers with a look that was equal parts nerves and resolve.

"You've got this," she said, her voice steady.

Alex managed a thin smile. "See you on the other side."

They stood together in the hush, the world narrowing to the space between breaths. Down the hall, a bailiff called for counsel to gather; court would begin soon. The NovaTech office felt a thousand miles away.

Maya squeezed Alex's shoulder, then turned back toward Jordan. Alex straightened his jacket, exhaled, and let himself believe, just for a moment, that the truth might be enough.

———

The jury filed in, the scrape of chairs and the rustle of notepads fading into silence. Judge Price's eyes found Jordan. "Your first witness?"

"Alex Carter," said Jordan.

Judge Price nodded at the clerk, who summoned Alex from the waiting area. As Alex moved toward the stand the room tilted, or maybe he did. He caught the rail, smiling at the jury as if to apologize for being human.

"Mr. Carter," Judge Price said, "would you like a moment?"

"I'm okay," he said. Then the letters on the witness placard blurred and doubled. He blinked them into one. Sat. Swore.

Jordan approached the lectern, his tone gentle but precise. "Good morning, Alex. Would you please introduce yourself to the jury?"

Alex nodded, voice steadying as he spoke. "My name is Alex Carter. I'm the Chief Technology Officer and co-founder of NovaTech."

Jordan offered a reassuring nod. "Let's go back to the beginning, Alex. How did NovaTech come to be?"

Alex hesitated, a small smile flickering as memory softened his features. "It started at a conference, actually. I was working at another company, a big company. Good people, but... they weren't interested in new ideas. I'd been obsessed with telemetry. How to process all the messy, real-world data that comes in from sensors, medical devices, you name it. I thought there had to be a better way, something more adaptive, more... human."

He glanced at Maya, who watched from the plaintiff's table, her expression unreadable but intent.

"I was venting to another engineer in the hallway, probably too loudly, about how my company just wanted to do things the old way. I said something like, 'If I have to flatten one more data stream into a spreadsheet, I'll lose my mind.'"

A ripple of laughter swept the jury and Alex relaxed a little.

"Maya overheard me. She came over, introduced herself, and said, 'Maybe you should stop trying to fix someone else's house and build your own.' I thought she was joking, but she wasn't. She asked me to explain my idea. How I'd let data streams keep their 'accents' instead of forcing everything into the same mold. She listened. Really listened. And then she said, 'If you're serious, let's talk about what it would take to build this for real.'"

Jordan nodded. "And did you?"

Alex smiled, a little sheepish. "I quit my job two months later. Maya and I started NovaTech in a rented room with a whiteboard and a coffee machine that barely worked. We brought in Ethan, who was fresh out of school but brilliant. We spent months chasing the idea. How to make a system that could breathe, that wouldn't break when the world got weird."

Jordan let the moment breathe. "Can you explain, in simple terms, what you invented?"

Alex leaned forward, finding his rhythm. "We built a kind of translator... for signals that don't want to agree on what they are.

"Most systems force data into neat little boxes, ironing out the quirks and outliers. But in the real world, those quirks are where the truth hides. Our system learns how the streams relate, preserves what makes each one unique, and when things get rough, it doesn't panic. It slows down, queues the data, and waits for the storm to pass. It breathes, instead of breaking."

He glanced at the jury, searching for understanding. "It's like teaching a choir to sing together but letting every voice keep its accent. You get harmony, not just volume."

As Alex finished his explanation, Helen Brooks, seated in the front row, hair pulled back in a tight bun, paused her note-taking and looked up, her eyes narrowing in concentration. Next to her, Tom Collins leaned forward, elbows on his knees, nodding as if things had finally clicked.

Jordan smiled. "And why was that important?"

Alex's voice softened. "Because systems fail where people get hurt. If you drop the wrong data in a hospital, someone could miss a warning sign. Losing a shipment in logistics might cost money, but sometimes it's medicine, or food. We wanted to build something that could handle chaos without breaking."

Jordan nodded, shifting to the technical. "Can you walk us through how the system scales? How it 'breathes'?"

Alex gestured as if drawing in the air. "We monitor the system's health: queue lengths, CPU, memory. When things get busy, the system automatically adds more resources. When things calm down, it lets them go. It's not just about speed, it's about resilience. We built it so the system could adapt in real time, not just crash or freeze."

Jordan paused, letting the explanation settle. "Was that obvious? Was it something anyone could have done?"

Alex shook his head. "I wish. It took us months. Some of the pieces existed, sure, but no one put them together this way. We tried so many approaches and they all failed. What worked in the end was the sequence, the willingness to let the system wait instead of break. That wasn't in the textbooks.

"See, we had to figure out how to put several things together." Alex was now in his element. "First was using a decoupled architecture. Something that separated the data ingestion, transformation, and storage layers using messaging queues, like Apache Kafka or RabbitMQ. That makes sure that a backlog in the transform layer doesn't affect data ingestion and allows each layer to scale independently.

"Then we had to design stateless processing units: transformation logic embedded within stateless microservices or functions. That was crucial for scalability. And we had to package the transformation services as containers using Docker and manage them with a container orchestration platform. We used Kubernetes because it has built-in mechanisms for managing and scaling containerized applications.

"The hardest part was the breathing mechanism; the dynamic scalability. We needed to implement automatic scaling based on actual workload metrics; event-driven autoscaling that could adjust the number of processing instances according to the length of the queue in the messaging system. When the queue backlog grew due to data spikes and other fluctuations, the autoscaling needed to kick in, adding processing instances, and then shrink them as the queue emptied.

"There were other components, of course: monitoring systems, queuing systems, and more. They're detailed in the patent, and I can explain if you wish."

Jordan smiled, his voice gentle. "Alex, why did you build this?"

Alex looked at the jury, his voice quiet but clear. "Because I wanted fewer places where systems fail and people get hurt. I wanted to prove you could build something honest, something that breathes, and have it matter."

Jordan let the silence linger, then nodded. "Thank you, Alex. No further questions at this time."

Alex exhaled. The weight of months lifting, if only for a moment.

Judge Price adjusted her glasses and nodded to the defense table. "Ms. Whitaker, you may proceed."

Marla stood with a measured calm. She approached the lectern, her voice smooth and unhurried.

"Good morning, Mr. Carter."

Alex nodded. "Good morning."

Whitaker smiled, polite but distant. "You agree, don't you, that engineers in your field often read the same research papers, attend the same conferences, and face the same technical challenges?"

"Yes," Alex replied. "That's true."

"And it's not uncommon, is it, for two teams to arrive at similar solutions to the same problem?"

"They can try," Alex said, his voice steady.

"But they can, correct?"

Alex hesitated, then nodded. "Yes. It's possible."

Whitaker held up a laminated chart. "These performance curves. Hardly unique, are they? Two teams could end up with similar results, even if they never spoke?"

Alex studied the chart, then addressed the jury. "Curves are easy to draw. But the way ours bends under pressure, the way it recovers from overload; that's no accident. It's a fingerprint, not just a line."

Whitaker's smile didn't waver. "A fingerprint? Or just wishful thinking?"

Alex met her gaze. "It's engineering."

Whitaker moved on, flipping through her notes. "Let's talk about dynamic scalability. You testified that your system adds and removes resources automatically, based on workload. That's not a new idea, is it?"

Alex shook his head. "The general concept isn't new. But the way we applied it to telemetry, the way our transform layer orchestrates scaling in real time based on queue length and data anomalies. That's what's new."

Whitaker pressed. "But you'd agree that cloud platforms, for years, have offered autoscaling based on CPU or memory usage?"

"Yes, but—"

She cut him off. "And you used open-source libraries in your product, correct?"

"Everyone does. We disclose that."

"So, Titan using similar libraries isn't evidence of copying. It's evidence of using what's available."

"Libraries aren't architecture," Alex replied quietly. "They're bricks, not blueprints."

Whitaker's tone sharpened. "You sent Titan technical details, performance data, even failure modes, because you wanted a deal. You wanted their distribution, their money."

"We wanted a partner," Alex said, quiet but resolute.

"And when you didn't get it, you sued."

"When they launched our work, we sued."

Whitaker paused, letting the silence fill with implication.

"Before filing your patent application, you didn't conduct or review any formal prior art searches, did you?" Marla asked sharply.

"We didn't commission any formal, professional patent search. But as part of our development process, my team and I reviewed several existing solutions, primarily open-source implementations. We found a couple of general-purpose data stream processing libraries, but they couldn't handle anomalous data very well. That's when we figured we were on to something.

"Our patent attorney told us we needed to provide all of that prior information to the patent examiner when we filed the application, so we did."

"Speaking of 'your team,' you wrote in an email to your team that the solution was 'easy' once you saw the pattern. Isn't that right?"

Alex's jaw tightened. "I said it was easy in hindsight. It wasn't easy when everything we tried kept failing. Like I said, it took us months to get it right."

"But it's true, isn't it, that "dynamic scalability" was a well-known concept in general computing and networking prior to you filing your patent application?"

"The general concept of 'dynamic scalability' in an abstract sense was known, but its specific application and implementation within our unique telemetry processing system, particularly how our transform layer autonomously orchestrates and scales resources in direct response to specific data metrics and queue lengths in real-time, wasn't known." Alex was firm.

"We engineered a specific technical solution to a particular problem. Processing high-volume, unpredictable telemetry data streams efficiently and reliably. That's not something general scalability methods use in broader networking or web services."

"You called it 'breathing.'" Marla said. "That's what you say is unique right?"

"Yes."

"But your patent doesn't use that term, does it?"

"The patent doesn't specifically say 'breathing,' but it describes it." Alex picked up a copy of the patent that he had used when Jordan was asking questions.

He quoted:

The present disclosure provides a telemetry processing system comprising a data ingestion layer, a transform layer, and a storage layer. The transform layer (e.g., component 305) employs a dynamic scalability module (310) to ensure efficient handling of fluctuating telemetry data workloads.

Specifically, the dynamic scalability module (310) monitors key performance metrics of the transform layer, including but not limited to: data processing queue lengths, CPU utilization, and memory consumption of individual processing nodes. The system continuously evaluates these metrics against predefined thresholds.

Upon detecting that a metric exceeds a high-water mark threshold (e.g., queue length surpassing 80%), a scaling decision logic within the module (310) automatically initiates provisioning of additional computational resources, such as new containerized instances or virtual machines, to the transform layer. This resource orchestration is performed dynamically, leveraging cloud-native architectures that enable near-instantaneous scaling capabilities.

Conversely, when metrics fall below a low-water mark threshold for a sustained period, indicating a decrease in workload, the module (310) automatically deallocates underutilized resources to optimize operational costs and resource utilization. This approach ensures the system can process vast amounts of sensor data simultaneously, regardless of the volume, without compromising performance or reliability.

"All this discussion about the dynamic scalability module 310 handling fluctuating telemetry data workloads is what I call 'breathing.'"

Whitaker looked down at her notes and flipped a couple of pages. "No further questions."

Judge Price turned to Jordan. "Redirect?"

Jordan shook his head. "Not at this time, Your Honor."

Alex let out a long breath, tension in his shoulders finally easing as he rose from the witness chair. He caught the edge of the rail for balance, then stepped down, acutely aware of the jury's eyes tracking him. Some scribbled notes, others watched in silence, the weight of his testimony still hanging in the air. The courtroom was quiet, save for the soft creak of the chair as he left the stand, the echo of his words lingering long after he'd taken his seat.

# ELEVEN

THE COURTROOM BUZZED a bit as Maya was called and took the stand. The courtroom lights were harsh and unblinking. She adjusted the microphone, folded her hands, and let her gaze settle slowly on the jury.

Jordan approached, his tone gentle but purposeful. "Ms. Singh, thank you for being here. Could you please introduce yourself to the jury?"

Maya nodded. "My name is Maya Singh. I'm the CEO and co-founder of NovaTech."

Jordan smiled. "We've heard about NovaTech's invention. I'd like to talk about the company itself. When you started NovaTech, what did you hope to build?"

Maya took a breath. "I—that is, we: Alex and I. We wanted to build a company that mattered. Not just a product, but a place where people could take risks, tell the truth, and try to do things the right way. My parents taught me that work is a promise you keep to yourself and to others. That's what NovaTech was for me. A promise to build something honest, and to protect the people who believed in it."

Jordan nodded. "Let's talk about the journey that brought you here. After you received your first patent, what was NovaTech's next step?"

"We're a small team, but getting the patent confirmed that we had something special. We reached out to Titan Corp, hoping for a partnership. We thought that if we could prove ourselves in a pilot, we'd have a chance to scale our technology and make a real impact."

Jordan's voice was soft. "Can you describe what that pilot with Titan was like?"

Maya's eyes flickered with memory. "It was intense. Titan's team was sharp, skeptical, and very thorough. They asked for architecture diagrams, then performance data, then failure modes. Every week, the questions got more specific. Details we hadn't put in our pitch deck. At first, we were flattered. We thought it meant they were serious about working with us."

Jordan leaned in. "Did you share everything they asked for?"

"We were careful. We used NDAs, watermarks, tracked every document. But yes, we answered their questions. We wanted to show we could be a good partner. We believed that if we played fair, they would too."

Jordan paused, letting the jury absorb this. He pulled a paper from his binder. "Did Titan ever sign a term sheet or make a formal commitment?"

"No."

"Did they ever stop asking for technical detail?"

Maya shook her head. "No. They kept asking for more information, but they never committed. We kept hoping. Every new request felt like we were getting closer. But the deal never came."

Jordan's tone was gentle. "What happened next?"

Maya's voice was steady, but there was an ache beneath it. "One morning, we got an email. Titan was 're-evaluating strategic priorities' and wouldn't be moving forward. No explanation, no feedback. Just... done. A few weeks later, they launched a product that looked and sounded just like ours. Same architecture, same language, even the same quirks we'd spent months solving."

"How did you know their product used your work?"

"The architecture was the same," she said. "And it failed in the same place. We had a bottleneck in our transform layer when input streams spiked. They advertised a fix with the exact same tradeoff we'd made, latency for stability. Even the inflection points on their throughput curves matched ours."

Jordan let the silence linger. "How did that feel?"

Maya looked at the jury, her voice quiet but clear. "It felt like betrayal; not just of us, but of the idea that if you work hard and play by the rules, you have a shot. We lost more than a deal. We lost trust. In them, and for a while, in ourselves."

Jordan nodded, his voice low. "What did you do next?"

"We fought. We gathered every document, every email, every trace of what we'd built and what we'd shared. We tried to get answers, but Titan wouldn't talk. So we did the only thing left, we went to court. Not because we wanted a fight, but because we couldn't let them erase us."

Jordan walked Maya through a handful of exhibits: the nondisclosure agreement. Foundation. Admitted. A series of redacted emails, requests from Titan for increasingly precise *clarifications*. Foundation. Admitted. The final email severing the relationship. Admitted.

He stopped there, letting Maya's words settle in the room. "Thank you, Maya. No further questions at this time."

Maya exhaled, her hands still folded, the weight of her story now shared with the room.

———

Marla Whitaker, Titan's lead counsel, approached the lectern and offered Maya a polite smile. She turned to the jury.

"Ms. Singh, you said you're the CEO of NovaTech, correct?"

"Yes." *Stay calm*, Maya thought. *Don't let her set the tone.*

"You decide when to file lawsuits on behalf of your company?"

"I do, in consultation with our board and counsel."

Whitaker nodded, flipping through her notes. "Let's talk about the pilot with Titan. You testified that Titan kept asking for more information, and you kept providing it. That's because you wanted a deal, isn't it?"

"We wanted a partnership, yes."

"And you were hoping for Titan's distribution, Titan's resources, Titan's money?"

"We wanted the chance to build at scale. That's what partnerships are for."

Whitaker's tone sharpened. "But Titan never signed a term sheet. Never made a formal commitment. Isn't it true that you kept sending more details, more performance data, even after it was clear Titan was noncommittal?"

"We answered their questions under NDA. We believed they were serious."

Whitaker raised an eyebrow. "Or perhaps you were just desperate for a deal? NovaTech needed cash, didn't it?"

Maya's jaw tightened. *Don't apologize for ambition. The jury needs to see you believe in what you built.* "We needed a path to market. That's what every startup needs."

Whitaker let the silence hang, then continued. "You testified that Titan's product launch felt like a betrayal. But isn't it true that you and your team used open-source libraries in your own product?"

"Everyone does. We disclose that."

"And Titan used open-source libraries too?"

"So they've said."

"So the fact that Titan uses the same libraries isn't evidence of infringement, is it? They're there for everyone to use, right?"

"They're just libraries," Maya replied. "Sure, anyone can use them, but it's how you use them that matters. "

A couple of jurors looked up at that. Whitaker pressed on.

"Ms. Singh, you wanted Titan's validation. When you didn't get it, you sued. Isn't that right?"

Maya's voice was steady. "When they launched a product that used our work, yes, we sued."

Whitaker's tone was cool. "You could have walked away. You could have pivoted. Instead, you chose litigation. Isn't it true that NovaTech's investors were pressuring you for results?"

"Our investors wanted us to protect what we'd built and what they'd invested in."

Whitaker paused, then held up a document. "You sent Titan a series of increasingly detailed technical answers, even after weeks of silence. Isn't it possible you gave away too much, hoping for a deal that was never coming?"

Maya met her gaze. "We answered their questions in good faith. We believed in partnership. We believed in the rules."

Whitaker let the silence stretch.

Her tone sharpened as she flipped to a new page in her binder. "Ms. Singh, let's talk about the leak of information regarding the Titan pilot. Are you aware that confidential performance metrics from your pilot with Titan appeared in an industry newsletter?"

Maya's jaw tightened. "I am aware that pilot metrics were reported in the press."

Whitaker nodded, turning to the jury. "And those metrics, latency, throughput, explainability, were not supposed to be public, were they?"

"They did not include any code or proprietary architecture. They were high-level results."

"But they were subject to a non-disclosure agreement with Titan, correct?"

Maya hesitated. "We took care to avoid disclosing anything confidential. The numbers were anonymized."

Whitaker pressed, "Ms. Singh, isn't it true that after weeks of silence from Titan, you authorized the leak of those metrics to generate industry buzz and force Titan's hand?"

Maya's voice was steady, but quieter. "We were under immense pressure. Our investors wanted proof of traction. We needed to show the market that our technology worked."

Whitaker's voice was icy. "So you broke confidentiality to create leverage for NovaTech. Isn't that right?"

"No," Maya replied, her voice firming. "We did not break confidentiality. We shared only what we believed was permitted. General performance results, not proprietary details."

Whitaker let the silence hang, then addressed the jury. "Ms. Singh, do you understand that leaking even anonymized metrics can undermine trust with potential partners? That it can make your company look desperate, or even reckless?"

Maya met her gaze. "I understand the risks. I also understand what it's like to be erased by silence. We did what we thought was necessary to survive."

Whitaker closed her folder with a snap. "Nothing further."

Judge Price nodded. "Redirect?"

Jordan stood, his tone calm but clear. "Ms. Singh, just a few questions. You've been asked about the leak of pilot metrics. Did NovaTech ever disclose Titan's proprietary code, architecture, or confidential business information to the public?"

Maya shook her head. "No. We were careful to share only general performance results. Numbers that reflected our technology's capabilities, not Titan's secrets."

Jordan nodded. "And why did you feel it was necessary to share those results at all?"

Maya glanced at the jury. "Because we were being erased. We'd spent weeks working in good faith, answering every question, hoping for a partnership. When Titan went silent, we needed to show the world that what we'd built was real. We wanted to survive, not to betray anyone's trust."

As Maya spoke, Linda Wu, who had earlier frowned at the mention of the leak, lowered her pen and studied her with new interest. Frank Dorsey, today wearing a blue shirt instead of his USPS uniform, nodded almost imperceptibly, as if understanding the impossible position Maya described.

Jordan's voice softened. "Did you believe you were acting within the bounds of your agreements?"

"Yes. We never intended to violate confidentiality. We believed we were acting in good faith."

Jordan nodded, then addressed the jury. "Ms. Singh, in your experience, what happens to a small company when a giant partner stops answering calls?"

Maya's answer was quiet but steady. "You disappear. Unless you fight to be seen."

A ripple of movement passed through the jury box. Marta Alvarez, the small business owner nodded slightly and underlined a phrase on her notepad. Even the auto mechanic, Derek Foster, who'd seemed skeptical before, now sat upright, eyes fixed on Maya

"Maya," he said, using her first name as if it were simply the name of a person, not a role, "if Titan had signed a license, would we be here?"

"No," she said. "We would be building."

"Nothing further."

The judge excused her. As Maya left the stand, she passed Alex in the aisle. His smile was tentative and small, but it reached his eyes.

Judge Price looked over her glasses at the jury. "We'll break for lunch. Please remember my instructions. Do not discuss the case, do not read about the case, and do not form opinions until you have heard all of the evidence."

# TWELVE

TECH LEDGER | SOFIA MARTINEZ
**Trial Brief**

Courtrooms have a way of shrinking people; today, the opposite happened. NovaTech's CTO, Alex Carter, traced a line from problem to principle, and jurors leaned in when the math stopped sounding like math. Carter made it clear: "Our system breathes because we chose a sequence others rejected." In other words, the **order** is the invention.

Later, CEO Maya Singh's testimony brought the company's journey, and its anxieties, into sharp relief. Cross-examination focused on NovaTech's handling of confidential pilot data and the pressures facing startups in Titan's shadow. With both technical and emotional narratives now in play, industry watchers say the jury's response could set a precedent for how Silicon Valley will define partnership, risk, and survival.

Trials are telescopes: the further you look, the less you see around the edges. This morning's testimony narrowed the view:

Was NovaTech's choice obvious before they made it? Could their decision to leak information about the Titan pilot turn the jury's sympathies? Expect Titan to keep hammering on that theme and to counter Carter's protestations of invention with experts expounding on known tradeoffs and predictable optimizations. If everything is inevitable, nothing is infringement.

A FEW BLOCKS AWAY, in a rented conference room at the Centennial Hotel, a turreted redbrick mansion now repurposed for business and comfort, Titan's legal team gathered around a polished table. The air was thick with the scent of coffee and the faint tang of rain-soaked pavement. Here, far from the formality of the courthouse, strategy took precedence over ceremony.

Marla closed the door and lowered her voice. "Alex was sympathetic. When his knees buckled, I thought they'd carry him out like a fallen flag."

Richard Hale stood with his back to the window, jaw hard. "Juries love a martyr until they see the facts."

Marla pressed her lips together. "The judge likes clean lines. When those internal emails surface, we won't have lines, we'll have stains."

Richard's eyes cut to Claire, who had slipped into a back row of chairs like a question mark. "Anything you want to share, Claire?"

She held his gaze and felt the ground shift beneath her. "Just that juries hear what they need to hear."

"Then let's make sure they need to hear us," he said.

Claire gathered her notes. "I'm heading back. I've got some emails to answer."

The voices of her colleagues echoed behind her as she stepped into the hallway. Outside, the rain had eased, leaving the small New England town washed and waiting. Claire moved quickly, her mind already shifting to the next battle. Anything to put distance between herself and Richard Hale.

# Thirteen

The courtroom's afternoon light slanted through high windows, catching dust motes, and the edge of the jury box crowded with notepads and furrowed brows. Jordan Reyes stood, buttoning his jacket, and addressed Judge Price with a calm that belied the stakes at hand.

"Your Honor, the plaintiff calls Dr. Samuel Lin."

A tall, soft-spoken man in his early sixties, with silver hair and a measured presence, took the stand. After being sworn in, he adjusted his glasses and offered a brief, reassuring nod to the jury.

From the lectern, Jordan asked, "Dr. Lin, would you please introduce yourself to the jury?"

Dr. Lin looked at the jurors. "My name is Samuel Lin. I'm a professor of computer engineering at UC Berkeley, and I consult for companies on scalable data systems and telemetry infrastructure."

"Could you briefly describe your background for the court?"

"I hold a Ph.D. in computer science from Caltech. I've spent over thirty years researching distributed systems, published extensively, and advised both startups and major tech firms on telemetry, anomaly detection, and cloud architecture. I've also served as an expert witness in several patent cases involving data processing."

"Your Honor, we move to qualify Dr. Lin as an expert in telemetry processing systems and dynamic scalability."

Judge Price glanced at Marla Whittaker. "Counsel?"

"No objection, your Honor."

"So qualified," announced Judge Price.

"Dr. Lin, are you familiar with the patent at issue in this case?" asked Jordan.

"Yes," confirmed Dr. Lin. "I've reviewed the patent, its claims, the prosecution history, and all relevant technical materials."

"Could you explain, in simple terms, what a telemetry processing system is?"

"Certainly. Telemetry systems collect data from remote sources, like sensors in industrial equipment or business applications, and transmit it for analysis. The data is often messy, arrives unpredictably, and must be cleaned and transformed before it's useful."

"And what is a 'transform layer?' I believe that is described in the patent?"

Dr. Lin nodded. "The transform layer is the core of the system. It takes in raw, unstructured data and processes it; cleaning, normalizing, and enriching it so downstream systems can use it. In NovaTech's invention, this layer is dynamically scalable: it can automatically add or remove processing resources in real time, based on the incoming data's volume and complexity.

"Think of it like a set of lungs for data. When the flow increases, the system inhales, scaling up resources. When things calm down, it exhales, scaling back. That's what makes it resilient."

Jordan asked, "Why does dynamic scalability matter?"

"Because telemetry data is unpredictable. One moment it's quiet, the next, a sudden spike, perhaps due to a network outage or another unusual event. A rigid system might crash or, if it is designed for these worst case scenarios, waste resources by having them on-line when they are not needed. NovaTech's system adapts on the fly, scaling up to handle surges, then scaling down to save costs. This is especially crucial for anomaly detection, where outliers can overwhelm a fixed-capacity system."

"Let's turn to Claim 1 of the patent." Jordan brought the claim up on screens around the courtroom. Several of the jurors leaned in for a better view as Dr. Lin read it aloud:

1. A telemetry data processing system comprising:

at least one processor; and

at least one memory unit communicably coupled to and storing instructions executable by the at least one processor to perform a transform layer method, the method comprising:

receiving a data stream comprising time-series telemetry data;

monitoring a characteristic of the received data stream, the characteristic comprising at least one of data volume, data velocity, or an anomaly indicator;

dynamically determining a required processing resource level for a transform layer operation based at least in part on the monitored characteristic, the transform layer operation configured to process the telemetry data into a modified data format;

comparing the determined required processing resource level to a currently allocated processing resource level for the transform layer operation;

automatically allocating additional processing resources to the transform layer operation via a resource management module when the determined required processing resource level exceeds the currently allocated processing resource level;

automatically deallocating excess processing resources from the transform layer operation when the determined required processing resource level is less than the currently allocated processing resource level; and processing the telemetry data using the dynamically allocated processing resources.

"Could you summarize what it covers?" Jordan asked.

"Claim 1 describes a telemetry processing system with a transform layer that dynamically allocates processing resources based on real-time monitoring of data characteristics, like volume, velocity, or anomaly indicators," explained Dr. Lin. "If the system detects a spike, it automatically provisions more resources; when the spike passes, it deallocates them. This ensures both reliability and efficiency."

"Now, have you reviewed the accused Titan product?"

Dr. Lin adjusted his glasses. "Yes. I reviewed technical documentation, source code excerpts, internal emails, and the product's own marketing materials."

Jordan asked, "In your expert opinion, is Titan's product a telemetry data processing system that performs a transform layer method as described in Claim 1 of NovaTech's patent?"

"It is," replied Dr. Lin. "Titan's architecture includes a module that ingests telemetry data, processes it through a dynamically scalable transform layer, and uses real-time metrics to trigger autoscaling. Just as recited in Claim 1."

"Could you walk the jury through how Titan's system meets each element of Claim 1?"

Dr. Lin rotated slightly in his chair to look directly at the jury members.

"Certainly.

"First, Titan's system receives time-series telemetry data from multiple sources. Time-series data is simply a sequence of points recorded at successive intervals. Imagine taking a temperature measurement every so often. These intervals may be regular, such as every second, but they need not be. Imagine, for example, dozens of sensors in a hospital or a factory, each sending readings every second. That's a flood of data, fluctuating between steady flow and sudden spikes."

He gestured gently toward the claim text on the screen. "Second, the system monitors characteristics like data volume and anomaly indicators. If, say, a temperature sensor suddenly reports a dangerous spike, the system recognizes that as an anomaly and prepares to process more data, faster.

Helen, the retired teacher in the front row of the jury box, nodded and scribbled *spike = anomaly* in the margin of her notepad.

Dr. Lin continued, "Third, the transform layer then determines how many processing units it needs. If the data flow surges, it automatically spins up more resources. Think of it as opening extra lanes on a highway during rush hour. When traffic eases, it closes those lanes to save energy and cost.

He paused, letting the analogy settle. Collins, still in his Red Sox cap, looked up from his notes, eyebrows raised in understanding.

"Titan's system does this dynamically, in real time, using container orchestration. Software that manages these resources automatically. This is not just a theoretical feature; I've reviewed logs and stress test results showing Titan's system scaling up and down in response to real-world data spikes, just as NovaTech's patent claims.

"Did you find any evidence that Titan's system operates in a substantially different way or achieves a substantially different result than that recited in Claim 1?" Jordan's question was designed to provide the jury with an alternative, finding infringement under the doctrine of equivalents.

Dr. Lin shook his head. "No. The technical documents and test results show that Titan's system behaves in the same way, for the same reasons, and achieves the same results as the patented invention. In fact, some of the terminology and failure modes are identical to those described in NovaTech's documentation."

"So, even if Titan's system isn't identical in every detail, it functions in substantially the same way, for the same purpose, to achieve the same result?"

"Yes, it does," confirmed Dr. Lin.

Marta Alvarez, in the back row, tapped her pen thoughtfully, glancing between Dr. Lin and the claim text.

"What evidence did you rely on for your conclusion?" queried Jordan.

"I relied on Titan's internal architecture diagrams, code comments, and emails, some of which explicitly reference NovaTech's pilot results and design choices." Dr. Lin continued. "I also reviewed the stress test data, which shows the same 'breathing' behavior under load that Nova-Tech pioneered."

One by one, Jordan took Dr Lin through each of the documents he used to compile his expert report and analysis. It wasn't glamorous, but it was a master class in getting evidence admitted, building a record Jordan knew would be crucial to support any verdict. Judge Price watched from the bench approvingly. She appreciated the professional manner in which Jordan handled his task. So much so she had to be careful not to let the jury see her slight smile as Jordan worked his way through the myriad documents.

Fortunately for the jurors, Dr. Lin had a way of making even the mundane fascinating; a skill honed from years of teaching bored undergraduates the fundamentals of computer engineering. He explained each item carefully, noting its significance, and in doing so helped round out the story of NovaTech's breakthroughs and how they appeared time and again in Titan's system.

After about an hour, Jordan had his record. He asked carefully, by way of summation, "Dr. Lin, in your expert opinion, does Titan's product infringe Claim 1 of the patent?"

Dr. Lin was calm and confident in his reply. "Yes. In my opinion, Titan's product literally infringes every element of Claim 1."

"Thank you, Dr. Lin. No further questions at this time."

Jordan sat. The jurors wrote in their notebooks, a few exchanging glances as if weighing the testimony together.

Judge Price nodded to the defense table. "Ms. Whittaker?"

———

Marla rose, her expression composed, a legal pad in one hand and a binder of materials in the other. She approached the lectern with measured steps.

"Good afternoon, Dr. Lin."

"Good afternoon."

"You've testified as an expert witness before, correct?"

"Yes, several times." Dr. Lin's voice was almost soothing.

"And you're being compensated for your time in this case?"

"Yes, I am."

"Your compensation isn't dependent on the outcome of this trial, is it?"

"No, it is not."

Marla nodded, then turned to the jury. "Dr. Lin, you understand your role here is to educate the jury, not to advocate for NovaTech, correct?"

"That's correct."

"Let's talk about your methodology." Marla looked at her notes. "You based your opinions on materials provided by NovaTech's counsel, correct?"

"I reviewed those materials, yes, as well as technical documentation and public information."

"You didn't personally inspect the source code of Titan's product, did you?" Whittaker's tome was sharper now, though her demeanor hadn't changed.

"I reviewed code excerpts and technical documents, but not the entire source code."

"So your opinion is based on what NovaTech's team and their lawyers gave you, not on an independent inspection?"

Dr. Lin remained calm. "On the materials provided, yes."

A juror in the second row, pen poised, glanced up at this.

"Let's look at Claim 1 again." Marla gestured to the screen. "You agree that for infringement to occur, every single element of the claim must be present in the accused product?"

"Yes, that's my understanding," confirmed Dr. Lin.

"Now, you testified about 'dynamic scalability,' the system's ability to automatically adjust resources. That's not a new idea in computer science, is it?"

"The general concept is not new, but—" Dr. Lin began.

Marla cut in. "Cloud platforms have offered autoscaling for years, haven't they?"

"They have, but the specific application—" Again, his response was cut off.

"So, Titan's use of autoscaling isn't, by itself, evidence of infringing NovaTech's patent, is it?"

Dr. Lin remained unfazed. "Not by itself, no."

"And you'd agree that Titan's product uses open-source libraries, just as NovaTech's does?"

"Yes, that's common in the industry."

"So, using the same libraries doesn't mean Titan infringed NovaTech's patent, correct?"

"Correct."

Marla moved on. "Let's talk about configuration. Titan's product, as you understand it, requires an administrator to set scaling parameters, right?"

"There are configuration options, yes."

"So, if an administrator has to manually configure scaling, that's different from a system that automatically provisions resources, isn't it?"

Dr. Lin looked directly at Marla. "It depends on the implementation, but yes, manual configuration is different from fully automatic scaling."

Derek Foster, seated in the front row, underlined the distinction between *manual* and *automatic* in his notes.

"You didn't perform any independent tests to verify how Titan's product handles varying loads, did you?"

"No," said Dr. Lin. "I relied on the documentation and test results provided."

"So your opinion is a paper analysis, not based on hands-on testing?"

"It's true I did not do hands-on testing, but the paper analysis, as you've called it, was quite extensive. During the pilot, detailed logs documented the NovaTech system's response. I reviewed and compared similar logs provided by Titan concerning its product."

Marla nodded but didn't linger, her expression unreadable. "You're aware that the law requires damages to be apportioned only to the value created by the patented invention, not unpatented features?"

"Yes."

"And you didn't perform any analysis to separate the value of the transform layer from the rest of Titan's product, did you?"

"That wasn't my assignment."

"Let's return to the prior art." Marla turned a few pages in the binder in front of her. "You agree that dynamic scalability and transform layers were both known concepts before NovaTech's patent?"

"The general concepts, yes."

"So, combining known elements, dynamic scaling and a transform layer, could be seen as an obvious step to someone skilled in the art, couldn't it?"

"Not necessarily," said Dr. Lin. "But I believe that's for this court to decide."

Marla paused, then delivered her final line. "If you learned that Titan's product handled scaling differently than described in Claim 1, say, through manual configuration or a different algorithm, would that change your opinion?"

"If the implementation were materially different, yes, it could."

Marla nodded. "No further questions."

She returned to counsel table, leaving a faint tension in the air as the jury scribbled notes and exchanged glances.

———

Jordan stood and walked over to the lectern. His tone was calm, but purposeful.

"Dr. Lin, just a few questions."

Dr. Lin nodded, hands folded.

"Dr. Lin, you were asked about the general concept of autoscaling and transform layers being known in the industry. In your expert opinion, what makes NovaTech's patented approach different from what came before?"

Dr. Lin turned slightly toward the jury. "What's unique is how NovaTech's system combines real-time monitoring of data characteristics with dynamic, automated scaling, specifically within the transform layer. It's not just that the system can scale, but that it does so in direct response to unpredictable, real-world telemetry spikes, and does it automatically, without manual intervention. The architecture and the sequence of operations are what set it apart."

Jordan nodded. "You were also asked whether you performed hands-on testing of Titan's product. Did you have access to Titan's full source code or the ability to run independent tests?"

Dr. Lin shook his head. "No, I did not. My analysis was based on the technical documentation, logs, and materials provided in discovery, which is standard in these cases when the accused product is proprietary."

"Based on all the materials you reviewed, did you see any evidence that Titan's system handled scaling in a fundamentally different way than what's described in Claim 1?"

"No. As I said, the evidence showed Titan's system dynamically allocates and deallocates resources in response to telemetry spikes, just as the patent claims. If there were a fundamental difference, I would have noted it."

Jordan paused, letting the jury absorb this. "Finally, Dr. Lin, in your expert opinion, does the combination of features in NovaTech's patent: real-time monitoring, dynamic resource allocation, and automated scaling within the transform layer, represent a non-obvious advance over the prior art?"

Dr. Lin's reply was steady. "Yes, it does. The specific way these elements are combined and implemented is not found in the prior art. It's a novel and valuable contribution."

Jordan smiled slightly. "Thank you, Dr. Lin. No further questions."

As Jordan returned to his seat, Foster underlined *novel* in his notes, while Jenna Price exchanged a brief, thoughtful glance with Carla Ramirez.

Judge Price looked to the defense. "Any recross?"

Marla shook her head. "No, your Honor."

Judge Price nodded. "Thank you, Dr. Lin. You may step down."

She surveyed the counsel tables and the jury box. Her voice was clear and even.

"Ladies and gentlemen, we'll recess for the day. Please remember: do not discuss the case with anyone, not even with each other, nor conduct any research or read about the case in any form, including online or on social media. We'll reconvene at 1:00 p.m. tomorrow as I have a criminal calendar in the morning. Court is adjourned."

As the courtroom emptied, Jordan gathered his files and caught up with Maya, Alex, and Ethan in the hallway.

"You all did great today," he said, his voice low but steady. "Go get dinner. Get some sleep. We need everyone sharp tomorrow."

Maya nodded, exhaustion and adrenaline warring in her chest. "You're not joining us?"

Jordan shook his head. "I have to meet with Marla and the judge about some jury instruction questions. I'll catch up with you in the morning."

Alex managed a tired smile. "Don't let them wear you down."

"I won't," Jordan said. "But I want you all rested. Tomorrow's going to be a big day."

They parted ways at the courthouse steps, the city lights flickering on as the team headed into the night.

# Fourteen

**Tech Ledger | Sofia Martinez**
**Trial Brief: The Quiet Part Out Loud**

Yesterday's session wrapped with NovaTech's expert mapping of Titan's architecture, down to its "breathing" transform layer, against the patent claims. But today, the real inflection point arrives: Titan's internal emails, which we reported on a few weeks ago, are likely to go before the jury.

What's at stake? The emails show Titan's product strategy team not just benchmarking NovaTech's pilot, but actively mapping NovaTech's failure modes, stress curves, and even "breath policy" into their own stack. Such explicit references to NovaTech's design choices, especially under NDA, might be enough to convince the jury that Titan's so-called parallel development was really calculated appropriation.

For the technically inclined: watch for language about dynamic resource allocation, topology-preserving transforms, and the infamous "mirror their flow" directive. This internal correspondence could expose Titan to willful infringement and injunctive relief.

The industry is watching. If NovaTech can tie Titan's internal strategy to the code running in production, it's not just a win for one startup. It's a warning shot across the bow for every Goliath in the Valley.

Court resumes at 1:00 p.m. We will be watching.

THE COMFORT INN breakfast nook was quiet except for the faint hum of the mini-fridge and the tap of Ethan's fingers on his laptop. Maya sat at the small table, coffee cooling beside her, eyes fixed on her phone as she reread Sofia Martinez's Tech Ledger piece.

Alex hovered nearby, arms folded, watching the city wake up. "She's right," he said quietly. "Today's the day everything changes."

Ethan didn't look up. "Or the day we find out nothing ever does."

Maya forced a smile. "We've done the work. Jordan's ready. We're ready." She glanced at the clock—still hours until court. "Let's go over the timeline one more time. If the jury sees the pattern, they'll see the truth."

Alex nodded, but his jaw tightened. "I just hope the truth is enough."

Ethan closed his laptop, finally meeting Maya's gaze. "If it isn't, at least we'll know we didn't let them erase us quietly."

Jordan came down the stairs and joined the group, looking tired but focused. "Morning. Eat something. Hydrate. Today's going to be a long one." He set his briefcase down and pulled out a stack of notes.

"Remember this isn't about surprise," he said. "It's about foundation. Clean, simple, unassailable."

Maya nodded, fingers resting on one of Jordan's binders like it was a living thing.

Jordan tapped the binder. "Custodian first: authentication, business-records certification, hash verifications. Then provenance: Titan's legal hold, chain of custody, audit logs. Only after the jury sees the spine do they see the pages."

"And Richard?" Maya asked.

Jordan's mouth thinned into a line you could balance a coin on. "He'll explain, then he'll rationalize, then he'll remember he's under oath. We'll take him to the emails last, when the room is already with us."

Alex's palm hovered over the table, trembled, then landed. "You really think the words will be enough?"

"I don't," Jordan said. "I think the choices will be."

————

Across town, at the Centennial Hotel, Richard Hale stood at the window of the function room now serving as Titan's war room. His suit jacket draped over a chair; he stared down at the manicured lawn in front of the Victorian-style building. Marla Whittaker sat at a table, laptop open, scrolling through the Tech Ledger article with a frown.

"They're framing it as a turning point," she said, nodding at the screen. "If those emails come in, we're not just defending code. We're defending intent."

Richard's jaw tightened. "We stick to the story. Independent development. Industry best practices. No one admits to anything."

Marla looked up. "The chain of custody is clean. The custodian will authenticate the emails. After that, it's about context. We make it clear: benchmarking isn't theft. Parallel development isn't copying."

Claire Donovan poured herself a cup of coffee, her hands steady but her eyes shadowed. She hesitated, then said quietly, "But if they ask about 'mirror their flow'—"

Richard cut her off. "We don't give them more than they already have. We answer what's asked. Nothing more."

A silence settled over the room. Marla closed her laptop. "We'll be ready."

Richard straightened his tie, glancing at his reflection in the window. "We have to be."

————

When the NovaTech team arrived, the courthouse felt different. As if the walls themselves were bracing for what was to come. The usual bustle was muted as even the security guards seemed to speak in softer tones. Everyone sensed that something was about to break open; a secret ready to detonate, a truth that could change everything.

They spent the lunch hour huddled in a small anteroom behind the attorneys' lounge. The lounge was a throwback to a time before WiFi access and outlets overflowing with phone chargers. Paneled in walnut it smelled faintly of old leather, aged wood furniture, and well-worn books. The carpet had learned to swallow footsteps, and the only sound was the distant echo of voices from the main corridor and the occasional rattle of rain against the window.

Jamie sat at the far end of the table, sleeves rolled, a legal pad angled under the harsh fluorescent glare. No code, no screens. Just graphite and guilt. He looked smaller than usual, his shoulders hunched, the lines of exhaustion and regret etched deep in his face. Every so often, he glanced at the door, as if half-expecting someone to call him away.

He looked over at Maya. "Thanks for letting me help."

Maya was by the window, arms folded, watching rain stripe the glass in perfect diagonals. Her tone was steady, surgical. "This helps the case," she said. "It doesn't reset trust."

Jamie didn't flinch. "I know." His pencil moved on the pad, tracing Titan's mimicry like a confession in diagrams. Each arrow a scar, each box a breadcrumb tracing back to betrayal. He paused, staring at the page, then added another note; as if the act of drawing could somehow make amends.

Alex sat nearby, flipping through a binder of exhibits, his foot tapping a nervous rhythm against the leg of his chair. Ethan hovered by the coffee machine, pouring himself a cup he wouldn't finish, eyes darting between Jamie and Maya. The tension in the room was palpable, but beneath it was a sense of shared purpose. A fragile unity forged in the crucible of the trial.

Jordan entered, closing the door quietly behind him. He set his briefcase on the table and surveyed the team. "We're up first after lunch. Custodian, then Richard, then Jamie, then Claire. The order matters.

The story matters. We're not just proving what happened, we're showing why it matters."

He looked at Jamie, then at Maya. "Everyone ready?"

Maya nodded, her gaze still on the rain. "We're ready."

For a moment, no one spoke. Only the rain and the soft scratch of Jamie's pencil filled the room. Outside, the city waited. Inside, the fuse was lit.

———

By 12:45, the NovaTech team had made its way into Judge Price's courtroom, the hush of the hallway giving way to the charged stillness of the gallery, the jury box, the judge's bench. Maya took her seat at counsel table, with Alex and Ethan settling in behind her in the gallery and Jordan organizing his notes for the coming examination.

At 1:00 p.m. sharp, Judge Price reclaimed her bench and had the jury brought in. She nodded to Jordan, "Counsel, bring your next witness."

"The plaintiff calls Steven Kwan," Jordan said, "Titan Corporation's records custodian."

A compact man in a charcoal suit made the long walk to the witness stand. He took the oath and adjusted his glasses with the care of someone who liked his world legible.

Jordan approached with the lightest of touches. "Mr. Kwan, what do you do at Titan?"

"I'm the Director of Information Governance. I oversee document retention and legal holds, and I certify records for litigation."

"Are you the custodian of Titan's email archives?"

"Yes."

"Did you receive a litigation hold related to NovaTech following Titan's receipt of a notice of infringement?"

"Yes."

"Did you collect and certify emails from Richard Hale and others pursuant to that hold?"

"Yes."

Jordan set a slim stack on the rail: certification, hash values, chain-of-custody log. "Are these true and correct copies of Titan business records kept in the ordinary course?"

"They are."

Marla Whitaker, Titan's counsel, rose. "Objection to Exhibit 74 on hearsay grounds and under Rule 403. Prejudicial effect outweighs probative value."

Judge Price glanced over her glasses. "Business-records exception applies; these are the defendant's own emails. As for 403, the fact that evidence is damaging does not make it unfair. Objection overruled."

The first tremor moved through the gallery. The jurors leaned almost imperceptibly forward, as if a tide had drawn their ankles.

Jordan nodded. "Mr. Kwan, please read the sender, recipient, date, and subject line of Exhibit 74."

Kwan cleared his throat. "From: Richard Hale. To: Product Strategy Thread. Date: March 3rd of last year. Subject: 'Cost vs. Control.'"

"Please read the first three lines of the body."

Kwan's voice was steady. "Why pay for what we can build? Keep them talking. Map what we need, then we cut bait."

A small, collective exhale swept the jury box, like a bird changing direction.

Jordan didn't move. He let the hush find its shape, then placed Exhibit 75 on the rail.

"Mr. Kwan, sender and date?"

"From: Richard Hale. Date: June 9th."

"And the first two sentences?"

"They're eager. Use it. Ask for stress curves and failure modes—call it diligence. Flip to internal once we have a path."

Marla stood. "Objection, context. These are cherry-picked phrases."

Jordan looked at Judge Price. "The rest is in evidence, Your Honor. We'll publish the full thread to the jury."

"Objection noted. Overruled."

Jordan lifted a hand to the AV tech; the courtroom screens blinked awake. The full thread bloomed: timestamps, replies, the banal scaffolding of email around words that bore the moral density of lead. In a reply from a middle manager: *Legal's fine as long as we stay "indepen-*

*dent." Use public language.* In a follow-up from Richard: *We will. Keep the architect in the loop—mirror their flow. The trick is to look inevitable.*

No more gasps; just silence, vast and attentive.

Jordan walked them through authentication like a teacher in a lab: server logs, message-ID hashes, the archive map showing where the emails slept before the subpoena shook them awake. He asked Kwan whether anyone at Titan had flagged these emails as privileged. "No," Kwan said. "They were routed as business communications."

Jordan turned to the jury. "We publish Exhibits 74 through 81 in full." He looked back to Kwan. "Thank you."

"No further questions," he said, and sat.

Marla rose and tried to cauterize the wound. "Mr. Kwan, you're not here to interpret these emails, correct?"

"Correct."

"You're not here to tell this jury what Mr. Hale meant."

"Correct."

"You don't know whether these phrases referred to NovaTech at all."

Kwan blinked. "The threads include NovaTech's name in the subject line on a number of these."

Marla paused a fraction too long. "Nothing further."

————

"The plaintiff calls Richard Hale."

A murmur rustled the benches. Richard buttoned his jacket as if to armor himself, then took the stand. He swore in a voice that held.

Jordan approached with an expression that could have been politeness or could have been restraint. "Mr. Hale, you're Titan's Senior Vice President of Product Strategy."

"I am."

"Your team's responsibility includes partnerships with external technology companies."

"Yes."

"And decisions to pursue, or not pursue, those partnerships."

"Yes."

Jordan lifted Exhibit 74. "This is your email?"

"It appears to be."

"Your words: *Why pay for what we can build? Keep them talking. Map what we need, then we cut bait.* What did you mean?"

Richard didn't look at the screen. He looked at the jury. "We evaluate dozens of opportunities a quarter. 'Keep them talking' means maintain engagement while we assess fit. 'Map what we need' means map *our* requirements to either an internal solution or a viable partner. 'Cut bait' is a business colloquialism for ending discussions. It's not sinister. It's strategy."

Jordan considered him like a physicist listening to a magician. "And 'why pay for what we can build'?"

"Innovation often arises independently," Richard said smoothly. "If we can develop internally, that's responsible stewardship of shareholder capital."

Jordan nodded, as if the ground between them had finally leveled. "Let's find more ground." He displayed Exhibit 77: *Ask for stress curves and failure modes. Call it diligence.* He stepped closer. "Was that diligence?"

"It's diligence to understand whether a solution can scale."

"And *flip to internal once we have a path*," Jordan read. "Internal what?"

"Internal roadmap."

"To build what?"

"Capabilities in the same general problem space," Richard said. "We never used NovaTech's proprietary materials. Our path was independent."

Jordan let the claim hang there, fragile and exposed, like a chandelier. "Exhibit 79," he said, and the screen obeyed. *"Cut them off before Q3. If we miss, we miss. We can't license what we'll own."*

Richard's jaw flexed. "That's about timing and market windows."

"And the line, *'We can't license what we'll own'*?"

"We believed our internal approach would be distinct."

Jordan held his gaze. "You believed it, or you wrote it?"

"Both."

"Let's see the rest," Jordan said softly, as if to himself, and the next email filled the screen: a response from a product lead: *Mirror their flow. The trick is to look inevitable.*

"Did you instruct your team to 'mirror' NovaTech's architecture?" Jordan asked.

"No," Richard said. "I told them to benchmark."

"Benchmarking uses publicly available data," Jordan said. "These threads reference NDA materials: *failure modes, stress curves, degradations at scale.*"

Richard's smile had shifted into one that seemed to polish itself behind closed doors. "We asked questions to test claims. That's what diligence is."

"Diligence ends when you end discussions," Jordan said. "You ended discussions. Then you launched."

Marla was on her feet. "Argumentative."

"Sustained," Judge Price said. "Counsel, move on."

Jordan didn't look away from Richard. "Of course." He lowered his voice. "Mr. Hale, do you recognize Exhibit 81?"

Richard glanced, and in that glance something flickered. "Yes."

"Please read the highlighted portion."

Richard wet his lip. "We're at ninety percent parity on structure. Delta left is smoothing heuristics and the transform layer under spike conditions. Borrow if you must. Just don't get caught using their language."

A sound rippled through the courtroom, neither a gasp nor word. The jurors sat very still, the way people do when they are memorizing.

Richard tried to smile but realized the tool he intended had fractured. "That came from an overzealous subordinate. Not my direction."

Jordan's tone didn't change. "The 'overzealous subordinate' wrote, *'Per RH guidance.'* Are you RH?"

Richard's eyes flicked to Marla, to the jurors, back to Jordan as if searching for a kinder sky. "The phrase 'per RH guidance' is aspirational shorthand. People invoke leadership names to legitimize their own interpretations."

"Do you disavow the guidance?"

"I disavow any instruction to 'borrow.'"

"Do you disavow 'just don't get caught'?"

Marla stood once more. "Objection, argumentative."

"Overruled. Answer the question."

Richard's voice thinned. "I would not use that language."

"But your team did," Jordan said. "In an email produced by your company, kept in the ordinary course, authenticated by your custodian, sent during the exact window when you were 'keeping them talking.'"

Richard's hands folded, unfolded. "We built independently."

"Parallel evolution," Jordan said. "Inevitable paths."

"Yes."

Jordan let the word sit between them until it cooled. Then he turned to the jury. "No further questions."

Marla stood slowly, as if the air had thickened.

"Mr. Hale," Marla said, "did you ever direct anyone to copy NovaTech's proprietary materials?"

"No."

"Did Titan's engineers use open-source libraries and public research?"

"Yes."

"Is it common in your industry to arrive at similar solutions?"

"Yes."

"No further questions."

She sat. The line had been drawn: common tools, common paths, an industry of echoes where nothing was ever exactly stolen because everything was always already there.

———

Judge Price looked at Jordan. "Mr. Reyes?"

"Plaintiff calls Jamie Tran."

Jamie walked slowly to the stand, shoulders hunched, eyes fixed on the floor.

"Please state your name and your role at NovaTech," began Jordan.

"My name is Jamie Tran. I was a software engineer at NovaTech. I worked on the integration and documentation pipelines for the telemetry project."

"Jamie, I know this is difficult. Why are you here today?"

Jamie looked at the jury, his voice quiet. "Because I made mistakes. I want to tell the truth about what happened. About what I did, and why."

"Let's start at the beginning." Jordan's voice was consoling. "Did you have access to sensitive technical materials at NovaTech?"

"Yes. As part of my job, I had access to the documentation bucket, source code repositories, and internal test results. I helped prepare materials for the Titan pilot and for other potential partners."

"During the period when NovaTech was running its pilot with Titan, did you access or share any materials outside the company?"

Jamie hesitated, then nodded. "Yes. I did. Titan's people reached out to me. At first, it was just questions about integration, things that seemed routine. But then they started asking for more: specific test results, architecture diagrams, even internal notes about how we handled failure modes."

"Did you provide those materials?" Jordan's voice remained calm.

"I did. I sent them documentation and technical details that were supposed to be confidential. I tried to hide it; masked the access as health checks and used a dormant service account. I knew it was wrong, but I did it anyway."

"Why?" Jordan asked.

Jamie's voice finally cracked. "My daughter was sick. We were fighting with insurance, and the bills were piling up. Someone from Titan said they could 'help.' That if I sent what they needed, they'd make sure the hospital got paid. I told myself it was just one time, just a few files. But it kept going. Every time Titan asked for more, I sent it. I thought I could fix it before anyone noticed. I thought I could keep my job and save my family."

"Did anyone at NovaTech know what you were doing?"

"No. I hid it from everyone. Ethan, Alex, Maya. I lied to people I cared about. I'm sorry."

For a moment, no one moved. The weight of Jamie's confession seemed to settle over the room and Jordan waited a beat before resuming.

"Let's talk about what you sent. Did you provide Titan with information that went beyond what was shared under NDA?"

Jamie steadied himself. "Yes. I sent them internal architecture diagrams, stress test results, and notes about how our transform layer handled data spikes. I also sent them sample code and configuration files. Things that weren't part of the official pilot materials."

"Did Titan ever ask you to use specific language or avoid leaving a trail?"

"Yes. They told me to avoid using NovaTech's terminology, to 'mirror the flow, not the nouns.' They wanted to replicate our system without making it obvious. They said, 'Just don't get caught using their language.'"

"Did you see any of the features or terminology you shared appear in Titan's product?" asked Jordan.

"Yes.' Jamie nodded. "When Titan launched their platform, I recognized the architecture, the way the system handled failure, even some of the variable names. It was ours. Just dressed up in their colors."

"Jamie, why are you testifying today?"

Jamie looked at the jurors. "Because I want to make it right. I can't undo what I did, but I can tell the truth. NovaTech built something real. Titan took it, and I helped them. I'm sorry."

Jordan nodded. "No further questions."

A heavy silence lingered as Jamie lowered his gaze.

Marla was on her feet quickly. "Mr. Tran, you admit you violated NovaTech's trust and company policy?"

"Yes." Jamie's voice was flat.

"You acted alone, correct? No one at Titan forced you?"

"They pressured me," protested Jamie. "They offered help if I sent what they wanted. But I made the choice."

"You were not authorized to speak for NovaTech or to interpret the NDA?"

"No, I wasn't."

"No further questions." Marla sat as quickly as she had risen.

———

Judge Price looked at Jordan. "Next witness?"

Jordan's pause felt like a stone skipping once across a still pond. "The plaintiff calls Claire Donovan."

The room changed temperature. Marla's head snapped up. Richard went very still.

Claire walked from the back row to the stand the way a person walks over the last piece of ice in spring. She took the oath, hands steady. When she looked at Maya, it was not apology. It was acknowledgement.

Jordan approached with care. "Ms. Donovan, your role at Titan?"

"Senior Manager, Partnerships and Integrations."

"Were you part of the team evaluating a potential partnership with NovaTech?"

"Yes."

"Did you attend internal meetings about strategy for that evaluation?"

"Yes."

"Did you receive the emails we just showed the jury?"

"I was on most of those threads."

"Did the phrase 'keep them talking' refer to NovaTech?"

"Yes."

"What did 'map what we need' mean in those discussions?"

"Identify the elements of NovaTech's system we wanted in Titan's internal build."

Marla rose. "Objection. Calls for speculation."

"She was in the room," Jordan said. "Foundation laid."

"Overruled."

Jordan's voice flattened into steel. "Ms. Donovan, did Richard Hale direct the team to mirror NovaTech's architecture?"

Claire's eyes found Richard's. In them lived the first meeting, the handshake, the years of small silences that had turned into a wall. "He said we should benchmark aggressively. In practice, we took the flow NovaTech showed us and replicated it feature for feature."

Richard held her gaze. "That's not true."

Claire's expression didn't move. "It is."

"Did you ever object?" Jordan asked.

Claire inhaled like a diver before the plunge. "At first, I argued for partnership. Later, I stopped arguing."

"Why?"

Her voice didn't break. It just became more honest. "Because I liked my job," she said.

"Why are you testifying now?"

"Because I don't like who I am when I keep quiet."

You could feel the jury remember their own lives in that sentence, and the whole room seemed to tip an inch toward her.

Jordan slid one last exhibit onto the rail. "Ms. Donovan, do you recognize this meeting note from your account?"

"Yes."

"Please read the section titled 'Action Items.'"

Claire read. "*RH: Mirror flow; change terminology; avoid doc trails in chat. CD: Prep asks to Nova—stress curves, failure, call diligence.*"

"Who is 'RH'?" Jordan asked.

"Richard Hale."

"And 'CD'?"

"Me."

"Thank you," Jordan said. "No further questions."

Marla stood, gathered, tried to make a floor where there was none. "Ms. Donovan, you've been advised that Titan is considering downsizing and that you position is one that may be eliminated, correct?"

"Yes."

"You leaked internal materials to the press."

"I provided documents to a reporter," Claire said evenly. "The court has them now because Titan produced them in discovery."

"You're angry."

"I'm accountable," Claire said. "There's a difference."

Marla looked at the jury and found no purchase. "No further questions."

Judge Price glanced at the clock, then at the jury. "We'll take twenty minutes. Please be back by the top of the hour."

# Fifteen

When Judge Price called the recess, no one moved at first. The jurors were slow to stand, as if disentangling themselves from a long, taut cord. A few exchanged glances, as if searching for the right words to carry with them out of the room.

In NovaTech's row, Jordan exhaled for the first time in an hour. Maya sat with her hands folded so tightly her knuckles showed white, then released them and felt blood rush home. Alex stared at the blank screen on the far wall where the last email had burned out and left a ghost. Ethan closed his eyes and saw a server room at 2:13 a.m., frost in his lungs.

Across the aisle, Richard stared at a point just past the jury box, a man rehearsing explanations for a mirror that finally reflected. Marla touched his sleeve, not unkindly, and he didn't seem to feel it.

Claire didn't look at anyone until she reached the hallway. Then she looked at Maya. No nod, no ceremony; just a moment of recognition between people who had stood in the same weather on opposite shores.

———

The hallway swelled with voices like a pipe organ warming. Microphones bloomed anew. Cameras found faces.

Sofia Martinez stood to one side, phone in hand, choosing which words to send into the world with the knowledge that words could tilt a day. She watched Claire walk past without stopping and typed four lines that added no heat and carried all the light they needed.

*In court today:*
*Emails authenticated.*
*Directive language read aloud.*
*Insider confirms context.*

Jordan shepherded the team toward the elevator bay. "We'll get a limiting instruction on any arguments about privilege," he said, more to keep everyone thinking linearly than because anyone had asked.

Maya moved with him, and for the first time in months her stride matched his. "Do we have enough?" she asked.

"We have enough to survive a motion," Jordan said. "We have enough to make a jury's silence feel like assent."

"And to win?"

He didn't answer. The doors opened. Inside the elevator, the four faced the mirrored panel and briefly saw themselves as a single, strange new organism that had learned to move together: the lawyer, the builder, the sentinel, the witness they hadn't known they needed.

---

### TECH LEDGER | SOFIA MARTINEZ
#### Language on Fire

Most trials hinge on interpretation; some hinge on phrasing. Today, jurors read Titan emails that said the quiet part out loud: "Why pay for what we can build?" Defense counsel called it shorthand; the room heard intent.

The witness who authenticated the thread, an insider turned truth-teller, didn't look like a revolution. That's how revolutions arrive.

"Copying in tech rarely looks like a heist," one expert told me last year. "It looks like confidence plus access." The jury now has both on paper.

NovaTech still has its damages expert left to testify and Titan will counter with technologists that return us to claim charts and constructions. But you can't un-read a sentence once it lands. Words linger. So do silences.

The courthouse lights cast an unfamiliar gold across the damp sidewalk. Maya sat on a bench outside and let the cold work on her.

Alex lowered himself beside her, careful with his breath. "That felt like something," he said.

"It was," she said.

Ethan stood a little apart, phone in hand, watching the server logs remotely because habit felt like prayer. Jordan returned with coffee he didn't seem to taste and news he didn't rush to share.

"They want to talk," he said, and for a heartbeat everyone's body remembered sleep.

"About settlement?" Maya asked.

"About the terms of a conversation about settlement," Jordan said. He sat, set the cups between them. "We'll hear them. Then we'll decide whether justice feels like a check or a verdict."

Maya nodded, eyes on the courthouse door. Inside, the exhibits were sleeping, the transcripts were cooling, the day was writing itself down.

"Whatever we decide," she said, "we do it awake."

Jordan smiled, small and not unkind. "Awake is how we got here."

They didn't toast. They didn't hug. They sat for another minute in a quiet that wasn't triumph and wasn't defeat. Then Jordan herded them toward the courthouse door. It closed behind them, leaving the quiet outside, waiting for whatever came next.

# Sixteen

Judge Price nodded to Jordan. "Your next witness?"

Jordan stood. "Plaintiff calls Dr. Eleanor Vance."

Dr. Vance made her way to the stand and took the oath, voice steady.

Jordan approached. "Dr. Vance, please state your name and professional occupation for the court."

"My name is Eleanor Vance. I am a principal economist specializing in software and data processing systems."

"Where are you currently employed, and what is your role?"

"I'm with Insight Analytics, where I lead the technology valuation practice."

"Could you describe your educational background?"

Dr. Vance looked at the jurors. "I hold a Ph.D. in Computer Science from Stanford University, with a focus on distributed systems and software economics. I also have a master's in applied mathematics."

"Do you hold any professional certifications relevant to software economics, patent damages, or data processing systems?"

"Yes. I am a Certified Licensing Professional, a member of the American Intellectual Property Law Association, and a member of the

Licensing Executives Society, where I am a past chair of the technology transfer committee."

"Have you published articles or papers in these fields?" Jordan asked.

"Yes. I have published over twenty peer-reviewed articles on software valuation, patent damages, and economic modeling for data systems. One of those papers was cited by the Federal Circuit recently in connection with a methodology for computing patent damages."

"Have you previously testified as an expert witness in patent litigation?"

"Yes, I've testified in about two dozen patent cases for both patent owners and accused infringers."

Jordan turned to Judge Price. "Your Honor, we move to qualify Dr. Vance as an expert in patent damages related to software and data processing systems."

Judge Price nodded. "Dr. Vance is so qualified. Proceed."

"Dr. Vance, were you engaged by NovaTech's counsel to perform a damages analysis in this case?"

"Yes."

"What specific task were you asked to perform?"

"I was asked to calculate the damages suffered by NovaTech as a result of Titan's alleged infringement of NovaTech's patent concerning a novel transform layer within a telemetry processing system."

"What materials did you review in preparing your analysis?"

"I reviewed financial data, technical specifications of Titan's accused product, marketing materials, and the expert infringement report of Dr. Lin." Dr. Vance shifted in her seat. "I also found and studied copies of licensing agreements concerning other telemetry systems, although those were between different companies."

"How did you locate those other licensing agreements?" Jordan queried.

"I found them as attachments to publicly available SEC filings of Synapse Telemetry, a software vendor. They date from a few years ago, but as they were related to the field and involved a competitor of Titan, I considered them to be somewhat relevant to my analysis. In particular, the licenses related to a telemetry processing system that relied on manual calibration of processing resources."

"Did you rely on any specific data, facts, or methodologies standard in your field?"

"Yes. I applied the hypothetical negotiation framework as of the date of first infringement, using standard economic principles and reliable data to determine a reasonable royalty rate and base."

"Are these methods generally accepted in your field?"

"They are."

Jordan paused. "Before discussing your financial analysis, can you briefly explain the patented invention as you understand it?"

Dr. Vance took a sip of water. "The patent covers a novel transform layer within a telemetry processing system. Its key innovation is dynamic scalability: automatically adjusting processing capacity to handle varying data loads, optimizing resource use and performance."

"How does dynamic scalability provide value?"

"It allows the system to automatically scale up during peak loads and scale down during low activity, preventing bottlenecks and reducing costs. A significant improvement over static systems, such as the one for which I reviewed the prior licensing agreements."

"Did you consider Dr. Lin's findings that Titan's product practices the claimed invention?"

Dr. Vance replied. "Yes. I relied on Dr. Lin's conclusion that Titan's architecture, especially its data handling and scaling modules, implements the claimed dynamic scalability feature."

"Based on your analysis, have you formed an opinion on the damages NovaTech is entitled to?"

"I have."

"What is that total damages figure?"

"$131.2 million."

Jordan remained calm. "Could you walk us through how you arrived at this figure?"

"I calculated damages based on a reasonable royalty: a rate that a willing licensor and licensee would have agreed to in a hypothetical negotiation at the time infringement began. I considered relevant factors including the royalty rates specified in the prior licenses I mentioned, the utility and advantages offered by the invention, the relative positions of NovaTech and Titan, both with respect to one another and in the industry at large, and the extent to which Titan would have benefitted from the invention. I also assumed this would be a non-exclusive license, as over time NovaTech would likely have sought to commercialize its technology in other respects."

"How did you determine the appropriate royalty base?" Jordan asked.

"I identified the smallest saleable infringing component, the Telemetry Processing Module, as the royalty base. I detail this in my report."

"Why use this module's revenue rather than a total telemetry processing system product's revenue?"

Dr. Vance's voice took on a professorial tone. "To ensure proper apportionment between patented and unpatented features. The patented transform layer drives a significant portion of demand for this module and, ultimately for the overall system. However, other aspects of the system are not covered by the patent and therefore are not appropriate to include in my calculations."

"How did you determine a reasonable royalty rate?" Jordan continued.

"As I said, I analyzed comparable licenses in the industry for similar technologies and patents. I also used my experience with negotiating other licenses in this field and arrived at a rate of 8% of the royalty base."

"Did you analyze how the patented feature impacts Titan's cost savings and performance?"

"Yes," said Dr. Vance. "The dynamic scalability feature is responsible for substantial cost savings and performance improvements, justifying the proposed royalty rate."

"In summary, what is your final opinion on the total reasonable royalty damages owed to NovaTech by Titan?"

"$131.2 million."

"Do you believe your calculation provides fair and adequate compensation for Titan's unauthorized use?"

"I do."

"Thank you, Dr. Vance. No further questions." Jordan turned and returned to his seat.

———

Marla Whittaker rose, notes in hand, and approached the witness stand.

"Dr. Vance, you understand your role as an expert is to be objective and impartial, correct?"

"Yes."

"You're being compensated for your time in this case?"

"I am."

"Your opinions are based entirely on the information and assumptions provided to you by NovaTech's counsel, right?"

Dr. Vance studied Marla. "I reviewed the materials provided by counsel, along with public records and independent research."

"If any of the facts or data you relied upon were incorrect, your opinion could change?"

"That's correct."

Marla looked at the jury. "You understand that the law requires any damages award to be apportioned only to the value created by the patented invention itself, not unpatented features?"

"Yes," replied Dr Vance, her tone even.

"Let's talk about the patented technology. The patent-in-suit relates to a 'transform layer' within a broader telemetry processing system, correct?"

"That's my understanding, yes."

"A telemetry processing system has many other components besides this transform layer. Data ingestion, storage, visualization, and so on?" asked Marla.

"Yes."

"Those other components are not covered by the patent-in-suit?"

"As far as I know, they are not."

"Titan's product is a complex system that includes all these various components, not just the transform layer, isn't that right?" Marla again looked at the jury.

"Yes, that's right," replied Dr. Vance.

"Did you perform any analysis to separate the value generated by the patented transform layer from the value generated by the many other non-patented components?"

"As I said, I apportioned the royalty base to the smallest saleable unit, the Telemetry Processing Module. It incorporates the patented feature."

"But you would agree that customers purchase the accused product for its entire functionality, not just for the transform layer?"

Dr. Vance frowned slightly, reluctant to concede Marla's point entirely. "The transform layer is a key driver of demand for the module, but yes, customers consider the full system."

"The 'dynamic scalability' feature you cited is a general software engineering concept used in many non-infringing contexts, isn't that true?"

"Dynamic scalability is widely used, but the patented implementation remains novel."

"You did not, in your report, attribute a specific percentage of the final product's value to the dynamic scalability feature alone, did you?"

Dr. Vance remained unruffled. "I apportioned value based on the module, not a percentage of the entire product."

Marla shifted tactics. "Let's discuss alternatives. You're aware that damages must consider whether acceptable non-infringing alternatives were available at the time infringement began?"

"Yes."

"Is it your position that no acceptable non-infringing alternatives existed?"

Dr. Vance paused. "As I mentioned, Synapse Telemetry does provide a telemetry processing system, but it relies on manual calibration of processing resources. It lacks the specific transform layer that allows for automated, that is, dynamic, scaling provided by NovaTech's invention. So, while it is an alternative, I'm not convinced everyone in the industry would consider it to be an 'acceptable' one. Nevertheless, it did form part of my analysis."

Marla consulted her notebook. "Are you aware of the dynamic telemetry processor offered by Chorus? Isn't that an alternative system

available on the market at the time of the hypothetical license negotiation?"

"I am."

"Chorus' telemetry processor includes a scalability observability
pipeline that provides some dynamic scalability, albeit through a
different technical implementation, isn't that right?"

Dr. Vance answered easily, "Yes, but its performance and scalability
are not equivalent to the patented invention."

"Did you review the technical specifications for Chorus' telemetry
processor?"

"I did. I spent an afternoon with Dr. Lin going over the Chorus
system and he was able to point out several areas where it failed to adapt
to outliers as well as NovaTech's system. I believe he covered that in his
report."

Marla pressed on undeterred. "As the Chorus system was an available and acceptable substitute, NovaTech may not have been able to
command the 8% royalty rate you say is appropriate, would you agree?"

"If it were truly equivalent, that might be the case, but my analysis
found it was not."

"Another factor affecting your royalty rate calculation was the other
license agreements you mentioned?"

"Yes."

Marla leaned forward slightly, "None of those licenses involved the
exact patent-in-suit or a purely comparable technology, did they?"

"As I said, they involved similar technologies, but not the exact
patent claim."

"Those license agreements involved software technology covered by
several patents, not just one, correct?"

Dr. Vance nodded. "That's correct."

"You did not adjust the royalty rates from those portfolio licenses to
account for the fact that only one patent claim is at issue here?"

Dr. Vance shook her head. "Actually, I considered the scope of the
licenses and adjusted my analysis accordingly, but the rates reflect
industry practice."

Marla considered for a moment but said finally, "No further questions." She returned to her seat, and the courtroom settled into a hush

as the jury absorbed the exchange. Dr. Vance simply waited on the stand, her gaze steady.

———

Judge Price looked at Jordan. "Any redirect, Mr. Reyes?"

Jordan shook his head. "No, Your Honor."

Dr. Vance gathered her notes and stepped down from the witness stand, her testimony complete.

Judge Price turned to Jordan. "Anything else?"

Jordan stood. "The plaintiff rests, Your Honor."

Judge Price nodded and looked at the jury. "Court is recessed for the day. Please remember my instruction not to discuss the case. We'll resume tomorrow at 8:30 with the defense's case." With that, she left the bench.

The courtroom exhaled; a quiet, collective release. The jury filed out, and the NovaTech team lingered in silence, the day's battles settling into memory.

———

The rain had stopped, but the air outside was still heavy. Jordan arrived last, his suit rumpled and carrying a folder. Maya, Alex, and Ethan were gathered around the small table in the breakfast nook, the remains of takeout scattered between them.

Jordan set the coffee down and slid into a chair. For a moment, no one spoke.

Alex broke the silence. "That was a day."

Ethan nodded, rubbing his eyes. "I keep replaying Dr. Vance's testimony. I think the jury was with her."

Maya's voice was quiet but steady. "They listened. That's all we can ask for now."

Jordan glanced at the folder. "I met with Marla to go over Titan's settlement offer. She says they're 'open to creative solutions.'"

Alex leaned forward. "Is it real, or just a tactic?"

Jordan shrugged. "Either... Or both, though not what we asked for.

They're willing to drop the IPRs and pay something, but nowhere near $130 million. More like $10 million. They're betting we'll blink before the verdict."

"Would you take it?" Ethan asked.

Jordan looked at Maya. "It's not my call."

Maya considered. "We came this far for a reason. If we settle, it's because it's right for NovaTech. Not because we're tired."

Alex looked over. "I want to win. But I want to survive, too."

Jordan smiled, tired but genuine. "You should talk to your board and run the numbers. But tonight, we rest."

Ethan raised his cup. "To tomorrow."

Maya nodded. "To whatever comes next."

They sat together in the quiet, the day's battles settling into memory. For the first time in weeks, the silence felt earned.

# SEVENTEEN

DINNER HAD BEEN SERVED on white linen. Grilled salmon, roasted vegetables, and small, elegant desserts. The clink of silverware had faded, replaced by the low murmur of conversation and the occasional scrape of a chair. Marjorie Thorne, Titan's General Counsel, sat at the head of the table, her posture composed, a cup of espresso in front of her.

Marla Whittaker entered, closing the door behind her. Richard Hale looked up from his plate, his expression tight. Two junior lawyers, one in a Titan polo, the other in a crisp dress shirt, sat further down, quietly reviewing annotated printouts of the day's exhibits between bites.

Marjorie set her fork down. "Well?"

Marla set her bag down. "I spoke with Jordan. He listened, but he didn't commit to anything. He said they'd talk to their board."

Richard's jaw flexed. "So they're feeling good."

Marla nodded. "They have every reason to. Their expert was solid, and the jury was with them. They know it."

One of the junior attorneys asked in a low voice, "If they think they're winning, why even talk settlement?"

Marjorie answered, her tone measured. "Because even a strong case can go sideways with a jury."

"What's their number?" asked Richard, pushing his plate away.

"They want the moon. One hundred thirty million. Our offer didn't move them."

"We're not going higher," Marjorie said. "Not unless the board tells us to."

The other junior lawyer looked up. "So what do we do tomorrow?"

"We put on our case. Show the jury we built this system ourselves. The engineers testify, then our experts. We keep it clean and focused. No drama, just facts."

"And if the jury doesn't buy it?" Richard asked from his seat.

"Then we're ready for appeal," interjected Marla. "But we're not conceding anything tonight."

A silence settled. Rain tapped the window. The city outside felt far away.

Marla gathered her notes. "Get some rest. Tomorrow, we show them Titan doesn't fold."

The team nodded, subdued but resolute. Marjorie lingered by the window, watching the reflections blur and reform, already thinking three moves ahead.

———

The morning greeted them with a cold mist, leaving the courthouse steps slick and shining. Lawyers clustered in small groups under the portico, clutching coffee and last-minute notes. Inside, there was a low hum of anticipation.

Marla paused just outside the courtroom doors, spotting Jordan at the end of the hall. She approached, her expression composed.

"Any reason to pause things?" Marla asked quietly.

Jordan shook his head. "None."

Marla nodded, lips pressed thin. "See you inside."

They entered the courtroom together, the jury already assembling, Judge Price's bench empty but expectant.

Moments later, Judge Price took her seat. "Ms. Whittaker, you may call your first witness."

———

"The defense calls Michael Chen."

A man in a navy suit, took the stand and was sworn in.

"Mr. Chen, what is your role at Titan?"

"I'm a senior software engineer. I've worked on the telemetry processing system since its inception."

"Did you participate in the design and development of the transform layer at issue in this case?" Marla asked.

"Yes. I was part of the architecture team."

"Did you or your team have access to any confidential NovaTech materials during development?"

"No," said Chen. "We used only internal documentation and open source libraries."

"Can you describe the process Titan used to develop the dynamic scalability feature?"

"We benchmarked several open source solutions and designed our own module to meet Titan's performance requirements. We did not use or reference NovaTech's proprietary information."

"Did anyone instruct you to copy NovaTech's technology?"

"No."

"Thank you, Mr. Chen. No further questions."

Jordan stood and walked to the lectern. "Good morning, Mr. Chen."

"Good morning."

"You testified you're a senior software engineer at Titan?"

"That's correct."

"And you worked on the architecture team for the telemetry processing system?"

"Yes."

"You told the jury you did not have access to NovaTech's confidential materials during development?"

"That's right," confirmed Chen.

Jordan leaned forward. "Let's talk about what you *did* have access to. You attended meetings where NovaTech's pilot results were discussed, correct?"

"I attended some meetings, yes."

"In those meetings, did you review performance metrics, stress curves, or failure modes provided by NovaTech?"

"I saw some summary data, but nothing proprietary."

"Nothing proprietary. Mr. Chen, are you familiar with the term 'breath policy'?"

"I've heard it," Chen replied noncommittal.

"Did Titan use that term before the NovaTech pilot?"

"I don't recall."

Jordan looked at the jury. "You don't recall. Let's look at Exhibit 79. An internal Titan email, dated during the pilot. The subject line is *NovaTech—Breath Policy*. You're copied on this thread, correct?"

"Yes."

"In this email, Titan's product lead writes: 'Their breath policy buys integrity at the cost of latency. Can we replicate this tradeoff in our stack?' Did you respond to this email?"

"I may have." Chen shifted in the witness chair.

"You did." Jordan clicked the reply on the screen. "You wrote: 'We can model their queue management and see if it holds under our load.' Is that correct?"

"That's what it says."

"So, you were tasked with modeling NovaTech's approach to queue management, as described in their pilot, yes?"

"We were benchmarking approaches." Chen voice faltered.

"Benchmarking. Did you use NovaTech's pilot data as a reference point?"

"We used public data and what was shared in meetings."

"What was shared in meetings, under NDA?"

Chen paused. "I believe so."

"Mr. Chen, you testified Titan's system was developed independently. But you were present for discussions about NovaTech's architecture, you received emails referencing their 'breath policy,' and you were asked to model their queue management. Is that all correct?"

"Yes," Chen said quietly.

"Did anyone at Titan ever instruct you not to use NovaTech's terminology in your code or documentation?"

"There was a suggestion to adopt internal language."

"A suggestion. In Exhibit 81, another email," Jordan displayed it, "the directive is: 'Mirror their flow. The trick is to look inevitable. Just don't get caught using their language.' You're copied here as well?"

"Yes." Chen's answer was hollow.

"Did you adhere to that directive?"

"We used our own terminology."

"But the architecture, the sequence of operations, the tradeoff between latency and integrity, those were modeled after NovaTech's pilot, weren't they?" Jordan pressed.

"We evaluated multiple approaches."

"Including NovaTech's?"

Chen looked down, his voice barely audible. "Yes."

Jordan let the answer hang for a moment, then nodded. "Thank you, Mr. Chen. No further questions."

Marla rose.

"Mr. Chen, just a few additional questions.

"You were asked about emails referencing NovaTech's 'breath policy.' When you received those emails, did you or your team copy NovaTech's code or proprietary algorithms?"

"No, we did not."

"When you say you 'modeled their queue management,' what does that mean in the context of your work at Titan?"

"We benchmarked different approaches, including public information and our own designs, to see what worked best for our system."

"Did you ever have access to NovaTech's source code or internal technical documentation?"

Chen looked directly at Jordan. "No, I did not."

"You were shown an email that said, 'Mirror their flow. The trick is to look inevitable. Just don't get caught using their language.' Did you interpret that as an instruction to copy NovaTech's invention?"

"No. I understood it as a reminder to use our own terminology and to make sure our work was original."

"As far as you know, was Titan's telemetry system the result of independent engineering?"

"Yes, it was." Chen's confidence had returned.

"Thank you, Mr. Chen. That will be all for now."

Chen left the stand, walking straight out of the courtroom without a backward glance.

———

Marla, perhaps sensing the need to bolster Titan's narrative through sheer repetition, called two more engineers, each a member of the team responsible for the telemetry processing system. Their testimony, though earnest, covered familiar ground: independent development, reliance on open source libraries, and categorical denials of ever using NovaTech's code or confidential materials.

On cross-examination, Jordan methodically walked each witness through similar sequences of emails, meeting notes, and technical overlaps that had unsettled Chen. The answers varied in phrasing but not in substance; each engineer insisted Titan's work was original, even as the documentary record suggested a more complicated truth. If Marla's strategy was to make the story of independence more believable by sheer volume, hoping the jury might finally accept it after hearing it enough times, from enough voices, then the effect was more numbing than clarifying. By the time the last engineer stepped down, the courtroom felt caught in a loop, the line between coincidence and coordination growing ever thinner.

With her "fact" witnesses exhausted and the jury's patience tested, Marla turned to her next, and most important, witness: Titan's technical expert, Carleton Nord.

Nord took the stand when called, settling into the witness chair with the calm assurance of someone who had spent years explaining complex systems to skeptical audiences. Marla approached, a fresh stack of exhibits in hand.

"Dr. Nord, would you please state your name and professional background for the record?"

"Certainly. My name is Carleton Nord. I'm a principal systems architect at Helix Consulting, where I specialize in distributed computing and scalable data infrastructure. I hold a Ph.D. in Computer Science from MIT, with a focus on real-time data processing. Over the past twenty years, I've designed telemetry and analytics platforms for several Fortune 500 companies, published more than thirty peer-reviewed articles, and served as a technical advisor on multiple industry standards committees. I've also testified as an expert in a number of patent cases involving cloud architecture and data pipelines."

Marla nodded. "Have you had the opportunity to review the patent at issue in this case, as well as the technical documentation for both NovaTech's and Titan's telemetry systems?"

"I have. I've reviewed the patent, its prosecution history, the parties' technical documentation, source code excerpts, and the expert reports submitted by both sides, including Dr. Lin's."

"Your Honor, we move to qualify Dr. Nord as an expert in distributed systems and scalable telemetry architecture."

Judge Price nodded. "So qualified."

Marla turned back to Nord. "Dr. Nord, can you briefly describe for the jury what Titan's telemetry processing system does, and how it handles dynamic scalability?"

"Of course. Titan's system is designed to ingest, process, and analyze large volumes of telemetry data from a variety of sources. Industrial sensors, medical devices, logistics networks, and so on. The architecture is modular: data is ingested, normalized, transformed, and routed to downstream analytics. For scalability, Titan's system uses a combination of open-source orchestration tools and proprietary scheduling algorithms. The system can scale up or down in response to load, but the scaling is governed by administrator-defined policies, not by the kind of real-time, fully automated feedback loop described in the patent."

Marla nodded. "Dr. Lin testified that Titan's system 'breathes' in the same way as NovaTech's patented transform layer. Do you agree?"

"No, I do not. While both systems can scale, the mechanisms are fundamentally different. NovaTech's patent claims a transform layer that automatically and continuously monitors queue lengths, CPU, and other metrics, and then triggers resource allocation in real time, without manual intervention. Titan's system, by contrast, uses scheduled scaling and threshold-based alerts. An administrator sets the parameters: when to add resources, when to scale back. There's no autonomous, self-tuning feedback loop at the transform layer."

Marla displayed a diagram. "Can you point out for the jury where Titan's system differs from what's claimed in the patent?"

Nord leaned forward. "Certainly. Here—" he indicated the transform module. "Titan's system uses a stateless microservice architecture, but the scaling logic is external. The transform layer itself does not make scaling decisions. Instead, a separate orchestration layer, configured by the operations team, manages resource allocation based on pre-set schedules and batch analytics. The patent requires the transform layer to dynamically determine and allocate resources in direct response to monitored characteristics. Titan's does not."

Marla deliberately turned a page in her notes, drawing the jury's attention. "Dr. Lin also testified that Titan's system uses the same 'breath policy' and queue management as NovaTech. What's your view?"

Nord shook his head. "The term 'breath policy' is not used in Titan's code or documentation. While both systems address queue management and latency, Titan's approach is conventional: it uses standard queue backpressure and circuit breaker patterns, widely available in open-source libraries. There's no evidence Titan implemented the specific feedback-driven scaling described in the patent."

"Did you find any evidence that Titan's engineers copied NovaTech's code or proprietary algorithms?"

"None whatsoever. I reviewed the codebase and the development history. Titan's system was built using open-source components and internal design documents that predate the NovaTech pilot. The similarities are what you'd expect from two teams solving the same technical problem with industry-standard tools."

"In your expert opinion, does Titan's telemetry processing system infringe the asserted claims of NovaTech's patent?"

"No, it does not. The key claim elements: dynamic, autonomous scaling within the transform layer, are not present in Titan's system. The architecture, while superficially similar, is implemented in a fundamentally different way."

"Thank you, Dr. Nord. No further questions."

———

Jordan waited for Marla to retake her seat, collected a slim folder, and approached the lectern.

"Good morning, Dr. Nord."

"Good morning," Nord replied.

"You testified that Titan's system uses 'scheduled scaling' and 'administrator-defined policies,' correct?"

"That's right."

"But Titan's system does monitor queue lengths, CPU usage, and other performance metrics in real time, doesn't it?"

"It does monitor those metrics, yes."

"And when those metrics cross certain thresholds, the system can trigger the allocation of additional resources?"

"If the thresholds are set, yes."

Jordan leaned forward. "So, the system is capable of dynamically allocating resources in response to monitored characteristics, just as the patent describes?"

Nord looked at the jury. "The difference is that Titan's system requires those thresholds to be configured by an administrator."

Jordan pressed. "But once those thresholds are set, the system acts automatically, correct? No one has to manually approve each scaling event?"

"That's correct."

"So, if the patent claim describes a system that 'monitors characteristics' and 'dynamically allocates resources' when certain conditions are met, Titan's system does that, doesn't it?"

Nord searched for a gap in the argument. "In a general sense, yes, but the patent describes a more autonomous feedback loop."

"The patent doesn't require the system to invent its own thresholds, does it? It just requires that the system monitor, compare, and allocate resources dynamically."

Nord was a little less forceful. "That's one way to read it."

"And Titan's system, as you've described it, monitors, compares, and allocates resources dynamically, based on real-time data?"

Nord again tried to insert a wedge into the knot Jordan was tightening. "Yes, but only within the parameters set by the administrator."

Jordan moved to another item. "Let's talk about the transform layer. You said Titan's scaling logic is 'external.' But isn't it true that the transform layer is the component that receives the benefit of the scaling? That is, when more resources are allocated, it's the transform layer that processes more data?"

"The transform layer benefits, yes."

"So, from the perspective of the system's operation, the transform layer is dynamically scalable in response to monitored characteristics?"

Nord had to concede. "That is one characterization. It is not one that I would necessarily use."

"And you've told us that Titan's system, like NovaTech's, uses queue management and latency monitoring to decide when to scale?"

"It does."

"So, the main difference you're pointing to is where the scaling logic resides? In the transform layer or in an orchestration module?"

"That's correct."

Jordan now made it plain. "But the patent claim doesn't specify where the scaling logic must reside, does it? It just requires that the system monitor, compare, and allocate resources dynamically."

"That's a possible interpretation."

"So, if the jury finds that Titan's system meets all the functional requirements of the patent claim, monitoring, comparing, and dynamically allocating resources, then Titan's system would infringe, wouldn't it?"

"That would be for the jury to decide."

"Thank you, Dr. Nord. No further questions."

———

Marla stood, returning to the lectern with a measured calm.

"Dr. Nord, just a few clarifying questions.

"You were asked about Titan's system monitoring metrics and its dynamic resource allocation. In your expert opinion, is there a meaningful technical difference between a system that acts entirely autonomously and one requiring an administrator to set scaling parameters?"

Nord nodded. "Yes, there is. In Titan's system, the administrator defines both the thresholds and the scaling logic. The system neither makes those decisions autonomously nor adapts its own parameters in real time. That distinction is significant compared to what the patent describes."

"Does the patent require that an administrator be involved in setting those parameters?"

"The patent describes a system that continuously monitors and adapts without manual intervention. If an administrator has to set or adjust the thresholds, it's not fully autonomous as claimed."

Marla continued. "You were also asked about where the scaling logic resides. Why does that matter?"

Nord pointed at the earlier diagram. "The patent claims require the transform layer itself to perform the monitoring and scaling. In Titan's system, those functions are handled by an external orchestration layer, not by the transform layer. That's a key architectural difference."

"In your professional opinion, does Titan's system meet all the requirements of the asserted patent claims?"

"No, it does not."

"Thank you, Dr. Nord. No further questions."

With Dr. Nord's testimony complete and the technical battle lines clearly drawn, Marla turned next to the question of money.

———

"The defense calls Mr. Julian Croft."

A tall, composed figure in a tailored suit took the stand. After being sworn in, Croft settled his notes and looked toward the jury.

"Please state your name and professional background for the record."

"My name is Julian Croft. I am an intellectual property valuation specialist and managing director at Croft Analytics, a firm that focuses on economic analysis and damages assessment in technology and patent litigation. I hold a Master's degree in economics from the University of

Chicago and have spent over twenty years advising clients on IP valuation, licensing, and damages. I've testified as an expert in more than thirty patent cases, including several involving software and data processing systems."

"Have you reviewed the materials relevant to this case, including NovaTech's patent, the accused Titan product, and the damages report submitted by Dr. Vance?"

"Yes," Croft replied. "I have reviewed all of those materials, as well as Titan's financial records, industry licensing agreements, and the technical expert reports from both sides."

"What were you asked to do in this case?"

"I was asked to independently assess the appropriate measure of damages, if any, that would be owed by Titan in the event the jury finds infringement. My task was to determine a reasonable royalty, if one were owed, and to evaluate the methodology and conclusions of NovaTech's damages expert."

Marla leaned slightly. "Let's start with the basics. In your opinion, what is the correct approach to calculating damages in a case like this?"

Croft adjusted to face the jury. "The law requires that damages be no less than a reasonable royalty for the use of the patented invention. The goal is to determine what Titan and NovaTech would have agreed to in a hypothetical negotiation at the time of first alleged infringement, taking into account the value of the patented feature and the availability of alternatives."

"Do you agree with Dr. Vance's approach?"

"I did not. Dr. Vance used the revenue from Titan's entire Telemetry Processing Module as the royalty base and applied an 8% rate, resulting in a damages figure of $131.2 million. In my opinion, that significantly overstates the value attributable to the patented feature."

"Why is that?" Marla asked.

"The patented feature, a particular approach to dynamic scalability in the transform layer, is only one small part of a much larger, multifunctional product. Customers purchase Titan's system for a broad spectrum of features: security, analytics, integration, and reliability among them. Since the patented feature does not drive demand for the entire module, using the module's full revenue as the royalty base is inappropriate."

"What did you do differently?"

"I identified the smallest saleable unit that actually practices the patent, then apportioned value to the specific feature at issue. I also considered the availability of non-infringing alternatives: other telemetry systems on the market offering dynamic scaling through different means. Such competition would have limited NovaTech's bargaining power in any negotiation."

"What royalty rate did you find appropriate?"

"Based on comparable licenses in the industry, most of which are for single software features or small portfolios, the typical royalty rate is well below 1%. I selected a rate of 0.5%, which is consistent with industry practice for a single, non-core feature."

"And what did you use as the royalty base?"

"I used only the incremental revenue attributable to the patented feature, not the entire module. After apportionment, the royalty base is a small fraction of what Dr. Vance used."

"What is your total damages figure?"

Croft looked at his report. "If the jury finds infringement, the total reasonable royalty damages would be $4.6 million."

"Did you consider whether Titan could have used a non-infringing alternative?"

"Yes," said Croft. "In fact, that is one reason why the damages would be so low. There were several available alternatives at the time, including products from Chorus and Synapse Telemetry, which offer dynamic scaling through different technical means. Titan could have integrated one of these alternatives at minimal cost, limiting the value of the patented feature."

Marla summed up. "In your professional opinion, is Dr. Vance's $131.2 million figure reasonable?"

"No, it is not. It is vastly inflated and does not reflect the value of the patented feature in the context of the market or the product."

"Thank you, Mr. Croft. No further questions."

———

Jordan got to his feet, a single sheet of notes in hand.

"Good morning, Mr. Croft."

"Good morning," Croft said amiably.

"You testified that you're an intellectual property valuation special-ist, correct?"

"That's right."

"And you've served as an expert for both patent owners and accused infringers?"

"I have."

"In this case, you were retained by Titan?"

"Yes."

Jordan glanced at his notes. "Let's talk about your methodology. You said you identified the 'smallest saleable unit' that practices the patent. That's the component you used as your royalty base, correct?"

"Correct."

"And you didn't use the revenue from the entire Telemetry Processing Module, as you say Dr. Vance did?"

"No, I did not."

"Instead, you apportioned value to what you considered the patented feature?"

"Yes."

"That apportionment is based on your judgment about how much value the patented feature contributes to the product, correct?"

Croft nodded. "That's right."

"There's no single, objective formula for that apportionment, is there?"

"It's based on industry practice and my professional experience," Croft replied.

"So, two experts could look at the same product and reach different conclusions about how much value the patented feature contributes?" Jordan asked.

"That's possible."

"You also testified that there were 'readily available alternatives' to NovaTech's patented approach. You mentioned Chorus and Synapse Telemetry?"

"Yes."

"Did you review technical evidence showing those alternatives performed as well as NovaTech's system in real-world deployments?"

"I reviewed product literature and market reports."

"But you didn't conduct independent technical testing or review source code for those alternatives, did you?"

"No, I did not."

"And you have no training or expertise in computer system design or cloud system architecture like Dr. Vance, correct?"

Croft remained steady. "I have no formal degrees in those areas, but in my work, I have studied many such systems and am familiar with their operation."

"So your conclusion that Titan could have switched to an alternative 'at minimal cost' is based on marketing materials, not technical analysis or personal technical expertise?"

"It's based on the information I had available," replied Croft.

"Let's talk about the royalty rate. You selected 0.5%, correct?"

"That's right."

"You agree that some licenses in the industry, especially for foundational or enabling technologies, can command higher rates?"

"In some cases, yes."

"And you agree that if the patented feature is critical to the product's performance, the parties in a hypothetical negotiation might agree to a higher rate?"

"If it's critical, yes."

"You also testified that Dr. Vance's $131.2 million figure is 'vastly inflated.' But if the jury finds that the patented feature is a key driver of demand for the module, your damages figure would be too low, wouldn't it?"

Croft countered. "Not necessarily. Even if the jury finds it was a key driver of demand the overall damages may still be proper given the alternatives that were available. Having Titan's name associated with a product, regardless of what technology is 'under the hood,' is what a lot of people will gravitate to. Customers may well take the fact that Titan chose to integrate another solution to mean the particular implementation is not what's important."

"Even under those conditions though, you agree that the proper amount of damages depends on how much value the jury believes the patented feature actually contributed to Titan's product?"

"Yes, that's correct."

Jordan stepped away from the lectern. "Thank you, Mr. Croft. No further questions."

Judge Price looked at Marla, and she walked back towards the lectern.

"Mr. Croft, just a few clarifying questions."

"You were asked about your apportionment of value to the patented feature. Is it common in your field for experts to use professional judgment and industry practice when determining apportionment in patent damages?"

Croft nodded. "Yes, it is. As I said, there's no single formula, every case is different. We rely on accepted economic principles, comparable licenses, and our experience to make a fair assessment."

Marla continued, "You were also asked about your review of alternatives. Did you rely on the same types of industry sources and market data that are standard in IP valuation work?"

"Yes," Croft replied. "Product literature, market reports, and industry analyses are routinely used to assess the availability and viability of alternatives. That's standard practice."

"And in your experience, is it unusual for a damages expert to rely on such sources when technical testing is not available?"

"Not at all. It's very common, especially when the alternatives are commercial products with published performance data."

Marla paused. "Finally, Mr. Croft, does your conclusion about the appropriate royalty rate and damages reflect your best professional judgment, based on the evidence and your experience?"

"It does."

"Thank you, Mr. Croft. No further questions."

———

When she got back to Titan's table, Marla glanced at her notes, conferred briefly with her colleagues, then nodded to the judge. "Your Honor, the defense rests."

Judge Price looked over the courtroom, then addressed the jury. "Ladies and gentlemen, we'll break for lunch. Please remember my instructions: do not discuss the case or conduct any research. We'll resume at 1:30. Court is in recess."

The courtroom doors opened, and the low hum of conversation began as counsel gathered their papers and the jury filed out, the weight of the morning's testimony still hanging in the air.

# Eighteen

Jordan met Maya, Alex, and Ethan in the hallway as the courtroom emptied for lunch. "Go get something to eat," he said, tucking a folder under his arm as he stepped aside. "I'm going to the attorney lounge to polish my closing."

Maya hesitated. "What about rebuttal?"

Jordan shook his head. "Don't need it. They didn't hammer invalidity, and I think both the judge and the jury want to get this over with. Marla probably figures they have a better shot with the PTAB since they're arguing obviousness, and a jury isn't likely to go there."

He glanced at the closed courtroom doors. "She's betting that even if we win, their damages guy gave the jury enough reason to settle for a small number, so the risk feels worth it."

Alex managed a tired smile. "So we're really almost done?"

Jordan nodded. "Almost. Eat something. The waiting is the hardest part."

He turned away, leaving the team standing in the hallway, the weight of the trial settling like a quiet fog as the lunch crowd drifted past.

———

The courtroom settled as Judge Price returned to the bench. She glanced at the plaintiff's table.

"Mr. Reyes, do you have any rebuttal or further evidence to present?"

Jordan rose. "No, Your Honor."

"Very well." Judge Price nodded, then turned to the jury. "Ladies and gentlemen of the jury, both sides have now rested. We will proceed to closing arguments. Mr. Reyes?"

Jordan stood, buttoned his jacket, and walked to the lectern. He paused, allowing the silence to settle, before beginning:

"Ladies and gentlemen,

"Thank you for your attention and patience throughout this trial.

"You have heard a story that began with a problem. A problem that kept Alex Carter awake at night, searching for a way to make systems breathe, to keep people safe. You have seen how Maya Singh built a company on that solution, how NovaTech shared its work in good faith, and how Titan took what was offered and made it their own.

"You've seen the evidence: the architecture diagrams, the stress curves, the emails that said the quiet part out loud: 'Why pay for what we can build?'

"You heard Jamie Tran's confession, a story of desperation and regret, and Claire Donovan's courage in telling the truth.

"You saw Titan's own words, authenticated and undeniable, mapping NovaTech's innovation onto their product.

"Our technical expert showed you how Titan's system mirrors NovaTech's, feature for feature, tradeoff for tradeoff. Our damages expert explained the value of what was taken. Not just lines of code, but years of work, trust, and ingenuity.

"Titan's experts told you that everything NovaTech built was obvious, that it was just another step in a long march of progress. But ask yourselves: If it was so obvious, why did Titan need NovaTech's answers? Why did they ask for stress curves, failure modes, and the secrets behind stability? Why did they say, 'Just don't get caught using their language'?

"Let's review . . ."

Jordan spent the next several minutes going over the exhibits used by Dr. Lin that explained the claims and the infringement in detail. He noted how Titan's expert was forced to agree that the only difference he could point to was where the scaling logic resides. "Something not explicitly required by the patent claim," he emphasized. He covered Dr. Vance's careful methodology in arriving at her damages number, pointed out her expertise in both technical and economic matters, and reminded the jury that her calculations were based on an apportionment due the patented transform.

As he drew to a close, Jordan looked at each member of the jury in turn.

"This case is not about punishing success. It is about protecting the promise that innovation is rewarded, not stolen. It is about the difference between inspiration and appropriation, between partnership and predation.

"You have the power to decide what kind of story this becomes. Is it the story of a company that dared to solve a problem and was punished for its openness? Or is it the story of a jury that saw the truth, weighed the evidence, and chose justice?

He turned and looked briefly at Maya. "On behalf of NovaTech, I ask you to find for the plaintiff."

Returning to the jury. "Protect the work. Protect the promise.

"Thank you."

With that, Jordan left the lectern and took his seat.

———

Judge Price nodded to Marla.

She stood, smoothed her notes, and addressed the jury with calm conviction:

"Ladies and gentlemen of the jury,

"Like Mr. Reyes, I want to thank you for your attention throughout this trial.

"You have heard a compelling story from NovaTech. A story of innovation, ambition, and disappointment. But this case is not about stories. It is about facts, law, and the reality of how technology evolves.

"You have seen that Titan's engineers, like NovaTech's, worked to solve complex problems using tools and techniques standard in our industry. Dynamic scalability, transform layers, and autoscaling are not secrets. They are the building blocks of modern data systems, taught in universities and implemented in open-source platforms long before NovaTech's patent.

"Our technical expert, Dr. Nord, showed you that Titan's product was built independently, using publicly available methods. He explained that the architecture and algorithms in question were well-known, and that Titan's system does not automatically provision resources as described in the patent. Titan's approach is distinct, and the similarities are the result of common engineering solutions, not copying.

"You heard from Mr. Croft, our damages expert, who explained that NovaTech's claim for damages is vastly inflated. The patented feature is only a small part of a much larger, more complex product. Customers choose Titan's system for its reliability, integration, and breadth of features. Not for any single technical detail.

"NovaTech's witnesses spoke of betrayal and emotion, but emotion is not evidence. The law requires proof. The proof that Titan took something unique, something not already in the public domain, and used it without permission is missing.

"Ask yourselves: If the solution was so novel, why do so many systems use similar approaches? If Titan truly copied, why do the technical details differ? Why did NovaTech keep sending information, hoping for a partnership, if they believed their secrets were at risk?

"This case is about the line between inspiration and monopoly. If every improvement in technology can be claimed as exclusive, progress will stall. The law protects true innovation, but it does not reward overreach.

"On behalf of Titan, I ask you to find for the defense. Protect fair competition. Protect the freedom to build on what is known.

"Thank you."

Marla looked at Judge Price and then returned to her seat.

———

Judge Price adjusted her glasses and addressed the jury, her tone measured and clear.

"Ladies and gentlemen of the jury, it is now my duty to instruct you on the law that applies to this case. Please listen carefully, as you must follow these instructions in reaching your verdict.

"First, you are the sole judges of the facts. It is your responsibility to weigh the evidence, assess the credibility of the witnesses, and decide what actually happened. My role is to instruct you on the law.

"The plaintiff, NovaTech, claims that Titan Corp. infringed its patent. Titan denies infringement and contends that the patent is invalid. The burden is on NovaTech to prove infringement by a preponderance of the evidence. That is, that it is more likely than not that Titan's product contains every element of at least one asserted claim of the patent.

"Titan, in turn, must prove any claim of invalidity by clear and convincing evidence. A higher standard, meaning it is highly probable that the patent is invalid.

"You must consider each patent claim separately. Infringement can be found in two ways: literal infringement, where every element of the claim is present in the accused product, or under the doctrine of equivalents, where the accused product performs substantially the same function, in substantially the same way, to achieve substantially the same result.

"If you find infringement, you must then consider whether Titan has proven that the patent claim is invalid as obvious. In deciding obviousness, consider what a person of ordinary skill in the field would have known at the time of the invention, the differences between the prior art and the claimed invention, and any evidence of commercial success, long-felt need, or copying.

"If you find infringement and validity, you must determine the amount of damages. Damages must be adequate to compensate Nova-Tech for the infringement, but no less than a reasonable royalty. You must not award damages as a penalty or out of sympathy.

"If you find infringement and validity, you must determine the amount of damages. Damages must be adequate to compensate Nova-

Tech for the infringement, but no less than a reasonable royalty. You must not award damages as a penalty or out of sympathy.

"If you find that Titan infringed a valid claim of the patent, you must also determine whether NovaTech has proven, by a preponderance of the evidence, that Titan's infringement was willful. Willful infringement refers to conduct that was intentional or in reckless disregard of NovaTech's patent rights. It does not require that Titan acted with malice, but it does require more than mere negligence.

"In deciding willfulness, you may consider all of the facts and circumstances, including whether Titan knew of the patent, whether Titan reasonably believed it did not infringe or that the patent was invalid, and whether Titan attempted to conceal its conduct or acted in a manner inconsistent with good faith.

"If you find willful infringement, you should indicate that finding on the verdict form. You should not, however, increase or alter the damages amount based on willfulness. Any increase in damages, if appropriate, will be decided later by the Court.

"Remember, your verdict must be based solely on the evidence presented in this courtroom and the law as I have given it to you. You must not be influenced by sympathy, prejudice, or public opinion.

"You will receive a verdict form with specific questions. Answer each question as instructed, and all jurors must agree on each answer.

"If you have any questions during deliberations, write them down and give them to the bailiff. I will bring you back into court to address them.

"Thank you for your attention and service. You may now retire to the jury room to begin your deliberations."

———

The jury room was quiet at first. Nine strangers sat around a battered oak table; the door was closed, the world outside suspended.

Helen Brooks cleared her throat. "All right, everyone. We've heard a lot. Let's start by listing what matters most."

Carla Ramirez spoke up. "Shouldn't we decide on a foreperson first? Before we get to the details?"

"That's right," said Derek Foster, the auto mechanic. "We should put someone in charge first."

"Okay," said Helen. "Who should be the foreperson?"

"Why don't you do it Helen?" Frank Dorsey, the postal worker, looked at her. "You're used to running a classroom, and this isn't much different." He looked at the others, "Anyone object?"

"Fine with me," said Carla. The others nodded.

Helen took a breath, feeling the weight settle on her shoulders "Fine. "So, what matters most?"

Walter Greene, the retired firefighter, spoke for the first time. "The technical stuff was dense, but I keep coming back to those emails. 'Why pay for what we can build?' That sounded... deliberate."

Marta Alvarez, the small business owner, shook her head. "But Titan's expert said those techniques were common. If everyone uses dynamic scaling, is it really stealing?"

Linda Wu, the nurse, tapped her pen. "It's not about stealing, Marta. They explained that even if there's no copying, there can still be infringement. Anyway, Jamie's testimony hit me. He was desperate, but he admitted what he did. That takes guts. And it shows Titan got things they shouldn't have."

Tom Collins, the IT guy in the Red Sox cap, shrugged. "The law says we need proof of infringement, not just similarity. Did Titan cross the line, or did they just follow the industry?"

Marta Alvarez said, "I keep thinking about Maya. She built something, and it got taken. But business is tough. Isn't it just competition?"

Helen nodded. "Let's take it one question at a time. Did Titan use NovaTech's invention?"

Carla frowned. "Their product looks a lot like NovaTech's, but the defense expert said the architecture was different. I'm not sure."

Frank added, "Claire's testimony made it sound like Titan wanted to copy, but the emails could mean a lot of things."

Helen raised a hand. "Let's vote. Just to see where we stand."

They passed slips of paper. The votes were split.

Foster, the auto mechanic, sighed. "Great. We can't even agree on the first question."

Linda Wu suggested, "Let's go around the table. One by one."

As each juror spoke, the room filled with debate, empathy, and the weight of responsibility. Some voices wavered, others held firm. The clock on the wall ticked, indifferent.

After a while, Helen stood. "We've all had our say. Let's vote again and see if anyone has changed their mind."

This time, the votes were still split, but not by as much. Helen glanced at the clock, then at the faces around the table. People looked tired, uncertain.

"We're not there yet," she said quietly. "Let's call it for today."

She knocked on the door for the bailiff. The jury filed out, faces solemn, each carrying the case with them into the night, knowing their decision would shape the story's end.

# NINETEEN

**TECH LEDGER | SOFIA MARTINEZ**
Trial Brief: Jury at an Impasse in NovaTech v. Titan

After days of testimony and high-stakes argument, the fate of NovaTech v. Titan now rests with the jury. But as the sun set on the federal courthouse this evening, there was still no verdict.

The nine jurors, charged with deciding whether Titan Corp. infringed NovaTech's patent and, if so, what damages are owed, spent the afternoon behind closed doors, reviewing evidence and the judge's instructions. By late afternoon, they emerged looking tired and contemplative, offering no hint of which way the decision might go.

Legal experts say the case is a rare test of both technical nuance and corporate ethics. "Patent trials are always complex, but this one has the added drama of whistleblowers, internal emails, and the very real question of what counts as innovation versus imitation," said one attorney following the case.

For NovaTech, tonight is another anxious wait in a budget hotel, hope and dread in equal measure. For Titan, it's a test of nerves and narrative control. For the industry, the outcome could set a precedent for how Silicon Valley's biggest players treat the upstarts who challenge them.

Deliberations resume tomorrow morning. Stay with Tech Ledger for continuing coverage.

IT WAS STILL misty when Maya, Alex and Ethan left the fluorescent hush of the Comfort Inn's lobby. With nothing left to do but wait, they wandered south, following a narrow sidewalk past a few neat houses, budget hotels, and utility poles, until the path gave way to the wild edge of the South End Marsh.

The marsh was a broad, silvered expanse, ringed by reeds and tangled brush. Pools of water reflected the low clouds, and the air smelled of wet earth and distant pine. They paused at a roadside pull-off, watching a pair of egrets stalk the shallows, their white shapes ghostly in the dusk.

Alex shoved his hands into his pockets. "I used to think if we just built something good enough, the rest would take care of itself."

Ethan snorted, boots squelching in the mud. "Turns out, the world's messier than code."

Maya didn't answer. She watched the birds, how they moved: patient, deliberate, unhurried by the storm. For a moment, she let herself imagine what it would feel like to be weightless, to drift above the fight.

A gust of wind sent droplets pattering from the trees. "Let's head back," she said. "Before we get drowned."

They trudged up the informal path, shoes soaked, jeans spattered with mud. By the time they reached the Comfort Inn, the sky was nearly dark and their breath steamed in the cold.

Jordan was waiting in the lobby, suit jacket draped over one arm, phone in hand. He looked tired, but his eyes were sharp.

"Marla called," he said, as they shook off their coats. "She's upping the offer. More money. And she floated the idea that maybe there's room at Titan for some of you. If you want it."

Alex's jaw tightened. "A job at Titan? After all this?"

Ethan shook his head. "They want to buy us out, not just the tech."

Maya looked at Jordan, then at her team. "We didn't come this far to be absorbed. Not for a check, not for a desk at Titan. We built something real. We see this through."

Jordan nodded, relief flickering in his eyes. "I'll tell her no."

They headed inside, the lobby's warmth a small comfort against the damp. Ethan was already on his phone, scrolling through takeout menus. "Thai or pizza?" he called over his shoulder.

Maya managed a tired smile. "Surprise us."

As the door swung shut behind them, the marsh faded into memory. A brief pause before the waiting began again.

————

Across town, the Granite Restaurant glowed with quiet confidence. White tablecloths, flickering candles, and the low hum of conversation rising above the clink of glassware. Outside, the rain streaked the windows, but inside, the air was warm and fragrant with roasted root vegetables and seared scallops.

Richard Hale sat at the head of the table, posture relaxed, eyes half-lidded as he surveyed the room. Marjorie, Titan's General Counsel, was to his right, her expression unreadable as she picked at a plate of cider-glazed duck. The two junior lawyers, both in crisp shirts and new shoes, sat further down, trying to look as if they belonged.

Marla returned from a brief call, sliding into her seat with a practiced smile. She set her phone face-down beside her wine glass.

"Jordan says it's a no," she reported. "NovaTech isn't interested. Not in the money, not in a seat at Titan."

Richard barely glanced up from his plate. "Of course not. They want their day in the sun. Let them have it."

Marjorie's fork paused midair. "Juries are unpredictable, Richard. You know that as well as I do. We've given them every chance to be reasonable."

Richard shrugged, swirling his wine. "We've given them what they wanted—a fight. If they lose, they'll say the system was rigged. If they win, they'll be a footnote by next quarter."

One of the junior lawyers cleared their throat, glancing at the menu as if it might offer billing guidance. "Should we, ah, prepare a new draft of the settlement memo? Or—?"

Marjorie's gaze was sharp. "You'll prepare whatever's needed. But tonight, you'll also enjoy your dinner. This is New England, try the cod."

The table fell into a brief, awkward silence, broken only by the arrival of the next course: local oysters on a bed of seaweed, garnished with pickled shallots and a drizzle of something bright and green.

Richard raised his glass, the gesture casual yet final. "To Titan. May we always have the best table in the house."

The junior lawyers echoed the toast, uncertain but eager. Marla managed a small, tight smile. Marjorie's eyes lingered on the empty chair at the end of the table. Claire's chair, now empty, as if she'd never been there at all.

Outside, the rain continued. Inside, the team dined on uneasy confidence.

———

Helen Brooks stood at her kitchen sink, rinsing out her mug as the last of the evening news faded from the living room. Her husband, Bill, leaned against the counter, watching her with gentle curiosity.

"Long day?" he asked.

She nodded, drying her hands on a dish towel. "You could say that."

He smiled, trying to coax her out. "Anything you can tell me?"

Helen shook her head, a rueful smile on her lips. "You know I can't. The judge's orders."

Bill sighed, not for the first time. "I just worry about you, that's all. You look tired."

Helen glanced at the stack of court papers on the table—jury instructions, her own careful notes. "It's... a lot to think about. I'll be glad when it's over."

He squeezed her shoulder. "I'll keep the tea warm."

She managed a grateful smile, but as she sat at the table, pen in hand, the silence pressed in. The city outside was quiet, but inside her mind, the arguments and faces from the courtroom replayed, over and over.

———

Tom Collins pulled into his driveway just after nine, the Red Sox cap still on his head. The porch light was on, and through the window he could see his teenage daughter hunched over her laptop, earbuds in, oblivious to the world.

Inside, his wife, Karen, was waiting at the kitchen table, a plate of reheated lasagna set aside for him.

"Hey," she said, as he dropped his bag by the door. "How's it going? Any news?"

Tom shook his head, slumping into the chair. "Can't talk about it. You know the rules."

She smiled, teasing. "Not even a hint?"

He grinned, but it didn't quite reach his eyes. "Not even a hint. I'll tell you everything when it's over. Maybe."

She reached across the table, squeezing his hand. "Just remember, it's only a job for them. For you, it's just a few more days."

Tom nodded, but as he ate in silence, he found himself replaying the day's debates, the faces of his fellow jurors, the weight of the decision that waited for him in the morning.

———

As midnight passed, the city outside the courthouse slept uneasily, caught between restless hope and apprehension. In hotel rooms and suites, in silence and in whispered conversations, everyone waited for morning.

———

The courthouse was waking earlier than most of the businesses in Concord. By the time Maya and the team arrived, the morning sun was glinting off wet pavement and the flag snapping in a light breeze. She paused at the security checkpoint, clutching her bag a little tighter than usual, and nodded to the guard who now recognized her by sight.

Inside, lawyers clustered in corners, meeting with clients in low voices before morning calendar calls. The Titan team had claimed their usual bench, Marjorie and Richard deep in conversation while the junior lawyers shuffled papers and refreshed their inboxes, trying to look indispensable.

Jordan found Maya near the elevators when she got off. For a moment, they stood together in the hush, watching the flow of people.

"Sleep?" he asked, voice low.

She shook her head. "You?"

He smiled, but it didn't reach his eyes. "Didn't even try."

They shared a moment of silence, the kind that comes only at the end of a long campaign. Then Jordan squeezed her shoulder, gentle but firm. "Whatever happens, we did the work."

Maya nodded, drawing a steadying breath. "See you on the other side."

He peeled off toward Marla, and Maya made her way to where Alex and Ethan waited, both fidgeting with their phones, eyes darting to the clock.

In the jury room, Helen Brooks had already arranged the chairs around the battered oak table, her notes stacked neatly in front of her.

"Morning, everyone," she called, her voice brisk but kind. "Let's get settled. We've got work to do."

Tom Collins slouched into his seat, Red Sox cap in hand. Marta Alvarez set her thermos on the table with a sigh. Linda Wu offered a tired smile, glancing at the clock.

Helen clapped her hands softly—more encouragement than command. "All right, let's pick up where we left off. We owe these people a decision."

As the door closed, the world outside faded, and the room became its own universe. In the hallway and in the lounge, the lawyers and parties waited. Pacing, whispering, checking their watches and phones. The courthouse clock ticked on, indifferent to hope or dread.

———

As the morning advanced, the jury was making progress.

Marta Alvarez and Walter Greene had huddled at one end of the table, discussing the emails.

"'Why pay for what we can build?' That doesn't sound innocent," said Marta.

"It was intentional," Walter nodded. "They knew about NovaTech's patent. They kept asking for more details, then cut them off."

Linda Wu, having overheard, stood and moved to the two. "But is that enough? Even if they had the details, did they actually use NovaTech's patent?"

Others of the group, sensing this might, at last, be going somewhere, started gathering.

"I keep coming back to the stress curves. The expert said Titan's system reacted the same way under pressure. That's not a coincidence," Tom said, his certainty evident.

"But their guy said it's just good engineering. That anyone would end up there."

"No, Marta." Tom shook his head, flipping back in his notebook. "Remember what Dr. Lin said. 'Telemetry data is unpredictable.' He said that because of that, the transform layer has to determine how many processing units to use. That the test results show that Titan's system behaves identically to the NovaTech one. He even said some of the terms Titan used were those described in NovaTech's documents. That's not just good engineering, not just a coincidence."

"I agree," said Frank. "You don't get that by just trying to solve the same problem. Look, if you and I were going to build a... I don't know, say, a birdhouse, we might both end up with something that keeps the rain out. But the odds of us using the same wood, the same nails, cutting the same little window in the same spot, painting it the same color? Unless one of us was looking at the other's plans... pretty much zero."

The other jurors were listening. Carla nodded, tapping a finger on the table. "Exactly. And here, it's not just the outside that matches. The test results, the way the system handles spikes, even the language in the logs. Titan's stuff lines up with NovaTech's almost line for line. They had the blueprints and they just went ahead and built what they showed.

"Yeah," Marta said, coming around to the others' views. "If it was just a similar idea, I guess I could buy coincidence. But this? This feels like they had the answer key."

Helen looked around the table. "I think that's what the law means by infringement. Not just solving the problem, but solving it the same way, with the same steps."

There was more debate. Derek Foster, the mechanic, wanted to look at the patent again to see where the "breathing" was described.

Helen gently pointed him to the claim at the end of the document. "Look here, Derek. It says, 'monitoring a characteristic of the received data stream,' and then 'automatically allocating additional processing resources to the transform layer.' That's what Dr. Lin said was meant by 'breathing.'"

"Alex said that was the hardest part to figure out," said Carla. "He said they tried lots of ways to solve the problem, but it took months."

"That's why I don't buy that Titan just happened to get to the same place on their own." Tom sensed the group was close. "They needed to know how NovaTech did it. They kept asking for more. They drained those people dry."

Helen looked at her group. "Jenna? You've been quiet this morning. What do you think?"

The young college student looked at Helen. "I don't know. I mean, this all sounds fine and everything. And I liked Maya, but Titan is just... everywhere. I mean they make pretty much every tech thing I own. I'm sure they have tons of people working on stuff all the time. Why would they have to use anything from NovaTech?"

Helen kept her voice quiet. "Well, remember what the other experts talked about. They said other companies had solutions. Synapse and Chorus. But NovaTech's was just better. Maybe Titan thought that if they were going to have to go up against Chorus and Synapse, they needed the best. And the best was NovaTech."

Jenna thought about it. "I guess that's possible."

"More than possible," Tom said. Remember Hale's email? 'Mirror their flow.' He's telling their people to use NovaTech's design exactly. If something is mirrored, it's not just similar, it's identical."

Jenna smiled faintly. "That makes sense. I hadn't thought about it that way before."

Helen glanced around. Faces that had started the day with uncertainty now looked assured. Her group was ready. "Why don't we take a vote?"

This time, when the little slips of paper were counted, there were nine votes for NovaTech.

Helen smiled at everyone and read the first question on the jury form aloud: "Has NovaTech proven, by a preponderance of the evidence, that Titan literally infringes Claim 1 of the patent?" With a flourish, she ticked the box for *Yes*.

She continued reading the instructions. "If you answered 'Yes' to Question 1, proceed directly to Part B regarding validity."

Helen looked up, her voice gentle but firm. "Okay, before we do that, let's take a break and get some air."

Chairs scraped back from the table. But some lingered, aware that their verdict had begun to take shape.

———

Unaware of what had just transpired, Maya paced the courthouse hallway. While Alex and Ethan were somehow able to sit on the bench outside the courtroom, Maya could not keep still. She stared at her phone. When that got no result she stared at the courtroom door, and, unable to move it by force of will, back at the phone.

Jordan strolled back towards the group. "They're taking their time," he said, trying to sound casual.

"Maybe that's good," Maya replied, though her voice was tight. "Means they're being careful."

Alex managed a thin smile. "Or maybe they're arguing about lunch."

Ethan snorted. "I'd kill for a sandwich right now."

They fell silent, the weight of the moment pressing in. Down the hall, the Titan team clustered by the windows, their junior lawyers shuffling papers and pretending to be busy.

Maya glanced at the clock. "Almost done," she whispered, more to herself than to the others.

———

Their break over, the jurors returned. The morning's tension had been replaced by a sense of camaraderie. Reaching the first decision had replaced uncertainty with focused energy. Helen glanced at the verdict form, then at her group.

"All right," she said, "let's move on to validity."

They debated, but this time as people moving with a shared purpose rather than doubt. They talked about code libraries and other ways in which dynamic scaling and transform layers had been used. And they read, and reread, the patent claim and wondered aloud just what obvious was supposed to mean. There were disagreements, but the earlier momentum carried them forward. Soon the slips of paper were counted, the boxes ticked.

Shortly before noon, Helen gathered the pages of the verdict form, checked them twice, and knocked on the door for the bailiff.

In the hallway, Maya looked up at the sound, heart pounding. Down the corridor, the Titan team straightened in their seats. The waiting was over.

———

The courtroom was a cathedral of stillness. No cameras, no chatter; just the hum of fluorescent lights and the anticipation of which story would live.

Maya sat at the plaintiff's table; hands folded so tightly her knuckles looked carved from stone. Alex was beside her, pale but upright, his breath shallow and steady. Ethan hovered behind them, a silent sentinel. Jordan stood with his binder closed, as if the war had already been fought and all that remained was gravity.

Judge Eleanor Price entered with the economy of someone who understood the cost of time. She took her seat, adjusted her glasses, and spoke in a voice that carried like a bell.

"Has the jury reached a verdict?"

Helen Brooks stood. "We have, Your Honor."

The clerk took the verdict form, unfolded it, and read aloud in a tone that made every syllable sound like law.

"On question 1, 'Has NovaTech proven, by a preponderance of the evidence, that Titan literally infringes Claim 1 of the patent?' Answer, Yes."

The words landed like a stone on a still pond. Ripples moved through the room—gasps, exhales, the soft percussion of relief. Maya felt her chest loosen and tighten at the same time. Alex closed his eyes, a single tear breaking free before he could stop it. Ethan gripped the back of Maya's chair like he was holding the earth steady.

The clerk continued.

"On question 2, 'Has Titan Corp. proven, by clear and convincing evidence, that Claim 1 of the patent is invalid as being obvious?' Answer, No."

The courtroom was completely still.

"On question 3, 'What amount of monetary damages do you find NovaTech is entitled to receive as a result of the Defendant's infringement of Claim 1?' Answer, 'one hundred thirty-one million, two hundred thousand dollars.'"

There was a pause, short, but charged, before the clerk read the final line.

"On question 4, 'Has NovaTech proven, by a preponderance of the evidence, that Titan's infringement was willful?' Answer, Yes."

Another ripple passed through the gallery. Not loud. Not dramatic. Just the unmistakable sound of a truth acknowledged. Maya didn't exhale; she felt the verdict pass over and through her like a long-dreaded wave finally breaking.

Judge Price nodded once, as if the verdict were something she had always known. She looked at Marla. "Ms. Whittaker?"

"We'd like to poll the jury, Your Honor."

"Madam Clerk." Judge Price spoke to the clerk of the court.

One by one, the clerk asked the jurors, "Is the verdict as read your true and correct verdict?" One by one they each answered, "Yes."

"Thank you, ladies and gentlemen of the jury," Judge Price said. "Your service is complete. Now that the case is over, you are free to discuss it with any person you choose. By the same token, however, I would advise you that you are under no obligation whatsoever to discuss this case with any person.

"If you do decide to discuss the case with anyone, always bear in mind that the other jurors fully and freely stated their opinions with the understanding they were being expressed in confidence. Please respect the privacy of the views of the other jurors. If you took any notes during the trial, they should now be destroyed. You are discharged with the court's sincere appreciation."

The trial was over.

———

For a moment, no one moved. Then the room fractured into motion. Reporters rushed for the doors while the lawyers gathered papers like shields. Titan's team folded inward around Richard Hale, whose face looked carved from something brittle.

Maya stayed seated. Her hands were still clasped, her breath still shallow. Jordan touched her shoulder lightly. "You did it," he said.

She shook her head. "We did it."

Alex leaned close, voice hoarse. "It's over."

Maya looked at him, at the man who had built the thing that started all this, and felt the ache of what "over" meant. It meant money. It meant headlines. It meant Titan bleeding in ways that would make other giants think twice. But it didn't mean the years back. It didn't mean the marriage saved. It didn't mean the innocence restored.

# TWENTY

THE OFFICE WAS quiet for the first time in months. Two days had passed since the verdict—two days since Maya had received the brief text from Ravi: *Proud of you*. The adrenaline had faded, replaced by something ambiguous. Jordan had told them the judge wanted to talk, and he had stayed behind in New Hampshire. That didn't sound good.

Maya arrived, setting her bag down with more care than usual. She stood for a moment in the doorway, listening for signs of life in what now seemed an unfamiliar place. She heard someone rummaging around in the lab and walked in to find Alex at the whiteboard. He was drawing, a bit aimlessly, while Ethan sat in the corner, eyes on the screen but mind elsewhere.

No one spoke. There was nothing left to say about the trial, the verdict, or the number on the verdict form that now felt both monumental and fragile.

There was a knock at the door and Maya turned to find Jamie standing there. He looked thinner than she remembered.

Maya broke the silence. "You're here."

Jamie nodded. "I wanted to thank you. For letting me... for letting me try to make things right."

Ethan looked up, his voice steady but tired. "Penance isn't a password, Jamie. But it's a start."

Jamie nodded again, eyes on the floor. "I know. I'll do whatever it takes."

Maya's tone was gentle but firm. "If you stay, it's with conditions. Transparency. Audits. No solo access. Forgiveness is a process. We'll walk it if you do."

Jamie exhaled, the sound shaky but real. "I'll walk."

No one shook hands. The only movement was the soft click of Maya's coffee mug against the table.

———

Across town, in his glass-walled office high above the city, Richard Hale stood at the window, watching as the morning filled the sky. Marjorie Thorne entered, a folder in hand.

"Phase two," she said, setting the folder on the table. "PTAB."

Richard didn't turn from the window. "What does Marla say?"

Marjorie's voice was cool. "We're not out of the woods. But she tells me that as long as we agree to a bond, it's a good bet Judge Price won't enter judgment or hold a hearing on an injunction until the Board rules. The bond's just money. The real fight is in Alexandria now."

Richard nodded, jaw tight. "We win this, the rest is noise."

Marjorie didn't answer. She watched Richard for a moment, then left him alone with the city and the silence.

———

Back at NovaTech, Maya poured coffee for the team. The ritual felt almost normal. She wondered if this was what victory was supposed to feel like. For a moment, the office was just a place to work, not a battlefield. But outside, the weather was changing.

# TWENTY-ONE

"WASN'T he supposed to be here by now?" Ethan's frustration seeped into his voice.

Alex looked over. "Relax. The plane was probably just late getting in. He'll be here."

Jordan had called between connections in Denver and told the team he would come to their office after his flight, no matter the time. Maya stood by the window, arms folded, staring at a list of action items that already felt obsolete.

The door opened and Jordan stepped in, rain on his jacket. He looked tired. More tired than after the verdict, Maya thought.

Jordan set a folder on the table. "We have news," he said, voice steady but low.

Alex looked up, hope and dread warring in his eyes. "Good or bad?"

Jordan managed a thin smile. "Depends on how much you like déjà vu."

He took a breath, then continued. "Titan posted a bond this morning and Judge Price entered an order. She's staying entry of judgment and the injunction hearing. She'll wait until the PTAB finishes with the IPRs."

Ethan's chair scraped back. "Wait. So after all that, the trial, the verdict—they just... hit pause?"

Jordan nodded. "That's how it works. Titan filed their IPR petitions before the trial, and because they posted a bond, the judge is holding off. No injunction, no final judgment; not until the Patent Office decides what to do."

Alex's voice was tight. "How long?"

"If the Board institutes trial, maybe fourteen months from now," Jordan said, "Maybe longer. If they don't, we move forward and Judge Price will hear our motion for an injunction."

Maya's jaw clenched. "And if they do?"

Jordan's tone was grim. "Then we fight the whole thing again. On paper, this time. No jury. Just three administrative judges and a stack of documents."

Ethan shook his head. "So what do we do now?"

Jordan opened the folder, spreading out drafts of the preliminary responses his team had been working on behind the scenes. "We have two weeks to file our POPRs. Patent Owner Preliminary Responses. We need to show the Board that Titan's petitions don't even deserve a hearing. That the patent wasn't obvious, that it wasn't just a remix of old ideas."

He looked at each of them in turn. "We're going to use this fight to explain what makes our invention matter. Not just to us, but to anyone who cares about building something new."

Alex's hands trembled as he reached for one of the drafts. "We already proved it once," he said, voice tight.

Jordan nodded. "Now we prove it again. Different room, different rules. But the same truth."

The team gathered around the table, the reality of the new battle settling in.

———

A few days later and almost midnight, the conference room was bright with the glow of laptops. Drafts of the POPRs were spread across the table, annotated in three colors. Used coffee cups outnumbered people.

Jordan stood at the whiteboard, marker in hand, reviewing a claim chart. Dr. Lin sat beside Alex, flipping through a binder thick with prior art references. Ethan scrolled through a draft on his laptop, brow furrowed.

Ethan broke the silence. "Tell me again," he said, looking at Jordan, "why are we filing these things? How does this work, exactly? I mean, we already won in court."

Jordan set down the marker and leaned against the table. "The PTAB, the US Patent Office's Patent Trial and Appeal Board, can review a patent even after it's issued. Titan filed IPR petitions arguing the patent should never have been granted because it's claims are 'obvious' in light of prior art. If the Board thinks they have a case, they could institute a trial. If not, we're safe. These responses are our shot to convince them not to even open the door."

Alex shook his head. "But we already proved this wasn't obvious. No one was selling anything like this before. And besides, the jury..."

"True," said Jordan. "The jury said Titan didn't prove invalidity. The last USPTO Director felt strongly that juries should be respected, but he's gone now and the standard for proving obviousness at the Board is different than it was in court."

Dr. Lin looked up, a tradeoff weariness in his eyes. He'd been through many such paper wars before. "And besides, Alex, in patent law, it's not about whether there was an existing commercial solution. At least, it's not only about that. The question is: Would a person of ordinary skill in the art, that's someone with the typical background in this field, have found your invention obvious based on the entirety of what was already publicly known? That's what the Board cares about."

Ethan frowned. "So, even if nobody built it, if they think it was obvious, we're sunk?"

Jordan nodded. "Pretty much. The law says an invention can be obvious even if it's not on the market, as long as the pieces were out there and it would have been obvious to put them together. The Board can use a single reference, or a combination of prior art references, as long as they articulate a reason why someone would have combined them. That's called making a 'prima facie case of obviousness.'"

Alex threw up his hands. "I don't even understand that word anymore."

Jordan thought for a moment. "Imagine a world where everyone has a pencil. There're great. You can write with them, you can sharpen them and write some more, but if you make a mistake then what? You have to stop, put down your pencil, reach into your pocket and get out an eraser to clean up the mistake. Then you have to put the eraser away, pick up the pencil and start all over again.

"Now, imagine you're a clever guy who one day realizes the solution is a pencil with an eraser on the end. Voila: no more separate pencils and separate erasers. Suddenly, these two can be united, so whenever someone makes a mistake, they just flip the pencil over, erase, and carry on.

"The question is: Would it have been obvious for someone skilled in making pencils to stick an eraser on the end, just because both things existed?"

Dr. Lin jumped in. "If a published article or patent suggested combining them, or if it was common sense among pencil makers, then the Patent Office might say, 'That's obvious, you just combined two known things in a predictable way to get a predictable result.' But if no good reason existed to combine them, or if putting them together solved a problem no one anticipated, or if unforeseen difficulties had to be overcome to join the eraser and the pencil, then it might not be obvious."

Ethan leaned forward. "So it's not enough that nobody sold a pencil with an eraser before. If the Board thinks it would have been an easy, logical step, they can say it's obvious?"

"Exactly," Jordan said. "And it gets even trickier. The Board can use multiple references, say, a patent that describes a pencil and a separate article about erasers, and argue that a 'person of ordinary skill' would have put them together."

Ethan scrolled to a section in the draft. "And you told us it's not just about what's in the references, right? There's this *KSR* precedent?"

Jordan nodded. "The *KSR* decision changed everything. The Supreme Court ruled you can't dismiss obviousness simply because the prior art lacked a recipe for attaching erasers to pencils. Instead, you ask whether a skilled person, our pencil maker toiling in the factory, applying ordinary creativity and common sense, would have been motivated to combine the teachings of disparate references—maybe even references that don't pertain to pencils and erasures, as long as it is something a pencil maker would consider—as the patent claims. It's a flexible standard; the Board can even say, 'It would have been obvious *to try* this combination, even if no one actually did.'"

Ethan just shook his head. "So even if you're the first to actually do it, you can lose your patent if they think it was just waiting to happen?"

Jordan nodded. "That's why we have to show not just that we were first, but that what we did wasn't an obvious next step. We need to explain why our combination, our sequence, our choices, weren't just predictable or routine."

Dr. Lin added, "And we have to do it on paper, with references and logic, not just with a story."

Alex flipped through a stack of highlighted patents. "And prior art is... what exactly?"

Dr. Lin answered, "Prior art is any public knowledge or technology relevant to your invention at the time you filed. Patents, published articles, even blog posts. Anything that could show your idea wasn't new or was an obvious next step."

Alex's voice was tight. "So they can just second-guess the patent examiner? Even though there's already been a prior art search? Even though the patent already issued?"

Jordan sighed. "Yes. Because the system isn't perfect. Patent examiners have to search a massive universe of prior art: patents, papers, products, even YouTube videos. They might miss something, interpret a reference differently, or simply fail to see how two pieces fit together. The standard for obviousness is subjective: what one examiner deems obvious, another might not. The PTAB is supposed to be a second set of eyes, to catch mistakes or close calls."

Dr. Lin added, "And sometimes, the rationale for combining references isn't clear. The examiner has to make specific findings and explain why a skilled person would have made the leap. If they don't, or if they get it wrong, the Board can step in."

Alex let the binder drop from his hands, clattering against on the floor. "So we're fighting ghosts. Old papers, hypothetical engineers, and the Board's idea of common sense."

Jordan smiled. "Welcome to my world. That's why these responses matter. We have to show the Board that Titan's case is just hindsight. That our invention wasn't obvious, even if the pieces were out there. We have to connect the dots for them, or they'll connect them for us."

Ethan looked at the draft on his laptop. "We already proved this once. Now we have to do it again, but on paper, with no one to look in the eye."

Jordan nodded. "Different room, different rules. But the same truth. Let's make sure they see it."

The team got back to work, as Jordan began to walk them through the final edits before the clock ran out.

———

### Tech Ledger | Sofia Martinez — Opinion
**The Second Front: How IPRs Can Unmake a Verdict**

The USPTO has a new Director with deep roots in representing Big Tech. On her first day, she's issued a memo: henceforth, all institution decisions for post-grant reviews will be centralized under her Office. As the rumors suggested, we learn yet again that procedure is power wearing polite shoes.

The PTAB's promise had been consistency. While not everyone enjoyed the way the Board had been handing down decisions since it was created in 2012, everyone at least agreed its process had been, mostly, transparent. Like them or not, the Board's judgements were carefully reasoned and laid out for everyone to see. This afforded petitioners and patent owners alike some sense of predictability. Together with the previous Director's policy of "settled expectations," where a patent that has already been adjudicated in another forum deserves respect, patent owners had come to believe that their hard won victors would not be second guessed.

With the new Director's announcement, that semblance of fairness is gone. The new reality is predictability of a different kind: patents tried once in the light, get tried again in the shade.

Jordan read from his laptop. "The new Director just issued a memo: She will personally decide all institution questions. The era of 'settled expectations' is over...This means every patent is fair game. Even ones a jury just upheld. The Director can erase years of work with a single decision."

"So everything we wrote in our briefs about the jury's findings is going to be ignored?" Maya asked, her voice hollow.

Alex was pacing by the window. "They can erase us with a memo." His voice was even more bitter than yesterday's coffee from the hissing machine. "All that testimony, all those nights—gone."

Ethan was quiet, staring at his hands. "So, we're back at square one?"

Jordan closed the laptop, his voice heavy. "We're not done yet. But the rules just changed."

———

The video call connected with a familiar chime. Alan, Priya and Jonas appeared against blurred backgrounds.

Maya took a breath and started. "Thanks for making time. I wanted to update you on the IPR situation and the new developments out of the Patent Office."

Alan nodded. "We saw the Tech Ledger piece. Is it as bad as it sounds?"

Maya didn't sugarcoat it. "We got our preliminary responses filed before the Director's announcement. The petitions and our responses are in the record. But the memo changes the playing field. From now on, all institution decisions go through the Director personally. Jordan says the old policy would have respected a jury verdict, but he thinks that's gone now. There's no guarantee our win in court will mean anything."

Priya leaned forward. "So what does that mean for us, practically?"

"It means," Maya said, "that even though we did everything right, the new Director might institute review anyway. And, if he does, the standard is different. The Board only has to find obviousness by a preponderance of evidence. That's more likely than not. They can look at the same prior art the jury looked at and reach a different conclusion."

"And now, one person controls the gate," sighed Alan.

Jonas frowned. "Is there anything we can do?"

"Wait," Maya said. "We made the best record we could. We showed why our invention wasn't obvious, why the jury got it right. But we need to be realistic: the process is more political now. The Director's background is with Big Tech."

Alan's voice shifted, more businesslike. "And while we're fighting, what's happening with Gen 2? We're getting pressure from the OEMs. The litigation put us behind, and we can't afford to lose momentum on the next generation telemetry system."

Maya nodded. "I know. We've had to triage, but I've already told the team: Gen 2 is back on the front burner. We're reallocating resources now that the filings are in. Some of the smaller OEMs have come back to the table since the verdict, but they want to see progress. So do I."

Priya's tone softened. "And the numbers? How long can we keep this up?"

Maya hesitated, then answered honestly. "We're limping along. The verdict helped, and the news coverage brought a few OEMs back, but sales are still slow. The cost of this fight is real. We're watching every dollar. If the Board institutes review, it's another year—at least—before we see any real closure. But as long as we have customers, and as long as we have a shot, I'm not giving up."

Jonas nodded. "We just need to be sure we're not betting everything on the lawsuit. The business has to keep moving."

Maya managed a tired smile. "I agree. We're not giving up on the fight, but we're not putting the company on pause, either. I'll keep you posted as soon as we hear anything from the PTAB. And I'll send a Gen 2 update by the end of the week."

Alan nodded. "Thanks, Maya. Just keep us in the loop."

The call ended, leaving Maya rubbing her eyes and staring at her reflection in the darkened screen.

# Twenty-Two

**Tech Ledger | Sofia Martinez**

**From Verdict to Limbo: NovaTech's Patent Win Put on Hold by PTAB**

The American patent system once promised that a jury's verdict was the final word. But for NovaTech, last month's $131 million victory over Titan Corp is now "on hold," and the fight is far from over.

Earlier today, the Director of the USPTO issued a terse, clinical decision: "Petitioner has shown a reasonable likelihood of prevailing on at least one challenged claim." In plain English, that means Titan's challenge to NovaTech's patent will move forward, and the jury's verdict is suspended, possibly for good.

For NovaTech's team, the news is a gut-punch. The PTAB's process is designed for efficiency, but critics say it can erase years of work with a single decision. "It's like winning the Super Bowl, only to have the league say the rules changed after the game," said one industry insider.

As the legal battle shifts from the drama of the courtroom to the bureaucracy of a "paper court," NovaTech faces a new kind of exhaustion: complex filings, mounting bills, and the slow erosion of hope. For CEO Maya Singh, the hardest blow may be personal. After fighting for recognition and finally winning, the system says it's not enough.

The next phase will test not just NovaTech's technology, but its faith that justice can survive the machinery of process.

———

JORDAN READ ALOUD SO the room could hear. "*Petitioner has shown a reasonable likelihood of prevailing on at least one challenged claim...*" He turned a page. "*...on each ground...*" Another. "*...we institute on all claims, all grounds.*"

Maya held her breath until it made a small sound in her throat. "It's not a decision, but it's a decision."

"They've opened the gate," Jordan replied. "Now we try and shut it."

He pointed to a paragraph that felt like a door closing softly. "*We reserve secondary considerations for finality; Patent Owner has not established nexus at this stage.*" He looked at Alex. "Your proof that the market loved what you built is framed as irrelevant because it might not be 'tied' to the exact claim language."

Alex shook his head. "We used that language to describe the thing. Now the language erases the thing."

Ethan stood at the window, watching cars negotiate the rain. "They'll call praise 'anecdote' and copying 'convergence.'"

Jordan spoke softly, almost to himself. "Courtrooms are about telling your story. You stand in front of a jury, you look people in the eye, and you fight for what's right. Here," he gestured at the decision, "it's not about stories. It's about paper. The Board doesn't see witnesses sweat, doesn't hear voices crack. They read the arguments and check the boxes."

He paused, searching for words. "Sometimes, the system isn't built to find the truth, it's built to finish the process."

Maya looked up, her voice barely a whisper. "So, what do we do?"

Jordan managed a tired smile. "We keep fighting. But don't mistake the verdict for justice. Sometimes, all you get is the record. From here on, it's about filings, declarations, and deadlines."

Jamie looked up, voice small. "Do we even have a chance?"

Jordan nodded. "We always have a chance. But we're starting on the back foot. Statistically, petitioners win more often than patent owners. And having the Director say there's a reasonable chance they should win doesn't help. When the person at the top says, 'this looks like obviousness,' it's hard for the judges to say different."

The team sat with his words, the weight of the system settling over them like a slow fog. Outside, the city moved on, indifferent and unaware.

————

In the executive suite at Titan, Richard Hale saluted Marjorie with his coffee mug as she walked in.

She didn't bother to sit. "It's done. The Director instituted review on all grounds. Every claim, every petition. We're moving forward."

Richard wore a thin smile. "I heard. Just like we planned."

Marjorie nodded. "The system works for those who know how to use it," she said, her tone clinical and voice edged with quiet certainty.

Richard turned to the window, eyes sharp. "Let them have their verdict. The real fight was always going to be here. Now it's just process. Paper and patience."

Marjorie scrolled through her messages. "We'll see. Marla's team is already drafting the next round based on NovaTech's preliminary responses, but they'll have to come up with something new in order to address the Director's decisions."

Richard poured himself some more coffee, the gesture slow and deliberate. "Let's make sure our people know what's at stake. No surprises. If NovaTech wants to bleed for another year," he said, slowly and deliberately, "let them."

Marjorie's voice softened, just a fraction. "They'll fight. But the odds are with us now."

Richard raised his mug in a silent toast. "To process. And to knowing which room matters."

Rain streaked the windows as Marjorie left to put out another fire.

———

NovaTech's Patent Owner Response was due in just ten weeks and they'd already burned a week chasing nexus like a cat chasing a red dot.

Jordan stood at the whiteboard, marker in hand, and circled two phrases in Claim 1:

*dynamically determining a required processing resource level for a transform layer operation based at least in part on the monitored characteristic*

*automatically allocating additional processing resources to the transform layer operation via a resource management module when the determined required processing resource level exceeds the currently allocated processing resource level.*

He stepped back, the marker squeaking as he underlined "transform layer," "dynamic scalability," and "automatically allocating."

"Here's the problem," Jordan said, voice tight. "The Board doesn't care if customers love our system. They care if they love *this*," he said, tapping the claim language, "and only this."

Maya flipped through a stack of glowing customer testimonials and frowned. "But every letter talks about reliability under load, zero data loss, the system 'working great.' It's the dynamic scalability that provides those results. That's why they love it."

Jordan shook his head. "Unless the evidence says, 'We bought Nova-Tech because of its transform layer's dynamic scalability, as described in Claim 1,' it's just noise. The Board calls that 'insufficient nexus.'"

Alex, frustrated, pointed to a highlighted email from a hospital CIO and read aloud, "Your platform handled a telemetry surge without a single dropped packet. Our old system would have crashed."

He looked at Jordan. "That's the transform layer. That's the whole point."

Jordan nodded, but his tone was grim. "Unless the email spells out that it was the dynamic, real-time scaling of the transform layer, the feature recited in the claim, the Board will say it could be any part of the system. Or just good engineering. Or even luck."

Ethan paced, muttering, "So all the proof that we changed the industry..."

"Is irrelevant," Jordan finished. "Look, maybe if we actually had an OEM signing a patent license, that would carry the day. The Federal Circuit has been pretty clear: people might buy a product for all sorts of reasons, but the only reason someone signs a patent license is because of the patent. Even if it's not the only reason for the deal, there is a direct line between the claims and the license. And that's a 'nexus' even the Board can't ignore. Otherwise, if it's just software, unless we can show it's because of the specific technical feature in the claim, it just doesn't cut it. That's the game."

Maya's voice was quiet. "So we need declarations from customers, engineers; anyone who can say: 'We chose NovaTech because of the transform layer's dynamic scalability, as claimed.' Otherwise, the Board will say there's no nexus, and all this," she gestured at the pile of testimonials, "gets boxed up and ignored."

"Declarations might help," Jordan started, "but the Board will be wary of litigation bias. They won't take assertions made after the fact at face value. They want those declarations, assuming we can even get them, to reference pre-litigation evidence showing that the purchase decision was based on. or substantially tied to, the claimed feature, not just general performance metrics."

A heavy silence settled. The only sound was the scratch of Jordan's marker as he wrote, in block letters:

NEXUS = PRAISE → FEATURE → CLAIM LANGUAGE

Jordan looked at the team. "We need to bridge it. Tonight, we start calling. We need every customer, every engineer, every partner to say, in their own words, that what mattered was the transform layer's dynamic scalability. Not just that it worked, but that it worked because of what's in Claim 1."

The team fanned out, the grind beginning again.

———

Marla's conference room was sterile; an impersonal space off an impersonal lobby that nevertheless boasted an impressive view and uncomfortable furniture. The kind of space that had become popular with big firms: expensive-looking but not welcoming.

Jordan sat opposite Dr. Nord, Titan's technical expert, at one end of the long table. The court reporter had arranged her stenotype near the end of the table, facing Dr. Nord. It was connected to her laptop that ran computer-aided transcription software to provide a real-time feed for the lawyers both in the room and at Titan headquarters. The court reporter also wore small headphones and had placed small, but very high quality, mics on the desk so that she could capture every word of the deposition.

Marla, seated next to Dr. Nord, looked at Jordan. "No videographer?"

Jordan smiled back. "No. I never use one for an IPR depo. The Board doesn't want the video, so it's not worth the time or trouble."

"Ready to get started?" the court reporter asked.

Marla nodded and Jordan said, "Let's swear in the witness please."

The court reporter administered the oath. Dr. Nord raised a hand, recited the familiar words, then settled back in his chair, hands folded neatly on the table.

"Dr. Nord," Jordan began, "you provided a technical report for this case, correct?"

"Yes, that's right," Dr. Nord replied.

"In that report, you concluded that Claim 1 of NovaTech's patent was obvious based on the combination of the Swanson and Agarwal references, is that correct?"

"Yes."

"And your opinion is based on what a person having ordinary skill in the art, a PHOSITA, would have known or been able to do at the time of the invention, right?"

"Yes."

"You believe that combining the teachings of Swanson and Agarwal would have been routine or common sense for this PHOSITA?"

"That it would have been obvious to such a person, yes." Dr. Nord stated.

"Since the time of your report have you changed your conclusion that the invention would have been obvious?"

"No."

Now Jordan opened his binder to the *Swanson* tab, glancing at the real-time transcript scrolling on his laptop. He slid copies of Swanson across the table. "Let's start with Swanson. It's Exhibit 1005. Swanson describes dynamic scaling in the context of cloud storage platforms, is that right?"

Dr. Nord examined the document Jordan had passed him, "Yes."

"Cloud storage platforms typically manage I/O requests, data availability, and storage capacity, not real-time, high-velocity data processing pipelines like a telemetry system, correct?

Dr. Nord responded carefully, "That is generally accurate as a description of their primary function, yes. A cloud storage platform has different end goals from a telemetry system. However, the core engineering principle taught by Swanson, dynamically allocating compute resources based on a monitored load metric, is a widely applicable concept. A PHOSITA would recognize that the 'load' in both cases ultimately translates to CPU usage, memory consumption, and I/O pressure on the underlying hardware. The application of this universal principle to a different type of data flow is a routine engineering adaptation."

"You would agree, though, that the operational constraints and performance requirements for a storage system are not the same as those for a real-time data transformation layer?"

"The specific metrics might differ, but the operational constraints and performance requirements remain similar in principle. A storage system is highly constrained by latency for I/O operations and ensuring data consistency and availability. A real-time data transformation layer is tightly constrained by data throughput, processing time, and queue depth to prevent backlogs.

"Yet, the core technical problem in both situations is identical: how to monitor the system's load in real-time and automatically provision the necessary underlying computational resources to maintain performance and avoid system failure. The engineering solution, using a resource management module triggered by a monitored characteristic, is transferable and obvious to a person skilled in the art."

Jordan pressed. "Does Swanson mention 'telemetry systems' specifically?"

"No."

"Does Swanson teach anything about a 'transform layer operation' within a data pipeline?"

"Not specifically, no."

"Isn't it true that storage scaling often involves different metrics, like IOPS or capacity, than processing scaling like CPU utilization or queue depth?"

Dr. Nord leaned forward. "That's true on a superficial level. The business metrics or application-specific metrics a manager might look at are different: a storage admin cares about IOPS and capacity, while a data engineer cares about queue depth and CPU utilization in a processing layer.

"But a PHOSITA would understand that these are merely different manifestations of the same underlying resource management problem. Both IOPS in Swanson and CPU utilization in the claimed invention are 'monitored characteristics' used to infer system load.

"The core teaching of Swanson is that you identify any relevant metric that indicates resource need and use it to trigger a universal resource management module. The selection of the specific metric relevant to a given application, whether it's IOPS or queue depth, is a routine design choice and does not require an inventive step."

Jordan turned to another tab in his binder, *Agarwal*. He passed copies of the Agarwal patent to Dr. Nord and Marla. "Now let's turn to the Agarwal patent. Exhibit 1007. This patent describes an event-driven architecture for a real-time analytics system, correct?"

"Yes," Dr. Nord agreed, "that's how it is described in the Abstract."

"Agarwal focuses heavily on the architecture and flow of events, does it not?"

Dr. Nord straightened in his seat. "Yes, Agarwal does describe an event-driven architecture. However, Agarwal highlights the critical need for systems to be responsive and handle high throughput. Agarwal doesn't explicitly describe the mechanism for dynamic scaling in detail, but it clearly identifies the problem: the need for a system robust enough to handle unpredictable event streams in real-time."

Jordan continued. "Agarwal doesn't describe a 'resource management module' for automatically allocating additional processing resources, does it?"

"That specific phrase, 'resource management module,' might not be in Agarwal, no. But Agarwal has an architecture that manages data flow between different stages. To make such a system operate effectively in the real world, one must include some form of resource management."

"Agarwal doesn't suggest how to dynamically scale the underlying infrastructure in response to load, does it?"

Dr. Nord shook his head. "You are correct that Agarwal does not provide a detailed blueprint for the specific *mechanism* of dynamic infrastructure scaling. Agarwal focuses on the architectural flow of data events. But it suggests the need for such a mechanism by describing high-throughput and unpredictable event loads. Any PHOSITA understands that real-time systems dealing with variable loads must scale to function reliably and efficiently."

"So, you are saying that Agarwal describes an architecture, not the specific mechanism for dynamic infrastructure scaling?"

Now Dr. Nord nodded. "Yes, that's a fair characterization: Agarwal describes the system at an architectural level. It provides the framework and the purpose of the system.

"But that distinction between architecture and mechanism is exactly why the invention is obvious. Agarwal establishes the need for reliable, real-time data processing capabilities within that architecture. A PHOSITA encountering that architectural need would simply turn to routine, known engineering solutions for resource management."

"Your argument that the invention is obvious hinges on a

PHOSITA being motivated to combine Swanson's storage solution with Agarwal's analytics system, correct?"

"Yes. But modern software architecture is highly interconnected. A competent software engineer working on real-time analytics architectures, Agarwal's field, would certainly be expected to have standard competence in related fields like cloud computing infrastructure, resource management, and general scaling techniques, which is what Swanson describes. They don't need to be an expert in cloud storage architecture, but they would be generally familiar with common, established techniques for dynamic resource allocation within standard cloud environments. The techniques in Swanson exemplify exactly that: standard, well-known engineering practices for resource efficiency. The PHOSITA would possess the combined knowledge of basic resource management practices and real-time architecture design, making the combination straightforward."

"Where in either reference is the PHOSITA specifically directed to look at the other reference, or a similar type of system?" Jordan asked.

"There isn't," replied Dr. Nord. "But it's my understanding that the law only requires that a PHOSITA would have had a reason, motivation, or suggestion to combine the known elements to achieve a predictable result. In this case, Agarwal describes a system that presents a clear problem: How do you manage variable, real-time data loads efficiently? Swanson provides a well-known, established engineering solution for dynamic resource allocation that addresses exactly that type of variability. The motivation for a competent engineer to combine these would not come from the references themselves, but from common sense and the desire to build an efficient, working system. If you have a problem and a known solution exists in the general engineering toolbox, combining them is an obvious step."

"Isn't it true that combining two separate systems can introduce new technical challenges, such as latency issues when provisioning resources in real-time?"

Dr. Nord leaned back. "Any implementation of a complex system will involve engineering challenges; that's just a reality of software development. But these are the kinds of challenges a PHOSITA is expected to overcome.

"The potential for 'latency issues' is a known factor in any dynamic cloud resource provisioning. Swanson provides a solution for managing the latency associated with provisioning new resources by anticipating needs and pre-warming resources, or by managing the queue depth during the ramp-up phase.

"Overcoming these routine integration issues does not make the underlying concept of combining the two systems non-obvious. A PHOSITA would possess the skills to troubleshoot and mitigate these standard latency problems using well-known optimization techniques."

Unfazed, Jordan kept pressing. "If the PHOSITA required expertise from two distinct fields to combine these ideas, doesn't that suggest the invention was non-obvious?"

"That characterization assumes these are entirely separate and unrelated fields, which I would argue is incorrect." Dr. Nord said.

"Computer engineering, cloud infrastructure, and data processing systems are highly related and overlapping domains. The PHOSITA isn't just a basic coder; they are a competent professional who stays abreast of industry best practices across relevant cloud technologies. The PHOSITA is expected to know how basic resource management works and how real-time data architectures function.

"The knowledge required to combine the general concepts in Swanson and Agarwal falls within the expected skill set of an ordinary engineer in this field at that time. It does not require extraordinary expertise or an inventive leap to bridge these two disciplines."

Jordan continued for a while longer, but he knew Dr. Nord was a practiced witness unlikely to deviate from his earlier declaration. Now and then Jordan scored a sound bite: Dr. Nord had agreed Agarwal describes a general need for an analytics system, but not how to implement dynamic scaling, and Swanson's metrics for scaling cloud storage are not the appropriate ones to scale a real-time processing or transform layer. That, and a couple of other items, were probably the best that could be achieved.

Eventually, Jordan said, "Thank you Dr. Nord. No further questions."

Marla nodded. "No questions."

The court reporter unplugged her mic; the deposition was over.

———

Invoices arrived like relentless weather. The NovaTech experts wrote declarations the size of novellas; the printers clicked and sighed and drank reams of paper. A courier took three bankers' boxes to the copy store and returned with a receipt that looked like a joke.

As days blurred into weeks, birthdays were missed, dinners skipped, and the calendar shed pages at an alarming rate. Gen 2 slipped behind schedule, causing Alan and Jonas to first demand, then plead for more focus. All that pressure just led to Ethan and Alex snapping at one another over misplaced exhibits and cold coffee. When Maya forgot to approve a bank transfer, other employees asked why their paychecks hadn't been deposited on time. The grind was relentless, and the cracks were showing.

As the filing deadline grew close, Maya found herself reviewing redlines of draft Patent Owner Responses until the letters blurred, then refocused to hurt her again. Ethan built a retrieval index for their exhibits and named it *Athena*. Alex marked up the expert declarations with the tenderness of a teacher correcting a child who had nearly understood. Even Jordan, usually unflappable, left a meeting early, muttering about "just one night's sleep."

Two weeks before the Responses were due, Jordan called a strategy session.

"We got what we expected. Nord admitted Agarwal doesn't teach dynamic scaling, and Swanson doesn't mention telemetry or transform layers. But we need to make our argument bulletproof."

He pulled up a draft on the screen. "Here's our core: The invention isn't just a mashup of Swanson and Agarwal. It's a leap neither reference suggests."

Alex nodded, rubbing his eyes. "Swanson's about cloud storage: IOPS, capacity, durability. Agarwal's about real-time analytics, but it's all architecture and event flow. No one in storage is thinking about queue depth in a transform layer; no one in analytics is thinking about storage scaling."

Ethan added, "And neither one points to the other. There's no hint in Agarwal to go looking for a storage solution, and Swanson's not talking about real-time, high-velocity data at all."

Jordan typed as they spoke. "Exactly. The PHOSITA in cloud storage is solving a different problem than the PHOSITA in real-time analytics. Titan wants the Board to believe these fields are interchangeable, but they're not. The engineering challenges are fundamentally different."

Maya flipped through a stack of annotated references. "Agarwal says the system needs to be robust, but it's silent on how to actually scale resources. Swanson's dynamic scaling is tied to storage metrics, not the metrics that matter for a transform layer."

Jordan nodded. "That's our second pillar: Even if you tried to combine them, you wouldn't get what we built. The invention identifies the right monitored characteristics for the transform layer and links it to a resource management module. That's not in Swanson. That's not in Agarwal. That's us."

Jamie cleared his throat, hesitant. "I, uh, went back through the old design docs and commit logs. There's a note from the first week we tried to scale the transform layer, before we even had the resource manager. It's in the comments; I flagged it." He slid the pad across the table, not quite meeting anyone's eyes. "It shows we were solving a different problem than Swanson. We weren't thinking about storage at all."

Jordan took the pad, scanning the page. "Thanks, Jamie. Maybe we can work this in somehow."

Jamie nodded, relief flickering across his face. "I'll keep digging. There might be more." He slipped out quietly, the door clicking shut behind him.

After a moment, Jordan looked at Maya. "He's trying."

"I know," Maya said. "But it's still raw."

Alex brought them back. "We're not just theorizing. Our system actually achieves efficient, reliable scaling for bursty telemetry data. Manual provisioning always left us with either lag or wasted resources. This is the first time we hit the equilibrium."

Ethan grinned, despite himself. "It's why the customers love it... even if the Board doesn't care."

Jordan smiled, but it was thin. "That's our third point: the result was new and unexpected. If it was so obvious, why did it take months of trial and error to get it right?"

He looked at each of them in turn. "We need to hammer this home. The invention is more than the sum of its parts. It bridges two unrelated fields and adapts a technique from one domain to a new environment to solve a unique problem. That's not obvious. That's invention."

Maya nodded, resolve hardening. "Let's get it on paper. Every word counts."

Jordan returned to redlining the draft, the team's voices overlapping as they refined each point.

# Twenty-Three

**Tech Ledger | Sofia Martinez**
**Countdown to Alexandria: What a PTAB Hearing Is (and Isn't)**

Think of a PTAB hearing as an executive summary measured by a stopwatch: sixty minutes per side, a three-judge panel, no jury, minimal drama by design. The record is closed. The goal is clarity on paper, not catharsis in person.

"You don't tell a story at the PTAB; you prune one," said attorney Jordan Reyes. "Every sentence is a risk of running out of time."

For NovaTech, the task is narrow and exacting: Prove that the path to their invention wasn't paved by a collage of older papers, without leaning on the very human proof a jury found persuasive. Expect phrases like "motivation to combine," "reasonable expectation of success," and "nexus." Expect the red timer to matter. What you shouldn't expect: closure. That arrives weeks later in a PDF.

———

THE HEARING ROOM was smaller than Maya expected, and cleaner than any room that had held this much harm had a right to be. No jury box, no gallery. Just a raised bench, two counsel tables flanking a lectern, and a digital clock on the bench that blinked a relentless red: 60:00.

Nine months had passed since NovaTech had filed its Responses. In that time, their expert had been deposed, Titan had filed its Replies, and NovaTech had filed Sur-Replies. The last word before the Board would hear oral argument.

June in Alexandria and the weather was hot and humid. Their flight into Reagan National Airport had been delayed due to thunderstorms and the team had only arrived at the Embassy Suites opposite the King Street metro station after midnight.

On the walk over to the USPTO headquarters that morning, Maya's phone buzzed. A text from Ravi: *Hang in there. You're stronger than you think.* She smiled a little.

The two of them had run into each other a few weeks ago at the corner café they used to frequent. He was picking up a package, she was grabbing coffee. Their conversation had been brief and awkward. Just enough to remind her of what she'd lost, and what might still be possible.

Now on the 10th floor of the Madison Building, Maya took her seat with Alex and Ethan on either side.

Ethan leaned forward and whispered to Jordan at the counsel table. "Sixty minutes. That's all we get?"

Jordan didn't look up from his notes. "That's all anyone gets."

The panel entered. Three judges in suits, no black robes, faces unreadable. The lead judge nodded. "Good morning. Each side will have sixty minutes and may reserve time for rebuttal. Petitioner will go first followed by Patent Owner. Is each side ready to proceed?"

Marla, fresh and precise, rose first. "Ready for Petitioner."

Jordan stood, "Ready for Patent Owner."

"Petitioner, you may begin."

Marla took her place at the lectern, her voice crisp and confident.

"Motivation to combine doesn't require poetic necessity. Just a good reason and the expectation you won't break something."

She spoke of combinations, of substitutions, of predictable results.

"You have Dr. Nord's testimony concerning the highly interconnected nature of modern software architectures. His opinion that a PHOSITA working on real-time analytics architectures would also have competence in related fields like cloud computing infrastructure and resource management. It would have been well within the PHOSITA's ability to combine Swanson's core teachings concerning identification of relevant metrics for a given application with Agarwal's understandings that systems need to be responsive and handle high throughput. A general knowledge of basic resource management practices and real-time architecture design makes the combination straightforward, inevitable, and predictable."

She repeated the words "would have been obvious to a person of ordinary skill" so many times that Ethan almost expected one to materialize out of thin air.

Marla went briskly through her slides, fielding the odd question along the way. After about 40 minutes, sensing the judges had heard enough, she stopped. "I'll reserve the remainder of my time for rebuttal."

Throughout Marla's presentation, Maya hadn't looked away from the bench. The lack of challenges from the judges when Marla had reduced NovaTech's creative choices, the parts that made their system real, to a mere swap of parts made her think the PTAB must regard everything as just a spreadsheet of right answers waiting to be assembled by anyone with steady hands and hindsight.

"Thank you, Ms. Whittaker," the lead judge said. "Mr. Reyes, let's hear from Patent Owner."

Jordan rose, set his binder on the lectern, and began. "Good morning, Your Honors. This case isn't about whether pieces existed; it's about whether the path existed. Whether a skilled person would have seen a reason to take these specific steps, in this order, when the record says the field was pulling in the opposite direction."

He put up a slide with a single claim chart on the screen. "Petitioner's map," he continued, "looks complete only because it's drawn with today's pen. The alleged 'motivation to combine' relies on assumptions imported from later work. When you strip those away, the road vanishes. The lab logs, the contemporaneous papers: they show an unresolved trade-off that our invention solved by making a system that breathes, not merely one that was faster.

"Without hindsight, Petitioner's references do not suggest the claimed transform layer unless you are willing to call a prophecy a photograph."

The judge in the middle seat leaned forward. "Counsel, are you saying a skilled artisan wouldn't consider smoothing heuristics and the transform layer constraints?"

Jordan pointed to a figure on another slide, one Alex had drawn. "Not in this way, for this purpose, in this sequence. The systems they cite punish that sequence. Ours breathes through it."

Alex whispered, "They're treating our choreography like Lego."

Maya's eyes never left the red timer. It blinked down.

Another judge, this one on the left. "Isn't this merely optimizing a known trade-off: stability over latency?"

Alex's breath caught. Maya felt the question like a physical blow. That was the choice that made their system humane. Alex whispered in the gallery, "We taught it to breathe." Maya touched his sleeve, grounding him.

"Respectfully, Your Honor, optimization presumes predictable improvement," Jordan said. "The record isn't about turning one knob. It's about changing the dance. Adapting ingestion and normalization so telemetry becomes usable under non-ideal conditions. The Petition never explains why a skilled person would expect that choreography to work then. It points to parts but doesn't supply the reason."

He kept the cadence tight: a line of text, a citation, a pause. The clock slid from 38:12 to 38:11 to 38:10, indifferent.

Now the judge on the right asked, "You argue secondary considerations. Specifically, praise and adoption. But where's your nexus?"

"The nexus," Jordan said, "is the claim language itself. The market evidence ties to the dynamic scaling limitation. The one the Petition treats as a passive substitution. Our customers valued that improvement. The expert declarations, ours and theirs, agree it wasn't a free lunch at the time."

He turned a tab; and put up a demonstrative: two logs, two outcomes; one brittle, one resilient.

The lead judge glanced at the clock. "Claim construction," she said. "Your 'transform layer operation.' Is that format-level or semantic?"

"Semantic," Jordan answered, "as the specification makes plain and as our district-court record showed. The Petition's format-level reading is what lets the collage slide together. Remove that, and the glue doesn't hold." He did not say the name of the trial judge. He didn't need to.

In his seat, Ethan scribbled *timer = tyrant* in the margin of his legal pad, then scratched it out, suspicious of poetry in a place that pretended not to hear it. The red digits blinked: 22:47.

The questions kept coming, careful blades shaving the argument down to the bone. Why not this combination? Why not expect success? Why not a simpler swap? Jordan stayed inside the record. He declined every invitation to sentiment. He did not tell them about the hospital pilot that had failed and the call where the tech lead said *fix it, and we'll reschedule.* He did not tell them about the night Maya learned to cry in ways that leave no tears. He told them where the citations ended. He told them what did not follow.

"Counsel," the lead judge said, "if we disagree on your reading of 'transform layer operation,' does your position collapse?"

"No," Jordan replied. "Even under their narrower reading, they need a why. They don't have one. And the expert's 'predictable' result assumes data hygiene that the record shows did not exist."

He closed his binder, the gesture quiet, decisive. "If there are no other questions, I'll reserve ten minutes for rebuttal."

Marla returned to the lectern. "Predictable," she said again, and again, as if the word could do the work of proof. "Counsel's choreography is just Lego with better lighting." When the bench pressed her for the why, she pointed to hindsight and called it common sense.

Alex stared past the lawyer at the clock, watching it tick ever downward. He'd always known time was a parameter, but he hadn't known it could be a weapon. He thought about the whiteboard where he and Ethan had argued about moving normalization upstream; he could still feel the plastic marker cutting into his palm when he'd written we need both. In this room, both felt like an indulgence.

"Patent Owner rebuttal."

Jordan took the lectern one last time. "Two points," he said, voice measured, clock-aware. "First, on motivation: the Petition's reasons are post hoc. They lean on outcomes discovered after the alleged combination. The contemporaneous record points the other way. Second, on expectation of success: their expert treats resilience as a constant. It wasn't. Our limitation. The dynamic scaling that unifies telemetry semantically wasn't a neutral swap; it was a choice with cost and courage. The Petition never explains why anyone, then, would have bet a product on it."

He let the silence sit for one count. Two. The red digits: 02:14.

"With that we'll submit the case."

The lead judge thanked counsel. The three rose, collected papers, left with the practiced economy of people who believed in schedules.

———

Outside the hearing room Maya's eyes stung. Alex leaned against the wall, whispering, "They turned our choreography into Lego."

Maya's voice was barely a breath. "And asked why dancing wasn't obvious."

Ethan stared at the floor, hands in his pockets. "Sixty minutes. That's all we were worth."

Jordan flexed his hands, shaking out the ache. "We preserved every issue. Whatever happens, we can take it up."

Maya nodded, but the red timer still pulsed behind her eyes.

# Twenty-Four

**TECH LEDGER | SOFIA MARTINEZ**
**PDFs That End Wars**

When a jury speaks, you get applause or outrage. When the PTAB speaks, you get a PDF. No confetti. No cameras. Just a tidy "Final Written Decision" uploaded at 9:03 a.m., stamped with the words every founder dreads: "All challenged claims unpatentable." The sound is not a gavel. It's a quiet click on a link followed by a hollow silence.

For NovaTech, closure came not in a courtroom, but in a document: precise, bloodless, fatal. "The real drama at the PTAB is deferred," attorney Jordan Reyes had once told me. "You prune for months, then a panel decides if you're holding a living branch or sawdust." This morning, the Board decided. The branch is gone.

———

IN THE TEN weeks since Alexandria, Maya had practiced the discipline of forgetting. The IPR lived in a folder she refused to open; every calendar block read **G2**. Gen 2 was getting close. The build was more or less stable and the first demos had drawn interest: not promises, but calendars and NDAs. For the first time in months, NovaTech moved to the rhythm of releases instead of reply briefs.

Then the ping.

**Subject**: FWDs.
**From**: Jordan Reyes
Maya—final decisions just posted. The Board found all asserted claims unpatentable. Call me when you're ready.

She clicked. The language was antiseptic: *We find Petitioner has shown by a preponderance of the evidence that claims 1–18 are unpatentable.*

Words that felt like a bell tolling somewhere far away, then stillness. The jury's victory had been frozen months ago; this morning, someone had unplugged it.

She forwarded the links to Ethan and Alex, then to Jamie with a single line: *We'll regroup at 10.* Her fingers hovered over Ravi's name— an old habit, a half-remembered impulse to reach for the voice that had once steadied her. She let them fall back to the desk. The PDFs stared back unblinking.

———

They gathered in the conference room: Maya, Jordan, Ethan, Alex, Jamie. The air felt thin.

"They accepted Titan's motivation to combine and reasonable expectation of success," Jordan said, his voice steady. "And they said we failed to prove a sufficient nexus between the commercial success and industry praise and the claims to make a difference."

Ethan frowned. "How do they say Gen 1's traction isn't tied to the claims?"

Jordan tapped a paragraph. "Two moves: claims not commensurate in scope, and attribution to unclaimed features. They point to comments in the record that suggest buyers loved the UI and ease-of-deployment, but those features are not in the claims. They acknowledge sales but say the success wasn't shown to stem from the specific architecture we claimed."

"So, good job, but not enough," Ethan finished, eyes red.

"Not for the Board," Jordan said. "For the jury, yes. But this isn't a question of persuasion. It's record sufficiency measured with a microscope."

Jamie stared at the header: BEFORE THE PATENT TRIAL AND APPEAL BOARD. "So that's it? We're done?"

"No," Maya said, her voice quiet and even. "We're not done. We're down." She forced herself to breathe. "Jordan, talk to me about an appeal."

Jordan folded his hands. "Federal Circuit review. Deferential on fact. Substantial evidence is the standard. We'll argue legal missteps, misconstruction, and that the Board ignored key secondary considerations. But facts? If there's any reasonable reading of the record that supports their findings, the panel's conclusions stand."

Alex exhaled hard. "So we need error. Not outrage."

"Exactly," Jordan said. "It's a long road. But there is a road."

———

In a windowed corner of Titan's campus, Richard Hale swiveled from his monitor as Marjorie Thorne appeared in the doorway.

"Board went our way," Richard said. "All claims."

"No champagne," Marjorie replied. "Just emails."

"Already sent," Richard said, holding up his phone.

Marjorie nodded. "No victory laps. And get the team a quiet dinner tonight. We've earned a meal without depositions in the middle."

As Marjorie departed, Richard gazed out the window. He knew what the PR statement would say: *We respect the process; innovation thrives when ideas are free to compete.* There would be no mention of Claire, or of emails that sounded like orders dressed up as weather, or of a jury that had once found a different truth.

His phone buzzed with a note from a headhunter with a subject line that assumed the future was already arranged. He turned the phone face down and looked at his reflection. It looked back, waiting for the correct angle to return authority to the eyes.

He picked up the phone anyway.

————

By noon, the district court's ECF ping matched NovaTech's. The entry was short, almost polite:

> ORDER: The injunction hearing set for next Tuesday is VACATED as moot, in light of the Patent Trial and Appeal Board's Final Written Decisions invalidating the asserted claims. The Court MAINTAINS THE STAY pending resolution of any appeal. A STATUS CONFERENCE is set for October 15 at 9:00 a.m. — Judge Eleanor Price.

Maya read it twice. *Moot.* A word that sounded like a door closing.

"Judge Price isn't moving until the Federal Circuit speaks," Jordan said. He'd already flagged the order for the team, highlighted the date, added an agenda.

————

At 3:00, the faces appeared in a grid: Alan, two partners from the fund who never remembered to unmute, and a consultant whose Zoom background remained fixed on the Alps as though altitude could imply wisdom.

Alan didn't bother with small talk. "Let me be direct," he said. "We have a Board decision that guts our patents. Talk to me about options. And more importantly, talk to me about whether those options matter."

Jordan leaned in slightly, clasping his hands. "We can request rehearing or go to the Federal Circuit. But the question isn't availability, it's viability. Appeal buys time but not certainty. The odds of reversal are low. The expense is real. And even if we win, it will be a year or more before anything helps you."

The consultant shifted in front of his mountain peaks. "So you're saying the appeal's a long shot."

Jordan nodded. "A long shot that burns cash and distracts the company. At the Federal Circuit the question isn't whether the judges would have decided the case differently. It's whether there's enough of a record to support the Board's decision. If so, that's the ballgame. Meanwhile Titan gets to keep building. They have wind at their backs."

Alan rubbed his forehead. "Cost?"

"Low six figures," Maya said. "More if we push every argument. Less if we narrow. But even the lean route is expensive."

"Business impact?" one of the fund partners asked, finally unmuted.

Alex straightened. "Gen 2 is close, but we're not there. Without protection on the architecture, we're exposed. We can still ship, but the upside is blunted. Licensing leverage evaporates, competitive positioning weakens, investors will ask what moat we have left."

Maya added quietly, "And teams are shaken. They won't say it out loud, but they're scared."

"Brand impact?" the consultant asked.

Maya forced a thin smile. "We've been the company that keeps getting up. That story still holds. But I won't pretend this didn't land hard."

Silence descended—heavy, almost humid; the kind that makes people recalculate everything they thought they understood.

Finally Alan exhaled.

"Okay. Appeal is off the table."

Maya blinked. "Off?"

"We're not funding it," Alan said. "Not when the odds are this low and the burn is this high. We need to be stewards of the capital we have left."

Ethan looked down at the table. Alex's jaw tightened.

"And Gen 2?" Maya asked, though she already felt the answer forming like a bruise.

Alan hesitated. "That's the real conversation. Without patent protection, this board has serious concerns about putting more money into a product that may never command the margins or defensibility we projected. We need to consider whether extending resources on Gen 2 is still rational."

Alex flinched. "You're considering canceling it."

"We're considering all scenarios," Alan said evenly. "No decisions yet."

The consultant cleared his throat. "We're not saying it's dead. But investors don't love funding technology that someone else can replicate freely."

Jordan shot Maya a sympathetic glance.

"Look," Alan said, trying for gentle. "You three built something extraordinary. But we're at an inflection point. The patent loss changes the math. We need to revisit the roadmap, the cash position, and whether doubling down makes sense."

Maya kept her face still, but something inside her felt like glass under pressure.

"Understood," she said.

"We'll reconvene next week with models," Alan said. "I'm not promising anything. But we owe it to everyone—employees, investors, you—to evaluate objectively. Hard decisions may be ahead."

The call ended with a few muted nods, the consultant disappearing back into his synthetic Alps.

Maya and Jordan walked toward the door in quiet tandem. At the window, she stopped. The city sprawled outward, indifferent, sun catching on mirrored buildings like a rebuke.

"They're going to kill it," she said quietly.

Jordan didn't sugarcoat. "They might."

"If Gen 2 dies, we lose everything."

"You lose a version," Jordan said. "Not the vision."

She didn't respond.

"Look," he continued, "you knew patents were one leg of the stool. They're gone. Now you find another leg. Another partner. Another structure."

Maya closed her eyes, jaw trembling just once. "Death knell."

Jordan shook his head. "A bell," he said. "Bells don't end things. They signal something needs attention."

Maya stayed late.

The office emptied around her, a tide receding. Screens dimmed. Voices faded. The HVAC clicked on—a low hum, steady, almost like breathing.

She opened a blank document and typed: *Next Steps After PTAB Decision.*

Deleted it.

Typed: *We will find a path.*

Deleted that too.

Finally she wrote: *We move forward.* She stared at the words. They felt less like a rallying cry and more like a vow.

A message from Ravi flashed across her screen: *Saw the news. You'll figure it out. You always do.* She looked at it for a long moment before sliding the phone under a stack of papers, face down. There would be time later for bridges. Tonight was for keeping the lights on.

She closed her laptop, stood in the quiet, and whispered to no one: "We move forward."

# TWENTY-FIVE

**TECH LEDGER | SOFIA MARTINEZ**
**After Patent Collapse, What Future—If Any—Remains for NovaTech?**

When the Patent Trial and Appeal Board invalidated NovaTech's patent last month, the shockwaves traveled far beyond the courtroom. Once seen as a rising star in next-generation telemetry analysis systems, the battered startup has spent the past weeks navigating a void left by the sudden loss of the intellectual property that anchored its market narrative.

According to multiple sources familiar with the matter, NovaTech's board quietly declined to pursue an appeal to the Federal Circuit, citing steep legal costs, long timelines, and the low likelihood of reversal. The decision, while fiscally conservative, effectively shuttered the last legal avenue for NovaTech to restore its competitive moat.

The implications were immediate. The company halted internal funding for the completion of its long-awaited Gen 2 platform

—hailed by early insiders as the "realization of the NovaTech thesis"—placing the ambitious project in limbo. Several employees, speaking on condition of anonymity, described the moment as "a gutting," "a stall-out," and "the clearest sign yet that the runway had turned into a cliff."

Despite a loyal customer base and pockets of strong internal morale, investors have grown increasingly wary. Without patent protection, NovaTech now faces a market where competitors can replicate the architecture without fear of infringement; a reality that undermines both valuation and long-term defensibility.

Rumors have circulated for weeks that the board has begun exploring "alternatives," a term often synonymous with acquisition talks or controlled wind-downs. While the company has not issued any public statements beyond a terse acknowledgment of the PTAB decision, insiders report that senior leadership has been "exploring multiple scenarios" to preserve team and technology.

Analysts across the sector are asking the same question: Is Nova-Tech preparing for a strategic pivot, a sale, or a sunset?

————

Morning came in pale, uncertain streaks, the kind of light that made the office windows look frosted from the inside. Maya sat alone at her desk, the silence heavy enough to feel structural, like the building itself was holding its breath after the board's decision the day before. Gen 2 was stalled. The patent was gone. Funding was frozen. In the span of a single meeting, the future had shrunk to a narrow, airless corridor, and every path forward seemed to dead-end in a different kind of loss. She stared at the blank legal pad before her—Next Steps scrawled at the top—and realized she had no steps left that didn't feel like surrender.

Her phone buzzed. The name on the screen made her sit up: Daniel Cho.

She swallowed the grit in her throat and answered.

"Didn't mean to catch you this early," Daniel said, voice low, the soft hum of a car engine audible beneath it. "Couldn't sleep. Figured you probably weren't either."

Maya leaned back in her chair. "What's going on?"

A brief pause, filled with something heavier than hesitation. "I wanted to talk before anything gets... formal."

Her spine stiffened. She already knew the tone—measured, deliberate. The kind that preceded proposals that changed trajectories.

"Helios has been following everything," Daniel continued. "And look, I won't sugarcoat it. The PTAB decision, the funding freeze— your board's in a corner. You are, too."

"We're figuring it out," Maya said, even though the words felt thin, more muscle memory than truth.

"You're trying," Daniel corrected gently. "That's not the same."

She closed her eyes just long enough to steady herself. "If this is about Gen 2—"

"It is," Daniel said. "And it isn't. The board loves what you built. They believe in the architecture, the thesis, the team. But they also see a stalled roadmap, no patent shield, and investors pulling their horns in. And they're not wrong to be cautious."

He paused.

"Helios is willing to back you, but we need assurances that Nova-Tech doesn't drive off a cliff or stall before getting out of the garage."

Maya rubbed her forehead. "Then lead the next round. Take a board seat. Take two."

Daniel exhaled—soft, controlled, and unmistakably pained. "Maya, Helios doesn't take concentrated risk without control. It's our culture. You saw it in the pilot onboarding—the way those questions came at you. We don't put millions behind a product we're not positioned to steer if things go sideways. It's cultural. It's governance. It's how we manage downside."

"We don't need steering," Maya said, sharper than she intended. "We need partners."

"And we want to be," Daniel said quietly. "But not with a single vote on a board that can't even agree whether Gen 2 deserves another month of life. One disagreement and we've thrown good money after bad. We've watched too many high-potential startups implode because the founder and the investors locked horns at the worst possible moment."

His voice sharpened a little. "And I think you know that's a real possibility."

Maya didn't answer.

Daniel continued, softer now, almost apologetic. "If Helios is going to put real capital behind NovaTech—capital that actually stabilizes the company, that funds a multi-year roadmap, that gives Alex and Ethan and the rest of your team security—we need to know that when the hard decisions come, we're not just observers."

Maya let out a bitter, humorless breath. "So you become the adults in the room."

"You know what I mean. You've been carrying the world on your shoulders. With full ownership, we can carry some of it with you."

"And without ownership?"

"Without ownership," Daniel said, "we're spectators with expensive tickets."

Maya stared out the window then turned to face the quiet rows of desks waiting for a future they no longer had a clear claim to. "You're asking me to give up my company."

"No," Daniel said. "I'm asking you to give it a future."

A beat. "And to keep leading it. Just not alone."

Silence stretched; the kind that sat between two cliffs, wind howling through the hollow. Finally Daniel said, "I don't want to pressure you. And I'm not going to sell you on it over the phone. But I'm sending something over. Read it. Talk to your team. If this isn't right for you— I'll respect it."

A soft chime sounded. An email.

"I have to jump," Daniel said. "But Maya... whatever you decide? I meant what I said when we first spoke. You built something extraordinary."

The line clicked off.

Maya stared at the email notification glowing on her lock screen: *Helios Term Sheet.* She didn't open it. Not yet. Instead she sat in the quiet, the early light glinting off the abandoned monitors, letting the weight of the moment settle into the room like dust.

Only after several minutes did she double-click the attachment and begin to read.

———

By the time Maya reached the office, the sky had lifted to a flat gray, the kind that made everything look washed and temporary. The space was quiet—too early for most of the team. The hallway lights hummed with the same weary persistence she felt in her bones.

She printed the term sheet without sitting down, the pages warm against her palms, then messaged Alex and Ethan: *Can you both come in? Need to talk.*

Alex arrived first, hair still damp, expression already wary. Ethan followed a minute later, cup of tea in his hands, eyes scanning her face before he took a seat. "What's going on?" he asked. Not hostile. Braced.

Maya set the three stapled packets on the table, one in front of each of them. "A proposal," she said. "From Helios."

Alex didn't touch his. Ethan flipped immediately to the first page and froze. "A full acquisition?" he said, voice small but sharp.

Maya nodded.

Alex gave a dry, humorless laugh. "This is what I walked away from. You remember that, right? This exact life? Reporting lines, umbrella orgs, quarterly integration committees—"

"Read it," Maya said quietly.

They did.

Silence stretched, punctuated only by the thin rustle of pages.

Helios would acquire NovaTech outright but NovaTech would operate as a semi-autonomous division: *NovaTech Labs @ Helios.* Eighteen months of roadmap control; staff retained; full Gen 2 completion and upgrades funded. A commitment to shield the tech from internal assimilation during the transition.

Ethan got to the last page first. His brow tightened. "And then this," he said, tapping the line with the back of his pen. *Integration review scheduled twenty-four months post-close.*

Alex looked up sharply. "So they get to take us apart later. Great."

"It's not a guarantee of assimilation," Maya said.

"It's the opposite of a guarantee," Alex shot back. "This is 'we'll leave you alone until we don't.'"

Ethan set his packet down, rubbing his thumb over the corner. "Maya... this is big. This is everything changing."

"I know," she said.

Alex pushed back from the table, arms crossed. "So what; we become a lab inside the machine? A little fenced-in innovation zoo they feed at budget season?"

Maya met his eyes. "It's how we survive."

Alex scoffed. "We've been surviving."

"No," Maya said softly. "We've been enduring. Barely."

Ethan looked between them. "She's not wrong, Alex. Our runway's a cliff edge. Titan's win hurts us in every conversation. The investors are nervous."

Maya leaned forward, palms flat on the table.

"This isn't about selling out. It's about giving people we hired—people who trusted us—a safety net. It's about giving our investors an off-ramp that isn't a total loss. And giving ourselves a chance to finish what we started without bleeding out along the way."

Alex didn't answer.

She continued, voice steady but warm. "Gen 2 isn't done. Our upgrades aren't done. The pilot isn't stable. We need more people, more time, more burn than we can raise under the cloud we're under. Helios gives us the runway *and* the shield to finish the work."

Ethan spoke quietly. "And the integration review?"

"That," Maya said, "is our horizon line. If twenty-four months go by and Helios can't understand who we are or why we matter, then we walk away. Together. Clean. With something new to build."

Alex stared down at the printout, jaw tight, breathing slow. "This is the opposite of what we dreamed," he murmured.

"I know," Maya said. "But it protects what actually matters."

He didn't look up.

"Our team," she said. "Our people. This thing we built that deserves to exist long enough to prove itself."

Ethan nodded slowly. "It's not the dream. But it might be the path."

Alex stayed quiet for a long time. Finally, he closed the packet and tapped it once against the table, not angrily, but deciding. "You really believe this is how we do right by everyone?"

"Yes," Maya said. "I do."

"And you think we can still be... us? Even inside Helios?"

"I think we stay us until they prove we can't," she said. "And if that day comes, we're smart enough to start again."

More silence.

Then Alex let out a long, exhausted breath—the kind that comes after fighting something inside yourself and losing in the most necessary way. "Okay," he said finally. "Let's talk it through. Really talk it through. But... I'm not walking away from this team."

Ethan gave a small, relieved nod. "Then we're aligned."

Maya exhaled as the tension in her shoulders eased by a fraction.

\*\*\*

The conference room felt too small for what the three of them were about to do. Maya set her laptop in the center of the table, angled so Alex and Ethan could see. The screen reflected the fluorescent lights overhead, giving everything a faint, sterile glow.

The faces of the board slowly populated the screen: Alan first, then Priya with her immaculate office in the background, then Jonas from what looked like an airport lounge, earbuds already in place.

"Maya," Alan said, leaning forward. "Good morning. You said there was something urgent."

"Yes," Maya said. "Thank you all for making time."

Alex shifted beside her. Ethan sat very still.

Maya began. "Helios reached out yesterday with an acquisition proposal."

The board members did not look surprised; they looked prepared.

She shared the term sheet on the screen. Three sets of eyes scanned it quickly—these were people who spent their lives parsing deals. Alan was the first to speak. "So they're proposing a full acquisition with Nova-Tech operating as a semi-autonomous division."

"NovaTech Labs @ Helios," Maya clarified.

Priya nodded. "Eighteen months of roadmap control. That's generous."

"And staff retention," Jonas added. "All headcount preserved."

Ethan looked down, but they kept reading.

"They're funding Gen 2 to completion. That alone is... well, frankly, more than we can do right now," Alan said.

"And they're committing to shielding the architecture from assimilation during that period," Maya said. "We can finish the work without being swallowed on day one."

A long silence followed, the kind where no one wants to say the first bad thing.

It was Priya who broke it. "It's a lifeline," she said simply. "Let's call it what it is."

Alan nodded. "I agree. The offer respects the work. The people."

Jonas tapped the screen. "But we need to acknowledge the last line."

Everyone looked: *Integration review at twenty-four months post-close.* Priya leaned back. "That's the risk point. They can revisit autonomy then."

"They can decide to fold everything in," Jonas said. "Or restructure. Or—"

"—or keep NovaTech exactly as is," Maya finished. "If we're delivering. If the tech proves its value at scale."

Alan studied her face. "Do *you* believe that's possible?"

"I do," Maya said. And she meant it—maybe not with certainty, but with conviction.

"And your team?" Priya asked.

Alex spoke first, voice calm but edged. "It's not the future I wanted. Not when Maya and I founded this thing." He looked straight into the camera. "But I understand the reality. And I'm not walking away from our people."

Jonas nodded approvingly.

Ethan spoke next. "The review clause scares me. But the alternative —limping forward with a shrinking runway, or laying people off—it's worse."

"And we'll be stronger in twenty-four months than we are now," Maya said. "If it doesn't work, we walk away with our heads held high. Together."

The board absorbed this. Alan folded his hands. "Let's talk fiduciary duty. Does this serve our investors better than raising another round under current conditions?"

"Yes," Priya said immediately. "A new round would be brutal—valuation slashed, preferences stacked. This gives them a soft landing."

"And our employees?" Jonas asked quietly.

"It gives them stability," Maya said. "Salaries protected. Roles intact. Health insurance uninterrupted. Burnout deferred instead of accelerated."

Alan nodded once, decisively. "It's the humane option." He exchanged glances with the others. The kind that signals something solidifying, the decision crystallizing. Finally, he said, "Maya, Alex, Ethan—NovaTech has been through the kind of struggle that kills good companies. You built something remarkable. And you built it with integrity. This"—he gestured toward the term sheet "is a way to preserve that integrity and that work."

Priya added, "It isn't surrender. It's stewardship."

Jonas closed the PDF on his screen. "I'm ready to vote."

Priya nodded. "Same."

Alan looked at each face in turn. "All in favor of moving forward with the Helios proposal?"

One by one, the board members raised their hands.

"Approved," Alan said. "Unanimous."

A softness entered his voice. "Maya... you've done right by this company. Now let Helios help you carry it the rest of the way."

The call ended, screens blinking back to reflections of the three founders.

No one spoke. The silence thickened with everything they had been and everything they were about to become. Finally, Ethan let out a slow breath. "Well," he said, voice thin but steady. "There's no going back now."

Alex leaned back, staring at the darkened screen. "Good," he murmured. "Then let's move forward."

Maya closed the laptop. "Together," she said. And for the first time in a long while, she felt the smallest ember of hope.

# Epilogue

The first rays of sunlight caught the chrome edge of the chair in the new office. Smaller than the one she had had at Titan, but with windows that opened. Claire Donovan stood by one now, watching the dusk settle across a row of mismatched desks. The startup was barely two years old, its logo taped to the glass, its ambitions still scrawled in dry-erase marker on the walls. She liked the messiness of it. The way people argued over code and laughed too loudly, the way nobody seemed afraid to ask for help.

Her new title was "Director of Partnerships," but the job was simpler than that. She listened. She built bridges. She tried to remember what it felt like to believe in something before the politics and the paperwork. Some days, she caught herself waiting for the other shoe to drop: a compliance ping, a veiled threat, a calendar invite with no agenda. But the only alerts now were for birthdays and bug fixes.

Claire opened the window a little wider and let the air in.

———

Across town, in NovaTech's new offices, even after six weeks the team was still settling in. The surroundings were a dramatic change from their old space. More glass. More light. More brushed-metal surfaces that caught the sun and bounced it into corners they hadn't known existed. But the team was growing into it; the way a transplanted tree eventually claims the soil it's given.

Maya walked down the main corridor, passing clusters of people leaning over laptops, laughing softly, arguing over whiteboard sketches. The familiar hum of intensity had returned, but without the frantic edge that once tinged every conversation.

Gen 2 was getting final touches and the early Beta reviews—internal Helios teams, select enterprise partners—were better than she'd dared to hope. Phrases like *"astonishing performance gains"* and *"architecturally elegant"* were appearing in feedback threads. Even Helios's famously conservative CTO had used the word *"impressive."* That one had made Ethan print the email and tape it to his monitor.

At the café-style kitchen island, Maya stopped to fill her new travel mug with coffee. The mug had been a present from Ravi, who had come by the new office to offer congratulations. Their conversation had been brief, but the awkward silences it included felt less like absence and more like possibility.

Jamie was at the counter, chatting with two new hires, and he looked up as Maya entered. "Morning, Maya!"

"Morning," Maya said, smiling. "How's onboarding going with the Beta partners?"

Jamie grinned. "They're obsessed; which I'm taking personally, obviously."

The warmth in his voice still caught Maya off guard. Six months ago, she wouldn't have imagined this version of Jamie: steady, engaged, part of the team's center of gravity again. Helios had slotted him into a role that balanced ambition with room to heal. It had turned out to be good for everyone.

"Stand-up in ten," Jamie said, raising his mug.

"Wouldn't miss it," Maya replied. She kept walking.

Alex was in the engineering bay, sleeves rolled up, eyes on a screen filled with performance graphs trending steadily upward. He looked... good. Grounded. Still occasionally bristly at corporate nonsense, but calmer now that the existential threat wasn't suffocating them.

"You see the new stress-test results?" he asked without looking up.

"I did," Maya said.

He exhaled slowly, the kind of breath released when numbers finally match vision. "We're going to nail this."

"We are," she agreed.

Ethan was in one of the glass breakout rooms, meeting with a product lead from Helios. He waved her in, but she gestured that she'd catch him later. He nodded, already deep in discussion. He'd grown into this part of the job—the bridging between NovaTech's DNA and Helios's machinery. He was good at it. Better than he gave himself credit for.

People were working. People were laughing. People were planning next quarters, not next weeks. And despite the quiet awareness that the 24-month integration review waited on the horizon like a distant shape, one they couldn't yet identify, they were confident. Cautiously. Deliberately. But confident.

They would prove themselves. They would earn their place as Nova-Tech Labs @ Helios. They would stay themselves.

Maya reached the new conference room, the one with the absurdly large monitors, the view of the city, the table that could seat three times more people than their old office ever could. On the far wall hung the original patent, brought over from the old space, its frame polished, its glass replaced after what seemed like years of scuffs.

Beside it, a second nail waited.

She carried the new frame under her arm. The empty frame. The one she had promised the team she'd hang when the time was right.

There had been debate about where it should go. Engineering wanted it in the lab, product wanted it in the hallway; but ultimately, it belonged here. In the room where decisions were made. Where futures were shaped. Where the next chapter would begin.

Maya held the frame for a moment, feeling the cool edge of metal beneath her fingertips. People filtered in behind her. Alex, Ethan, Jamie, others from the team. Conversations dimmed as they noticed what she was doing.

Without ceremony or speech, she lifted the frame and hung it on the waiting nail. It settled with a soft, satisfying click. Beside the old patent, the empty frame gleamed in the morning light—huge, untouched, unapologetically blank.

Alex stepped forward, hands in his pockets. "Looks good there."

Ethan nodded. "Feels right."

Jamie smiled. "Room for something big."

Maya stepped back, looking at the two frames side by side. "What we built," she said quietly. "And what we build next."

The team stood with her, watching the frames reflect the city outside—the past and the future, anchored together on a single wall. Maya let the moment settle, warm and full and steady. "Alright," she said, turning back to the room with a small, determined smile. "Let's get to work."

And with that, the next chapter began.

———

# Thank You

Thank you for spending time in the world of *The Litigation Protocol*. If you connected with the story, the characters, or the ideas behind it, I would be genuinely grateful if you took a moment to leave a review.

Reader reviews, no matter the length, make a meaningful difference—they help new readers discover the book, support the broader Patent Wars series, and let me know what resonated with you.

The Patent Wars will resume in
*The Innovation Protocol*.

# About the Author

Tarek N. Fahmi is a practicing intellectual property attorney with more than three decades of experience guiding startups and global technology companies through the high-stakes world of patent strategy, prosecution, and litigation. His work spans industries from semiconductors to software to advanced communications systems, and his career has taken him through the U.S., Europe, and Asia as he helps clients build and defend complex patent portfolios.

Fahmi draws extensively on real-world experience—attorney-client dynamics, strategic inflection points, procedural bottlenecks, and the human pressures inside the legal machinery—to bring authenticity to the Patent Wars series. His writing blends legal precision with narrative momentum, illuminating how innovation, power, and institutional design collide in the modern patent system.

*The Litigation Protocol* is his debut fictional exploration of the forces shaping today's technology battles, told through characters who must navigate both the promise and the peril of the systems meant to protect them.

www.ingramcontent.com/pod-product-compliance
Lightning Source LLC
Chambersburg PA
CBHW050526110726
47899CB00005B/1607